THE PROBLEM WITH GOD

The Claddagh Trilogy

by Evan Geller

ISBN: 1494253267
ISBN 13: 9781494253264

DEDICATION

To Jack, the Bulldog
Requiescant in pace, Canis magnifica
Hoya Saxa!

URIEL

by Ralph Waldo Emerson

It fell in the ancient periods
Which the brooding soul surveys,
Or ever the wild Time coined itself
Into calendar months and days.

This was the lapse of Uriel,
Which in Paradise befell.
Once, among the Pleiads walking,
Seyd overheard the young gods talking;
And the treason, too long pent,
To his ears was evident.
The young deities discussed
Laws of form, and meter just,
Orb, quintessence, and sunbeams,
What subsisteth, and what seems.
One, with low tones that decide,
And doubt and reverend use defied,
With a look that solved the sphere,
And stirred the devils everywhere,
Gave his sentiment divine
Against the being of a line.
"Line in nature is not found;
Unit and universe are round;

In vain produced, all rays return;
Evil will bless, and ice will burn."
As Uriel spoke with piercing eye,
A shudder ran around the sky;
The stern old war-gods shook their heads,
The seraphs frowned from myrtle-beds;
Seemed to the holy festival
The rash word boded ill to all;
The balance-beam of Fate was bent;
The bounds of good and ill were rent;
Strong Hades could not keep his own,
But all slid to confusion.

A sad self-knowledge, withering, fell
On the beauty of Uriel;
In heaven once eminent, the god
Withdrew, that hour, into his cloud;
Whether doomed to long gyration
In the sea of generation,
Or by knowledge grown too bright
To hit the nerve of feebler sight.
Straightway, a forgetting wind
Stole over the celestial kind,
And their lips the secret kept,
If in ashes the fire-seed slept.
But now and then, truth-speaking things
Shamed the angels' veiling wings;
And, shrilling from the solar course,
Or from fruit of chemic force,
Procession of a soul in matter,
Or the speeding change of water,
Or out of the good of evil born,
Came Uriel's voice of cherub scorn,
And a blush tinged the upper sky,
And the gods shook, they knew not why.

PROLOGUE

Arthur Schlessel was not a stupid man. He wasn't a scientist or a theoretical mathematician, not a cosmologist or philosopher. He was a businessman. But he was a very good businessman, and he knew people. He understood their desires, their motivations. He was smart that way, and it had made him extraordinarily successful. He sat at the desk, staring at the small pile of items before him, understanding this fact and regretting it. He wished he didn't know.

Arthur was still in his somber, charcoal gray suit; his funeral suit. He always wore this suit to funerals, never to any other occasion. He seemed to be wearing it a lot lately. He loosened his tie and unbuttoned his collar. Arthur closed his eyes and remembered watching his friend slump forward in this same chair, slump forward and die, his friend's face coming to rest on this same pile of stuff on his desk. What was this shit, anyway? A computer hard drive, sitting in a nest of crumpled yellow paper; notes, scribbled equations, doodling and scrawled obscenities visible on their face. What was this shit, that had been piled like some offering before his dead friend? Arthur feared he knew. He put his head in his hands and cried.

"Got a match?"

Arthur looked up to see Chuck leaning against the door. He, too, was still dressed from their friend's funeral. Well, maybe not Chuck's friend, maybe not since the deceased had caused that twist in Chuck's nose. Arthur shook his head.

"Too bad."

CHAPTER 1

Father Julius Zimmerman was in Hell. Hell, it turned out, looked and smelled an awful lot like Helmand Province in Afghanistan. He wasn't surprised. He was dripping in sweat. Of course he was, it was hot as Hell in here. He sat in an armored personnel carrier with his squad. It was stifling, as usual. He turned to smile at his squad mates, noticing that they were all dressed in the same cowled woolen robes he had worn as a novice. As his buddy next to him turned to smile back, Zimmerman saw that the other man's face was a skull, smiling. Julius started to scream.

The explosion lifted the APC straight into the air. It crashed back to earth with a grinding shriek. The air in the small vehicle became a stifling, putrid miasma that smelled of death. Julius twisted violently to free himself of the wreckage entangling him. His eyes snapped open and his breath caught in his throat. Jack, his English bulldog, was staring at him, muzzle drooling on the bed and nose nearly touching his own. Dog breath. Julius screamed again, for real this time. Jack almost blinked.

"Shit, Jack," Julius yelled, "You scared the crap out of me." Julius fought to disentangle himself from the blankets that had twisted around him as he thrashed through his nightmare. He finally succeeded and

1

swung his feet over the side of the bed, sitting up. He bent to scratch Jack's head.

"Ready to go, huh?" Jack stared back, unblinking. Julius didn't think the dog ever blinked. Julius went to get up, putting his hand in the small pond of drool Jack had left on his bed. "Aww, shit, Jack. I just washed these sheets." Jack stared back. "Don't get so upset," Julius said. "It's okay. I'll take care of it. Don't be so hard on yourself." Jack just stared at him. Julius scratched the dog's head again and went into the bathroom.

Zimmerman came out in his Georgetown hooded sweatshirt and shorts. He grabbed his phone off the charger and dropped it in the water-proof bag with a handful of dog snacks and a bottle of water. "Let's go, buddy. You got point." The dog shuffled out as Julius held the door open. Zimmerman followed outside into the predawn darkness, carrying the bag. The early morning chill was refreshing, dew on the grass stretching down to the river. Julius forced himself not to check his six as he followed Jack's waddling ass down to the boathouse.

Jack sat watching on the dock as Julius flipped the two-man scull off the rack. "Two-man scull, two men's skulls," Julius muttered to himself as he lowered the craft into the water. It was heavy, almost a hundred pounds and ungainly, but Julius expertly flipped it into position next to the dock with a soft splash. He dropped the bag into the back of the boat and held it steady to the dock. "What are you waiting for?" he growled at the dog. Jack twisted his head quizzically for a moment, then padded over and dropped like a bowling ball into the boat. The dog took a seat behind the bag, facing front. Julius slipped into the front seat, facing backwards towards Jack, stretching arms and legs as he slid the seat back and forth on its silent mechanism. Julius had just greased the tracks and oarlocks yesterday. He liked quiet.

"Clear to the rear," Zimmerman announced quietly. "Clear to the front?" he asked the dog. Jack stared past Zimmerman and said nothing. "Good to go, then." Zimmerman pushed off from the dock. He fitted his long graphite oars to their locks and began an easy pull upstream to the middle of the Potomac. It was still dark, but a lighter purple over the Gothic towers of the university hinted at the dawn to come. Zimmerman started to pull harder, settling down to his warm-up cadence. He stared back at the dog staring at him. "When are you going learn to row? I'm getting a little tired of hauling your fat ass up and down this river." Jack tilted his head. "You know what I'm talking about, dog-breath. Getting a little jiggly around the middle. No snacks until we clear the Chain Bridge." Jack lay down on the ditty bag, settling his muzzle on his paws. He looked sad.

Zimmerman began to slowly increase his cadence, sliding and pulling in concert to the soft splashing of the dipping oars. Despite the cold, a sheen of sweat appeared on his forehead. He concentrated on his breathing. He was an "empty-lung technique" guy, inhaling steadily during the power stroke, emptying his lungs slowly during the recovery, his chest empty and his knees tight in, squeezing every bit of air out at the catch, then the cadence beginning again, his powerful chest filling with air as he pulled with his back and shoulders, pushed with his legs and felt the trembling boat shoot forward through the glassy water. He was a human metronome, a sweating piston pumping within the scull's smooth cylinder, watching his wake curve gracefully downstream.

Jack's head came up off his paws. He made a thrumming sound with his throat and looked at Julius. "What?" Zimmerman asked between breaths. "You say something?" A second later they passed under the Chain Bridge. "Oh. You said bridge, huh? Fine, go ahead. Lard-ass." Jack chose not to reply to this, instead nuzzling into the ditty bag and coming out with a dog treat. "Just one, lard-ass. It's Wednesday, we're going for distance today. Better make 'em last." Jack made his sad sound and settled into chewing on the snack.

Julius settled into his endurance cadence. He no longer wore a heart monitor or brought along his little electronic metronome. After four years of rowing three times a week, his body knew what to do. He didn't think. That was the best part. He pulled, the oars splashed, the water slipped by. He felt a trickle of sweat travel the length of his spine. He kept to the middle of the river, somewhat narrower here as he headed north, the yards and yards drifting behind him marked by the little whirlpools left by his curved oar blades. Silence, if you didn't count the loud snuffling of Jack polishing off his treat. Jack looked into his eyes, head tilted.

"No more. Not until the next bridge." Jack made his sad sound again, a deep thrum ending with a higher note that always sounded to Julius like his ex-wife saying "Fuck you." Pity, that. He breathed, pulled harder but no faster. The water flowed past, the river making its slow turn to the west. Julius could see the dawn threatening to break behind them as he fought to race away. Sweat started to drip down his nose. Pulling, breathing, pulling, breathing. Jack started to snore.

Jack's head came up and Zimmerman knew he must be nearing the Beltway bridge. How long had he been rowing? He didn't know, didn't wear a watch. Pulling, breathing. A drop of sweat rolled into his eye and he tried to blink it away as the huge mass of the bridge passed darkly overhead. Julius could hear the early morning traffic noises as he shot like an arrow out from under the bridge. Sweat in both eyes now and it wouldn't blink away. He couldn't see, was blinded by the sweat and the sun rising like a searchlight over the bridge, straight into his eyes.

"Dammit!" he said out loud, shipping his oars and rubbing at his eyes with the heels of both hands. He had been in a trance, moving at speed like a perfectly tuned machine, hadn't been thinking or feeling or anything and then—stupid sweat, stupid sun, he thought. He looked back at Jack, who was waiting to be told he could get his snack. Something caught Julius's eye, however, something about the bridge. He looked up, squinting into the sun which was intensely bright, exactly behind the bridge. Something on the bridge—a person. Standing by the railing, a person, silhouetted by the bright sun behind. A girl, he thought, the light streaming through a loose white dress or something, her figure in dark relief within. He stared, transfixed, his eyes watering from trying to squint into the sun. It was a vision, he thought. An angel, an angel from heaven. He could make out a ring of fire, a red halo about her head, lit from the sun behind. Everything else about her was in shadow. As Julius watched, she raised her arms, outstretched. Jack barked, once. An angel, he sees it too, Julius thought. Just then, the vision started to shrink. Zimmerman stared, confused, until he realized that she wasn't shrinking. She was falling, pitching head first over the side of the bridge.

"Holy shit!" Julius snapped out of his trance and struggled to unship the oars. His boat was whispering away from the bridge, farther and farther as he watched the figure fall silently, slowly. She hit the water with a sickening splash and disappeared. Jack made his sad sound. Waves lapped at the boat.

"Shit, shit, shit," Julius said as he struggled to bring the scull about. This was exactly what the small boat was designed not to do. He fought the craft, backing one oar and pulling hard with the other, the graphite bending and locks creaking with the strain. It seemed to take forever to bring it around, to start the pull back to the bridge. "Do you see her, Jack? Is she there?" Jack barked, once; now hopping past Julius to the bow, front paws on the gunnel, staring ahead. He barked again, his stub of a tail wagging. Julius kept shooting glances over his shoulder to try to see ahead but could only see Jack's butt wiggling emphatically side to side. "Get down, Jack. Down, dammit! If you fall in, you're gonna sink like a rock!" Jack turned to look back at Julius. He made the 'fuck you' sound. Then he returned to looking forward.

Julius thought he was getting close, but wasn't sure until Jack started barking. Jack almost never barked, almost always in the context of pizza. He was barking like a crazy dog now, though. He kept looking back at Julius, then to the water. Julius used the oars to brake the boat to a stop. He got up on his knees and scanned the water. He saw nothing. Jack was hopping up and down with his front paws on the gunnel, barking. Jack never hopped.

"Dammit, Jack! Get down here, you're gonna fall in." Julius wished again that the stubborn animal would wear his life jacket once in a while. Jack had always refused, making the sad sound whenever Julius put it on him. Julius had made him wear it once, despite Jack's complaining. The next morning he found it chewed to shreds.

Jack was looking just ahead of the boat now, steadily alternating barks with thrumming sounds, not hopping anymore. Julius was trying to think what to do, not even certain he had really seen the girl. But Jack had seen her, too, he was sure. As he stared at the same spot in the river as Jack, her white figure rose to the surface. Silently, her inert form surfaced, face down, her arms outstretched. A formless white dress clung gauzily to her. She didn't move.

Without a thought, Julius rolled over the gunnel into the river. The boat rolled as he dropped smoothly underwater, knocking Jack off the gunwale. Julius came up, suddenly realizing that his jump must have rolled the boat. He looked from the floating girl to the boat. No Jack! "Oh my god!" Julius stretched for the boat as Jack's head came up. He had been knocked into the bottom of the boat, but now stood with paws on the gunwale again. He barked and looked at the girl. Julius just shook his head and turned to swim for the girl. Julius was a strong swimmer; most ex-Navy SEALs were. He was at the girl in three strokes and rolled her face up, treading water. He brought his arm under hers and around her chest. Julius could feel her breathing. She's alive. He turned with her, twisting to see where he was, where was his boat. Where was his boat? He turned and saw his boat, and Jack still standing on the gunwale, looking at him. The boat was moving downstream, moving with increasing speed away from him. Jack stared, twisted his head questioningly.

"Stay, Jack! Stay! Don't jump! Stay in the boat!" Julius looked at Jack, at the receding boat, back down at the girl in his arms. He looked back to Jack, now moving more swiftly with the current. "I'm sorry, Jack. I'm sorry." The boat was moving faster.

Fuck you.

Julius swam for the riverbank, carefully holding the girl's head above water. By the time he had pulled her ashore, the boat had disappeared downstream.

CHAPTER 2

Julius pulled the limp girl up onto the riverbank. He knelt beside her and confirmed that she was still breathing. "Hey!" he yelled into her ear, shaking her. No response, her eyes remaining closed. "Shit," he whispered to himself, realizing his cellphone was still in the boat. The boat, with Jack. "Shit," he said again, looking downstream. No boat, no Jack.

Julius clambered up the muddy bank to the road. It was daylight now and traffic building. Julius stepped right onto the highway, waving his arms above his head. Two cars managed to swerve past him but he kept moving farther into the lane until the next car was forced to screech to a halt. More screeching as multiple lanes of traffic came to a stop. Julius strode purposefully to the car in front of him. The guy inside, dressed in a suit and swearing inaudibly, glared at him through the driver's window. Julius knocked on the window.

"What?" the driver mouthed.

"Open the window," Julius commanded, gesturing. The window slid down. "Phone. I need your phone. It's an emergency." The man stared at Julius, then looked ahead, obviously thinking of taking off. Julius grabbed the top of the steering wheel. "It's an emergency," he repeated.

7

The guy looked at Julius and handed over his phone. Julius let go of the steering wheel. "Thanks. Be just a second."

Horns started to blare from behind the car. Julius held up his hand, gesturing to the traffic. "Shut up, this is an emergency," he yelled at them. He dialed 911 and reported the girl on the riverbank, just west of the 495 bridge, that he needed an ambulance. He hung up and handed the phone back to the driver. "Thanks," he said. "You can go now." He stepped back to the side of the road, allowing traffic to resume.

Julius checked on the girl, then scrambled back up the embankment to wait on the shoulder of the road, staring at the oncoming traffic. The ambulance appeared several minutes later, red lights flashing. Julius flagged it down. He led the paramedics down the bank to where the girl still lay, breathing but unresponsive.

"How'd you find her?" the paramedic asked, checking her pulse as his partner opened their equipment box.

"I was rowing, just passed under the bridge. Looked like she jumped," Julius answered.

"I was pushed," the girl said softly, eyes still closed. The three men looked at her in surprise.

"She's conscious?" the other paramedic asked. Julius shrugged, but the girl said nothing more despite their further efforts to arouse her. Julius had to help carry the girl, once strapped in a stretcher, up the riverbank to the ambulance.

"Thanks," the paramedic said to him, breathing hard with the effort. "Are you riding with us?"

"Do I have to?" Julius asked. "My dog is still in the boat, drifted downriver."

"You got some ID?" the paramedic asked. Julius shook his head. "Then you better come with us. Police might want to talk to you."

"Shit, really? What about my dog?"

"Gonna have to swim for it, I guess," the paramedic said, gesturing Julius into the jumpseat next to the stretcher. He took the other seat and fastened his seatbelt. "Better put on the seatbelt. Jimmy drives like a lunatic." He banged on the wall behind them twice. The siren started up as the rig lurched into traffic.

"Any chance we're heading to Georgetown Hospital?" Julius asked the paramedic.

"No way," the man replied. "Gotta take her to Suburban, this side of the highway."

"Shit."

It was three hours before they let Julius leave. The police, having interviewed him twice and taken his personal information four separate times, declined his request to be dropped at the University. Julius grabbed a taxi from in front of the hospital. He had the cabbie wait while he sprinted upstairs to his room in the dorm to grab some money. As he opened the door to his room, Jack lifted his head from the pillow.

"Really? Sleeping? On my pillow?" Jack said nothing and just laid his head down. Julius grabbed a twenty from his desk and ran downstairs to pay off the taxi. When he returned, Jack was snoring. A large puddle of drool had formed on his pillow. Julius's ditty bag was at the bedside. The dog treats were gone, he noticed. "Hey," he called to the dog, shaking him awake. "How'd you get home?" Jack looked at him sideways. "You bring back the boat?" As Jack wasn't answering his questions, Julius headed back out to the dock.

"You're supposed to bring back the boat, Father," the equipment manager said, smiling.

"Yeah, sorry about that. Where'd you find it?" Julius asked.

"Not far upstream, in the shallows. Hiker found it and rowed it back, with Jack sleeping on your bag. Nice old guy. Found your phone and figured out you lived here from the recent calls, he said. Was wondering if the dog took the boat out by himself and just got tired of rowing."

"Something like that."

"Really? Because I never saw Jack row much, you know? With his really short arms and all. Not much of a swimmer, either, I bet."

"You get his name? The hiker?"

"Yeah. Figured you'd want to give him a call to thank him. If you weren't drowned or anything." He handed Julius a piece of paper he fished from his pocket.

9

"I'll send him one of Jack's autographed publicity shots, maybe a couple of tickets to next week's game."

"Sounds about right, Father."

"Boat's okay?"

"Just a lot of drool and dog treat crumbs in the bottom."

"I'll come by after my class to clean it out."

"Already did, Father. Thanks for offering. Just glad you're alright."

Julius trotted back to his room to shower and change. Dressed in his dark gray suit and collar, he loaded his papers into his messenger bag. He took a minute to rescan the page with the pictures of his students in this afternoon's class. He had spent an hour last night memorizing each of their faces, but just wanted to be sure. They all looked so young, he thought. "You coming to class?" Julius asked the dog. Jack opened one eye but didn't lift his muzzle from the pillow. "Rough morning, huh? Fine, you take a little R and R. I'll see you later." Julius slung the bag over his shoulder and left.

CHAPTER 3

Julius waited in the hallway, watching the students go into his classroom. When the soft bell from his phone signaled three o'clock, he followed a student into the room. He closed the door behind him and strode to the front. Julius tossed his messenger bag on the desk. Turning to the blackboard, he wrote "FR. ZIMMERMAN" in large, block letters. He turned back to the class, slapping the chalk dust from his hands.

"Good afternoon. My name is Zimmerman. This is THEO-001, The Problem of God." Someone began knocking on the door. A student from the back row started to get up to open it. "Please stay seated. As your schedule indicates, this class begins at three. Not 3:02, not 3:10, not 3:15. If you cannot attend at three, please reschedule to a time that is more convenient.

"I am aware that this class is a requirement for you. I am aware that none of you are planning to pursue a career in theology. I am acutely aware that two of you are taking this course for the second time." More knocking on the door led the student in the back row to shake his head at the face pressed up against the window. The face disappeared.

"Fourteen of you are first semester freshmen. Nine of you are sophomores, three juniors. Mr. Hagstrom," and here Julius looked Hagstrom

11

straight in the face, "is a senior. As this course is required for graduation from Georgetown University, Mr. Hagstrom will have special motivation to do well, so that he should not cost his parents an additional twenty thousand dollars in tuition." Julius and Mr. Hagstrom exchanged a brief smile. Julius walked up the side of the room as he continued.

"I'm sure almost all of you are carrying laptops in your bags. Several of you have already set them up on your desks. Mr. Simeon," and here he came to a stop in front of Mr. Simeon, "is already typing frantically upon his computer. As I doubt that I have yet said anything worthy of recording, I presume that you are posting a tweet, something to the effect of 'this prof is a dick.'" Scattered laughter accompanied Mr. Simeon's blushing.

"It's like you read my mind, Mr. Zimmerman." The young man smiled up at him, still blushing brightly.

"Sadly, that's not difficult, Mr. Simeon. You may refer to me as Father Zimmerman or just Father." He turned to address the entire class. "I have no problem with the use of computers during class and I am not so foolish as to expect you to refrain from texting or blogging or skating about the web while I am speaking. Do as you may, you are all adults. Please be advised, however, that your participation in discussion is critical to this course. By critical, I mean to imply that your grade will strongly reflect your participation. Fully one fifth of your grade will depend upon my completely subjective opinion of your participation. If the university would permit it, I would base your entire grade upon your participation but, unfortunately for all of us, that is not possible. Therefore, the remainder of your grade will be split between examination results and the score you will receive on two writing assignments. This will require you to write and require me to grade your writing. As I say, that's a chore we'll just all have to deal with.

"More's the pity, ladies and gentlemen, because you are not here to learn to write an expository essay. I am confident you will be taught that skill in other courses required of you. You are in my class to learn to think. That is why your participation is critical. This will be a discussion class and I therefore expect you, I demand you, to discuss. If you do not discuss, if you do not volunteer your thoughts and opinions, I will wrest them from you. You will not hide from me or your colleagues in this class. If you participate in a serious fashion on a regular basis, you will do well in this class, I assure you. The only thing you need master to get an A in my class is the ability to put forth a reasoned and cogent argument." At this point, Julius stopped pacing in front of a young man who had been staring steadily at his fingernails since Julius began talking. "Mr. Adamsky," he said, looking down at the young man. "What is the only thing you need to master to get an A in my class?"

Adamsky looked up at Julius with a bovine stare. After a moment, he shrugged. Still staring at Mr. Adamsky, Julius asked "Mr. Sanchez, what is the only thing you need to master to get an A in my class?"

Sanchez looked up from his laptop. "I'm sorry, were you talking to me?" Scattered laughter.

"Ms. Chu, what is the only thing—"

"The ability to put forth a reasoned and cogent argument," a woman seated in the back answered.

"I'm sorry, Ms. Chu, what was it you said?"

"I said that the only thing you need to master to get an A in your class is the ability to put forth a reasoned and cogent argument."

"Yes, I believe I heard you say that. But what I was going to ask, before you interrupted, was what is the only thing more rude than inattention during a discussion. Do you have an opinion, Ms. Chu, as to what is the only thing more rude than inattention during a discussion?"

"Interrupting?"

"Yes, that is correct, Ms. Chu. And now you have succeeded not only in disappointing the instructor, but in stirring a general animus towards yourself amongst your colleagues as an overeager sycophant. Combined with the common stereotype of Asians as overachieving and inappropriately competitive, I'd say that you have your work cut out for you in the coming weeks, Ms. Chu." Chu opened her mouth as if to say something. "I'm sorry, Ms. Chu, were you going to say something?" Chu closed her mouth and shook her head, obviously seething.

"Impressive, Ms. Chu. Self-control, the ability to choose not to speak. Class should attend to her example. Many times, the critical decision is to decide to remain silent. What was it Voltaire said? 'Everything you express should be true, but not every truth need be expressed.' Of course, excessive self-control is also part of the Asian stereotype, so I'm not certain you're helping yourself here, Ms. Chu. And my singling you out for praise is certainly generating additional hostility towards you amongst your classmates." He flashed Chu a smile, which was not returned. He walked back to the front of the class and fished a book out of his messenger bag. He held it up.

"*The Problem of God*, by John Murray, S.J., the required text for this course. How many of you purchased this at the bookstore?" Every hand went up. "How many besides Ms. Chu have begun reading it?" Scattered laughter as several hands were raised. "Ms. Lapides, you raised your hand. You have read the text?" A young woman in the middle of the class nodded. "How much did you read?"

"All of it."

"Really, all of it?" She nodded. "I assume that you are an only child, Ms. Lapides."

Lapides turned crimson. "I had a brother..."

"I'm very sorry, Ms. Lapides. I'm very sorry for your loss. You know, you often hear it said that the greatest tragedy is for a parent to suffer the death of a child. But I don't think that is true. I believe the greater sadness is for a child to suffer the loss of a sibling." Julius met the young woman's gaze for a moment. He continued more softly, "What did you think of the book, Ms. Lapides?"

Lapides looked at him plaintively. "It was okay, I guess."

"Do you have your copy with you?" Lapides nodded. "Would you be so kind as to read from page two, the paragraph near the middle of the page, beginning 'The second epoch?' "

Lapides began to read haltingly, then with more conviction, "The second epoch of yesterday begins in the patristic age. Then, in consequence of the new issues raised in the Arian and Eunomian controversies, the biblical problem of God was transposed to a different level of discourse, the level of theological understanding. It came to be posited no longer simply in intersubjective and descriptive terms but in ontological and definitive terms. The new problem was, first, the relationship of the Logos-Son to the Father, and, second, the knowledge of and names of God." She looked up at Julius. "Should I keep reading?"

"No, that's fine. That was very well read. What do you think it means?"

"I'm sorry?"

"What do you think the author is saying in that paragraph?" Lapides looked down at her book and just shook her head. "Are you a smart person, Ms. Lapides?"

Lapides looked up at him, confused. "I guess. Pretty smart, I guess."

"You graduated from high school, top of your class, no doubt?" Lapides nodded. "Public or private school?"

"Public."

"Oh, I see. Anyone here graduate from a private school?" No one raised their hand. "Oh, come on. You're too modest. Twenty-one of you graduated from private preparatory school. Mr. Sturmley, you graduated from Cranbrook Academy, did you not?" Mr. Sturmley nodded from his seat in the second row. "A very prestigious and shockingly expensive institution. Valedictorian, if I'm not mistaken?" Sturmley nodded again, reddening. "Did you read the textbook before coming to class today?"

"Not all of it."

"But some of it?" Sturmley nodded. "Get past page two, did you?" Sturmley nodded again. "Great. What do you think the author is saying in that paragraph that Ms. Lapides so movingly recited?"

"I'm not sure."

"But you read it before coming to class?" Sturmley nodded again. "Anyone? Anyone have an idea what Murray is trying to say in that paragraph?" Silence. "Come on people, it's from the introduction, for heaven's sakes. Anyone?" Silence. "Should I have Ms. Lapides read it again? No, I think not. It wouldn't help, I assure you. I've tried reading that textbook at least twenty times and I, for one, can't make heads or tails of it." They all smiled at this. "There will be no assigned reading from that text. I apologize that the university lists it as required. I will be releasing you from class ten minutes early today. The bookstore is less than a five minute walk from where we are sitting. I encourage you to take the opportunity to walk straight over and return the book for a full refund.

I say that, knowing that only half of you will do so. The other half will instead use the gift of the time I have given you to pursue other, no doubt more important tasks, like emptying your bladder or purchasing a snack. You will do that because your parents have paid for your education and as part of that education, this book. You haven't worked for the money required to purchase that text, and therefore you don't care what it cost or that the money was completely wasted. No doubt several of you are much more upset that you wasted the time actually trying to read the ridiculous thing.

"Anyway," Julius continued, dropping into his chair, "you won't need it anymore. All the readings required for class will be posted on the website at least a week ahead of time. Those readings are required and required for a reason. Read them and understand them before showing up for class." He looked at his cellphone. "We meet at three on Friday. The topic for discussion will be miracles. Have a good afternoon." He watched them gather up their things and go. Like it'll be a miracle if at least half of you don't drop the class by the end of the day, he thought to himself.

CHAPTER 4

When Julius returned to his room, Jack was still asleep on the bed. The tide of drool now spread from the pillow and lapped at the headboard. The dog didn't awaken when Julius closed the door. He remained asleep as Julius changed out of his suit into jeans and a tee shirt, carefully rehanging the suit and shirt in the closet. Finally, Julius leaned close to the dog's ear and yelled, "Hey Jack! Time for a walk, buddy!" The dog opened one eye and stared at Julius. Slowly, Jack raised up off the pillow, first with his back legs and then with his front. He stretched once forward, then rocked to the back. He gave a shake and then stood on the bed, looking at Julius. He twisted his head slightly.

"Coming?" Jack jumped off the bed and stood as Julius held open the door. He lumbered out, tail wagging. Julius followed the dog out onto the commons, now crowded with students in various states of undress given the warmth of the sunny September afternoon. A couple of people said hello to Father Zimmerman. Over a dozen said hello to Jack. Students, grounds keepers, faculty all walked over to say hello to the university's mascot. Jack accepted the adoration of his fans with his usual aplomb. He trotted over to a tree and took a moment to relieve himself. As he turned to look for Julius, someone called out "Hey, Jack! Catch!"

A Frisbee sailed just over Jack's head. Jack stared disparagingly for a moment at the young man who had thrown it, then sauntered over to lay at the feet of Julius, who had seated himself on a bench under a tree. "Jack doesn't do Frisbee," Julius said to the young man who had trotted over to retrieve his Frisbee. "Next time throw a box. He loves boxes."

As one young coed after another came over to sit and pet Jack, Julius fished out his cellphone and the slip of paper the boatman had given him. He read the name, Robert Llewellyn, off the paper and dialed the number.

"Hello," a man's voice answered after several rings.

"Hello," Julius answered, "may I speak to Robert Llewellyn?"

There was a click, and then nothing. Julius listened a few seconds longer, incredulous. "What the hell? He hung up on me." He dialed the number again. The same voice answered. "I'm sorry," Julius said pleasantly, "we must've been cut off. Can I speak to Robert Llewellyn?"

"Listen, asshole, knock it off. I'm not in the mood." Then he hung up again.

Julius looked at the phone. "What the fuck?" he muttered under his breath. Jack gave him a look and the sad sound. "Not you, Jack." Julius checked the number against the numbers on the note and confirmed that he had indeed dialed correctly. He stashed the paper back in his pocket. Julius sat and watched the scene around him for a few minutes, then used his phone to search for the number of Suburban Hospital. After a couple of transfers he got through to Admitting and confirmed that a young Jane Doe had been admitted, still no name assigned. He noted the room number into a memo on his phone with a question mark after the note.

"Let's walk a little before dinner, Jack."

They walked around the campus for half an hour. When they had finished their walk, Jack and Julius joined their Jesuit colleagues in the dining hall for dinner. After dinner, Jack returned to the dorm room and Julius attended mass at the campus sanctuary. The rest of the evening was spent washing the sheets and reading Julius's well-worn copy of Spinoza's *Theological-Political Treatise* for the fourteenth time.

Jack got to sleep in late as Thursday was a day for running, not rowing. Jack didn't do running. He was still asleep, on the floor this time, when Julius came back from his run to shower. It being the first week of classes, Julius had an unusually light schedule. He knew he should head over to the library to do some research for the article that was due in six weeks, but the day was too spectacular to spend the morning interred amongst the book stacks. He was thinking of taking Jack over to the dog park when he saw the boatman's note sitting on his nightstand. He still hadn't figured that telephone call out, but it got him thinking about the strange events from yesterday. What the hell, he thought. He dressed in jeans and his collar.

Julius stopped next door to ask his neighbor to take Jack out sometime later in the morning, as he'd be gone awhile. He grabbed a book and headed out, walking across campus and over to M street. He cut across the GW campus and continued east until he finally got to the Metro station. It always irked him that there was no subway station closer to Georgetown. Someone had once told him that it was a purposeful oversight, to keep the common folk out of the tony neighborhood. That was stupid enough to probably be true, he thought.

After waiting a few minutes on the sparsely occupied platform, Julius stepped on a red line train and headed north. He had read only six pages of his book when it was time to get off at the Bethesda stop. He stood blinking in the sunshine as he stepped out of the station, deciding whether to walk or take the bus up Old Georgetown Road. As he was considering, the bus squealed to a stop right in front of him. Fate, he figured, stepping aboard and taking a seat.

Julius stood in front of the hospital as the bus pulled away. He wasn't entirely certain why he was here. Julius wasn't one to indulge a whim, but here he was. He headed through the glass doors and got directions to the room number he had noted on his phone. Nobody said a word to him as he navigated the corridors and finally stood in the doorway to the sterile little room. Julius stood there, staring at the young, red headed woman from yesterday, lying asleep in the bed. He hadn't noticed yesterday that she was so pretty.

"Just going to stand there and stare?" Her eyes were still closed, but she was smiling.

Julius gave a start. "May I come in?"

19

"Did you bring flowers?"

"No. I didn't know if—"

"Well, I think it's pretty damn thoughtless to visit someone in the hospital without at least bringing flowers, don't you?" She still hadn't opened her eyes, was still apparently speaking to the ceiling.

He stared at her, uncertain what to say.

"Tell you what," she continued in the direction of the ceiling, "why don't you go back downstairs and pick up a nice bouquet of flowers. And a couple of Snickers, while you're at it. Then you can come in." She turned to him and opened her eyes. She smiled at him.

"Sure. I'll be right back, then." He turned and headed back to the elevator, wondering again why he was even here.

Julius returned with a small vase of flowers from the gift shop and a couple of Snickers bars. The girl was sitting up in bed, dressed in a hospital gown with the covers pulled up to her waist, head propped on pillows. She watched him put the vase on the little bedside table.

"Bring over the card before you sit down," she said.

He blanched as he sat down. "I didn't get a card."

"No card?" He shook his head. "Hardly seems worth the effort without a card." She gave him a fetching smile.

"I didn't know your name. So, no card."

"You don't know my name?" She looked hurt.

"No, I'm sorry. My name is Zimmerman, Father Zimmerman." He offered his hand and she shook it gently.

"I was hoping you might know my name," she said after an awkward pause. He raised his eyebrows and was about to ask a question when she asked, "Why are you visiting me if you don't know who I am, Father? Is this one of those courtesy visits you have to do, to punch the little ticket you guys carry?"

"How did you know about that? Are you a priest?"

"No, but I dated one in a previous life."

"Well, I'm sure I speak for the Holy See when I ask you to please not share that with anyone outside of the profession."

"I am nothing if not discrete, Father. Zimmerman, was it?"

"It still is."

"Rebelling against your overly protective Jewish parents, I assume."

"Slightly more complicated than that. I am at a disadvantage in this conversation. I don't know what to call you."

"I'm afraid I can't help you with that, Father Zimmerman."

"Amnesia?"

"Slightly more complicated than that."

"Were you injured in your fall yesterday?"

"You know about my fall?"

"I rescued you. From the river."

"You did? How gallant of you, Father."

"Seemed the right thing to do at the time."

"Appearances can deceive, Father."

"I should have left you to drown? I must admit, I was tempted for a moment."

"Were you?"

"I had to abandon my dog to the river in order to save you."

"A difficult choice. I'm sure I wasn't looking my best at the time. What made you pick me over your dog?"

"I thought you might be an angel."

"Really?"

"Only for a moment. The sun was in my eyes. Besides, the dog is pretty much a pain in the ass."

"Did he survive your moral dilemma?"

"He did."

"I'm glad. I'd hate to have to lie here tonight thinking that you made the wrong decision."

She smiled sadly at him as he just stared at her, confused.

"Did you bring me Snickers?" she asked after a bit.

"I did." He handed over both bars. She unwrapped one and took a bite that consumed half the bar.

"Do you like Snickers, Father Zimmerman?" she asked, chewing.

"Not particularly, no."

"What candy do you prefer?"

"I'm more partial to Twizzlers, actually."

"Really? You shock me. I would think you more discriminating."

"Why do you say that?"

"Every year, Twizzlers is the most popular candy in movie theaters nationally. Did you know that?" He shook his head. "Also, they are made of no natural ingredients whatsoever. You might as well eat them with the wrapper still on."

"I didn't know that."

"Good thing you stopped by then, Father."

"Good thing. Since I'm here, would like me to pray with you, child?"

She polished off the last bite of the candy bar and licked her fingers clean of the melted chocolate. "I can think of nothing that I'd like less."

"I'm sorry?"

"Don't be. It's not your fault, particularly. But no."

Zimmerman was dumbfounded for a moment. "I don't know what else I can do to help you, young lady."

"Father, you've already done so much. You could stop calling me 'child' and 'young lady,' though. I think I'm probably older than you are."

This confused him even more. "Then we're back to the problem of what to call you," Julius said.

"Let's solve that problem in the most direct manner possible."

"What would that be?"

"You could leave." She smiled at him again.

"Really?" She nodded. He was at a loss for a moment, then said, "I guess I'll be going, then." She smiled. He stood and shook her hand. "God bless you, then."

"Yeah, whatever."

Julius spent the entire ride back to campus shaking his head and muttering to himself. He didn't know what to make of the woman. He couldn't decide if she had been rude to him, or playing with him, or if she was mentally defective in some way. He was completely at a loss, even more so as he replayed the conversation in his mind over and again while he rode the subway home. He had taken the time to visit her, had bought the woman candy and flowers—and she had pretty much tossed him out on his ear. He no longer thought that she might be an angel.

CHAPTER 5

Rowing on Friday was for speed and power, not endurance. Nobody fell from the sky and Jack and Julius both remained in the boat for the entire cruise. Julius was glad to be back to a normal routine. He spent part of the morning trying to do some research on his article, but his heart wasn't in it. He kept thinking about the strange woman in the hospital. Julius called the hospital and was told that the woman was still a patient, still listed as Jane Doe. Odd, he thought. She hadn't appeared ill or injured in any way, during his visit.

Julius had a yogurt for lunch on the commons with Jack, who also had yogurt for lunch. It was part of the slimming diet that Julius had put him on. Julius also tried to convince him that it was good for his coat. Jack was skeptical, but tolerated the kind with fruit on the bottom. Jack still resented the fact that he roomed with a priest who ate pizza about twice a year. He might as well be living in a monastery.

Julius tossed their empty containers in the trash and walked with Jack across the commons to White-Gravenor Hall. He waited as Jack peed on a shrub just before mounting the steps to the front door, then Jack followed Julius into the registrar's office. Jack accepted the fawning attention of the secretaries as Julius checked to see how many students had dropped his class over the last forty-eight hours. He smiled to see that only three had dropped. And he had actually picked up a student in transfer. He wondered if the Chu woman was still in his class.

"Let's go, Jack." The dog turned reluctantly from having his chin scratched and followed Julius down the hall to his classroom. They were almost a half hour early and the room was empty. Julius took his papers and laptop computer from his bag and placed them on the desk. He tossed the bag into the front corner of the room beside the wall of windows. Jack trotted over and lay down on the canvas bag. Julius sat at the desk and logged on to the university intranet. He pulled up his revised course list and checked on the name of the new student, surveying the young woman's picture and glancing over her biography. Another freshman. He brought up his course management spreadsheet and made the necessary changes. Jack began snoring from the corner. Julius looked over and saw the animal asleep on his back in the sun, all four paws in the air. Not the dog's best look. Drool was already to be seen darkening the fabric of his bag. Julius shook his head and made a mental note to get an old blanket for the corner.

Students began to trickle in and take seats. Julius glanced at his phone and smiled inwardly, noting that class didn't start for another fifteen minutes. Point made, then. He smiled at Ms. Chu as she took a seat in front of him. She didn't smile back, but took out her laptop and flipped up the screen. The room filled up, Jack kept snoring. Julius went back to working on his computer.

Julius's cellphone made a soft bong from its place on his desk, the face showing three o'clock. Julius got up and walked to the back of the room. As he reached to close the door, a final student scooted in, smiling apologetically. The new student, he noted.

"You made it, Ms. Steponowicz," Julius said to her, smiling and closing the door behind her. He pronounced it with a vee sound for the 'w,' as his grandparents always had. The young woman gave him a surprised smile and hurriedly took a seat. Julius walked back to the front of the room and wrote "Miracles" in large block letters on the board. He turned and half sat on the front of the desk, arms folded and legs crossed at the ankles.

"Thank you for joining us, Ms. Steponowicz," Julius said. "I'm wondering if you found out the reading assignment for today's class in time to review the materials."

"I did, Father," the woman responded, taking out her laptop and placing it on the desk.

"Very good. Perhaps then, you'd be kind enough to provide us with your definition of a miracle, to get this started."

There was a brief moment of silence as the young woman scowled at the screen of her laptop.

"Ms. Stepanowicz?" he repeated.

"Yes, Father. I'm sorry." She brightened. "A miracle is a certain unusual operation, producing such an effect, whose cause cannot in any way be explained through the ordinary laws of nature, but rather is wholly contrary to them, and therefore requires that these necessarily be suspended for a time and that others be substituted in their place." She looked up at him, smiling broadly.

"Really?" She nodded enthusiastically. "Is that your definition of a miracle, Ms. Steponowicz?" She nodded less forcefully, smile drooping. "I would, in that case, suspect you of misattribution, as your definition is suspiciously similar to that of Johann Muller, in his lecture entitled 'On Miracles.' I believe that if one does a Google search for 'definition of miracles,' it comes up as the third entry." Steponowicz's smile disappeared completely as she looked down fixedly at her computer. "I usually have no objection to the use of authoritative sources in our discussions, Ms. Steponowicz, but I do require that you cite those sources, not leave the class with the impression that the thoughts are your own." The woman was now blushing visibly. "In addition, I believe that I specifically asked for your definition of a miracle, not that of Herr Muller. So let me ask you again: What is your definition of a miracle, Ms. Steponowicz?" The woman looked up at him briefly, met his gaze, then looked down again at her computer screen. "Please, Ms. Steponowicz, close your computer." She did so, reluctantly. "Take a deep breath now, and think. Take your time and please tell the class your definition of a miracle."

"Passing this class, probably," the woman said softly. This was greeted with gentle laughter.

"That would be an example, not a definition, Ms. Steponowicz." The laughter stopped but was replaced by knocking at the door from the back of the class. A student looked over and started to rise from his chair.

"I believe, Mr. Fields," Julius said forcefully, "that I made it clear last class that the tardy would not be admitted. Please sit."

"But it's an old guy, with a collar, Father," the young man protested.

"Well, Mr. Fields, in that case, please let the old guy in. I apologize." Fields rose and opened the door. The portly, gray haired rector of the theology department, dressed in black suit and collar, came in and, smiling to Julius apologetically, took a seat in the back of the room. Julius acknowledged him with a nod.

"Welcome to our class, Father Pauley," Julius said. "We were just about to hear a definition of a miracle from Ms. Steponowicz." He turned back to the young woman.

"A miracle is an act of God," Steponowicz said.

"That's it?" Julius said. She nodded, reddening slightly again. " 'A miracle is an act of God.' Your definition does have the virtue of brevity, I'll grant you that. Ms. Chu, what do you think of Ms. Steponowicz's definition?" He walked back to lean against the blackboard and looked at Chu.

"It's okay," Chu said.

"Is it, Ms. Chu? I'm afraid that you're just overcompensating for our little fracas during last class, trying to win over your classmates with feigned admiration. What do you really think of her definition, Ms. Chu?"

Chu scowled at him. "Actually, it sucks."

"Is that your unvarnished opinion, Ms. Chu? Upon what do you base that opinion?"

Chu shrugged but said, "Her definition—"

"Her name is Ms. Steponowicz," Julius interrupted.

"Ms. Steponowicz's definition," Chu began again, stumbling slightly on the pronunciation, "infers at least two conditions. One is that she believes in God, though that is not explicitly stated in her definition. The other is that some events, miraculous events, are the work of God. That implies that she doesn't believe that all works are the works of God. And that implies that she really doesn't believe in God in the usual sense. It's inherently contradictory. So the definition sucks. In my opinion."

"Thank you for your opinion, Ms. Chu. Mr. Fields, maybe you can do better. Do you have a definition that Ms. Chu might find more acceptable?"

"Doubt it," he responded from the back of the class.

"Don't be crass, Mr. Fields. The old guy doesn't like it," Julius said, smiling at Father Pauley. Pauley just looked confused. "Take a shot."

"A miracle is an event contrary to nature and the result of divine intervention in the affairs of man."

"Ms. Chu," Julius said, "what do you think of Mr. Fields's definition?"

"I like it," Chu said, smiling. General applause broke out about the classroom. Fields did a double fist pump.

"Mr. Fields, congratulations. Please come up and write your definition legibly on the board."

"Serious?" the man asked.

"As death, Mr. Fields. Please," Julius responded, holding out a piece of chalk to the young man. Fields took it and began to write on the board, though not legibly.

"Is English your native language, Mr. Fields? Not Russian, or Mandarin?" Julius asked the man.

Fields turned to him. "Yeah, why?" The class laughed. Fields erased the board and started again, this time only slightly more legibly.

Julius turned to the class, gently shaking his head. "On January 15, 2009," he began, "US Airways flight 1549 took off from LaGuardia Airport in New York with 155 passengers and crew aboard. The airplane was a two engine Airbus A320. Three minutes into the flight, during climbout, the plane passed through a flock of Canadian geese, both engines ingesting sufficient bird mass to cause an immediate and complete loss of power. As you might surmise, this was not a good situation, occurring as it did during the most critical moment in the aircraft's flight. With insufficient altitude to reach an alternate landing strip, the odds at that moment of anyone surviving were approximately one in two hundred thousand.

"On that day, however, Captain Chesley B. "Sully" Sullenberger, a former fighter pilot and safety instructor, successfully performed the most difficult maneuver that any commercial pilot might attempt, a dead stick ditching of the plane safely in the Hudson River. Not only did he ditch the plane successfully, he did so in such proximity to the USS Intrepid museum and its associated wharf that watercraft in the area were able to rescue all aboard before the aircraft sank. The incident was immediately christened The Miracle on the Hudson."

Julius walked to the windows and gave Jack a nudge with his foot, as the dog's snoring had become a distraction. Jack rolled onto his side with a snuffle but remained asleep. Julius leaned on the window ledge. "Mr. Hixon, does that incident which I've just described meet Mr. Fields's definition of a miracle?"

Hixon looked up from his laptop. "No, I don't think so."

"Why not?"

"The incident doesn't meet either part of his definition. It wasn't contrary to the laws of nature and wasn't the result of divine intervention."

"How do you know that?" Julius asked him.

"Because, the pilot just used his skill to land the plane. It was a great job and all, but not a miracle."

"Do you believe in miracles, Mr. Hixon?"

"Yeah, I guess so."

"Why?"

"Because I believe in God."

"Have you ever witnessed a miracle, Mr. Hixon?"

"I don't think so."

"Then why do you believe they occur, Mr. Hixon?"

"Because the bible says so."

"And you believe in the literal truth of the bible?"

"Yeah."

"The given word of God and all that?"

"Yeah, I guess."

"So when we carefully consider the text of the bible and calculate that the given word of God makes it necessary for man to have existed on this planet for less than seven thousand years, you're okay with that. You don't believe in evolution, or the validity of the world's fossil record. You subscribe to the literal interpretation, the one that says that the sun and stars revolve around the earth."

"No, I didn't say that."

"I believe you did, Mr. Hixon. I believe your statement leads directly and unavoidably to a complete refutation of evolution, physics, and astronomy, and ultimately the greatest part of scientific theory as we currently understand it. You probably don't truly believe that planes can fly."

"I don't agree with that, Father. I didn't say that."

"You did, indeed. If you disagree with me, you are contradicting your own argument. If you are going to use the bible as a primary source, there are implications. Wouldn't you agree, Ms. Steponowicz?"

"Yeah, but I think he's right that it wasn't a miracle," Steponowicz said.

"For the reasons Mr. Hixon said?" She nodded. "You can return to your seat, Mr. Fields, thank you. Remind me to never ask you to write on the board again." Zimmerman paused and turned back to the class. "What if I told you that an eyewitness to the event stated that he clearly saw two huge, loving hands embrace the plane as it fell from the sky and gently lower it to the surface of the Hudson River? Would it be a miracle then, Mr. Daly?"

"Yeah, that would be a miracle then. But that didn't happen," Daly said.

"How do you know?"

"Because there were pictures and all. Nobody else saw any giant hands."

"What if the giant, loving hands were miraculously invisible, except to this particular witness? What then? Might the successful landing of Flight 1549 be a miracle then, Mr. Daly?"

"Yeah, but it wasn't. It was just a really great job of flying. 'Hands' dude was probably high."

"Beating the odds of one in two hundred thousand isn't miraculous enough for you, then?"

"No, it was just really lucky. That Sully was an ace, you know?"

"You're sure? Even if that one witness was quite adamant about what he saw? Even if this witness otherwise seemed to be a respectful, sober, God-fearing citizen? You're sure there was no miracle?"

"Well, no. I'm not positive. I wasn't there."

"What if I told you that fully eighty percent of the passengers on the plane, who were indeed there that day, used the word 'miracle' in describing their experience? What then, Mr. Daly?"

"They were just happy to be alive, that's all."

Julius looked at the clock. "On Monday, please come to class prepared to discuss miracles in greater depth. Write a three paragraph argument as to whether the incident we have discussed was a miracle, why or why not. I stop reading at the end of the third paragraph. Consider also, please, if you have witnessed a miracle in your short lives. And make sure to read and understand the assigned reading from Spinoza on the subject. Have a good weekend, ladies and gentlemen."

Julius bent and gathered up the drool soaked messenger bag from under Jack as the students filed out. He sat down and started putting away his papers when he noticed that Ms. Chu was standing in front of the desk.

"Yes, Ms. Chu?" he asked, looking up at her.

"Do we have a problem, Father Zimmerman?" the woman asked, arms folded across her laptop like a shield on her chest.

"We have a problem if you think we have a problem, Ms. Chu."

"I think I've been in your class exactly twice and both times you've given me a pretty hard time."

"I'm sorry you feel that way, Ms. Chu. I meant no offense, I assure you."

"So I don't have to worry that every class is going to be like that, then?"

"I make no promises, Ms. Chu."

"I like the class, Father. I don't want to have to change sections."

"Fine, then. I'll see you on Monday, Ms. Chu." He went back to putting his papers away. Chu stood before him for a moment more, then turned and left.

Julius looked up and saw Father Pauley still seated in the last row. Julius got up and walked back to sit with him. Jack followed and sat next to Pauley, letting the older man scratch his head.

"Hey, Pete," Julius greeted the man. "Good to see you."

"Julius, good to see you, too. Who's 'the old guy?' "

"That would be you."

"I was afraid of that. You were pretty tough on that one."

"That's what you pay me for, Father."

"I don't pay you that much, Julius."

"True. What can I do for you, Pete?"

"Are you very busy?"

"Oh, oh. This can't be good."

"It's not so bad. I need a favor. Father Sutton was supposed to moderate one of the sessions tomorrow, but he had to bow out."

"Really? Sutton loves that conference. Prepares for it all year. What happened?"

"He's having surgery in two weeks. Prostate cancer."

"Oh, I'm sorry to hear that. Is he going to be okay?"

Pauley shrugged. "God willing, he should be. He's not a young man, but they say they caught it early."

"I'll include him in my prayers this evening."

"Great. So you'll cover his session tomorrow?"

Julius nodded. "Sure, no problem. What's the topic?"

Pauley handed over a manila folder of papers. "Here's the list of presentations. The session is titled 'Secular Reasoning and Modern Threats to Church Dogma.' "

"Really? The war on Christmas? Who comes up with this stuff?" Julius asked, taking the papers from the other man.

"That would be me. You know, the old guy." He stood and clapped Julius on the shoulder. "Thanks, Julius."

"My pleasure, Pete. Give my best to Sutton when you see him."

CHAPTER 6

Julius sat at his desk that evening reviewing the raft of papers Pauley had given him. He went through the materials provided by each of the scheduled speakers. Several of the presenters had provided a full transcript of their planned lecture, others only a printed version of their Power Point presentation. He reviewed each of the attached biographies. It seemed his biggest challenge in moderating tomorrow's session was to be the proper pronunciation of the Polish priest's name for his introduction. The second biggest challenge was going to be staying awake throughout the entire, tedious session.

Julius went through the pages again, searching. The session was scheduled to include six presentations, but Pauley had given him materials relating to only five. He checked the program again. The last presentation was scheduled to be something titled "A New Existential Threat to the Moral Authority of the Church." The presenter was listed as Charles Parnell, PhD. That piqued Julius's curiosity—all the other speakers were senior Catholic clergy, their names followed by the suffix "S.J." He paged through the materials again and found the bio sheet for Parnell. While the others went on for several paragraphs, Parnell's was one sentence: "Charles Parnell is a doctor of philosophy, President and member of the

First Quorum of the Seventy." Zimmerman scratched his head. He had never heard of the First Quorum of the Seventy. He opened his laptop and typed the phrase into Google.

"Holy Mother of God," Julius whispered under his breath. Jack gave him a look. The man was a Mormon. He clicked on the top reference and was directed to the Church of Latter-Day Saints website. There was a list of the First Quorum of the Seventy, listed alphabetically, and there, indeed, was the name of Charles Parnell. What the hell was a Mormon doing as a presenter at Sutton's annual Georgetown Conference on Contemporary Theology? Zimmerman had attended half a dozen of the meetings in the past. He knew it was rare enough for a non-Jesuit to present at the forum, had never heard of anyone from outside the Catholic hierarchy even attending. Weird.

It now made more sense, though, that the materials were missing from Parnell's presentation. Obviously, Sutton had accepted his presentation not realizing who or what the man was. Once he figured it out, Sutton must've talked to Parnell and the man had decided to pull out of the conference. Julius thought of trying to reach Sutton to confirm his suspicions, but when he looked at his cellphone, he saw that it was after eleven. Too late to politely call the elderly priest recently diagnosed with prostate cancer, he thought. Julius would just have to be prepared to fill up the time scheduled for the missing talk somehow. He'd probably just open the panel up for general questions at the end. That usually was good for killing a half hour or so. He closed up his computer and took Jack out for his night time bathroom break.

The next morning, Julius gave Jack over to Steve, the young priest who lived next door in the dorm. Dressed in his best navy blue suit and collar, he walked over to Gaston Hall to set up for the conference. It wasn't scheduled to begin until nine, but Julius planned on arriving early to make sure he had everything ready.

When Julius arrived and checked in with the coordinator, he was surprised to find that his session was to be held in the main auditorium. He had assumed that his was to be one of the minor sessions, held in one of the smaller conference rooms. He walked into the ornate, 700-seat hall and stared. A table was set up on stage as well as the usual speaker's podium and large projection screen. He walked up the center aisle and mounted the steps to the stage. Julius glanced at the placards in front of the table and saw his own on the end closest to the podium, with "Moderator" under his name. There were six other placards, with Parnell's at the opposite end of the table. That's pretty strange, Julius thought. The coordinator got the news that I'd be subbing for Sutton in time to change the placard, but not that Parnell had cancelled. He put his messenger bag on the chair and went back up the aisle to find the coordinator.

Julius found the coordinator again outside the hall, talking to a bald guy wearing a white suit. They were both laughing at some quip the bald guy had made when Julius approached.

"Sorry, Ms. Elliott," Julius said. "I don't mean to interrupt, but there's been a minor mistake in the setup for my session."

The woman immediately turned to Julius with a look of concern. "I'm sorry, Father Zimmerman. What is the trouble?"

"Nothing serious, Ms. Elliott. Sutton probably just forgot to tell you. The last speaker, Parnell, has cancelled. We should remove his placard from the dais."

"I have?" the bald man in the white suit said, turning to Julius.

Julius turned to him and noticed that the man was also wearing white shoes. Who wears a white suit and white shoes to a religious conference? Zimmerman wondered silently. "I'm sorry, you are?" Julius asked the man in white.

"Parnell. Chuck Parnell. Who are you?"

Zimmerman blanched, looking at the man. He noticed now that he seemed older, probably early fifties or so. Almost as tall as Zimmerman, but thin as a rail. His suit hung on him like a scarecrow.

"I'm Father Zimmerman, Julius Zimmerman. I'm the moderator for this session."

"I thought Sutton was moderating."

"He was, but he was forced to withdraw at the last moment. I'm his replacement." Julius shook his hand. "I'm sorry, Dr. Parnell, I had assumed that you withdrew from the conference."

"Did Sutton say that? Why should I withdraw? What's going on, Zimmerman?"

"Please, Dr. Parnell, don't be upset. It's my mistake, I'm sure. I just assumed that you had decided to withdraw, because all of your materials were missing from the preparation package I was given." Parnell appeared to be looking about suspiciously. "Is there a problem, Dr. Parnell?"

"I didn't think so, not until you walked up, Zimmerman. Now I'm not so sure." He kept looking around and back to Julius. The man was anxious, to the point of almost twitching.

"Is there some reason that your presentation materials are missing from my folder, Dr. Parnell?"

"I didn't provide any." Julius raised an eyebrow. "Sutton was okay with it. I talked to him. He knew."

"As moderator, Dr. Parnell, you put me at a disadvantage, I'm afraid. May I review your materials prior to the start of the session? We have enough time, I believe."

"No, you may not. I told you, Sutton and I had an understanding. No advance materials, nothing to be published in the program or handouts except my name and the title of my talk."

"Really?"

"Yes, really. Sutton was fine with it."

"Well, I'm not sure that I'm fine with it, Dr. Parnell. And I'm the moderator now, not Father Sutton."

"What are you saying, Zimmerman? You kicking me off the program? Fine, just say the word, I'm out of here. Your loss, believe me. But tell me now, because I'm going to have to grab my stuff back from the projectionist guy. I'm not leaving anything here, that's for sure."

"No, Dr. Parnell, of course not. I'm not throwing you off. I'm saying that I'd like to review your materials before the session, so that I may moderate properly. I'm sure you know how these things work." He tried to look reasonable as the other man was getting visibly more agitated.

"Not gonna happen, Zimmerman. Just introduce me, that's all. You're going to have to hear it all at the same time as everybody else."

Zimmerman shrugged. "As you wish, Dr. Parnell." This is one weird guy, Julius thought—as if anyone gave a damn about the guy's lecture. Most of the audience would probably be snoring in their seats by the time this guy stood up to talk.

"I can give my talk, then?" Parnell asked. Julius nodded. "Okay, good. I came all the way from Salt Lake City, you know."

"Well, welcome to the nation's capital, Dr. Parnell," Julius said, turning to walk back into the hall.

"And no recording of any kind, Zimmerman! Sutton promised, no recording," Parnell called after him.

Zimmerman turned back to face the man. "That," he said, "you'll have to take up with Ms. Elliott, the coordinator. I'm just the moderator, Dr. Parnell. I look forward to your presentation." Elliott, he saw, had drifted away during the exchange.

"Oh, you're going to love it, Zimmerman."

"Please, call me Julius, Dr. Parnell."

"We're making history today, Julius!" The man looked liked he was about to jump into the air.

"If you say so, Dr. Parnell."

Julius returned to the stage and spoke with the technician. Together, they checked all the microphones. Julius tested the laser pointer and podium controls. Satisfied that all was ready, he took his seat at the table and watched the hall fill up.

Before long, the other presenters appeared and introduced themselves to Zimmerman. Each of the speakers took their chairs except Parnell. Parnell, Julius noticed, was pacing about the back of the hall, repeatedly leaving and re-entering through the back doors of the auditorium. He looked like an ice cream vendor walking about in that white suit, Julius thought.

Zimmerman's phone gave a soft bong from the table in front of him. Julius took the podium and called the session to order in his stage voice, then waited for the audience to settle into silence. He took a few minutes to welcome the attendees and express the regrets of Father Sutton for being unable to moderate this session as planned. After a few more platitudes regarding the earnestness of today's topic, he introduced the first speaker.

Two minutes into the first presentation, Parnell mounted the steps to take his seat on the dais, crossing in front of the speaker as he did so. Julius watched Parnell fidget in his chair as he monitored the time remaining for the first presentation. The first presenter finished with several minutes to spare, his conclusion prompting polite applause. Considerably more than it deserved, in Zimmerman's opinion. Julius retook the podium to introduce the second speaker and watched as Parnell left the dais to walk back up the center aisle, leaving the hall as Zimmerman finished the introduction and sat back at the table. Parnell returned and retook his seat in the middle of the fourth speaker's presentation, earning him a scowl from the priest at the podium. Parnell didn't seem to notice, but kept sitting at his end of the table, his knee bouncing nervously. During the fifth presentation, Parnell apologized to his neighbor at the table for spilling water onto his lap, speaking into the open microphone before him. Parnell, apparently oblivious to the fact that his comments were being broadcast at a volume equal to that of the presenter, then began to comment upon the relative unimportance of the speaker's topic. Julius had no choice but to walk down to Parnell's end of the table and switch off the man's microphone as discretely as he could, as the speaker continued droning on in apparent obliviousness. Julius returned to his seat and forced himself to listen to the man making no obvious point at the lectern.

Julius was trying hard not to rest his head in his hands. That certainly wouldn't do for the moderator. He scanned the audience before him and noted Father Pauley in the front row, looking amazingly attentive. Many others, however, had succumbed to obvious slumber, eyes closed and heads nodding rhythmically. Julius was certain that this was the single most tedious event in which he had ever been a participant—this from a man who had been forced to sit through countless military exercises, as well as many interminable Catholic ceremonies. Julius sat, dreading the last introduction he still needed to make. At least Parnell hadn't left the stage again. Zimmerman came back to attention as he heard the audience applaud without enthusiasm. He joined in, weakly.

After the speaker had returned to his seat, Julius took to the podium for his one sentence introduction of Dr. Charles Parnell. He looked over to the table and was horrified to see Parnell's seat again empty. He looked around anxiously, then jumped as Parnell tapped him on the shoulder. He had been standing directly behind Julius and now gave him a weak smile as those members of the audience still awake giggled slightly at the burlesque moment. Julius returned to his seat, unamused.

Parnell began inaudibly, having managed to noisily knock the microphone up in front of his nose as he placed his notes on the podium. This was compounded by Parnell's style of reading his presentation while looking straight down at his notes, chin on chest. Against his better judgment, Julius stood and repositioned the microphone for Parnell. Parnell came to a complete halt and looked lost for several moments. Parnell then gave Julius a quiet thank you and began his talk again from the beginning. Julius fought the urge to slap himself in the forehead.

"The moral authority of the Church," Parnell began again, "lies in the promise of eternal salvation. The moral authority of the Church," he said again in the exact same intonation, "lies in the promise of eternal salvation." Please don't let this man repeat every line of his presentation, Julius prayed to himself. "Without the promise of salvation as given us by Christ, where is the moral authority of the Church, or the motivation of the churchgoer? It is, of course, the universal fear of death that gives us our authority and our purpose. Our authority and purpose arise, of course, from the universal fear of death. And the unknown that follows death, of course."

Julius felt at that moment that the unknown that follows death may be a welcome relief from this man's style of public speaking. He forced himself to smile and pay attention. For a brief moment, Zimmerman blamed the stricken Father Sutton.

"I would like to report to you," Parnell droned on, "my fellow colleagues in Christ, today, to report to you today a very serious threat to our moral authority. I will report to you now an episode that threatens to explode—" here Parnell looked up at his audience and inexplicably smiled, "—to explode this authority by destroying our hold on this promise, our hold on this promise of salvation." Julius had no clue what the man might be talking about. He was fairly certain that every awake member of the audience shared his predicament.

"If this works," Parnell gave the audience another nervous smile, "I will now play for you a conversation recorded several years ago and which I have only recently become aware of recently in my possession. Please listen to this unedited, unaltered recording between Dr. Gabriel Sheehan, the deceased inventor of the well-known thought interpreting technology, and his late wife. This is a recording made in their lab. I'm going to play the recording now." A minute of silence followed as Parnell repeatedly stabbed at a button on the podium without result. As he began to glance about with a panicked expression, a hissing began loudly over the speakers, then diminished in volume as the recording continued:

"Hey, Gabe."

"Is it you, really? Leena?"

"Yeah, babe. You were expecting someone else?"

Julius listened more attentively. The woman's voice sounded familiar, but he couldn't place it.

"Where are you, Leena? I can't see you."

Zimmerman almost fell out of his chair as he turned to look at the screen behind him. It showed huge pictures of the two individuals speaking. He didn't recognize the man. The woman, he was sure, was the woman he had just visited two days ago in the hospital. He had to consciously make an effort to close his mouth.

"I'm dead, Gabriel. You figured that out, right?"

"How?"

"Haven't a clue on this end, honey. You'd know the answer better than me."

The recording ended with another hiss and Parnell cleared his throat.

"Yes, that's right," Parnell stated emphatically straight down into the podium. "You have just heard a recording between someone alive and someone who has passed into the great beyond, as it were, with someone who is indeed, actually already dead." Here Parnell looked up to his audience with obvious eagerness. He appeared somewhat disappointed in the faces he saw looking back. He continued doggedly, "This recording goes on to describe in great detail the actual existence and condition of a life that exists after death here on earth. It is an actual, verified recording between someone who is alive and someone who is actually, really dead." Here Parnell looked up from his notes to address the audience directly. "I believe," he concluded, "that this newly discovered evidence proving the certain knowledge of a life after death is the greatest threat to our authority as a church. Thank you for the opportunity to address you today this morning. Thank you."

Parnell's conclusion was greeted with awkward silence until Julius began to gently applaud. The applause was taken up weakly by the audience as Julius rose to take back the podium. Parnell just stood next to him until Julius gave him a little nudge and gestured him back to his seat.

"Thank you for that very interesting presentation, Dr. Charles Parnell. That concludes this session, ladies and gentlemen. Please join me in giving a round of applause to all of our speakers this morning." A smattering of applause mixed with the sound of the audience rising for the exits. Julius caught the eye of Father Pauley, still seated. Pauley stared back at him, looking deeply distressed. Julius just gave him a shrug.

Julius acknowledged the thanks of the speakers as he loaded his papers back in his bag. He couldn't help but notice Parnell still seated at the end of the table. He wasn't certain, but Julius felt that common decency and his role as moderator required him to go over and say a few kind words. The man looked deflated.

"Fascinating talk, Dr. Parnell," Julius said.

Parnell brightened and smiled up at him. "Did you think so? It is amazing, isn't it?" Julius could only nod. "I gotta tell you, though, Zimmerman. I was really expecting more of a reaction, you know?"

"Really?"

"Well, yeah. Come on, I just made the biggest announcement in the history of mankind, here for the first time, ever. I mean, this is bigger than landing on the moon, or the Rosetta stone, or anything, for chrissakes. Life after death." The man definitely looked disappointed.

"Well, I'm sure it just caught the audience by surprise."

"Is that what it was, you think?"

Julius nodded again. "Sure surprised me, I'll tell you." Julius smiled at him. He didn't bother to add that he knew for a fact that the putative dead person in the recording was alive and well just up the road. "Well, thanks for the presentation, Dr. Parnell. Have a safe trip back to Utah."

"Actually, I don't fly out until tonight. Do you want to get some lunch? I'm pretty sure Sutton mentioned lunch, after the presentation."

This caught Zimmerman by surprise. "Actually, I'm supposed to hand you over to Father Pauley," Julius said, turning to where Pauley had been seated. "But I see that he's left, I'm afraid."

"Oh, not a problem," Parnell said, smiling and rising to his feet. "Where should we go? Parnell declined Zimmerman's suggestion of a cafeteria on campus. They ended up seated in a back booth at The Tombs. Over lunch, Parnell told Julius of his discovery of the recording, of his relationship with the two individuals in the recording, of the world-shaking importance of the recording. After almost an hour, Julius could no longer contain himself.

"Dr. Parnell, I've got to tell you—"

"Please, Julius. Call me Chuck."

"Chuck, then. I've got to tell you something about your recording." Parnell waited, smiling between forkfuls of steak. "The woman in the recording, I think I know her."

"Really? No way, Julius. How could you? I mean, I've got to tell you, Helena really got around, you know? I mean, just from what I know about her, which isn't the half of it I'm sure, that woman really got around. She was something, I'll tell you. The strangest woman I ever met, that's for sure. Could swear like a sailor, too. One time—"

"I've met her, Chuck."

"It's possible, I guess. Like I said, she's—"

"Alive, Chuck. She's still alive. I met her two days ago."

Chuck looked at him confused, then smiled. "Not possible, Julius. She's dead. She's been dead almost four years now."

"I saw her two days ago, alive. I think someone is trying to trick you or something, Chuck," Julius said. "I'm sorry, but I'm sure it's the woman in your recording."

"Don't worry about it, Julius. Really." Parnell finished his lunch and put down his fork. "Someone who looks like her, sure, maybe. But it's not possible. I saw the woman die, watched her die. On video. Like thirty times, Julius."

Julius shrugged. The man didn't believe him, fine.

"She did have a twin sister, you know," Chuck said. "But she's dead, too."

Parnell made no effort to pick up the check, muttering something about "the moderator's prerogative." It was the most money Julius had spent in a year. Julius said goodbye as Parnell headed back to his hotel. Zimmerman checked on Jack and went to early Mass, still dressed in the navy suit. Sutton or Pauley, he wasn't sure which, owed him big time. Maybe both.

CHAPTER 7

Sunday morning was for church. No rowing, no running. Back home after services and changed into jeans, the plan to take Jack to the dog park had to be scrapped on account of rain. Jack didn't do rain. Actually, Jack's favorite activity on a rainy Sunday was a day-long classic movie marathon on the TV in the dorm's common room. Normally, Julius would've used the respite to work on his article. It wasn't due for another five weeks, but he was sure that Father Pauley would be asking for it early. He always did. Well, Pauley could cut him a little slack after yesterday's effort and expense. Julius shook his head, remembering his conversation over lunch with that queer man about his strange claim of proof of an afterlife.

Jack's snoring made working at the desk impossible. Julius thought about going to the library, but couldn't get yesterday's events out of his head. He put on his collar and a raincoat, left a bowl of water and food for Jack in case the dog regained consciousness, and headed for the subway.

Julius stood at the nursing station, dripping on the floor. The woman's hospital room was empty. He stood waiting as the ward clerk looked at her computer screen.

"I'm sorry, Father, I was wrong," the woman said, smiling apologetically. "She wasn't discharged after all. She was transferred, to room 240. Just yesterday."

"Thank you," Julius said. He headed back to the elevator. He was wondering if he should take the opportunity to head back to the lobby and get the woman another Snickers bar before he visited her. He certainly couldn't afford any more flowers. She had been pretty rude about the flowers, anyway, with that "no card" comment.

Julius found the appropriate hospital ward by following the signs. He stood staring at the door of the unit, locked. It was the psych ward. He pushed the intercom button on the wall and was buzzed onto the ward.

Julius looked around as he walked down the hall to the nursing station. He had never been on a psych ward before and felt uncomfortable. The place, however, looked deserted. He saw no patients at all. As he walked up the hall, he noticed the sign for room 240 and slowed to glance in. It also was empty. He continued to the nursing station.

"I'm here to visit the woman in room 240," Julius told the nurse at the desk.

"Are you a relative?" the woman asked.

"No, just visiting." Julius smiled uncomfortably at her. "I'm a priest," he added for no good reason, "it's what I do."

The woman smiled back. "That's fine, Father. I was just hoping you might be someone who knows something about her. Nobody can tell us anything and she's not talking."

"Really? What do you mean, not talking?"

"Just that, not talking. Not saying a word to no one."

"Is she here?"

"Probably in the day room. She walks around a lot." The nurse pointed him down the hall. Julius walked down the hall and found the dayroom. The woman was there, dressed in a hospital gown, and sitting with her legs tucked beneath her on the couch. She had her eyes closed, her face turned up to the light from the window. There wasn't much more than a suffused grayness, however, as it was still raining pretty hard outside. No one else was in the room, so Julius sat down on a chair opposite.

She smiled, though her eyes remained closed. "Either you're having a hard time finding another patient to minister to, or you have the most boring life in the world," she said.

He smiled back at her. "Well, that's a relief. The nurse said you weren't talking. I thought I might've come all this way in the rain just to stare at one another."

"A kinder man would find that sufficient, Father."

He lost his smile. The woman had an uncanny ability to put him on the defensive. "A more appreciative patient would be happy for the company."

"If you're looking for appreciation, Father, try the hospice unit down the hall. They tend to have lower standards." She opened her eyes to meet his, still smiling. He was starting to regret the trip. Again.

"Why are you here?" he asked.

She shrugged. "They don't know what to do with me, I guess. When they ran out of billable diagnoses on the regular ward, they tossed me in here. Probably billing under 'catatonia, undifferentiated' or 'traumatic amnesia.' Good for another ten or twenty grand, I'm sure."

"You're okay, then? You remember who you are?"

"I never forgot who I am, Father."

"Nobody knows your name," Julius said.

"You mean, nobody in this hospital knows my name."

"Yes, that's what I mean. And I don't know your name." She just nodded at him. "If you know your name, why won't you tell anyone? Why won't you tell me?"

"Like I told you, Father, last time. It's complicated. Don't take it personally. Believe me, if I was going to tell anyone, you'd be the first."

"Well, you don't have to," Julius replied, smiling a little too smugly. This isn't the way he had planned the conversation. He thought the whole discussion was going to be a lot more humorous.

"I know I don't. But thanks for being so supportive."

"No," Julius corrected, "that's not what I meant. You don't have to tell me, because I know who you are." The woman stopped smiling at this. She brought her feet to the floor in front of her and leaned forward, waiting. Now I have her attention, Julius thought. Not so high and mighty. "I met someone yesterday, someone who knows you." He waited, letting her chew on this for a bit. He waited for her to ask for him to continue, but she didn't. She just kept him fixed with her stare. She has green eyes, he noticed. He started to feel uncomfortable. Where were all the other patients, anyway?

"It's pretty quiet in here, huh?" Julius continued, deciding to try to defuse the situation a bit. "Not a lot of other patients."

"It's Sunday. They discharge everybody they can. Everybody else goes home on pass for the weekend. You want to take me out on pass, Father?"

Julius didn't think that was a great idea. "Honestly, I don't think they'd let me. Since I'm not family. You want to walk around a little?"

"You were saying you met someone who knew me. Yesterday, you said." She was still leaning forward, the hospital gown billowing around her like a tent. Julius really didn't like her body language; she looked tense.

"Yeah, weird guy," Julius went on. "He gave a presentation at the university. I teach at Georgetown, and they asked me to moderate a session at a theology conference yesterday. This guy gave a talk." She nodded at this, unsmiling. "Weird guy, really weird talk."

"What was his name?"

"Parnell. Dr. Charles Parnell. He's a Mormon minister or something, whatever they call they're officials. Pretty high up, I guess. Very strange man."

"Really, a Mormon? And a doctor?"

"Not a doctor, a PhD. In philosophy, from Salt Lake. But evidently pretty high up in the Mormon Church, a president of some quorum or something."

"But weird, you said?"

"Strangest guy I ever met," Julius said, a little relieved that the tension seemed to have lessened between them. He smiled. "White suit, white shoes. Couldn't sit still for a second."

"Ponytail?"

"Huh? Ponytail? No, the guy was bald. Completely bald." The woman just raised her eyebrows at this. "You know him?" She shook her head. "Well," Julius continued, "he thinks he knows you, poor fool. You were his whole presentation."

"I was?"

"Yeah, it was a little sad, really. He showed your picture, and another guy. You know, the guy who invented the mind reading company, I forget his name."

"He showed my picture? In his presentation?" Julius nodded. He had obviously gotten her attention, finally.

"Yeah, yours and that other guy."

"Why?"

Here, Julius smiled again. He leaned back in his chair to savor the delivery of his punch line. "That was the sad and weird part. His whole talk was based on believing you were dead." No reaction. No smile, no head shake. Weird, Julius thought, there should be some reaction.

"Really?" she said finally.

"Yeah, that was his whole point. He played a recording between you and the other guy. It was definitely you, I recognized your voice. But Parnell claimed that it was a conversation with the dead, because he knew you were dead."

"Weird."

"Yeah, like I said. Weird and a little pathetic."

"Why would he think I was dead, do you think?"

"Oh, he was convinced you were dead, over four years he said. I had lunch with the guy, didn't have a choice. He told me he had watched you die, on video, like thirty times. He was absolutely convinced that the recording was between that mind reading guy and you, after you died. He actually said, 'from the great beyond,' I think." Julius chuckled. The woman didn't, however. She didn't move. Julius was starting to feel uncomfortable again, though he wasn't certain exactly why.

"I felt kinda sorry for him, to tell you the truth," Julius continued. "I tried to tell him he was mistaken."

"You did?"

"Yeah." Julius knew he was taking a little risk here, but he wanted to see her reaction. "I told him he was mistaken, that the woman in his presentation wasn't dead. I told him that I was afraid he was being played in some way." She stared at him, unmoving. "I told him I had just seen you, alive. Two days ago." He watched her, waiting for a reaction.

"You told him that you'd seen me? Alive?" Her voice was soft, maybe a little too soft—menacing, Julius thought. He nodded. "You stupid, fucking moron!" she said, not softly.

Julius blanched. He didn't think he had been called that since leaving the Navy, certainly not since he'd divorced his wife. He was going to say something in response, but the woman suddenly shot off the couch and grabbed Zimmerman by the neck in a strangle hold. Julius was shocked. Without thinking, he reflexively brought both hands hard up between her forearms and broke her hold free. Their eyes met for an instant, just before the woman snapped her elbow across his nose and then punched him in the solar plexus. Julius doubled over and the woman grabbed his collar, throwing him to the floor.

Zimmerman wasn't certain what the woman was planning on doing next, but he wasn't about to wait to find out. He lashed out with his arm and caught her heel, sweeping it out from under her. He glimpsed her falling and twisted to face her, barely blocking a kick from her other leg aimed at his head. Shit, he thought, who the hell is this woman? The kick had been well aimed but off balance, landing her on her back. Julius was on top of her in a second, then found he had to block a flurry of strikes aimed at his head and face. He felt a rib snap as she got a shot into his side with her knee. He winced, but now he was really pissed. Zimmerman wadded her gown into her face as he sat heavily on her chest, pinning her arms with his knees. She struggled, but her something just over a hundred pounds wasn't going to budge his two sixty-five. Finally.

"Shit!" he exclaimed when he was finally able to take a breath. The rib sent a stab of pain with every inspiration. "You fight like a fucking Israeli!" He wiped at his nose and his hand came away bloody. He wiped off his hand on the woman's gown.

"Yeah, well you fight like a fuckin' girl," she replied from under him, struggling.

He smiled. "Like a girl, huh? Who's sitting on top, little lady?"

"Yeah, well, I'm wondering how you're going to explain sitting on top of me, asshole, when the nurses walk through that door."

This gave Julius a moment's pause. He realized at that moment that he was, indeed, sitting astride the chest of a woman patient who was naked beneath him, her gown gathered over head. This was going to take a little explaining. Zimmerman turned to look over at the door. She took that moment to snap her head forward, her forehead smashing into his testicles. He grunted and crumpled forward. She kicked hard off the floor and used his momentum to buck him off, his head hitting the wall behind her. In a split second, she was on him. Zimmerman's head was dizzy with the impact. He felt her knee in the small of his back, his right leg bent double and pinned in her crotch as she straddled him. His left arm was pulled painfully up behind his shoulder blade and to complete the situation, she grabbed his hair with her other hand and pulled his head back, hard. And his rib really hurt, too.

Damn Krav Maga, Julius thought to himself. Back in training, he always hated fighting against guys who used that technique. Why didn't anybody just punch you anymore? He lay face down on the floor, pinned and in pain. Zimmerman realized from his SEAL training days that in his current position this woman could certainly kill him in at least three different ways. He decided to look on the bright side, realizing that if she was going to kill him, she probably would've done it already. He decided to try charming her.

"Wanna go two out of three?" He tried to sound nonchalant, not like someone who was about to die painfully.

"Shut up," she hissed in his ear. "I'm thinking."

"Take your time. I'm good here." There was a brief pause during which he could hear her breathing raggedly, her breath hot on the side of his face.

"Okay, Julius fucking Father Zimmerman," she said, still holding his head back uncomfortably. "Here's the deal. I'm going to let you go in a second—"

"Oh, good. So you're not going to kill me then?"

"No, I wouldn't feel right about killing another priest, lucky for you."

"I'm sorry, did you say—"

"Shut up, dammit," she said into his ear. "I'm going to let you up. And you, Father Zimmerman, since you have completely fucked me and probably gotten me good and killed, are going to help me get out of here. Got it?"

"Sure, no problem."

She released her multiple holds and plopped down onto the couch. She blew a lock of red hair up off her forehead. Zimmerman painfully rose from the floor and sat with a grunt back in his chair. They stared at one another, both breathing heavily.

"Where the hell are all the nurses?" Julius asked.

"Probably playing cards at the nursing station. You got a little blood there, Father," she said, gesturing to her nostril. He wiped away another trickle of blood and wiped it on the chair cushion.

"Your gown's a little askew," he told her, gesturing. Her gown was mostly hanging, cape-like, behind her.

"Sorry," she said, blushing slightly. She pulled the gown around, covering herself.

"So, this is nice," Julius said, smiling.

"Glad you came to visit?" she said.

"Not so much." He winced as he took a deep breath.

"Rib?"

He nodded. "You were saying something about how I fucked you and probably got you killed."

"Yeah. Thanks for that, Father Zimmerman."

"How about we pray together?"

"Maybe later, after you get me out of here."

"Yeah, how exactly do you think I should do that?"

"Give me a minute."

"Just tell me again why I should do that? I mean, it did sound like a pretty good idea when you had me by the hair a minute ago and all—"

"Give me two seconds of grief, Padre, and I'll start screaming rape at the top of my lungs. Believe me, buddy, the way we look right now, nobody's gonna doubt it for a second."

Julius swallowed hard. Lady had a point, he had to admit. He was not happy that she seemed to be making all the points.

"Okay," she said, "this is how this is going to play out. First, I'll need some clothes. You got a car here?" He shook his head.

"Took the subway."

"Shit. I'll work on that after. First, I need you to get me some clothes."

"Yeah, how am I going to do that?"

"Don't play stupid with me, Father. Unless the Jesuits are teaching close quarters combat at the monastery, you were Special Forces of some sort. Don't pretend to look so innocent, chum." Julius lowered his eyebrows back to rest position. "Clean yourself up and get into the girls OR locker room, steal me some scrubs and shoes out of a locker. Size 6. I'm sure you've done tougher shit in your day." He nodded at her, serious now that he realized that he might really have to help this crazy lady escape.

"How'd you know I was a Jesuit?" he asked her.

"God's Marines, baby."

"I was never a Marine, honey."

"Delt? Greenie beanie? Some black ops group I never heard of?"

"Navy."

"A puke? Really? No shit."

"Nobody's called me that since I finished SEAL training."

"Until now, sugar." She smiled at him and gestured to her nose. He wiped away another drip of blood. "Go get me something cute to wear."

"How do you know I won't just walk straight out of here?"

"Because you know that by the time you make it back to Georgetown, the police will be waiting to arrest you for attempted rape and assault of a frail, defenseless psych patient."

"Frail, my ass."

"Hoya saxa, Father. Don't take too long, we got places to go."

CHAPTER 8

Zimmerman returned twenty minutes later with a pair of woman's small surgical scrubs and size 6 ½ shoes tucked under his arm. He sat down again across from his new accomplice in the day room.

"Have to stuff someone in a locker to get those?" she asked as he sat down.

"Like you said, I've done tougher shit in my day."

"Glad to hear it. You got a watch?" He shook his head. "Jeez! No car, no watch. I gotta get me a better partner."

"Be my guest."

"Maybe later, after we pray together. Count to a hundred, then."

"Yeah, then what?"

She rolled her eyes. "Then you stand up and walk out of here like the innocent priest you are, *mon frere*. Just make sure the nurses buzz the door open. Got it?"

"Doesn't sound too hard."

"Stay close to the right side of the hall as you walk down. You knew that, right?" He didn't credit this with a response. "Great. Start counting."

She took the clothing from him and left. He counted, and tried to think of exactly how he was going to ditch this woman. She had him in a bit of a bind. Zimmerman's past did make his position at Georgetown rather tenuous. Julius couldn't afford the girl reporting him, even if the accusation was bullshit. Well, not entirely bullshit, he realized—they had been fighting. And Julius didn't think many people would believe he was attacked by a woman about half his size. He would have to dump her in a way that prevented her from playing the rape accusation gambit. Nothing was coming to mind as he reached ninety-nine. Something would come to him, he was sure. He'd just have to see how this played out. Julius stood and walked nonchalantly past the nursing station. He gave the nurse at the desk a smile.

"Could you buzz me out, please?" he asked as he walked past. She nodded. As he approached Room 240, keeping close to the right side of the hallway, the woman emerged just in front of him. Now dressed in scrubs, she smoothly walked in front of Zimmerman as they passed through the buzzing door.

As the door clicked shut, she dropped back to walk by his side.

"Smooth," Zimmerman said. "Where to?" He looked around, hoping to see a security guard he could enlist. Nobody else was in the hallway.

"Stairway."

"Elevator's right here."

"Yeah, nice try, Zimmerman. When you came in, was there valet parking?" They went through the door into the stairway and started down together.

"Yeah, front entrance. Why?"

"You got to pick up your car, that's why." She turned to give him a smile.

"You are not asking me to steal a car."

"You're right. I'm not asking, Padre." She started going down the steps two at a time and Julius picked up his pace to stay with her. They came through the first floor door into the lobby. She continued, "I'll be in the valet lot. You grab the keys."

"Hey! I'm not—" She stopped dead in her tracks and gave him a cut-glass green stare. "You don't even know where the valet lot is," he finished weakly. She turned from him and hit the main entrance doors to the outside.

"I'll just follow this guy in the cute uniform, I guess," she said, starting to sprint after the valet running to get a car.

Zimmerman was left standing at the front entrance. Decision time, he realized. Let the crazy lady loose on the world as he went back inside to notify security? Not good enough, he thought. Besides, the girl had genuinely piqued his interest—Julius needed to know what this was about. She knew this Parnell guy, obviously. And Zimmerman had revealed something, maybe something that had really put her in danger. Julius shook his head. Besides, he realized, the girl really could report him. Actually, she didn't have to. He had already helped her off a locked ward. He'd have a hard time explaining how she had forced him into it. Julius realized he had two seconds to make this decision. Still high on the adrenaline from the fight, Zimmerman had to admit that this was a helluva lot more exciting than spending the afternoon at the library. 'Puke,' my ass, he thought. Looking around, he saw the locker with the rows of hanging keys. Zimmerman walked over and grabbed a set, turned and started walking quickly in the direction the valet and his new friend had run.

"Hey," Julius heard from behind him. "Can I help you, Father?"

Zimmerman just held the keys up in his hand as he strode away. "That's okay, I got it, son." He kept walking towards the lot without looking back.

The first valet passed him driving back to the entrance. When Julius got to the lot, he saw the woman standing next to a black Porsche. Julius just shook his head.

"Over here," he said to her, reading the number off the tag and heading to the spot where a brown Honda was parked. She walked over.

"Wrong car," she said.

He looked at her, puzzled. "What do you mean? I got the keys. Let's go."

She shook her head. "No fucking way we're taking that. That's our car," she said, pointing back to the Porsche.

"I am not going back and switching keys. No way, sister." He crossed his arms and tried to look determined. This woman was nuts, no doubt about it. She just stared at him. "You're kidding, right?" he asked. She didn't say anything. "That Porsche is probably a stick anyway."

"You can't drive a stick?"

He shook his head. "Never learned."

"I can't believe this. You really a freakin' Navy SEAL?"

"They don't teach manual transmission in BUD/S, lady. You do realize that we're standing in the middle of this parking lot stealing a car in broad daylight, right?"

"You're really going to make me go and switch the keys, tough guy?"

"You're really saying that we gotta steal a Porsche instead of a perfectly fine Honda? To which I am already holding the keys?"

"It's brown, Father. We can't leave here in a brown Honda, come on." He tossed her the keys. "Puke pussy," she muttered as she turned to sprint back to the hospital entrance.

"I heard that," he called after her. "Fucking nutcase," he added, more softly.

"Heard that," she called back over her shoulder.

She came back running much faster, waving the Porsche keys. Then Julius noticed the valets at the entrance pointing in their direction.

"I think they noticed," Zimmerman said as he ran behind her to the car. She got in the driver's side so he ran around and jumped into the passenger seat.

"Don't think that's going to matter," she said, starting the car.

"You say so," Julius said, not quite getting the door closed before the woman had the car squealing backwards out of the parking space.

"You're going to want to put on the seat belt, probably," she said. "Otherwise it makes that annoying dinging sound." Zimmerman's head snapped back into the headrest as she slung the car forward, shifting with her right hand as she buckled her seatbelt with the left.

"Might want to actually use the steering wheel," Zimmerman said, buckling his seatbelt.

"Driving tips from the guy who can't drive a stick?" She slalomed past the main entrance and gave a little wave as they bounced over the speed bump and tore away onto the main road. Zimmerman was shaking his head. The woman, however, was smiling broadly. "Man, these things have gotten a lot quicker in four years. Wow."

"I'm glad you're enjoying yourself. Just where are we going, any-way?" He started to check the mirrors for police flashers. "Holy Shit!" Julius exclaimed, grabbing the dashboard as she swerved at high speed around a car pulling out of a side street in front of them.

"Quite the joker, aren't you, Father?" she said, winking at him as she shifted through the gears. She was easily doing over eighty, he figured. "Not far. Just a few blocks up the road here." She fiddled with the controls to get the wipers going.

"We coulda walked," Julius said, releasing his death grip on the dashboard.

"Yeah, that would've looked special. A priest and a tiny lady surgeon, walking hand in hand down the street in the pouring rain. Like we just escaped the circus. No thanks, this is a lot more fun."

"Sure, we're having a lot of fun now. But in a couple of minutes, when we're face down on the ground with our hands cuffed behind us, not so much."

"We'll be gone by then, Father."

"We?"

"Well, I'll be gone. You may have some explaining to do, or running. You're choice." She suddenly braked hard and made a sharp left, down-shifted and accelerated, rear wheels screeching, snapping into a quick right turn. "I love this car. And you wanted to take the Honda." She steadily accelerated through the gears, passing other cars on Highway 191 like they were standing still. Still no sirens or flashers in his rear view mirror. They flew over the 495 bridge and she braked hard into a sweeping left hand turn, the engine screaming as she double clutched and downshifted, accelerating as she came out of the curve.

"So where are you going?" Julius asked, pulling his seatbelt tighter.

"7927 Deepwell Drive. The Robert Llewellyn Wright house. National landmark and my door outta here. Time to go home to fight another day."

"I'm sorry, what right house?" He grabbed the dash again as she slammed the brakes for a sharp left turn, power sliding into a residential neighborhood, then tweaking the steering wheel to bring the rear end back in as they entered another straightaway. She was smiling broadly.

"Robert Llewellyn," she said, hammering the shifter back up the sequence of gears. "You should check it out sometime. You know, a Frank Lloyd Wright house, coming up on the right here."

"Stop the car." He grabbed her arm on the stick. "Stop the damn car! Now!" She stood on the brakes and swerved to the curb, just barely tucking in behind a parked car.

"What? We're not there yet. It's a little farther up the road." She looked at him.

"I'm not sure. There could be a problem."

"What problem? What are you talking about, Zimmerman?"

He thought for a moment. "I don't know."

She looked at him quizzically. "You're weird, you know that?"

"Look, just do a drive-by, okay? I got a bad feeling."

"What? What bad feeling? Are you screwing with me, Julius?"

He shook his head. "Like this. What's this?" Julius asked, pointing at the sidewalk just ahead of them. She looked, and saw the man walking past them on the sidewalk. He was walking in the rain, dressed in a white bathrobe and slippers, apparently in no hurry.

She blanched and turned her head away towards the driver's side window, covering her face with her hand.

"Shit, I do not believe this!" she said. The man walked past.

"A little weird, I gotta admit," Zimmerman said.

"Shut up," she responded, backing the car and pulling back out into the street. "Keep your eyes open. It's the gray house with the flat roof, on the right." She drove slowly past the house. "Shit, shit, shit, shit, shit," she chanted softly as they drove past. She continued another hundred yards and pulled to the curb again.

"Shit is right," Julius said. "If they weren't your people, then you are screwed."

"You saw that, right?"

"Yeah, I saw that."

"Tell me."

"Guy on the porch with an automatic weapon, another guy—"

"Wait, how do you know?" she asked.

"Because the dude's sitting there with an automatic weapon sized blanket on his lap, and it's like eighty degrees out here." She nodded.

"What else?"

"Guy leaning on the fence across the street with a sidearm."

"How do you know? I didn't see him."

"Then you're blind. He had a jacket on, zipped up halfway. Definitely packing. Not to mention the third window from the end, somebody peering out the blinds, too."

"Yeah, saw that," she said. Zimmerman shrugged.

"I take it they're not yours, then."

"No, they're not mine."

"How about robe and slippers guy?"

"Hard to be sure, but no, not mine either," she said.

"Just as well. He looked weird."

She put the car in first gear and started to slowly pull away from the curb.

"Where are we going? Find your people?" Julius asked.

"Got no people, Padre. Just going." She slowly followed the looping residential road.

"Well, your safe house looks like it's blown. Time to get to GODD."

"Not really a time to go all Jesuit on me, Zimmerman."

"No, I meant your extraction point, your rally-evac location, whatever you call it. We called it the 'Get Out of Dodge Dot.' You know, on the map. GODD."

"Oh. Cute. Spec Ops lingo, got it. That there was it, Padre." She stopped at the light where the road joined back to Highway 191. As they waited at the light, a police cruiser slowly went past from right to left. As it passed, they both saw the officer's head swivel as he saw their car. "Shit," she said softly.

"Bingo," he agreed. She suddenly accelerated against the red light, cutting off oncoming traffic as she made a right onto the highway in the opposite direction that the cruiser had gone. Horns blared as she rapidly accelerated up the highway back the way they had come.

"That was fucking fast," she said, exasperated.

"This is DC, lady. There are more cops in this town per square foot than anyplace else in the world."

"Great." She slalomed around traffic, still accelerating. She saw the entrance for the 495 expressway and cut off a truck as she swerved to make the ramp, then accelerated again onto the Beltway. Zimmerman checked his mirror.

"Clear for the moment. Not long, though." She nodded, shifting and moving from lane to lane through traffic. She jumped on the brakes and suddenly exited off the highway onto the cloverleaf to Highway 190 heading south. No cops. "So where we going, sister?"

"Not really sure right now, Julius. Open to suggestions."

He shrugged. "Not my op. Not a clue."

"Pretend. Humor me." She took a hard right onto an exit and slowed onto a commercial road. She suddenly cut into a side road. She stopped, then accelerated in reverse into an alley. She stopped the car and leaned her forehead on the steering wheel. "I'm listening, Julius."

"Serious?"

"As the fucking angel of death, Father."

"I don't have a clue. I don't know who you are or why you're here. I don't know the mission, the parameters, the ROE. What are your assets, who's the opposition, what are their resources? How am I supposed to help?"

"You got a point."

"Damn right." He watched a car cross the end of the alley. She sighed.

"You say you teach at Georgetown, huh?" He nodded. "Live there?" Julius nodded again. She put the car in gear and pulled out of the alley.

"What? You think I'm taking you home? No way, lady." They both looked right as a siren started up. A police cruiser lit up its flashers and started to race toward them.

"Shit, there's a lot of cops in this town," she said. She accelerated the car down the street and exited the way she came, getting back on the expressway. Zimmerman watched in his mirror as the cruiser followed down the ramp.

"Still there."

"Yeah, noticed that. Help me here, Julius. Directions."

"I'm not giving you directions to my place. Are you nuts?"

"Good point. Okay, you said you took the subway to the hospital?" She was driving like a crazy person now, slaloming between cars, accelerating to stay ahead of the cruiser. She was actually pulling away, he noticed. The girl could drive.

"Yeah, so what?"

"Commuter lot? Park and ride?"

"Not sure."

"Think. Dammit, Julius, I could use a little help here."

"Yeah, I think there's a commuter lot. I don't commute, okay?"

"Don't get whiney. Parking structure or flat lot?" She swerved across four lanes of traffic and shot up an exit ramp, the cruiser shooting past and missing the exit.

"Nice."

"Yeah, you can flatter me later, if we don't crash first. Structure or flat?"

"Structure, right next to the station."

"Okay, that'll work. Get me there, Julius."

"Get you where?"

"The subway station! Stay with me here, Zimmerman."

He looked around to get his bearings. "I don't get out to Bethesda very often..."

"Stop whining and get us there, Father," she said, aggressively downshifting as she maneuvered through the side streets.

He saw a familiar corner, suddenly knew where they were. "Okay, right turn."

"Where?"

"Back there."

"Thanks, Julius," she swerved into the next right turn.

"Straight."

"I can do that."

"Next right. Shit!" A police cruiser, lights flashing, appeared straight ahead of them and crossed into their lane, approaching head-on. She snapped the car down the next right hand turn as the cruiser swept past, siren screaming a decrescendo. The parking structure loomed straight ahead. She wasn't slowing down.

"Uh, you're going pretty fast. Like really—"

Julius threw his arms over his face as they crashed through the entrance gate and onto the circular ramp. He cringed and held on to the dash with both hands. She circled the ramp at a ridiculously excessive speed, tires squealing, for four levels and then swerved out, yanking hard on the emergency brake and skidding to a 180 degree stop just outside a stairwell.

They both ran to the stairs and started down, two steps at a time. They came pounding out the door in time to see a police cruiser, sirens blaring and lights flashing, start up the ramp. They both immediately slowed to a walk. She took his hand as they walked into the subway station, took the escalator down to the platform. She looked around, and seeing no one, slid smoothly over the top of the turnstile. He did the same. A minute later, they boarded a train.

They sat down in the rearmost seat, facing forward. She put her head on his shoulder and closed her eyes. He took off his collar and put it in his pocket. He put his arm around her. They sat for a minute, catching their breath.

"Okay, Julius," she said softly, her head still on his shoulder. "Start talking."

"What?"

"What, what? You know what. How'd you know?"

"I'm not sure."

"Don't make me beat your sorry ass again, Zimmerman." He smiled at that.

"Robert Llewellyn."

"Yeah, so?"

"I got a message from a Robert Llewelyn a couple of days ago. The day you jumped off that bridge."

"I was pushed."

"Whatever."

CHAPTER 9

Zimmerman told her the story of the boatman's note, of the response he got when he called the number.

"Twice?" she said incredulously, her head coming up off his shoulder so she could look at him. "You called twice?"

"Yeah. The guy was pretty rude, too."

"Used your cellphone, of course."

"Yeah, of course," he agreed.

"Got it with you, Father?" she asked innocently.

"Sure do."

"Can I see it for a second?"

He smiled at her. She looked as innocent as a twelve year old all of a sudden. "Yeah, right."

"What? I'll give it right back. I just want to check—"

"What? You want to check how stupid I am? You're going to chuck it out the window. Not a chance, sister."

She pouted and put her head back on his shoulder. "I'm hurt that you don't trust me, Julius."

"You'll get over it. And it's not in that pocket, so stop groping." She sat up again.

"Then you toss it, Julius. You know it's a problem, don't be a dick."

"I'm not tossing away my phone. It's not a problem. You're just being paranoid."

She gave him a baleful look but said nothing, then stood up.

"Let's get off this train," she said, walking to the door.

"Where are we going?"

"Your place."

"I knew you were going to say that."

"Come on, Julius. We got to get back to walk the dog."

He raised his eyebrows. "More likely you're thinking of chucking him back in the river."

She gave him a hurt look as she stepped off the train. He followed. They walked along the platform to change trains home.

"They might have planted a tracker or something on him, you know."

"You're certifiable, you know that?"

"You said he was a pain in the ass, anyway."

"You know who else is a pain in the ass?"

"Hey, Jack," Julius said to the dog, opening the door to his room. Jack came waddling over, stump tail wagging. Julius tossed his keys on the desk and sat heavily on the bed. He watched Jack run over to the woman as she came in and dropped to her knees.

"Well, who do we have here?" she asked the dog. Jack came over, his whole rear end wagging, and proceeded to start licking her face. She rumpled his ears and gave him a pet on the back.

"Checking for implants?" Julius asked from the bed, smiling. "Might want to do a rectal, maybe they shoved it up his ass."

The woman and Jack were rolling on the floor, rough-housing. Julius watched. Jack wasn't often playful. Like, ever. Eventually, they both came over and flopped down on the bed next to Julius. Jack laid his muzzle on her stomach. She scratched his head between his ears. Jack thrummed.

"Careful, he drools," Julius warned.

"Don't we all, huh, Jack?" she said to him.

"Come on," Julius said, standing. "Let's go for a walk." Jack looked at him. "Come on, Jack. Rain stopped." Jack hopped off the bed with a thump and waddled to the door. Julius turned to the woman on the bed. "You coming?"

"Sure. I could use a walk."

The three of them walked slowly across campus. Jack stopped at several trees as they passed the commons. He acknowledged the occasional well wisher.

"That's one popular dog you got there, Julius."

"He's not really mine. He's the school mascot. I'm just taking care of him."

"Oh." They walked on together for a while, then sat down on a bench. They watched Jack walk around the commons, greeting his subjects.

"You're wrong, you know," Julius said. "About Robert Llewellyn."

"Am I?" she asked, still watching the dog and smiling.

"Yeah. Whoever left that message isn't a threat. Doesn't make sense. Just the opposite. I think it was a warning."

"You mean to scare you off?"

"No, not at all. A warning for you, about your safe house. Somehow, they knew I'd get you the message. Doesn't make sense, otherwise."

She nodded. "You could be right, Julius. Sometimes I can be a little overly suspicious. Or so I've been told." Jack came over and sat at her feet. She scratched his head between his ears.

Julius looked at her. "Who are you?" he asked finally.

"That's hard to say, Julius," she said, shaking her head as she kept scratching the dog.

"Why? It's hard to pronounce? I need a name. I got to call you something."

"Call me Joyce," she said.

"Can't call you that," he said. She looked at him, questioning. "That was my ex-wife's name. Pick another."

"Gee, Julius, you got issues. Call me Mary, then."

"Yeah, issues. Mary, then. Seems to me, Mary, that you're in pretty deep kimchee at the moment." She nodded at that. "That true what you said at the hospital? My fault?"

She nodded again. "Pretty much, yeah, Julius. Don't be too hard on yourself, though. I knew I was skating on pretty thin ice."

"So what did I do?"

"You, Julius, dropped a big fucking boulder through the ice. Then you pushed me in." He nodded at that. Julius stood up.

"Let's get something to eat, guys. Pizza, Jack?" Jack sprang to his feet. He barked.

They had pizza delivered to Zimmerman's room. Jack ate two pieces out of the box.

"No beer, huh?" Mary asked, eating her pizza while sitting on the end of Zimmerman's bed. "Can't have pizza without beer."

"That'd be great. Why don't you make a run to the convenience store at the end of the block?" Julius asked her from his seat at the desk. "Oh, right. You haven't had a chance to knock over a bank yet."

"You're angry, I can tell, Julius," she said, giving her crust to the dog.

"He's on a diet, okay?" Julius tried to grab for the crust but Jack beat him to it. "And yeah, Mary, I'm a little angry. You know, breaking my rib, getting me to help steal a car, that sort of thing. And all this after I bought you flowers."

"I'm sorry, Julius."

"Flowers weren't even in your room."

"They weren't?" He shook his head. "Yeah, I guess you're right. But there was no card."

Zimmerman stood and picked up the empty pizza box and stuffed it in the wastebasket. "So now what, Mary?"

She shook her head. "Fact is, Julius," she said, "my options are pretty limited at the moment." He sat back down, straddling the desk chair, listening. "Not the way this was supposed to play out, you know."

"Yeah, I got that impression a little while ago. Right about the instant you called me a stupid, fucking moron."

"I was angry."

"And now?"

"I've forgiven you, Julius."

"Oh, swell. So listen, Mary, now that we've had our fun today and dinner and all, how 'bout Jack and I walk you over to the shelter downtown and help get you signed in for the night, huh?" She shook her head. "You're shaking your head, Mary. Why are you shaking your head?"

"Sorry, Julius. I'd like to leave you alone, really. I mean, not that I didn't really enjoy our first date and all. Truth is, I don't see us getting serious, long term. You seem a lot more religious than I am."

"Yeah, I was thinking the same thing. So let's find you—"

"Can't, Julius," she said, shaking her head. "You know that. Every shelter will be on notice for the psych patient who stole a car. Sorry, can't go there."

He nodded. "Okay, you got a point. Where to then?"

She grinned at him sheepishly and gave a shrug. "Getting awful dark and dangerous out there, Julius," she said, finally.

"No way, sister," he said, shaking his head. "You are not crashing here." She gave him a puppy dog stare. "You're killing me here, you know that?"

"Just the one night, Julius. I think I'll be able to get some resources together tomorrow." She smiled again.

"Killing me."

She washed up while Julius took Jack out for his evening walk. When they got back, Mary was sitting at the desk with his laptop.

"Hope you don't mind. I needed to check some things for the morning."

"Mind? Why should I mind? I thought I had a password."

" 'Father SEAL' is not a password, Julius. It's just embarrassing."

"My turn?" he asked, pointing a thumb to the bathroom. She nodded and continued typing on the computer. Julius muttered something inaudible and disappeared into the bathroom. When he came out, he was dressed in pajamas. "Did you use—"

"—your toothbrush. Yeah, I hope you don't mind. I forgot mine."

He just stood behind her, shaking his head. Julius watched as she skated about the web, obviously researching Charles Parnell. Julius dropped onto the edge of the bed.

"So, should we pray together, Mary?" Julius asked from behind her.

She shook her head, still typing. She scowled at the screen. "Maybe later, Julius." He waited. Finally, she turned around to face him. "I don't really owe you anything, you know." He waited, meeting her gaze with raised eyebrows. "Really, this is pretty much your own fault. I'm the one getting screwed." He waited. She sighed and blew a curl of hair up off her forehead. "It's really complicated, Julius. I don't think you want to hear it, to tell you the truth."

"Oh, but I do."

"You really don't, Julius. It's very complicated."

"Seems we got all night, sister."

"I'm not a nun, Julius."

"What are you then, Mary?"

"Remember what you thought I was, when you first saw me?

"Yeah, I remember," he said. "I was never good with first impressions. Ask my ex-wife."

"Actually, Julius, you were closer than you realize."

"Meaning what, Mary?"

"Your friend, Dr. Parnell?"

"Way too weird to ever be my friend, believe me."

"Well, he is weird, I'll give you that. But he's not completely wrong."

"About what?"

"About me."

"I don't get it."

"Think about it, Julius." She turned back to the laptop and began typing again.

"What's to think about, Mary? Obviously, the guy's completely out to lunch. His whole point was that you were dead."

"Was."

"Was what?"

"Dead." He laughed. "Here," she said, standing up from the chair. "Have a seat." He took the desk chair. "Watch this." Mary leaned over him to start the video. It was a recording of a presentation her late husband had given over thirty years ago.

"What am I watching?" Julius asked.

"Just watch." The sound came up as a very young Gabriel Sheehan, inventor of mind interpretive technology, began his seminal lecture.

"That's the guy that Parnell showed," Julius said.

"Yeah, Gabriel Sheehan. My late husband," Mary said. "Just listen for a minute."

They listened as Sheehan began his lecture by introducing his research assistant, Helena Fianna. Mary leaned over to freeze the picture on the screen.

"That's the picture he showed of you," Julius said. "Thirty years ago, really?" She nodded. "You don't look bad for an old lady."

"Thank you, Father."

"So I should be calling you Helena, then." She shook her head.

"Search for Helena Fianna, see what comes up," she said. Julius typed in the search and hit enter. Only two hits, the first pointing to the video he had just watched. The other was her obituary.

He sat quietly for a moment. "Okay. So what's the play?" This time she said nothing. "Really, I'm impressed. A long con, got it. Like, a really, really long con, Mary. What's your angle?"

"No angle, Julius. It's not a con. That was me, then. This is me now."

"And the obituary?"

"That's real, too."

Julius closed the laptop and turned to face Mary where she was sitting on the bed again. "You're saying that Parnell's presentation was real? That in that recording, you're already dead?" She nodded. He smiled. "I don't believe it, Mary."

She smiled back, but not with any joy in it. "I don't expect you to, Julius. That's okay."

"So you're not going to tell me then?"

"Tell you what?"

"The truth. What's really going on."

"I did, Julius."

"I deserve better, Mary. I may have put my foot in it by telling Parnell you're alive, maybe I screwed something up for you, big time. I get it. But I crossed a couple of pretty bright lines today, also for you. I deserve something better than this, Mary. Or Helena. Whatever your real name is." She shrugged. "That's it then? Sticking with the 'back from the dead' story?" She nodded.

"Sorry, Julius. Really, I am."

"Don't look it, Mary. Helena. Whatever. In the morning, Mary, not my problem anymore. Right?" She nodded again. With an effort, he calmed himself. "We should—"

"Heads."

"I'm sorry?"

"Heads. I call heads."

"Yeah, I was going to say—"

"—that we should flip to see who gets the bed and who gets the floor. You use the quarter from the nightstand. I call heads and I win. I get the bed." She started to get in under the covers.

"Really? Not just back from the dead, huh? You can see the future?"

She snuggled into the pillow and gave him a shrug. She closed her eyes. Julius walked over to the nightstand and took his lucky quarter out of the drawer. He sat on the edge of the bed. "You sure you want heads?" She nodded, eyes closed but smiling slightly. Julius flipped the coin and caught it on the back of his hand. He looked down and swore softly to himself.

"Good night, Julius."

Julius grabbed the extra blanket and pillow from the closet. He lay down on the floor by Jack. Jack jumped up onto the bed and settled down next to Mary. Julius sighed and clicked off the light.

"Good night, Mary. Anything else about the future you want to tell me?"

"Not really," she said from the bed above him. "But if you really want to know..."

"Oh, I do, I'm sure."

"In about two hours you jump up here with me and we make wild, passionate love until the morning."

"Yeah, fat chance of that, sister."

"I'm not a nun, Julius."

"Yeah. Well, you're no angel, either. Night."

He didn't sleep. She snored as loud as Jack.

CHAPTER 10

"Hey, wake up," Julius said, shaking her. "Time to go rowing."

Mary stretched her arms up sleepily to encircle his neck. "I never heard it called that before," she said. "Just snuggle in right here, Julius." She pulled him down toward her.

He gently disentangled her arms. "No, I really mean rowing, Mary. Time to get up and get to the boat."

"You're kidding. What time is it?"

"Five."

"This is what you do every morning?" she asked, running a hand through her hair as she sat up.

"Just three days a week. Three mornings I run." She disappeared into the bathroom, shaking her head.

"And the seventh?" she asked through the closed door.

"Sunday is for our Lord, Mary."

She emerged from the bathroom. "Boy, you really need to get laid, Julius. Sorry, I used your toothbrush again."

"Yeah, that seems to be pretty important to you," Julius said, packing dog treats and water into the gunny sack.

"Dental hygiene?"

"Getting me laid. So much for your crystal ball, Mary."

"What? We didn't do it?"

"No."

"I figured I just slept through it."

"Come on, Jack." Jack went through his morning stretch routine, then just looked at the two of them. "Not so impressed with your fortune telling skills. Let's go."

They started out the door, Jack reluctantly taking the lead. "Free will, Julius. It fucks up everything," she said, following the dog into the hall.

"One way to look at it, I guess."

"That's what it says in the bible, Father Zimmerman. Chapter one."

"Can't argue with you there."

They followed Jack down to the boathouse. Julius held the scull fast to the dock while Mary and Jack climbed in the back.

"You don't expect me to row, do you, Julius?"

"Expect it? No. You could surprise me, though." He fitted his oars to the front seat.

"Was going to last night, but I fell asleep."

"Just as well, then." He climbed in and pushed off from the dock.

"What about Jack?"

"He doesn't row either. He's the coxswain. He barks cadence." Julius started to pull for the center of the river. He set an easy pace. Jack lay down on the bag. Mary turned and leaned against the back seat so that she could face forward and watch Julius. She watched him row for a few minutes.

"More like he snores cadence," Mary said, amazed that the dog could fall asleep so fast. "So this is what you do for fun, huh, Julius?" He nodded as he started to pick up pace. "Seems peaceful. Quiet. Relaxing."

"Usually."

"Always by yourself?"

"And Jack, usually. Unless it's raining. Jack doesn't like rain." He was breathing steadily now, pacing himself.

"Always the two man boat?" He nodded. "Many people know you do this?"

He thought for a couple of strokes. "It's not a secret. Probably three or four people, I guess. Maybe a few more."

"How many two man sculls does the school own?"

This he had to think about for a few more strokes. Finally, he said, "Two, I think. Never really thought about it." He went back to rowing quietly. Mary began to run her hands over all the surfaces of the boat, finally getting up on her knees to start feeling the outer hull. The boat began to rock with her clambering about. "Hey, down in back. You're rocking the boat, girl."

"I'm trying to think of a witty comeback, give me a minute."

"That gag has run its course, I think."

She grunted with the effort she was making at getting at something below the waterline. "Here we go," she said, falling back into the bottom of the boat with a lurch. "How about, 'somebody's fucking with us?' How's that?" She held out the small object she had ripped from the outer hull.

Julius stopped rowing. He slid forward on his seat to see what she was holding up. She handed it to him. He held it up to see it closer in the early morning light.

"Big deal." He tossed it over the side. Julius started paddling again, shaking his head.

"Somebody wants to know where you are, Julius." He just shook his head again and kept rowing. They passed under the Key Bridge.

"Can you give Jack one of his treats?" Julius asked her. She fished one out of the waterproof sack and gave it to the dog.

"Why would someone want to track you?" she asked him, sitting back down to face him.

"Guess they're afraid I'll fall out of the boat again," he said, smiling. She just arched an eyebrow at that. "I don't know, Mary. I'm just a priest. It's no secret where I am, or what I'm doing."

"Somebody cares."

"Maybe it's not me they care about, Mary."

"It's not my boat, Julius."

"It is this morning."

"Yeah, but how..."

"Maybe other folks have better crystal balls than yours, kiddo."

"You might be on to something there, Julius." He nodded.

"Actually," Julius said, "they probably put one of those on every boat, to keep track of them. Might have something to do with racing, even. To trigger the timers." They sat quietly as he continued to row them upriver. "Besides, they put tags on everything at this school. I shouldn't tell you this, but they even got one in Jack. Put one of those chips in him surgically when he was a puppy, right after I got him." Julius saw the look she was giving the dog. "Stop that! You better not throw him overboard." She smiled at him wickedly. "It's not a tracker, Mary. It's just an ID chip. Jeez."

His breathing became more labored and sweat began to run down his forehead. Eventually, they rowed under the 495 Bridge. Julius looked up, half expecting someone to fall onto them. Nobody fell, but as they pulled away, he saw someone standing on the bridge, standing at the same point Mary had been standing that day. He thought the man might be looking at them, but couldn't be sure. Julius pointed. Mary twisted around, looking. "Sun's in my eyes. What?"

"There was someone on the bridge, I think."

"Is that the 495 Bridge? My bridge?"

Julius nodded and resumed rowing. "Give Jack another treat, will you?"

"Dog gets a lot of treats, Julius." Julius nodded and kept his steady pace. "When do we turn around?" she asked him. "Do we have to keep going till someone falls out of the sky?"

Julius shipped his oars and let the boat glide. "Actually," he said between panting breaths, "this is the farthest I've ever rowed." He was soaked with sweat. Even this early in the morning, it was oppressively humid.

"That explains why you look so godawful tired, I guess," she said. "We're only halfway, you know."

Julius drank from a water bottle he took from the sack. He wiped sweat from his brow with the back of his arm. "You might have to row back."

"Maybe you should have one of Jack's snacks. You know, recharge."

Julius slowly brought the boat about. "I'm serious. Your turn."

"You're serious?"

"I'm tired. I didn't sleep well last night."

"Consumed with desire?" she asked.

"You snore worse than Jack. Switch seats. Don't capsize us." Julius slid off his seat and lay on his back in the bottom of the boat so Mary could climb over him. She stopped halfway and stayed there, lying on top of him.

"This is comfy. Pretty smooth, Zimmerman." She kissed him briefly.

"You're killing me here," he said, after.

"Julius, you have no idea what I'm capable of." She climbed past him and took the front seat. Zimmerman seated himself in the stern, facing her. Jack settled in his lap. He absently petted the dog. Mary started rowing.

"You ever row before?"

"Exercise machine. Once. Too boring."

He watched her row for a few minutes. "Don't think about the rowing, concentrate on your breathing. All the way in as you pull, all the way out as you come back. It's a Zen thing." She nodded and adjusted her breathing as he instructed. "That's it. Slow down. You're at racing cadence." He beat a slow tempo on his knee. She nodded again, slowed her rowing to match his tempo.

"At this rate," she said between breaths, "we should be back around nightfall."

He shook his head. She was starting to sweat already, he noticed. "No, if you can keep that up, we'll be back in plenty of time for lunch."

"Going to need a shower first," she said between breaths.

"Yeah, can't argue with you there," he said, watching her. Sweat was pouring off her now. He watched a rivulet run down her chest. She just raised her eyebrows at that, working too hard to make any rejoinder. "You're sweating pretty good. Want some water?"

She shook her head. "Girls don't sweat, Julius," she gasped at him. "We glow."

"Yeah, well, you're glowing like a pig. Not bad for a dead person. Try not to pass out." She just nodded, too out of breath to speak. "So, you mentioned you were married."

She nodded. "Was. Dead."

"So you're a widow." She tried to shrug as she rowed but it didn't work.

"It's complicated," she managed to gasp between breaths. "You," she grunted a breath, "divorced?" He nodded. "Why?"

"It's complicated."

"Julius," she gasped, "you're going to have to carry the conversation," another gasp, "for a while, okay?"

He smiled, watching her sweat. She was soaked through her scrub top. He was waiting for her to give up. Actually, she had already brought them a lot farther than he expected for a beginner. "War is hell, Mary." She nodded, gave him a look that clearly indicated that she wasn't in any position to make pleasant comebacks. "Let's just say that I left the service a bit screwed up. I wasn't much fun to be married to at that point. I think that's what she said." He watched her row some more, waiting for her to rest, which she didn't. "You can take a break there, Mary. River won't mind."

She kept rowing and just cocked her head, questioning. Same look Jack gives me, Julius thought. She kept rowing. "Really. Rest a little, then we'll switch back."

She gave him a wicked smile. "You just want," she said between breaths, "to get me on my back on the bottom," breath, "of this boat," breath, "huh, Zimmerman?" He shook his head, smiling. She kept rowing. The Key Bridge passed overhead.

"Wow. Almost home, girl. Pretty impressive. Of course, you're going with the current, lot easier. Still, not bad."

She grunted in reply and kept rowing.

She crashed them into the dock. Julius managed to grab a piling as they rebounded. Jack made his sad sound as he tumbled into the bottom of the boat, cursing. Mary collapsed on the oars, soaked in sweat and breathing hard.

"I think I'll throw up now," she said as he helped her up onto the dock. She staggered over to the lawn and collapsed, spread eagle on the cool grass. Jack came over and licked her face. Julius stowed the boat in the rack.

He walked over and stood over them. "Brunch or shower first?"

Mary looked up at him. She squinted, the sun behind him. "I'm better at running, you know."

"We'll see. Running's tomorrow. Shower first, then eat. Better chance it'll stay down." He gave her a hand up.

He sat on the bed and waited while she showered.

She poked her head out the door. "We could share. Save water." She smiled at him.

"That's okay. I'll pass." She closed the door again.

"Gonna use up all the hot water," she called out to him.

"Cold shower works."

She poked her head out again, wet hair streaming. "I'll bet it does," she said, winking at him. She disappeared back into the steamy bathroom. "Used to take a shower with my husband all the time."

"That how he died?" He heard the water turn off. After a few minutes, she emerged wrapped in a towel. She used another to dry her hair.

"It occurs to me, Julius," she said, "that I now have nothing at all to wear." She dropped onto the bed next to him. He stood up.

"Well, we can't have that, can we?"

"We can't?"

"No, we can't." He fished a tee shirt and a pair of running shorts out of a drawer and tossed them to her. She looked at the tee shirt. It read "Hale Eddy."

"New York indie rock, padre?"

"Left over from my younger, prewar days. My turn," he said, heading into the bathroom. "My God, it looks like someone drowned in here."

When he came out, she was using his computer at the desk again, dressed in the shorts and tee shirt. He proceeded to dress in his teaching outfit; slacks, collar, and sport coat.

"What's the plan, Mary?" he asked her, sitting down on the bed to put on his shoes.

"Thought you were buying me lunch," she said, turning to face him.

"I meant after."

She stood up and held her arms out as she did a pirouette. "Thought I'd walk into town and get something a little less ridiculous to wear. Maybe even underwear."

He laughed and nodded. "Good plan. You need some money?" She shook her head. "I don't even want to know."

"You?"

"I got a class to teach, over at White-Gravenor Hall. Ends at four. You can meet me there."

"Don't want me just hanging out here at the dorm, looking lonely? I could play with Jack."

"Whatever. Let's get something to eat." The dog's ears perked up. "Not you, lardass."

CHAPTER 11

Julius treated her to lunch at the dorm cafeteria, where they both ate free. Resources were running low at present. After lunch, he watched her walk off toward M Street looking like a twelve year old, his shorts reaching down nearly to her ankles. Laughing to himself, he took Jack out for a quick walk before dropping the dog back at the dorm. Julius then headed over for class, showing up early again.

He checked the assignments sent in by his class. Confirming that everyone had, indeed, sent in something, he randomly opened a few and skimmed the essays. He could only stand to read for a few minutes before he had to quit, appalled by the apparent inability of his students to formulate a reasonable three paragraph essay. He sighed and closed the laptop.

Julius watched as students drifted into class, though he was actually thinking about the morning's events. He wondered how Mary was planning to secure a wardrobe, then decided not to think too much about that. He wondered how much trouble he was getting into—had already gotten into. As his phone signaled three o'clock, he decided he wasn't going to think about that just now, either.

Julius walked to the back of the room and closed the door. He surveyed the room as he walked back to the front. It looked to him like a full house.

"I trust you all had an enjoyable weekend," he began, leaning against the desk. "Obviously, you didn't let my assignment take up too much of your time." This was met by general eye rolling as many of the students began to open their laptops. Not as many as last week, though, he noticed. Progress was being made. "Let us continue, then, on the subject of miracles—"

Julius was interrupted by a knocking at the door. He bounced onto his feet. "Jesus, Mary, and Joseph," he cursed, then reddened. Fields started to get up from his chair. "Not again, Mr. Fields. Another old guy? Or the same old guy?"

"No," Fields said, smiling. "It's Jack."

"Jack? Jack who?" The bulldog's face appeared in the window. Julius shook his head. "Let him in, Mr. Fields."

Fields opened the door and Mary walked in with Jack in her arms. She gave Julius an acknowledging nod and took a seat in the back row. Jack sat down at her feet. Julius was a bit stunned, staring at her. She was dressed up in some kind of designer dress, a bright print with a plunging neckline. Her hair was piled decorously on her head. She was wearing a necklace. And earrings. Where the hell did she get a necklace and earrings? he wondered. She had stopped smiling at him, he noticed. Now, she was giving him the tilted head, concerned look. He realized that he wasn't talking. He should be talking.

"Miracles," Julius managed to say. It took a minute to think of something else to say. "What did Spinoza have to say on the topic, Mr. Sullivan?" Julius sat on the desk, legs dangling. What the hell am I doing? he thought to himself, I never sit on the desk.

"He didn't believe in them," Sullivan said. Julius stood up again and paced the room.

"Why not?" Julius asked.

"He was an atheist," Sullivan answered.

"Where did you get that idea, Mr. Sullivan?" Julius asked, stopping his pacing to look at the man.

"From the reading."

"No, you didn't. The reading was an excerpt from Spinoza's work, *Theological Political Treatise*. At no point in that entire work does he make the statement that he is an atheist."

"He implies it, Father," the man continued.

"No, he doesn't," Julius responded, sounding a bit exasperated. "Ms. Wilkey?"

"Really, just the opposite, Father," the woman sitting in the back corner responded.

"Elaborate, please."

"Spinoza felt that it was heretical to think that an all-powerful God that created everything in nature would have to suspend those laws on occasions to work his will."

Julius nodded. "A quote to support that argument, Ms. Wilkey?" Wilkey began to fumble in her backpack for her laptop. "Mr. Fields? Do you agree?"

"With what, Father?" Julius spun to face the man and stared. "I agree that's what Spinoza said in the reading. I don't agree with Spinoza, though."

"Good enough, Mr. Fields. Do you have that quote yet, Ms. Wilkey?"

" 'If anyone were to maintain that God performs some act contrary to the laws of Nature, he would at the same time have to maintain that God acts contrary to His own nature—than which nothing could be more absurd.' "

"Excellent, Ms. Wilkey. It's a shame that you didn't bother to demonstrate your incisive reasoning on that poor excuse for an essay you submitted." Wilkey looked up from her computer initially smiling, then scowled at him. "So, Mr. Fields, you claim to be smarter than Baruch Spinoza?"

"No, not smarter. Just more religious, I guess."

"Don't screw this up, Mr. Fields. You're repeating the mistake that Mr. Sullivan just made. Spinoza's argument against miracles was not due to a lack of faith. Wilkey just explained that. Keep up. Why do you disagree?" Fields looked lost and just shrugged. "You disagree, Mr. Fields," Julius continued, "because it is at odds with your definition of a miracle, right?" Here Julius pointed to the definition still written on the board behind him. "You can read your own writing, right?"

Fields brightened. "Yeah, that's why. I knew that." The class laughed.

"So, it would seem that a true believer in God may or may not believe in miracles," Julius said. "Let us return, then, to the example at hand. Recall our discussion of Flight 1549, 'the miracle on the Hudson.' You have all now had the weekend to consider your opinions. Ms. Chu, was that a miracle?"

"No," Chu said from her seat in the front. "For the same reasons we talked about last week. It did not require the suspension of natural law."

"But Spinoza says that that's not the way God works," Julius said.

"I disagree."

"How fortunate I am to have a class full of students smarter than the great seventeenth century philosopher!" Julius exclaimed.

"I think it was a miracle, Father." A young woman from the middle rows had spoken, quietly. Julius turned to her.

"It's Ms. Lightley, isn't it?" he asked her. She nodded, looking down at her desk. "Please, continue."

She shrugged. Still looking down at her desk, she said, "I think it happened like you said. It was miraculous, the hands of God were invisible, but they held up the plane and saved those people. I believe it was a miracle." There was a loud guffaw from the back of the room. Everyone turned to look.

"Sorry," Mary said, blushing slightly. An awkward silence ensued. Julius had been studiously avoiding looking in her direction, had just about forgotten she was there. He stopped and forced himself to smile at her.

"Don't be sorry, Sister Mary," Julius said. "Thank you for gracing us. Please, continue." Mary met his gaze and arched an eyebrow.

"She sounds like Miracle Max," Mary said, trying for levity. The reference was obviously lost on the students. "You know: 'Sonny, true love is the greatest thing in the world. Except for a nice mutton, lettuce and tomato sandwich.' " She looked around the room and, seeing only uncomprehending stares, sighed.

"Ms. Lightley is a believer in magical thinking," Mary went on. Lightley and the rest of the class looked at her, waiting. "She has no basis for her statement, no foundation for her opinion."

"Ms. Lightley? Do you have a reason for your opinion that you may share with Sister Mary?" Julius asked.

"Well, yeah," the young woman said. She looked back down at her desk. "Like we were saying last week. I think it was impossible for that pilot to land the plane safely, after the engines went out."

"Am I going *mad*, or did the word 'think' escape your lips?" Mary said. She smiled as everyone looked at her again, aghast. "Princess Bride quote. Really." Julius fought the urge to shake his head, instead electing to subtly raise his eyebrows. He looked at her.

"That's your miracle?" Mary asked the other woman. The student nodded. Mary chuckled again, but more kindly this time. "Why?" Mary continued. "Because the odds were against him? You want to talk about odds? You want to talk about godawful impossibilities? What are the odds of a flock of geese choosing to fly like feathered kamikazes straight into both engines of the plane, huh? When in hell has that ever happened before, or since for that matter? Uh, never. That's your miracle, sister."

"No," Lightley said, distraught. She looked up to stare at Mary, wide-eyed. "That can't be a miracle!"

"Why?" Mary retorted. "Because it's bad? A miracle has to not just be impossible, but impossibly good?" Lightley nodded. "That's just horse-shit," Mary continued. "Who are you to say that? How do you even know what good is?"

"But they were all saved," the girl said, reddening.

"Great," Mary said sarcastically. "They were all saved, miraculously. Maybe one of the women on board that plane was even pregnant," Mary looked at Lightley, who smiled weakly and nodded. "Pregnant with a kid who will grow up to be some lunatic who will fly a plane into a stadium full of innocent tweens watching a freakin' Bieber concert. Still a miracle? Maybe the invisible giant hand of God was swatting the damn plane out of the sky in the first place, huh?" She glared at the girl. Lightley's eyes widened with shock and she looked down at her desk again.

Fields leaned to his neighbor and stage whispered, "That's one angry nun, I'll tell you." There was scattered laughter.

"Well, you make a good point, Sister," Julius cut in with feigned levity. "Taking more of an Old Testament viewpoint than we usually do in this class. But I think we'll leave the definition of good and evil for a later lesson." He smiled at Mary and turned quickly away. "Let's return then to the question of religious belief and the nature of miracles." He looked at the clock. Close enough, Julius decided. "Next time."

The class started to file out. Chu stopped in front of Julius long enough to say, "Nice move, Father. The nun almost makes you look sweet." Julius thought the woman may have winked at him before she turned to leave. He hoped not.

Mary and Jack came up to the desk where Julius was packing up his bag.

"Well, that was fun," Mary said.

"Hysterical," Julius said. He sat down and put his feet up on the desk. "Nice outfit. Stopped by the Salvation Army?"

"What?" Mary said, suddenly concerned. "I look bad?"

"Bad? Hell, no. I mean, not too bad at all." He was blushing. "I just meant, I expected something a little more plain, seeing as you had no money or anything."

Mary sat down at Chu's desk, smiling at his discomfort. "What fun would that be, Julius? A girl has to look nice, doesn't she?"

"Not sure they bought the Sister Mary thing," he said, pretending to do something with his papers.

"That one sure didn't," Mary said, nodding at the door.

"What one?"

"The pretty Asian girl. You know, the one who just winked at you, Julius." He blushed again. "Don't worry, Julius. I'll protect you." She leaned her elbows on his desk, chin in hands. "Can a poor, homeless waif buy you dinner, Father?"

He forced himself to stand up. "Seems only fair," he stammered. They led Jack outside.

They dropped Jack back at the room. Mary led Julius several blocks arm in arm to an elegant Italian restaurant, to which they somehow had reservations. They were on their second bottle of wine by the time the entre arrived.

Julius took a sip. He was no expert, but it tasted expensive. "Wow, that's great," he said.

"I'm happy you like it, Julius," she said, smiling at him and taking a long drink of her own.

"Are we going to have to run out the back after dessert?" he asked her.

"Of course not, Julius," she said. "I told you, my treat. Least I can do in return for your austere kindness."

"Well, thank you then, Mary. It's been my pleasure. I'm just curious—how did you go from not having any underwear this morning to ravishing Washington socialite?"

Her eyes lit up and she looked at him, putting down her glass. "Ravishing? Really? You think I look ravishing?"

He was blushing again so he took another drink of wine. "I was just saying..." he stammered.

"Please, Julius. Don't take it back."

"I wasn't going to, Mary."

"My real name is Grace, Julius. Please call me Grace."

He stared at her over his glass. "Grace, now? Not Mary? Not Joyce?"

"Certainly not Joyce," she said.

Julius was confused. "Why have I been calling you Mary, then?"

"Sorry, Julius. I have trust issues," Grace explained.

"I see. But Grace is really your real name?" She nodded. "Okay, Grace, then. So, Grace; what's going on? Who are you? What are we doing here?"

"We're having a nice, friendly dinner, Father Zimmerman. And your food is getting cold. Eat."

They both ate quietly for a bit.

"Enough about me," Grace said, having finished her glass of wine and gesturing for the sommelier. "Let's talk about Father Julius."

"We haven't talked about you," Julius said.

"Yeah, whatever." The sommelier, a young, elegant woman, recommended something that was lost on Julius but seemed to excite Grace a great deal. The sommelier left, smiling, to get the bottle. "You're going to love this next one, Julius. Better than anything you got at the monastery."

"What's that going to cost?" Julius asked between forkfuls of arctic char.

"She didn't say. An outrageous amount, I'm sure. Please don't keep bringing it up. I said this was my treat. Accept graciously, Julius. You know, like the beneficence of our Lord."

He smiled at that. "Maybe you should be a nun after all."

Grace choked on her food. She had to take a drink of water and shake her head at that. "So, Julius. How does a nice Jewish kid from Queens—"

"Chicago."

"Really, Chicago? Great town, Chicago." He nodded at that. "I knew a guy in Chicago."

"Why am I not surprised?"

"You ever get back there?" Grace asked.

"Couple of times a year. My folks still live there."

"Huh. Ever hear of a Mexican diner on State Street? Might not actually be there by now..."

"Only Mexican restaurant on State I know is Mariangela's. Wouldn't call it a diner, though. What?" Grace had suddenly snapped him a look.

She swallowed hard and looked sad for a brief moment. "Really? Mariangela's?" she asked. "Is it a good restaurant?"

"You're kidding right?" She shook her head. "The kid who owns it was on the cover of Fortune or something. Rags to riches story. I heard him interviewed once. Came across the border illegally, worked at a carwash in Utah. Now he's the poster boy for Latino entrepreneurship, owns like three or four top flight restaurants." He looked at her quizzically. "You've really never heard about this?"

"I haven't been paying attention to the news for a while. Nice kid, huh?"

"Yeah, nice. I'm a fan. He's a real believer. Not shy about it, either. In every interview, he tells this story about an angel that came to him at the carwash, changed his life. Most of these billionaire CEO types think it was all them, you know? Got to the top by their own drive and—are you crying?" He noticed that Grace had leaned back and was dabbing at her eyes with her napkin.

"Excuse me, Julius. I got some mascara in my eye. I'll be right back." He made an effort to stand as Grace quickly left for the lady's room.

When she returned, he was relieved to see her smiling at him. He helped her with her chair.

"Your parents did a good job with you back in Chicago, Julius," she said. She tried the wine that had arrived while she was gone.

"I hope it's okay. Since you were gone, I approved it. Tasted great to me. What do you think? As good as you hoped?"

"Every bit," she said, beaming. "You were about to tell me how a little Jewish kid from Chicago ends up as a Jesuit priest, with a stop in the middle as a Navy SEAL."

"No, Grace. I actually wasn't about to tell you about any of that." He pushed the remnants of his fish around his plate.

"You have to, Julius. I'm buying you a fantastically expensive dinner and sluicing you with great wine. You owe me dazzling conversation." He smiled and raised his eyebrows at that. "And later, of course, a whole night of wild sex." She smiled but his vanished. "Hey, that's just the way it is. I didn't make the rules."

"Mary—Grace. Whatever. I appreciate a running gag as much as the next guy. But it's getting old." He shook his head and took a long pull of the wine. It was exceptional wine. He realized he was mildly drunk.

"What? The shameless flirting? I'm not kidding, Julius."

He sighed heavily as he put his wineglass down. "I'm a priest, Grace. I swore vows. You know—poverty, obedience. Chastity."

"Give me a break, Julius. All you guys care about is sex."

"What? What guys? What are you talking about?"

"The entire Catholic church, Julius. On the ten point strategic plan, the top seven are about sex. Stop abortion. Stop the gays. Stop contraception. It's all you guys really think about."

"That's not true."

"Yes, it is. And out of respect for how much I care for you, Julius, I'm not even going to bring up your colleagues' penchant for child molestation." She smiled at him.

He reddened. "The church is charged with the protection of the sanctity of life, Grace. The most important work we do, that anyone can do, is shepherd life into this world. It's not about the sex, Grace. It's about the sanctity of life."

"Bullshit, father." She took another drink.

"Your opinion."

"I'm sitting across from a guy who used to kill people for a living and then swore off sex. Now he's lecturing me about the sanctity of creating life. Not really buying it, Julius. Don't see it working out for you." He reddened, jaw clenched. She had struck a nerve, she realized. She drank more wine and refilled his glass. "No kids from that marriage, huh?" she asked more kindly.

He shook his head and drank. "Came close. We just found out she was pregnant when I got deployed. But she miscarried, while I was overseas."

"Ouch."

He shrugged. "Happens. Worse things happen. Just wasn't meant to be."

Grace nodded. "Tell you what, Father. You kick up the sparkling conversation a few notches and maybe I won't activate my backup plan."

"Backup plan?"

"Yeah. I won't slip this Roofie into your next glass of wine and ravage you in your sleep."

"Can you do that?"

"It was just a backup, in case the wanton seduction fell short. I did have my heart set on you being conscious during the act, but I'm a girl who's willing to settle."

"I don't believe that." He took another drink. "So, Grace: Dressed to the nines, dripping in jewelry, and stocked with date rape drugs. You've had a busy day."

"Just a girl who loves to shop, Julius."

"Do I want to know details?" he asked, smiling slyly.

"I'll tell you later. After the surprise."

"Surprise?" She nodded gleefully. "I hope this isn't another shameless attempt to make me break my vows, Grace."

"Isn't everything in life just a shameless attempt to get you to break those vows, Father Julius?"

"Sometimes it does seem that way, Sister."

They ate dessert and coffee. She ate her dessert and most of his. Obviously, she wasn't counting calories. The third bottle of wine, the best of the night, stood empty. Inevitably, the check arrived. Grace produced a black American Express card from the small Louis Vuitton clutch. Julius just shook his head, making no effort for the check. He tried to look at the card as she signed the check but she spirited it away quickly.

"Don't be a boor, Julius. Just say thank you and give me a kiss."

"Thank you, Grace. It was a great dinner." He held her chair for her to stand. He kissed her cheek. "And I still feel conscious."

"Good. I wouldn't want you to sleep through the surprise."

"Yeah, you said that."

"Not that. Like you said, sex wouldn't be much of a surprise. But this will be, and just as much fun." She led him by the hand to the entrance. Julius was wondering what this girl thought was as much fun as sex. So far, she seemed pretty much of one mind. Grace produced a claim check from her clutch and gave it to the valet with a twenty dollar bill. The valet stepped to the curb, smiling, and opened the passenger door to the bright red sports car that had been parked in front of the restaurant since they arrived. It was a convertible, a 1987 Ferrari 328 GTS. The top was down.

"Wrong door, bud," she said to him. The valet apologized and ran around to open the driver's door. He handed her the keys. Grace got in and started the engine, smiling broadly at the sound as she blipped the throttle. She turned and smiled at Julius, who was still standing on the sidewalk.

"Is this the surprise?" he asked, "or the exciting police chase to follow?"

"Get in, Julius. It's a perfect night for a drive." Against his better judgment, he got in.

"Where are we going?" he asked as he buckled his seatbelt. He almost fell into her lap as she made a snap right turn away from the restaurant, engine revving a deep, rising musical note.

"Shenandoah Skyline Drive. It should be a great sunset."

"Is that far?"

"No clue. Why, you got other plans?"

He shook his head. "Just worried about Jack, that's all."

"He'll be fine, Julius. We'll be back early. In the morning."

CHAPTER 12

It was a magnificent drive. Once out of the city, Grace drove the sports car at speed through great swooping curves, along scenic ridges overlooking lush green valleys on either side. They drove into a spectacular sunset, as promised. As the sun dipped towards twilight, she pulled off onto a scenic overlook and stopped the car.

"Uh, oh," Julius said, smiling. "I feel my virtue is at risk. Dear God, shield me from this creature's temptations."

"Shut up, wiseass," she said, unbuckling her seatbelt. "Switch seats." She got out of the car.

"You're kidding, right? I told you, I don't know how."

"Get out." She held open his door. "You sound like a scared virgin."

"No, really. I'm not kidding. I can't drive a stick." She rolled her eyes. She hauled him out of the car.

"Get in and drive. It'll be fun."

"We're going to end up at the bottom of a cliff. Fun."

"Don't worry, Father. I'll be gentle. Believe me, in this car, on this road and with no traffic, you can't fuck this up."

She taught him to drive a stick, and how to double clutch, and how to drive really, really fast around turns. Grace made him realize that the lines on the road were just paint. The twilight turned a slowly deepening purple, stars appearing above them as they drove farther and farther west into the Virginia countryside. It seemed that they were the only ones out driving. He smiled continuously, punctuated with occasional gusts of laughter as he managed a particularly great downshift or accelerated hard out of a turn, having clipped the apex just so and cutting back across the double yellow line to swoop into the next bend on the stunning scenic drive. He actually whooped on one occasion.

Grace laughed with him, ignoring the occasional grinding of gears or redlining of the engine. She kept calling him Lieutenant Colonel Frank Slade, laughing each time she said it.

"Who's Frank Slade? Dead boyfriend?" he finally asked, swinging into another series of curves.

"You're kidding, right?" He shook his head. "You never saw 'Scent of a Woman?' "

"Don't think so," he said, looking at her for a second.

"Man, you need to get out a little, Julius," she said, shaking her head in the dark. "Probably can't tango, huh?"

"Don't know, I never tried." His ex-wife never liked dancing, he remembered.

"That would be a no, Julius. Not going to try to teach you heel and toe tonight, then."

"What's that? Some kind of Texas line dance?"

She laughed. "Get your mind out of the gutter, Father. No, it's a technique for shifting. Maybe next lesson."

He turned and smiled at her in the darkness. "So we're going to do this again?"

"Actually," she said sadly, "no. I think it's time to teach you how to do a really cool one-eighty, though. You might want to slow down a little."

"Why? Where are we, Grace?"

"Halfway, Padre. Time to turn around." She had him pull over at the next scenic overlook. They got out of the car and walked around for a bit in the dark, stretching their legs. They hadn't seen another car for hours. They sat on the hood of the car for a while, listening to owls hunting in the moonlight. There was a rustic bathroom at the overlook, but it was chained and locked. It took Grace a few minutes fumbling in the dark to find the tire iron in the car's trunk. They used it to snap the chain and they took turns at the restroom before getting back in the car.

She taught him a Scandinavian flick turn. Julius did a passable one-eighty on his third try. They headed back the way they had come, Julius driving at a more reasoned pace and keeping to his side of the road. Grace napped, her head propped against his shoulder, breathing sonorously in his ear.

When Grace awoke, there was a soft rose tint on the horizon ahead. She stretched and gave Zimmerman's knee a squeeze.

"Where we at, good-lookin'?" she asked.

"Not far from home, I think. Maybe another hour or less. We might beat the traffic." She nodded. "So, Grace, this is later. You said you'd tell me how you accomplished our little night on the town. Later, you said."

"No, I didn't."

"Yes, you did. Over dinner. I asked how you got the clothes, the jewelry, the date rape drug, and all. Remember? You said you'd tell me later."

"That was back when I thought you might tell me about how a Jew-ish kid from Chicago ends up as a priest."

"Maybe later," he said, looking over at her and admiring the morning light on her face, hair blowing behind her. He was trying to figure out about how old she was, but was pretty much at a loss. Somewhere north of forty, he was sure, but how much was hard to say. She sounded like she was a hundred years old sometimes, but when she smiled or laughed, she appeared younger than himself. He shook his head.

"What? What's wrong?"

"Just trying to figure you out, Grace."

"Maybe later, Julius."

They enjoyed a comfortable silence for a while, approaching civiliza-tion again. The sun was up now, but a thick morning haze cut the glare.

"I'll probably regret this, but I got to know, Grace. Come on. Yester-day you didn't even have an empty pocket."

"Can't just accept a gift graciously, huh, Julius?" He shook his head. "That's a shame." She paused for a bit. "Nothing evil, Julius. Don't worry."

"Come on."

"It's not complicated. You're going to be disappointed."

"I doubt it. And before you tell me—thank you. This was great. I had a blast."

She turned to smile at him. "I'm glad. You're welcome."

"Now tell me."

"I told you, it's not complicated. As it happens, the son of the Kuwaiti ambassador is a junior at Georgetown."

"Yeah, I knew that."

"Yeah, well, I ran into him on M Street. Actually, he kind of ran me over. At least, that's what it looked like. Nice kid."

"Wait. This is his car?"

"Yeah, you didn't notice the diplomatic plates?"

He shook his head. "We're joyriding in a car stolen from the Kuwaiti ambassador? Shit."

"No, Julius, don't be ridiculous. He lent it to me. To make up for running me over, kind of."

"You're kidding?" She shook her head. "And the clothes, the jewelry?"

"His Amex. Like I said last night, a girl has to be presentable."

"He lent you his credit card, too?" She nodded. "Why?"

"Julius, please. You're hurting my feelings."

Julius turned to stare straight ahead again. "He's expecting you, isn't he?"

"Of course he is. We have a date for dinner tonight, at L'Enfant Plaza."

His hands tightened on the wheel. "There's a hotel at L'Enfant Plaza," he said.

"I'm sure he's reserved a particularly nice room," she said, watching his face. "Is there a problem, Julius?" she asked.

He shook his head. "You're better than this, Grace."

"You don't know me very well, Julius."

"I know enough. Are you going to go?" He glanced over at her again. She shrugged. "Haven't decided yet. Not sure if I'm going to teach him a lesson about the dangers of running over the wrong gal, or allow him to experience the spectacular carnal creativity of an older woman.

Maybe both." She watched him for a while, but Julius said nothing, now studiously glaring at the road ahead. "A girl can't wait forever, Julius. We're only on this earth a short while, you know."

He shook his head. "Where should I drop you, Grace?"

"Drop me? We're going running this morning, remember?"

He had to smile. "We've been up all night, Grace. It'll be morning when we get back."

"Perfect."

CHAPTER 13

They parked the car illegally in front of Healey Gate and walked across campus to Julius's dorm. Jack was asleep on the bed amidst the forest of shopping bags Grace had dropped off the day before. Grace found the bag with the running outfit and shoes. She changed as Julius took Jack out for a quick walk to relieve himself. When they returned, Julius changed in the bathroom as Grace filled the dog's food and water bowls.

They ran at an easy pace. Grace followed a half step behind, letting Julius show her his usual morning route. They ran down the hill from Georgetown onto the Mall, up to the Capitol and back down towards the reflecting pool and the Lincoln Memorial. Halfway down the Mall they saw a small caravan of black Suburbans approach from the north along 17th Street. The cars pulled right up onto the Mall, forming a wide circle and forcing Julius and Grace to run towards the Lincoln Memorial. They ran up the steps and stopped at the top, both breathing heavily. They sat down at the top step, watching the scene unfold beneath them.

"What's going on?" Grace asked. She looked about, wondering if there was another way to run than back down the Mall. Didn't look like it.

"Helicopter coming in." Julius said, glancing behind.

"The President?"

"No. Marine One lands on the White House lawn. Could be the Vice President, though."

They watched as the huge helicopter appeared clattering behind them and settled onto the grass in the middle of the circled cars. Several individuals came and went between the helicopter and one of the black cars. The helicopter lifted off, the cars drove off the way they had come.

Grace shook her head. "Weird town," she said.

"It's special, that's for sure," Julius nodded. "Your tax dollars at work. Want to go?"

"Let's sit for a bit. I like it here."

"Tired, huh?" He smiled at her.

"Think what you want, darling," she said, staring out over the Mall. She remembered the one other time she had sat on these steps, watching the tourists below, holding her husband's hand and commenting that they really shouldn't be taking separate vacations. Separate vacations, she ruminated. Some vacation, this.

Julius watched her, her expression sad and distant. After a bit, she turned, noticing him looking at her.

"What?" she asked.

He shook his head. "What's the plan, Grace?"

She shrugged. "Lying low, Julius. Keep my head down for a bit, then see if things are a little less intense at the Llewellyn house."

He nodded at that. "What if they're not?"

"What? You tired of my company? Trying to get rid of me, Julius?"

"You could always hole up with the Kuwaiti kid," he said, not smiling.

"Lot of things I could do, Julius. If I have to. Not the first time living on the street, Padre." Grace studied him, wondering how this guy had gotten himself so tied up in knots. Julius looked out over the mall. She slapped his thigh. "Race you back," Grace said, suddenly standing and starting down the steps two at a time.

Julius stood, caught off guard. He nearly stumbled starting after her down the steps. "You don't even know the way back," he called from behind her.

"Then you might have half a chance of beating me," she called over her shoulder. She tore off to the left, following the way the Suburbans had gone, heading back to Georgetown.

By the time Julius caught up, Grace was sitting on the steps to the dorm. She pretended to have been there for longer than the ninety seconds she had beaten him by.

"Hope you swim better than you run, puke," she said, smiling.

He stopped at the bottom of the steps, hands on knees and breathing hard. "I do," he managed to gasp. "Don't say puke."

"Gonna throw up? Feeling pukish, Padre?" she asked.

He just shook his head. After a minute, he mounted the steps and let her back into the room. Julius lay down on the floor, the bed still being covered with high class shopping bags and a sleeping dog. Grace laughed as she stepped over him, closing the door behind her. She fished some clothes out of one of the bags and disappeared into the bathroom. Julius heard the shower come on.

Grace brushed her teeth as the water in the shower got hot, using Zimmerman's toothbrush, again. I really should pick up one of these, she thought. She climbed into the shower and let the hot water run on the back of her neck. Grace stood there, wondering how she was ever going to get back, wondering what would happen to her if she couldn't. She should've listened to Gabe, she thought. She should never have come here.

Grace looked up from her reverie. Julius was standing in the doorway, looking at her, his arms crossed as he leaned against the door. When she met his gaze, he didn't look away. She tried to read his expression, but couldn't. After a minute, he gave a little shake of his head and went back out. She finished her shower.

She came out of the bathroom, dressed in blue jeans and a tee shirt, toweling off her hair. Julius was seated at the desk, doing something on the laptop. She stood behind him and let her hair drip on him until he looked up.

"I'm sorry, Julius. I'll try to get out of your life as soon as I can."

He turned his chair to face her and took her hand. "I'm not sure that's what I want, Grace."

She sat down on the end of the bed, letting him hold onto her hand. "Geez, Julius. You've been in the Navy, a failed marriage, and the priesthood. When's the last time anybody gave a shit what you want—junior high?"

"You're sweet."

"Doesn't matter what you want, Julius. I'm sorry. It's probably what you need."

"Maybe," he said. "Doesn't seem that we've quite played this out yet, though. You got plans? You're not dressed for a date, sister." He tried a smile.

She gave his hand a little squeeze and smiled back. "I was going to go back to Bethesda, reconnoiter a little, you know? See if the coast is clear."

"You need somebody to watch your back?"

"Why? You know somebody?" He shook his head and tried to look wounded. "No, Julius, thanks. I'm not going to do anything stupid, just check things out."

"You'll be back then?"

She gave his hand another squeeze and dropped it. "Yeah, Zimmerman. You're not quite rid of me yet. I gotta get ready for my date later, you know."

His smile disappeared. "And then?" She just shrugged.

"What are you doing today?" she asked. "Taking Jack to the park?"

"Maybe. Have to go over to the library, spend a few hours researching a paper I've got to write. Come find me there, when you're done. We can both take him to the park."

"Sounds like a plan. Later, then," she said, standing. He looked up at her for an awkward moment, then did his little head shake again as she turned and went out the door.

That afternoon, Julius sat in his study carrel, a stack of old textbooks piled in front of him. He looked over the railing, watching Grace in the lobby two floors below. He had gotten some work done, finally. Most of the time, though, he was running through their conversations in his head, trying to figure her out. He could make no sense at all of the woman, no sense at all. He had watched her come through the library entrance a couple of minutes ago. Julius watched her walk around, looking for him.

Julius thought he recognized somebody else down in the lobby. Watching, he was fairly sure that the somebody else was Father Pauley. He didn't think that Pauley would be looking for his paper this soon, at least he hoped not. It seemed odd, however, as he watched. Pauley appeared to be loosely shadowing Grace's movements. Grace was moving somewhat randomly, checking desks and the rows of book stacks, but Pauley—he was sure now that that's who it was—maintained his distance in the lobby, but was consistently keeping her in sight. Odd, he thought.

Julius started to flush with anger. Shit, he thought, somebody told Pauley that some redhead was staying in my room. Shit, shit, shit. He closed the book and stood, watching the two of them perform their little *pas de deux* below him. I'll take care of this right now, he thought, explain to Pauley what was going on.

Just as Julius realized that he really didn't know what was going on, or what exactly he could say to Pauley, he saw the man suddenly turn away from Grace and walk quickly to the exit. Grace was looking up at Julius and waving; she had seen him when he stood up. He waved back and headed for the stairs to meet her.

"How'd it go?" he asked as he found her on the main level. He looked around for Pauley, but the rector had indeed left.

"Not so well," she said, following his gaze. "What's wrong, Julius?"

He shook his head. "Nothing. Just thought I saw someone I knew, just before I came down. Guess not. Not well? What happened?"

"Tell you later. Let's go get Jack."

They picked up Jack and walked him to the dog park. Grace wore a floppy white sun hat she had picked up in Bethesda, the wide brim partially hiding her face. They sat on a bench, watching Jack socialize with the other dogs.

"That your Julia Child hat?" Julius asked her, laughing.

"The chef? It's not a chef's hat, Julius."

"No, your undercover spying hat. She was a spy, you know. For the OSS."

"Really? I did not know that."

"So, what happened?" Julius asked.

"Same deal, different day. The house is still locked up tight as a drum. Not good. Not good at all."

"Who are they?

"Honestly? No clue, Julius. They don't look friendly, though."

"Bathrobe and slippers guy still walking around, too?"

She shook her head. "No, not sure where he went off to."

"But you knew him. You hid from him."

"No, Julius. I didn't know him."

"Why did you hide then?"

"Because he was wearing a fucking bathrobe, Julius."

"I don't understand, Grace."

"I know you don't understand, Julius. Believe me, you do not want me to explain it to you."

"Actually, I do." He looked at her, waiting. She shook her head and adjusted her hat.

"Fine, Julius. Just tell me when I start wasting my breath." He nodded. She watched the dog trotting around the park, he watched her as she talked. "The house—the Llewellyn house, isn't a safe house. It's how I got here. It's a kind of a gateway. I need to get back in so I can get out of here. Somehow. Only now, somebody doesn't want me to get back in. Which means that somebody doesn't want me to get back to where I came from."

"Which is where, exactly?"

"Let's leave that for later, okay?"

"Fine. Where does bathrobe guy come in?"

"He must have used the gateway, just like me. That's why I hid from him. I was afraid he might be following me."

"I'm lost already. Why does wearing a bathrobe mean he's following you?"

"I told you. It means he used the transport system, like I did."

"They give away free bathrobes?"

"No, they don't give away free anything. There's not supposed to even be anybody there, when you come out. You come out like the day you were born. You got to find something to wear."

"Really? Naked?" Julius asked. Grace nodded. "So he grabbed a robe?" She nodded. "You weren't wearing a robe, when you fell."

"No, Julius, I wasn't. I was wearing their fucking shower curtain. Didn't see any robes."

"Shower curtain? Really?" She nodded. "You know, now that you mention it, it did kind of look like a shower curtain, wrapped around you and all."

"Starting to make sense to you then, Julius?" She smiled at him.

"Not a bit, Grace."

"Didn't think so."

"We should get Jack." He stood up and headed over to where Jack was playing with a French bulldog. Grace followed as he reattached the dog's leash. They started back to campus.

"Your turn, Julius."

He shrugged as they walked. "Why bother, Grace?"

"It's what we do, Julius. I'm a good listener, and I'll probably, hopefully, be gone forever in a day or two. Couldn't hurt."

"What do you want to know?"

"Whatever you want to tell me, Julius."

"You're right about my parents being Jewish."

"No shit, Zimmerman." She smiled at him as they walked. "You don't look Irish, Father."

"But the Jesuit thing wasn't a way to get at them. That was the Navy."

"Yeah, not many Jewboy SEALS, I'm figuring."

"A few. But Mom and Dad had other plans for me."

"Doctor? Lawyer? Dad sure wasn't grooming you to be a Formula One driver, that's for sure."

"No, not a race car driver. Lawyer or doctor would've suited them fine."

"Not smart enough, huh?" They waited at a street corner for the light to change, watching the taxis and limos stream past.

"I was plenty smart, just not smart enough for them. Not once my brother died." The light changed and Julius stepped off the curb, Jack's leash in hand. Grace didn't move. Julius stopped in the middle of the street and looked back at her. "You coming?"

She caught up to him and they kept walking. "How old were you?"

"When I joined? Straight out of high school. They both nearly plotzed."

"I mean when your brother died."

"Oh. I was twelve."

"My sister died when I was twelve. Was he your twin?"

"Twin? No, he was older. My big brother. He was seventeen, a senior in high school. He was the smart one. And the athletic one, and the good-looking one."

"Sounds like a dick." Julius stopped dead and gave her a malevolent look. "Just saying."

"No, that was the worst part," Julius said, starting to walk again. "He was great, a great guy. Not a dick at all. He was great to me, especially."

"So why'd you push him down a flight of steps?"

Julius shook his head. "Probably should've. It would've been a whole lot less painful. Acute leukemia. He was diagnosed one week after he graduated, valedictorian. Never made it to his first day at Stanford."

"So you ran off to the Navy."

He nodded. "As soon as I could, day after graduating high school."

"Must've killed your folks."

"That's what I was trying for, at the time. And myself, of course. In a blaze of glory, make my brother proud."

They walked on in silence for a while, almost back to campus now.

"You know, Julius, you're not as fucked up as I thought."

"Oh, I am," Zimmerman said. "You don't know the half of it, Grace." He stopped again, suddenly.

"What is it?" Grace asked.

They had just stepped back onto campus. Julius watched the big man hurrying away from them, just ahead. From the back, he wasn't sure, but he thought it was Pauley, again. "Come on," Julius said to her. "We got to get this straight." He grabbed her wrist and pulled her along as he sped to catch up to the priest ahead of them.

This was just too much of a coincidence, Julius thought. Seeing Pauley twice like this, and now the man obviously trying to get away from them. "Father Pauley," Julius called to him. "Pete, wait up a second." Pauley stopped, reluctantly, but didn't turn around.

Julius caught up to the heavy senior priest, Grace and Jack in tow. Time to get this straightened out, Julius thought. "Father Pauley, let me introduce you to someone." Pauley turned around slowly, his face ashen. "This is—" Julius was cut off by Grace's piercing scream. Pauley fell to his knees, head bowed in supplication.

"Dear child," Pauley whispered huskily, "please forgive me."

Grace turned and ran.

CHAPTER 14

Julius watched her run away, then turned back to look at Pauley, still kneeling on the grass in front of him. Jack pulled away from his grasp, running barking after Grace, leash trailing behind. It took a minute for Julius to find his voice to ask Pauley, "Hell, Peter. What the hell is going on?"

Pauley said nothing, still kneeling and praying softly on his knees, his whole body now shaking with soft sobs. Julius was stunned. He knelt to try to help the older man up, but Pauley pushed him away, crying. Julius sat down in the grass, dumbfounded. He looked up to where Grace and Jack had run off, but they were gone.

After a while longer, Pauley stopped crying. He looked up at Julius. He tried to get up off his knees, but only managed to sit heavily in the grass. Julius stared at him, incredulous.

"What the hell is going on, Pete?" Julius asked quietly. Pauley could only shake his head for a minute.

He looked at Julius, eyes red-rimmed and filled with anguish. "Go find her," he croaked hoarsely. "Find her, Julius, and hide her. You have to take care of her."

"Why, Peter? What's going on?"

"Find her," the man said more emphatically, pushing at Julius.

"Why? Who is she?" Julius demanded.

"Get her back, Julius. Hide her somewhere. Come to me later, after she's safe. Go!" He pushed Julius roughly again.

It took Julius almost an hour to find her. He walked steadily in the direction she had run, calling for her, calling for Jack. Eventually, he heard Jack's bark in return. Julius found them, huddled in the shrubbery at the side of the Observatory. Grace was almost catatonic, her breathing ragged as she lay on her side, rocking and hugging herself. Jack stood over her, licking her face. Jack looked up, worried, as Julius crawled into the shrubs to hold her.

After some minutes, Julius was able to bring her out from her hiding place. He carried her back to the Jesuit residence, Jack following closely behind. Julius laid her down in his bed. Grace said nothing, still breathing in ragged spasms, her eyes squeezed tightly shut. Jack sat at the foot of the bed, looking back and forth between her and Julius, his head tilted with concern.

"I don't know, Jack. I just don't know, buddy," Julius told him, softly. "We'll just have to let her rest."

They let her rest. When Grace still lay curled up, unspeaking and unresponsive after several hours, Julius left to find Pauley. He left Jack behind to watch over her, muzzle inches from her face and staring with concern.

Julius found Pauley in the rector's apartment. The door was ajar. Julius knocked as he entered. The older man sat at his desk, the room almost dark. Pauley watched as Julius opened the blinds and sat down in front of him.

"Did you find her?" Pauley finally asked. Julius nodded. "Where is she?"

"Lying down, at my place. Jack's with her." The older man nodded at that, now looking out the window with an expression of never having seen this view before. Julius finally leaned forward and knocked hard on the desk. "Peter! Come on. What the hell is going on, Peter?"

The older man turned reluctantly to meet his gaze. He shook his head again.

"I'd hoped to never see her again," Pauley said. "It has always been my most fervent prayer, Julius. To never see her again." He turned his face to the window, looking like he was about to start crying again.

"Why, Peter? Who is she?"

"She didn't tell you? She didn't tell you about me?" Pauley asked, not turning from the scene outside.

"She's not talking. She's like in some kind of trance. I can't even get her to open her eyes."

"Poor child."

"That's all you can say? Poor child? The woman is in a state, Peter, like she's catatonic or something. You fell to your knees in front of her, begging forgiveness. What the hell is going on? What could she tell me about you? How the hell do you even know her?"

Instead of answering, Pauley stood up and made his way to the cabinet behind Julius. He brought a bottle of Irish whiskey and two glasses back to the desk. Pauley sat down and filled both glasses, drank off one of the glasses and refilled it. Pauley pushed the other glass towards Julius.

"You're going to want that," Pauley said.

Julius shook his head at the man. "I want some answers, Peter."

The older man shrugged and took another gulp from his own glass. "How did you find her?" Pauley asked.

"I fished her out of the Potomac five days ago." Pauley raised his eyebrows at that.

"And then you saw her picture at that idiot's presentation," Pauley said. Julius nodded. "What has she told you?"

"Almost nothing, Peter. Just like you're doing right now."

"Almost nothing, you say."

"She told me that the idiot was telling the truth."

Pauley nodded, again staring outside. "Do you believe her, Julius?"

"Of course not, Peter."

"You should, Julius. You should believe her." Julius stared at the other man, who would not return his gaze. "You need to take care of her. Protect her, Julius."

"Peter, I don't know what you're talking about. Believe her about what? The only thing I do know about her is that she can damn well take care of herself."

"Take a drink, Julius," Pauley said, pushing the glass forward. "You're going to need it, if you want me to tell you."

Grace kept her eyes squeezed tightly shut. Surely she was in Hell, she thought to herself. How else, she wondered, could he be here, here again with her? And the foul, fetid air she was breathing, surely this was Hell. She opened her eyes to see Jack, unblinking, staring at her with deep concern, his muzzle a fraction of an inch from her face. They shared a puddle of dog drool. A vision worthy of Dante, she thought to herself, focusing. *Lasciate ogne speranza, voi ch'entrate.* The dog licked her face.

Grace sat up and patted the dog's head. He had been worried about her. Grace sat on the edge of the bed, her face in her hands, thinking. She absently wiped drool off her face with a corner of Julius's bed sheet.

"Come on, Jack," she whispered, finally standing. "We gotta get out of Dodge." Jack barked, tail wagging.

CHAPTER 15

Pauley stared at the younger priest, watching as Julius took a sip of the whiskey. He waited until Julius had set his glass back down on the desk.

"Why, Julius," Pauley finally began, "are we celibate?"

Julius was taken aback for a moment, surprised by the strangeness of the question. "We're priests, Peter. It is our duty, a part of our devotion."

"Bullshit," the other man spat bitterly. Julius raised his eyebrows in surprise, remembering Grace's comment from the night before. "Since when does devotion require giving up love, or intimacy? What sense does that make? Who else does such a thing? It's an abomination, it's unholy."

"What are you talking about, Peter? It's our way, it's—"

"Bullshit," the other man repeated. "It has nothing to do with duty, or faith. It is the price we pay, Julius. The price we are asked to pay, for what we have to do."

Julius was lost. "What do we have to do, Peter?"

Peter looked at the other man with pity. "We are soldiers, Julius. We are the foot soldiers, soldiers in an unholy war that is almost upon us." The old man reached to refill his glass.

Julius stayed the other man's hand. "Enough whiskey, Peter. You're not making any sense. What war? What about the girl? What the hell is going on, Peter?"

"We are celibate, Julius, because we must be free. Free for sacrifice. In this battle, we must fight without encumbrance. We must be willing to give all, for God."

"Of course, Peter. Of course we are willing to die for God, for our faith—"

"Not die," Pauley snarled, striking his palm on the desk. "This isn't the damn Crusades. I'm not talking about dying in a blaze of sanctified glory. Nothing so dear, Julius. Death is nothing! A welcome passage, to an earned reward. It is not death I'm talking about, child."

"What then, Peter?"

"Lost," the old man said sadly. "We are to be lost, Julius." Pauley looked up and met the younger man's eyes, and already he looked lost.

Grace had changed her clothes, now in dark jeans and black shirt, her hair pulled back and bound up beneath a black watchcap. She crossed the commons, Jack following close behind. The Ferrari, she noted with relief, hadn't been towed yet. The usual rules don't apply to a red Ferrari with diplomatic plates, she thought. Grace opened the door and waited as Jack jumped in and sat in the passenger seat. Grace retrieved the keys from the visor where Julius had left them. She pulled on her seatbelt and started the car.

"Hope you like convertibles," Grace said to the dog, pulling out into the street. Jack lifted his face to the wind, smiling imperceptibly. *What dog doesn't like convertibles?*

They stopped at the McDonalds drive through. Jack didn't object when Grace ordered for him, a couple of cheeseburgers without the fixings. They ate together quietly in the car, parked behind the restaurant. They split the fries. Grace was forced to drink the entire chocolate shake herself; the dog never believed that 'chocolate is poison for dogs' bullshit, but Jack was embarrassed at his inability with straws.

They drove to Bethesda. Grace parked the Ferrari three blocks away from the Llewellyn house. She and Jack walked up the block slowly, across the street. The guard still sat on the porch, but the one across the street was gone. Nobody strolling around in a robe, either. They circled the block and returned to the car. The sun was going down. They took a nap, Jack lying with his snout in her lap.

"I don't understand, Peter," Julius replied softly.

"I wouldn't expect you to, Julius. Not yet."

"Tell me about the girl, then. Tell me about Grace."

"My little murderer."

"Come again?"

"You heard me, Julius. She killed me. Stabbed me in the heart, I think."

"You're not making sense, Peter."

"I deserved it, Julius. That and worse."

"What do you mean?"

"She was an orphan. Did she tell you? Her and her twin sister. Twelve years old, beautiful little girls. Orphans, in the old country."

"Ireland? You knew her when you lived in Ireland?"

"When I lived—that's right, Julius." He looked out the window again, remembering. He grew tearful as he remembered. "Her sister died, Julius. Fell from a window, to her death."

"What, Peter? What are you talking about?"

"I gave the girl last rites. I was their priest." He looked back at Julius, crying. "I loved them both. That's what—that's why she killed me."

"None of this is making any sense, Peter. I don't know why you're saying such things, none of it is true."

"It's all true, Julius."

"You're not dead, Peter."

"Appearances deceive, Julius. She killed me. She stabbed me in the heart."

Julius looked at the older man, watched as tears streamed silently down the other man's cheeks. Julius shook his head, not understanding.

"How can I help you, Peter?"

"Take care of her, Julius. Try to get her home. Without you, she'll be lost. Worse than death, Julius. So much worse. You have to help her."

"How? What do I have to do?"

"Get her to New York, I think. No way back from here, I'm sure. They know, they'll be watching for her."

"Who? Who's watching?" Pauley just shook his head. Pauley took the glass from the desk, his hand trembling as he drank. "Why New York?" Julius asked.

"She'll know. Tell her. Not here. She'll be taken, or lost. Not here, Julius." He looked pleadingly at the younger man. "Promise me you'll take care of her, Julius."

Julius nodded, rising from his chair. "I'll pray for you, Father Pauley. I'll pray for God to ease your mind."

"You'll be wasting your time, Julius. Just take care of my little girl."

It was dark. Julius opened the door and slid into the passenger seat. He looked over at Grace, asleep behind the wheel, Jack snoring on her lap. He shook his head.

"Hey!" Grace's eyes snapped open and she shot her fist towards Julius's throat. Julius was not surprised. He caught her fist in mid strike and held it fast. "Glad to see you're feeling better."

Grace pulled her hand free. She sat up, staring out the windshield and took a deep, shuddering breath. Jack lifted his head from her lap. "It's no good, Grace," he continued softly. "I talked to Pauley. Not that way. They're waiting for you."

"Is that what he said?" Julius nodded.

"He said we needed to go to New York," Julius said.

"I don't much care what that fucking old bastard said."

"We can't go in there, Grace."

"You're not going anywhere, Julius. I just need to get inside."

"They know you're coming. It won't work."

"Why are you here?" she asked him.

"He told me I had to help you." She snorted derisively at that.

"I don't care, Julius. If you're gonna help, then quit giving me shit and help." She started the car. "You better take Jack with you."

"What are you going to do, Grace?"

"I have to get back, Julius. I'm going home."

"Pauley said New York. He said you'd know how."

"Pauley is a child murdering bastard. He's full of shit and needs to die. Again." She handed Jack over with a grunt. "Dog feels like a lead cannonball." Jack gave her a disparaging look.

"This isn't going to work," Julius said.

"We'll see."

He silently shook his head in the dark. "What's the plan?"

"You and Jack ring the doorbell. I'm going in through the back."

"They must be guarding the back, Grace."

"We'll see, won't we?"

"Have you checked?" Julius asked.

"They've moved people around since this afternoon. No one's across the street now. Maybe they laid some people off."

"Pauley said they know you're coming."

"He probably told them," Grace said.

"Peter's not like that. Pauley's a good priest."

"Yeah, Julius. A good priest." She put the car in gear and pulled away from the curb. Grace drove around the block and pulled up in front of the Llewellyn house. It was barely lit from within. They could both make out the shape of the guard sitting on the porch. "It's been fun, Julius." She leaned over and gave him a kiss.

"Yeah, great. Good luck, Grace." Julius climbed out of the car with Jack and put the dog down on the sidewalk. He closed the door and watched as Grace pulled away. Then he turned to walk up the path to the front door of the house, Jack following behind. Five yards from the porch, he saw the guard stand up. Julius kept walking, mounting the steps to the porch.

"Hey, buddy," the guard said. "What are you doing?"

"Sorry," Julius said, mounting the last steps to meet the man on the porch. "I think I'm lost."

"You can't be here," the guard continued, walking forward and putting a hand on Julius's chest, the other hand holding an automatic weapon at his thigh. There suddenly came the sound of an Italian sports car redlining its engine from somewhere behind the house, followed by the sound of an Italian sports car splintering through a decorative wooden fence. The guard turned to the sound, giving Julius the opportunity to strike him once in the throat and then snap his knee into the man's groin. The guard doubled over, choking and dropping the weapon clattering to the floor. Julius grabbed the man's hair and slammed his head against the brick wall, then let him slump to the floor.

Grace crashed through the fence and slalomed the Ferrari through the backyard between two trees, spinning the rear wheels in a power slide through the flowerbed and ending by slamming broadside into the back of the house, pinning the rear door closed. There was a shout, and lights came on in the house. Someone crashed into the door from the inside and cursed. Grace stood up on the seat, listening. She could hear more shouts, footsteps bounding down stairs. No gunfire, though. That was good, she thought, that meant nobody had a line of sight to her.

Julius grabbed up the weapon and flattened himself against the front wall beside the door. He listened to the sound of crashing and shouts from the back of the house. Lights came on in the front living room. The front door burst open and a man charged onto the porch. Julius caught him across the face with the gun muzzle, dropping him. Julius spun and dropped to a knee just inside the front door, weapon raised and surveying the room. Empty. All the sound was coming from the back. Julius carefully advanced into the living room, crouching behind a chair. Jack decided to wait on the porch.

Grace stepped onto the top of the windshield frame, balancing momentarily before jumping and catching hold of the balcony railing. She pulled herself up onto the balcony and lay flat, watching. Several attempts were made to force open the rear door below her, without success. More cursing, more thundering footsteps on the stairs. She stood and flattened herself against the wall next to the balcony door. The door burst open and she stuck her leg out. A guard came running out, gun in hand and tripped, striking his head against the rail. Grace waited, and when no one else came out, she went inside. She turned off the light and crouched beside the wall, listening. Nothing. She advanced into the house, slowly.

"Oh, fuck me sideways!"

Julius heard Grace curse and stood up. Jack barked once from the front porch. Julius immediately dropped to the floor and a shot rang out from the direction of the kitchen. He heard the *whup* of a bullet going into a couch cushion behind him. "Not clear, not clear!" Julius shouted in Grace's general direction. Another shot rang out, this one also aimed in his direction. He was doing a great job of drawing somebody's fire, that much was clear. "Don't shoot, I'm a priest!" he shouted. Couldn't hurt, he thought. Julius waited, watching. The shooter appeared, advancing cautiously towards the front door, gun raised. Jack barked again and the man fired. "Who shoots at dogs and priests?" Julius asked, stepping up behind the man. As he spun, Julius clubbed the guy on the head with his gun butt and the man went down in a heap. Jack sauntered into the room and peed on him.

Julius quickly advanced through the ground floor, gun raised and rapidly panning each room, all empty. He raced up the steps two at a time and repeated the survey, gun raised, in each of the upstairs bedrooms, all empty. Finally, he burst into the bathroom. Grace was sitting on the toilet, head in her hands. She gave him a weak wave.

"Don't shoot." Julius lowered his weapon.

"What's wrong?" Julius asked. He was breathing heavily and slumped against the wall. Grace just pointed to the shower stall. It had been crudely bricked up, floor to ceiling.

CHAPTER 16

Pauley sat as his desk, staring at the book in front of him, the cover of this particular copy of "The Problem Of God" creased with wear. On a couple of occasions, Pauley had tried to witness the event, each time without success. Right now, he didn't have the emotional strength to do anything else but sit and stare.

There! My God, the elderly priest thought, that was it! He was certain that the book had shifted infinitesimally as he watched, as if he had blinked. But he hadn't blinked, he was sure. Despite knowing it had happened before, actually witnessing the event was heartening. There were others on his side, he wasn't really in this alone.

Pauley reached out and lifted the book, turned to the page marked by the unusual bookmark. He scanned past the familiar passages. There followed an italicized paragraph he was certain had not been there before:

Why do you doubt me? I see farther than you. Attend to the other matter, before it's too late. Leverage will be lost soon, with consequences that may be impossible to reverse. Her path is her own.

Pauley kept reading for a minute, but the rest was as he remembered. He replaced the book on the desk and leaned back in his chair. He looked out the window, considering the words: Her path is her own. He was shocked by the sentence. He had come to believe that such a thing could not be possible. He envied her deeply, sighing. He again felt the almost undeniable urge to grab up the book and turn to the end, but fought it with a shake of his head. He knew that would accomplish nothing, only make things that much more complicated. Things already seemed to be spinning out of control, he thought. I don't need more problems than those I already have.

Pauley heaved himself from the chair and picked up the book again. He walked to his bedroom. He pulled an old, battered leather suitcase from the closet shelf and let it fall open on the bed. Pauley threw his copy of "The Problem Of God" into the suitcase. He hated to travel, and Salt Lake City was very far away.

"We've got to go, Grace." She looked up at Julius but didn't move. "We've got to go." As if to punctuate his statement, the sound of a distant siren filtered through the bathroom window. "Let's go." He held out his hand and she took it without enthusiasm, allowing Julius to lead her out of the bathroom and down the steps. Jack fell in with them as they left through the front door. Grace pulled up short on the porch.

"Wipe down the gun and leave it," she said softly. He looked at her quizzically. "Don't they fingerprint SEALs? It'll take them two hours to blame this on you." He nodded and used his shirt to quickly wipe down the automatic weapon, lowering it to the porch.

"What about the car?" Julius asked.

"I already wiped it."

"No, I mean, how about we take it. We gotta put some distance between us and this house, fast."

Grace shook her head and started down the porch steps to the front walk, Julius and Jack close behind. "Sorry, Slade. No more crazy Ferrari fun, I'm afraid." She turned to look at the sound of approaching sirens. "Time to go." She broke into an easy jog and ran across the street, heading between houses as Jack and Julius struggled to keep up. After the fourth block, she pulled up and began to casually walk down the sidewalk. Julius walked up beside her, taking her hand. They waited a moment for Jack to catch up, then kept walking.

"Where to?" Julius asked. "Subway?" She nodded. "This way," he said, pointing.

They took the subway to Union Station in DC. Grace led them to the Amtrak ticket kiosk. Julius shook his head as she took out the black Amex card he'd watched her use at dinner.

"Not a good idea, my opinion," Julius said, watching her punch buttons on the kiosk. "The little diplomat's car is still at a crime scene, you know."

"Yeah, Julius, I know. Desperate times, Padre. And keep your head down, there's a camera at your three o'clock."

Julius turned his back to the camera and watched as Grace proceeded to purchase round trip tickets for two to New York, Philadelphia, Toronto, Montreal, Detroit, San Francisco, Salt Lake City, Chicago, Minneapolis, Los Angeles, and Miami. He smiled, watching the tickets pour out of the machine. He helped her gather them up.

"Where to really?" he asked.

"Your place." She wiped down the credit card and, holding it by the edges, slid it back in the machine.

"Somebody's gonna have a lot of fun for about twenty-four hours, I think," Julius said. They walked back to Georgetown. Julius had to carry the dog the last mile.

They slept in late, all three snoring in harmony in the little bed. By the time Julius opened his eyes, Grace was already showered, dressed, and sitting at the desk, tapping on his computer. Julius rubbed the sleep from his eyes and pushed Jack off his legs. The dog didn't wake up.

"Devising the plan, Evil Genius?" he asked of her back.

"Yeah," she said over her shoulder, still typing. "Step one, we get something to eat."

"I like your thinking. Give me ten minutes to shower and shave."

"I'll give you five minutes. Don't shave."

They left Jack sleeping and went to late breakfast in the cafeteria. Grace was devouring a mountain of institutional scrambled eggs and pancakes. Along with bacon and hash browns. Julius shook his head, watching her. He had finished his yogurt fifteen minutes ago.

"You planning on running a marathon later?" he asked.

She looked up from her plate. "Are all Jesuits judgmental masochists?"

He nodded. "Actually, 'Judgmental Masochism' is a year-long course at the seminary. It's a requirement."

"I knew some nuns who could've written the textbook."

"Blessed by a Catholic school education. You hide it well." She scowled at him. "Sorry. A bit out of line, there."

"More than a bit, Julius. You have no idea."

"Yeah? I'm listening." Grace went back to eating, shaking her head. "Not worth talking about."

"Come on, Grace. Ashamed of your rich white heritage that put you through Catholic prep? Sorority girl?" She continued eating, ignoring him. "What, it's okay to slam my tortured suburban Jewish roots, but you can't reminisce about Mumsy and Pops taking you out on the sailboat after church every Sunday? Tennis with Mom at the club while Dad worked hard at the firm to buy his little girl that sports car for her sixteenth birthday? That how you learned to drive a stick, from the chauffeur?"

Grace laid her knife and fork down on the table and stared down into her plate. "You done now?" she asked softly.

"You don't like opening up, do you, Grace? No problem pointing out how fucked up I am, but don't like to look in the mirror, huh?"

"Think what you want."

"I want to know what I'm involved with here."

"How much do you need to know as you're waving bye to my train?"

"Who says I'm waving goodbye? You bought me a ticket, kiddo."

"I bought lots of tickets, kiddo. None of them for you."

"I'm going with you, Grace."

She shook her head and smiled sadly at him. "You've got a class to teach, don't you, Julius? 'What is Truth?' and all."

"Pauley will take care of 'em."

Grace recoiled at that. "You do not want to let Pauley near those kids, Julius."

"You sound as crazy melodramatic as he does."

"That what you think he is? Melodramatic?" Julius nodded. "What'd he tell you?"

"Nonsense. Just like you. All I get is nonsense and bullshit."

"Maybe you should start listening to what people are telling you," Grace said.

"Maybe people should stop fucking with me and start telling me what's really going on. Not to complain or anything, Grace, but I kinda figured my days of being shot at were over when I left the service, you know?"

"I said ring the doorbell, not go all John McClane. What did Pauley tell you?"

"Nothing that made any sense, I told you."

"What exactly did he tell you?"

"Tell you the truth, I didn't get most of it. Talked about the old country. Told me to take care of you, called you his little girl."

Grace looked like she was going to vomit at that, but only said, "You need to stop listening to that old bastard. I'm not your problem, Julius, no matter what he tells you."

"Never thought you were, Grace."

"Why'd you come then?"

"Because I knew you'd try. And I knew it wasn't going to work. And you had my dog." He studied her: she looked very sad. "Mostly, the dog." She pushed the plate away.

"Don't you have a class to teach?" Grace asked.

"Not until tomorrow. I can play all day."

"Still want to protect me from the forces of darkness?"

"Not if they got guns, I don't," Julius said.

"They've got worse, I think."

"How about you quit with the drama and tell me what's going on, Grace? Maybe then I can really help."

Grace shrugged. "I told you before, I'm still playing defense. Haven't figured it all out."

"Give me the broad outlines."

Grace placed her palms flat on the table and sighed. "Fine, broad strokes. A few years ago, I was still married to that man in the video,

Gabriel Sheehan. I helped him develop the technology to interpret thought waves."

"Yeah, I'm familiar. Insight Technologies. Now pretty much defunct, right?"

"Yeah, I guess. Not really sure. Like I said, I've been off the ranch for a while."

"What does that mean?"

"Dead."

"Here we go."

"You want to hear this or not?" she asked. He nodded, smiling sardonically. "Whatever, forget that part if you want," she continued. "Broad strokes. At the end, the end of the company, Gabe made a discovery. A discovery that I was partially responsible for. Something that shouldn't have been discovered."

"Which was?"

"The afterlife." He raised his eyebrows. "The tape that Parnell played, the one you heard him present. That was part of it."

"You and your husband discovered what, exactly?"

"How to talk to the dead."

"Really?"

"No, not really. Just the one time. But that was one time too many," Grace said.

"Just gonna humor you here, broad strokes and all. Let's say I believe you, and that Parnell's recording is real. You were dead, right?" She nodded. "Are you still dead?" Grace just looked at him. "Okay, it seemed like a good question but I guess not. So you and your husband also discovered a way to bring you back from the dead. You're the Bride of Frankenstein?"

"No, Julius. I'm afraid that you're not taking this seriously."

"Oh, I am. Really, Grace. Just broad strokes, that's all."

"I just helped my husband develop a technique to communicate with me after I died. That's all you have to know."

"Oh, is that all? But it only worked once?" She nodded. "Just ignoring the dead person in the room, then, what's the big deal? It's over."

She shook her head, sadly. "It was supposed to be over. I didn't think it through. I had hoped that Gabe could just make it disappear, after we were done. I should've known better. Nothing disappears."

"And now that idiot Parnell has it."

"Chuck is a lot of things, but he's no idiot. Well, not in the usual sense. I don't think he knows what he has, or at least I hope he doesn't. But he knows enough."

"Enough to what?"

"Enough to show the world."

"Big deal. A recording that purports to prove an afterlife. I know there's an afterlife, every Christian knows there's an afterlife. Almost all of the world's major religions believe in some form of afterlife. Let him take his little tape to the New York fucking Times if he wants to."

Grace was shaking her head vigorously. "You don't know there's an afterlife, Julius. You don't even really believe there's an afterlife."

"Of course I believe in an afterlife. I'm a priest, Grace."

Grace shook her head. "You don't really, Julius. I'm sorry, but it's true. I can hear it in your voice, when you talk about your brother."

Julius looked at her coldly. "He was seventeen years old, Grace."

Grace nodded sadly. "Exactly."

"I don't get your point, Grace."

"You ever have to counsel a parent after the loss of a child, Julius? Not your brother—I mean, professionally?"

Julius nodded solemnly. "Just out of seminary. I had to work on a pediatric oncology ward for a month. It was horrible. I was sitting with parents every day, day and night. I almost quit."

"Why? Why is the death of a child so heartbreaking, Julius?"

"It's just a shame, that's all, Grace. To die so young, before a person even has a chance to live. It's not fair. That's what everyone believes, right?"

"It only seems unfair, Julius, because you're only seeing a part of their existence. You're like a child in this world, without perspective. If you could see the bigger picture, Julius, what happens after that child dies—what happened after your brother died—you wouldn't feel that way, believe me. You'd be fine with a child's passing, happy that your brother was someplace he had to be, someplace that was more important for him than Stanford. But you can't see that, so you don't believe me. And you can't make yourself feel better about it, no matter how hard you try, because you can't really know."

"And if I did really know? If I really believed you, Grace, you think that would make a difference?"

"All the difference in the world, Julius. If you—if the world—came to know for a certainty that death is not the end, then life on this world changes completely. Completely and forever. And not for the better, Padre. Not for the better."

"I don't see why you say that. I'm relieved. I'm happy to hear it. Why wouldn't everyone feel that way?"

"You don't really. You still don't believe me. If you did, you'd understand. It changes everything, Julius." Grace sighed. "It changes everything."

They stared at one another for a moment. He shook his head. "You're probably right. I'm still lost."

"Welcome to my world."

CHAPTER 17

Father Pauley sat across the desk from Charles Parnell. They were in Parnell's small office in Salt Lake City, snow-capped mountains visible through the large window.

"It was kind of you to see me on such short notice, Dr. Parnell," Pauley began.

"No problem, Father Pauley. I'm sorry you had to come all this way. We could've talked when I was in DC. You could've joined me and Father Zimmerman for lunch. At the Tombs."

"Yes, I'm very sorry to have missed you. That would've been pleasant, I'm sure."

"You saw my talk, though, right? You were there, I think. I remember Julius mentioned your name."

"Did he? Yes, I did see your presentation, Dr. Parnell." Pauley stared back at the man across from him, incredulous that he was again dressed in an all white suit. "Very interesting, Dr. Parnell. Startling, really."

"You were startled, then? I thought you would be. Actually, I thought I'd get a more passionate response. The audience seemed pretty reserved, at the end."

"I mean no offense, Dr. Parnell," Pauley said, unable to stop himself, "but I am embarrassingly unsophisticated in so many aspects of your religion. Is your manner of dress a uniform of some type? A reflection of your position within the hierarchy of the church?"

Parnell looked down at himself. "Why? What do you mean? What manner of dress?"

Question answered, Pauley thought. The man is simply an idiot. He shook his head dismissively. "No matter, I was just being curious. I should tell you, instead, the reason I'm here." Parnell appeared confused momentarily but brightened, nodding. "Of course, it relates to your presentation."

"Of course."

"Does the matter you presented represent your particular field of expertise?" Pauley asked.

"I'm not sure what you mean, Father."

"The study of matters relating to death and the afterlife. The subject of your talk. Is it your specialty? Does it comprise a significant part of your role within the church?"

"My specialty? No, I wouldn't say it's my specialty. Not until recently, that is." Pauley raised his eyebrows and waited for the man to continue. "And it's not really part of my official duties. I wouldn't say that."

"Would you say that your presentation represents the official position of the LDS church, Dr. Pauley?"

Parnell looked discomfited. "I really couldn't say."

Pauley studied the man closely. Unbelievable, Pauley thought to himself. He shifted uncomfortably in the little chair. "I'm sorry, Dr. Parnell. I'm old, and I don't do well with lengthy plane rides, I'm afraid. Would you object to continuing our conversation outside? It's a beautiful day and I would do better walking, I think."

Parnell brightened. "Sure, Father. No problem. We can walk over to the park."

In the elevator, Parnell started to say something, something undoubtedly related to his presentation. Pauley glanced at the two other men in the elevator with them, neither of them dressed like an ice cream vendor. Pauley cut off Parnell's nascent comment.

"You know, Doctor," Pauley said, "I've never been to your city before. It's beautiful. When does it start to get cold? October?"

"Yeah, I guess," Parnell answered, a little irritated to be interrupted so rudely. "I was going to say—"

"Here we go," Pauley interrupted again as the car came to rest. "I think this is the lobby." He waited for the others to exit the elevator, then led Parnell at a slow pace outside, allowing the others to move progressively farther ahead. Parnell opened his mouth to speak again. "You mentioned a park?" Pauley interjected.

"Yeah. This way," Parnell said, pointing to their left. Pauley nodded and adjusted their path. "I was going to say, Father Pauley, that my—"

"Explain to me," Pauley said, cutting off the other man again, "the nature of your role in the LDS church, Dr. Parnell."

Parnell stammered for a second, then said, "I'm a member in good standing, if that's what you mean."

"No, that's not what I mean. I'm certain you are, Doctor. I mean to ask what is your official capacity, your title."

"Well, we're a little different here than you guys, you know. No offense, Father Pauley. The LDS isn't really big on titles and stuff. We don't have bishops and cardinals, like you do."

"I am aware of that, Dr. Parnell. But you are, I believe, a member of the Quorum of the Seventy. Am I correct in this regard?" Parnell nodded. "President of the Quorum of Seventy, I believe? Certainly that is a position of some import, to be president of such a large quorum."

Parnell shrugged. "It's not really that big a deal, Father. We're advisory, mostly. And our positions are pretty transient. We rotate people a lot. The presidency is rotating, too."

"Advisory, you say," Pauley said, amiably. They were now entering the park. Pauley led them towards the river. "Advisory to whom?"

"The church as a whole, sort of."

"Surely there is some hierarchy, some leadership to whom you present your recommendations, is there not?" Pauley steered toward an open bench by the riverbank. It was warm, and he was starting to sweat, his collar chafing.

"Yeah, I guess. You're probably thinking of the Quorum of the Twelve. They pretty much are what you're thinking of, probably. You want to sit?" He gestured to the bench.

"That would be fine, if you'd like." They sat on the bench and watched the waterwheel in the middle of the river turn slowly. "A waterwheel," Pauley said.

"Yeah," Parnell said, smiling with pride. "This park was once part of Brigham Young's farm, you know."

"I did not know that," Pauley said, nodding appreciatively. "So are you also a member of this Quorum of Twelve? Or would you be joining them at some point, as part of this rotation you mentioned?"

Parnell snorted a laugh at this. "Not bloody likely." Pauley looked at him questioningly. "I mean, no. I'm not a member of the Twelve. Not going to be, either."

"Why is that, Dr. Parnell? You seem reasonably young and intelligent, a man of deep faith, undoubtedly. Surely with time—"

Parnell was shaking his head. "Not going to happen. A lot of reasons. Being reasonably young, for one. I think you have to be over ninety or so." He smiled at his little joke.

"And for another?" Pauley asked more seriously.

"And I came to to be a Latter-Day Saint relatively late in life. Not too much legacy, I'm afraid. None, actually. You've got to be third or fourth generation, I think, at least. Even better if your great-great-great grandmother used to date Brigham Young in high school or something like that, you know?" He smiled again at the other man.

Pauley nodded sagely, watching the relic of a wheel turn slowly in the river. "It's the way of the world, isn't it?"

Parnell watched the wheel slowly spin as well. "Yeah, whatever." They sat in silence for a minute. "I could tell you more about my discovery, Father. More than I presented at the conference." He looked at Pauley with a conspiratorial expression.

"That's very kind of you to offer. I'd like to hear all about it, at some point. I'm afraid my time with you today is limited, however, and I'll be needing to fly back home this evening."

"We could get dinner, later. Before you go."

Pauley shook his head. "I'm sorry, but that won't be possible. Tell me, Dr. Parnell, have you discussed your discovery, your presentation, with other members of your church?"

"Sure, a little."

"With whom, may I ask?"

Parnell shrugged. "Just a few of the guys in church, in the office. I worked with them on the mental health development, before. We talked about it."

Pauley nodded. "Were they encouraging?"

"I wouldn't put it that way."

"Anybody else? Anyone official? Did you clear your presentation with any official organ of the church? Discuss the matters you've discovered with the Quorum of the Twelve, or any of its members?" He looked intently at Parnell next to him.

Parnell shook his head. "No, nothing like that. Nothing official. It's not the way we work, like I said. We're much less formal, less—controlling—than the Catholic Church. No offense, Father."

"None taken, Doctor. Let's walk a little," Pauley said, standing. "Along the river looks pleasant." He led the other man away. Pauley thought that a man who had seated himself on the adjacent bench looked too interested in their conversation for his comfort. A minute later and farther down the river walk, Pauley began again. "Dr. Parnell, I hope to discuss your findings at great length in the near future. Now, however, is not the time."

"Really? But I thought you were leaving tonight."

"I am."

"When will we have a chance to talk about it, then?"

"I would like you to consider returning with me to Washington."

"Tonight? I couldn't—"

"Please hear me out, Dr. Parnell. I'm sorry to be so abrupt. We are only recently acquainted and you have every reason to be skeptical, but I think that it is of the greatest importance that you return with me to Washington. We would cover all of your expenses, of course, as well as providing you accommodations at the University."

"Is this about my discovery, my presentation?"

"Exactly so."

"It's such short notice, Father Pauley. I'd be happy to come out in a week or two, if you plan on covering my expenses. That would be better."

Pauley stopped walking and Parnell nearly bumped into him. Pauley turned to face the man. "I fear, Dr. Parnell, that if you do not return with me this evening, that next week will not be possible."

"Why is that, Father?"

"I believe that you will not survive until next week if you remain in Salt Lake City."

Parnell gaped at him. "What do you mean? I don't understand."

"At the risk of sounding melodramatic, Dr. Parnell, you are in danger here. It seems that you are unaware of the fact that your recent discovery, as you call it, has caught the attention of certain individuals. Individuals who feel very strongly about preventing your discovery from becoming public. Very strongly."

"You're screwing with me, aren't you?"

"No, Dr. Parnell, I assure you that I am not 'screwing with you.' I did not come all the way here today to screw with you. I came here to save your life. Perhaps you remain oblivious to the fact that we have been watched by at least two individuals during our entire time in this park, but that doesn't make it any less true. No, please don't look about like that, Dr. Parnell, that's not really helping or necessary. Let's start walking back to your office." He took a firm grasp of Parnell's elbow and turned him back on the path. He started walking Parnell back the way they had come. "That gentleman before us, for instance, the one leaning on the rail and looking out over the water. He was sitting on the bench beside us a moment ago. No, please don't stare at him as we pass. Thank you."

They walked past in silence. "I'm going to leave you now, Dr. Parnell. We must return to Washington. I left an envelope in your office, under the cushion of the seat which I was sitting upon. It contains a plane ticket. I urge you to use it." He stopped and smiled broadly at Parnell, who stood, gobsmacked. Pauley took the other man's hand and shook it vigorously, clasping his shoulder firmly with the other. "If you do come, it is critically important that you bring all of your papers, notes, anything that pertains to your discovery. Everything." He patted him on the shoulder, smiling broadly.

"There's a hard drive..." Parnell stammered.

"It would be particularly important that you bring that as well. Leave no trace of your work behind, I urge you. Tell no one that you are leaving or where you are heading. No one at all, do you understand?" Parnell nodded, speechless. Pauley released his grip on the other man. "I hope to see you tomorrow, Dr. Parnell. If not, may God have mercy on your soul."

"I'm sorry, what?"

Pauley turned and left the other man standing in the park.

Grace finished her coffee and leaned forward. "Listen, Julius. I need a favor." He raised his eyebrows, waiting. "How many kids in your class?"

"Twenty-five, last time I checked. It may be a few less, after Sister Mary tore one of my students a new one. Why?"

"No class this afternoon?" He shook his head. "Any way to get a hold of your students, today?"

"Not for certain. I have their email addresses and I can send them a message through the University intranet. No telling when they'd read it, though." He watched her thinking about this. "Why? What do you want from my students?"

Grace explained what she needed.

"Doesn't sound particularly dangerous," Julius said when she was finished. "Kind of a pain, really. You really think it's necessary?"

"That's what you're going to find out."

"Me? How?"

"How are you at counter-surveillance?"

He smiled, shaking his head. "Probably not a good time to tell you I washed out of sniper school, huh?"

"Seriously? Shit, you are such a loser. Why'd you fail?"

"Last phase, stealth and surveillance."

"Great. I'm partnered with the guy who flunked out."

"Less than one in thirty make it through, Grace. First in my class in marksmanship, though."

"Hoping that doesn't come in handy, actually."

"Me, too. So what do you want me to do?" Julius asked.

"Find a good, high vantage point in the station and just watch. See if anybody seems to be interested in your kids as they use those tickets."

"So you just want each of my students to get on the train with one of your tickets, have it punched, and then what? My class spends the week scattered around the continental United States?"

"No, as soon as the engineer—"

"Conductor"

"—conductor, whatever. As soon as he takes the ticket, tell them to walk down a few cars and get off. Tell them to come back to campus individually, not all leave together for the bar or anything."

"Sometimes the conductor doesn't take the ticket until the train's under way, you know."

She thought about this for a second. "Doesn't matter. They can just get on, walk down a couple of cars and get off. Shouldn't be hard. Tell them they all get extra credit. In your class, they're going to need it."

"Not if they end up in jail."

"Don't think there's much chance of that."

"What do you think? You really think someone's that interested in dogging you that they'd put a team to cover Union Station, just to see where you're going? Seems a little paranoid, or delusions of grandeur, you know?"

Grace frowned at him. "Thanks for your psychological analysis, Father. I told you, Julius, I'm on defense here. I don't know what's going on or what I'm up against. Guys with guns, though, that gets my attention. Shit, Julius, they bricked up the fucking shower. Was that a paranoid hallucination, Padre?"

He had to shake his head at that. "Okay. I'll set it up, see if I can get some kids to help. What about you?"

"I'm going to hide under your bed. With Jack."

"What? You're not coming to the station, see what's going on?"

"No way, Julius. I'll take Jack for a walk, though. Later."

"Gee, great. Thanks a lot, Grace."

"One other thing, Julius."

"Really? More?"

"Can you just get me into the library, before you go back to the room?"

"Research?"

"Something like that."

CHAPTER 18

Julius waited in the classroom. He had checked and found that, lucky for him, his classroom wasn't being used on the off days. He sent a blast email to everyone in his class through every channel he could think of, telling them he needed them for a project that would net them thirty points of extra credit for three hours work, give or take. And he'd be buying dinner for everyone who showed. Now, he was sorry he had thrown in that last part. He was seated at his desk, counting his funds. If everyone showed up, he was screwed. He didn't think there was much chance of that, however.

Julius looked at his cellphone. It was ten minutes after three. He had told them three. He started to think that it was a crazy idea, anyway. Some of the students would have class or be tied up, of course. Some of them probably thought he was a dick; no way they would come even if extra credit were promised. He'd give them twenty more minutes, then bail.

Chu walked in. She stopped inside the door, looking around the empty room.

"Would you like me to lock the door, Father? The others are late."

"No, that's okay, Ms. Chu. Thanks for coming. We'll give the rest a few more minutes."

"You knew I'd come didn't you? Being an overachieving Asian, possible extra credit and all." She sat down in a chair in front of his desk, smiling at him.

"I appreciate your coming. I know you must be very busy."

"Since I'm Asian, I must be taking a really hard schedule, huh?"

Julius shook his head, trying to think of something nice to say. He was saved from his inability to do so by a clot of fifteen students, all entering the room at once.

"Thank god!" one of the students wisecracked, giving voice to what Julius was thinking at that moment. "He hasn't locked the door on us yet." The rest laughed and they settled into chairs.

"Thank you all, each and every one of you, for coming," Julius said. "I know you're all busy. This, hopefully, won't take too much of your time." Zimmerman explained that he needed help with a social experiment, one that involved the illusion of traveling by train. He instructed the class on what he needed them to do.

Grace sat at the long row of computers on the main floor of the library. She turned her chair and angled the monitor so that she could see the reflection of the keyboard next to hers. She waited, pretending to do something meaningful. It wasn't long before a student took the seat next to her. Grace carefully watched the reflection of his fingers on the keyboard as he entered his user name and password. A few minutes later, he signed off, then headed upstairs into the stacks. Grace signed onto the University system with the man's login. Twenty minutes later, she had what she needed: a list of all the surviving structures designed by Frank Lloyd Wright and their dates of construction. She headed back to Zimmerman's room. Jack probably needed to pee.

Zimmerman leaned on the railing of the balcony overlooking the grand hall of Union Station. He watched the hundreds of people below him, scurrying to and from the gates like so many ants. His students were among them. He spotted them easily, as he had asked them to go home and get changed into one of their gray Georgetown tee shirts before showing up in the station. He had distributed the tickets earlier. The trains were scheduled to depart over a span of several hours and he had watched a steady stream of his students come and go.

Every train for which Grace had purchased a ticket was being watched, he was now certain. Over the last two hours, he had repeatedly noticed that his student would pick up a shadow as he approached the gate. The shadow was usually male, and though he couldn't be certain from this distance, they each appeared pretty young. They seemed about the same age as his students, in general.

Initially, he hadn't been sure. The whole thing was pretty subtle. But from this vantage point, over the last hour Julius became convinced as he watched the Kabuki dance played out below him. He had almost seen enough. Julius thought he should go down into the station and get a better look at the individuals doing the shadowing. Before that, however, he typed a text message to Chu, his student. He had made her project leader; because she was Asian, he explained. She had laughed at that. He sent off the text telling her to get a hold of the others and tell them the experiment was complete. Those students that hadn't arrived yet needn't bother.

"Excuse me, sir?"

Julius had just hit 'send' when he heard the voice behind him. He straightened and started to move away, towards the stairway.

"Sir, excuse me! Wait a second, please."

Well, he had said 'please.' Most people don't say please before shooting you. Julius stopped and turned to see a young man, late twenties, hustling toward him. Clean shaven, neatly dressed in a white dress shirt, no tie but a sport coat—Julius immediately got the impression the guy was going to start telling him about Jehovah. He smiled at the young man, who smiled back.

"Sorry to bother you, sir," the man said, a little out of breath. "Just a moment?" Julius shrugged at the young man, appraising him. He appeared unarmed. "I was wondering if I could..."

The other man reached into his coat. Julius stepped into him and grabbed his wrist in an iron grip. "Don't," Julius said, his face now close to the other man's.

The other man went white with surprise. "Ouch, hey!" He tried to back away but Julius held him fast.

"You were just wondering what?"

The other man was obviously scared and surprised. "Just if you could tell me if you've seen this woman. I have a picture. I was just getting my picture."

Julius patted the man's sport coat with his free hand and felt nothing suspicious. He released the man's wrist.

"Show me your picture." The other man gathered himself and produced a picture from his inside pocket, his hand trembling slightly. He held the photo out to Julius. Julius looked at it—the same picture of Grace that he had seen twice before. "No." Julius turned and walked away, down the steps to the main hall of Union Station. He headed for the subway to get back to his room, and Grace. Now he had seen enough.

As Julius headed across the large hall, scanning the crowded space, he could pick out a great number of young men and women with the look of someone passing out copies of The Watch Tower. He pulled out his phone as he walked, carefully avoiding eye contact. He dialed the number for the young priest who lived next door to his room.

"Hey, Steve," Julius said when the man answered.

"What's up, Julius?"

"You do me a favor?"

"Sure. What's up?"

"Could you go next door and—"

"You want me to get the cute redhead for you?"

Julius sighed. "Yeah, exactly. But make sure you get the cute one, not one of the other two I have living with me, okay?"

"Sure, Jules. Give me a second to get a shirt on, okay?"

"I'm sure she'd prefer if you didn't, Steve."

"Really? Just a second."

Zimmerman was almost at the subway entrance but didn't want to go in, as he was afraid he might lose the call. He heard some muffled conversation and Grace got on the phone.

"Damn, Julius. He's cute."

"Yeah, I'd thought you'd like that."

"What is it with you Jesuits? You're like the gays, all hunky and cut, you know?"

"Yeah, Grace, we're just like the gays. Listen, I'm on my way back. You want the good news or the bad news?"

"Give me the bad news. I always get the bad news first."

"I'm the same way. I can't enjoy the good news because I'm too afraid the bad news is going to be so much worse than the good news is good, you know?" Julius said.

He thought he heard Grace blow a ringlet of hair off her forehead, but he might have been imagining. "That's really fascinating, Julius. What did you find out?"

"Oh, yeah. So here's the bad news—there's about thirty guys crawling around this station, all looking for you."

"Shit."

"Yeah, shit. They're showing around your picture like you're the kid on a milk carton, you know?"

"Thirty? Really, thirty?"

"Yeah, maybe more. Really. But the good news is—hold it, I'm getting another call." The phone vibrated in his hand and he looked to see the caller ID.

"Just ignore it. What's the good news?"

"Shit!"

"I don't understand. Why is that good news?"

"No, shit. I've got to take this. It's Parnell. He's calling me."

"What? Chuck Parnell? Don't answer—"

Grace's voice was cut off as Julius switched calls.

"Dr. Parnell," Julius said. "This is a surprise."

"Is this Father Zimmerman? Is that you, Julius?"

The man sounded panic stricken, Julius thought. "Yeah, Dr. Parnell. This is Julius. What's wrong?"

"I can't talk. I need you to come and get me, Julius."

"Get you? Where are you?"

"I'm at the airport, in Baltimore. You've got to come get me. Pauley was supposed to be on the plane, but he never showed. He may be dead, I don't know."

"Dead? Father Pauley? What are you talking about, Dr. Parnell?"

"I can't talk, Julius. You have to help me. I've been here for over an hour already. I've probably been seen. It was freakin' impossible to get your number, dammit. Get up here, fast."

"Fine, Chuck. I'll be there in an hour."

"An hour? I could be dead in an hour, Julius. Get your ass—"

"Listen, Chuck. Settle down. I'm on my way now, but I don't have a car. I'll have to take the shuttle. It's going to be an hour, at least. Where should I meet you?"

"Just go to the international terminal. Go to where you meet arriving passengers. I'll find you."

"Just tell me where—"

"No, too dangerous. I'll find you." He hung up.

Zimmerman stared at the phone. Grace had hung up. He called back to Steve's phone. As he did so, he turned from the subway and headed to the Super Shuttle desk. "Yeah, sorry, Steve. Can I—thanks." He waited for Grace to come back to the phone.

"I told you to just hang up on the guy," Grace said.

"He's at BWI. He says he's in danger, that Pauley may be dead. He sounds frantic."

"Chuck wakes up frantic. He'll stop being frantic three days after he's dead. Who gives a shit?"

"I'm going to get him."

"Get him? Why?"

"He says he's in danger. Something's going on. It might have something to do with you, with this whole thing." He waited for her to respond but she was quiet for a little while. "Grace?"

"Yeah, I'm thinking. Okay, you may be right. Probably better if we have control of him—he may be the first asset we have in this mess."

"Asset? What do you mean? He's an idiot."

"Not as big as you think. Listen, bring him back and we'll stuff him in one of the dungeons or something, okay?"

"Dungeon?"

"Yeah, look at this place. There must be some dungeons, some torture chambers in this gothic horror show. Shit, Julius, isn't this where they filmed Rosemary's Baby?"

"The Exorcist."

"Yeah, exactly. Stuff him in one of the underground caverns and chain him to the wall."

"I'll get him a room at the hotel on campus."

"Is it a nice hotel?"

"Not particularly. Like two stars."

"Great. That'll seem like a dungeon to Chuck, believe me. I'll see you when you get back. Jack and I will wait up."

"It might be pretty late, Grace."

"You're worth it, Julius. Hey, what's the good news you were—"

"I gotta go, I'm at the shuttle and I'm going to try to catch this one. See you later."

"Hold it, Julius!"

"Yeah, what? I gotta hurry."

"Before you pick him up, at the airport. I need you to get a few things."

"Shit, Grace, what things? I'm not going to the mall."

"Get me a fifth of whiskey and a couple of rolls of duct tape. Got it?"

"What the hell are you talking about?"

"I told you. A fifth of whiskey, try to get Irish. Not that Glenfiddich shit. And make sure the duct tape is black. Two rolls, you better. Got it? Oh, and make sure you tell Parnell not to leave his room, don't talk to anybody. You'll bring him breakfast in the morning. Got that? And take his phone away from him."

"Take his phone? Why would he give me his phone?"

"Tell him it can be tracked, that the bad guys will find him and knock down the door and sodomize him. Listen, you better hurry, Julius, you're going to miss that shuttle. Love you."

"Love you, too." He shook his head, wondering why he had just said that. He tried to think of something else to say quickly, but she had already hung up.

CHAPTER 19

It was past midnight before Julius got back to his room. He sat on the side of the bed, pulling off his shoes and socks. Grace was propped up on the pillow, reading about Frank Lloyd Wright on Julius's laptop computer. Jack was asleep at the foot of the bed, snoring.

"So I put him in the room and told him to get some sleep," Julius continued. "He's completely lost it, I'm telling you. He's almost babbling, he's so panic stricken." Julius shook his head. "I've got to brush my teeth." He left for the bathroom.

"Did you get his phone?"

"Yeah. It's on the desk."

"Did he say what's going on?" Grace asked, getting up from the bed. She picked up Parnell's phone and started to go through the call log.

"Nothing that made any sense," Zimmerman said through a mouthful of toothpaste. He rinsed and spat. Julius came out of the bathroom dressed in his pajamas. He stood at the door of the bathroom staring at Grace as she stood at the desk, studying the phone. Grace was dressed in a nightie that looked like something one wears on a honeymoon. "You don't believe in flannel?" he asked her.

She turned and smiled at him wickedly. "Kuwaitis hate flannel. It's the desert, you know? You want to flip to see who gets the floor?"

"What good would it do? You already know what happens."

"True." She tossed the phone back on the desk and climbed into bed.

"Should I bother?" Julius asked. She shook her head, smiling. "Figured." He crawled under the covers next to her and turned off the light. "Night, Grace."

"Night, Julius." They lay quietly in the dark for a few minutes. "Hey, Julius."

"What, Grace?"

"You never told me the good news."

"In the morning, Grace. While we row. Night."

"And by rowing, you mean—"

"Rowing. As in a boat. Night."

"Night, Julius."

It was still dark in the room when the alarm went off at five. Julius rolled over and shook Grace awake.

"Am I still a virgin?"

"Doubt it. Time to go rowing," he said, heading for the bathroom. When he came out dressed in shorts and sweatshirt, he had to shake her awake again.

"I can think of better exercise, Julius. Burns calories, more fun. Relieves stress."

"You gonna wear that in the boat?"

She shook her head. "Give me a second, darling." Grace went into the bathroom and came out ten minutes later, washed and with her hair pulled back, wearing a dark gray Georgetown sweat suit. "Dog?" she asked. Julius nodded, giving the dog a shake. They waited for Jack to complete his stretching ritual. They headed down to the river.

Grace sat with Jack on her lap, watching Julius row. She shook her head.

"I hope I don't have to row us back again, Julius."

"Don't worry, we're not going that far. Today's for speed, not distance."

"You don't seem to be going very fast." He shook his head at this but said nothing. "So, Julius, you never told me the good news."

"What good news?" he asked, increasing his cadence.

"That's what I'm asking. Last night you said you had some good news and some bad. You told me the bad news already. Which is pretty fucking awful, by the way."

He nodded and waited until he had his next breath and began his pull. "Yeah, I guess you're not completely paranoid after all. Somebody's going to a lot of trouble to find you."

"And to keep me from leaving."

"Yeah, that too. Though I'm not really clear on that part."

"Yeah, get used to it, amigo. So what's the good news?"

"The people who are looking for you. I should've realized it after the episode at the Wright house."

"Realized what?" She had to wait while he got to the point in his cadence where he could talk again. "Geez, Julius, this hobby of yours sucks. We can't even have a decent conversation."

"I should have realized what we're dealing with. Last night just clinched it."

"So what are we dealing with that's such good news?"

"I don't know who or what they are, Grace. But I'll tell you this— they're sure not any kind of professionals."

She thought about this for a moment as she watched Julius row. "You're right. Those guys at the house acted like a bunch of Keystone Kops."

"No way they're pros, or even ex-military, I think. Not even Rent-a-Cop level, I'd say. And last night, those guys were just kids."

"Kids?"

"Yeah, like college age. They looked like Jehovah's Witnesses, you know? The guys and gals you see walking around the neighborhood that you need to pretend you're not home when they ring the doorbell."

"Huh. How'd you know they were looking for me, exactly?"

"Oh, they were looking for you, all right. They had every gate covered that you bought a ticket for. And they were showing around your picture."

"Shit."

Zimmerman shrugged as he slid forward to the catch. "Could be worse."

"True. But I still don't have a clue what's going on," Grace said.

"Yeah, that's a problem." He completed another stroke. "Maybe Parnell can enlighten us."

"Yeah, that reminds me," Grace said. "Did Parnell have anything with him when you picked him up? Briefcase, bag, anything?" Julius shook his head as he rowed.

"Not a thing. He came and found me, but he wasn't carrying anything except his phone."

"Shit. That's going to be a problem. Did you get the stuff I asked for?"

"I got the whiskey. Irish, at the duty-free shop. Jameson, not that Glenfiddich shit," Julius said.

"Great. What about the duct tape?"

"No, Grace. No duct tape. Turns out they don't sell duct tape at the airport. Who knew?"

"Gonna need duct tape. Black. And some other stuff," Grace said.

"Yeah, what stuff?"

"About a dozen tablets of Percocet."

"What?" Julius stopped in mid-cadence and looked at her.

"Or Vicodin. But Percocet would be better."

"Where the hell are we going to get narcotics? Why do we even need narcotics?"

"You need to row, Julius," she said, pointing at the oars. He started back up. "Come on, you must have some drugs at your place." Julius just shook his head at this. "Jesuits never get a toothache?" He shook his head again. "Father Steve next door probably has a stash. He's a party guy, I can tell."

"Doubt it."

"Then don't worry about it. I'll take care of the drugs. You get the duct tape. How about we turn this cruise around, Odysseus? Parnell's going to want breakfast and I've got some narcs to score."

They made it back without Grace having to row. Grace used the computer as Julius showered and changed. She went on the Georgetown

Hospital website and found the name of an oral surgeon on staff. Then she found the number for the campus infirmary. Julius came out of the bathroom, toweling off his hair, to hear Grace using Parnell's cellphone, speaking with a comical attempt at an Indian accent.

"I told you, Mr. Pharmacist, sir, I am oral surgery resident working with Dr. Keller, attending staff oral surgeon Georgetown University Hospital. No, I will not hold, Mr. Pharmacist, I am very busy doctor. My name? Dr. Rasmani Subramainian, resident doctor in oral surgery, as I have already told you. What? Just like it sounds, Mr. Pharmacist. Please, listen. Prescription is for Zimmerman, Julius. Zimmerman, yes, two em's, please do not make me spell everything we say, I have no time for this. Prescription is for Percocet five milligrams, dispense twenty tablets, no refills. Yes, twenty. Yes, generic is fine. My DEA number? I told you, I am calling for Dr. Keller, it is his patient but he is busy attending oral surgeon so I am calling in prescription for him. Yes, please use Dr. Keller's DEA number that you have on file, that would be fine. Date of birth? I'm not sure how old Dr. Keller is, Mr. Pharmacist. Oh, of patient. Let me check." She looked over at Zimmerman, who only shook his head. "Mr. Pharmacist, I do not have his date of birth, he has already left our office. I do not have that information, Mr. Pharmacist. I do know that Dr. Keller and I did a very painful extraction on Zimmerman, Julius and he will need the pain medicine very soon. Yes, yes, I will mail the cover script right away, right away. Yes, thank you very, very much Mr. Pharmacist. Bye."

Julius sat on the bed and pulled on his socks. "You sound like a brain-damaged Indian with an Irish brogue."

"You're going to want to hurry over to the pharmacy and pick up that prescription, Julius. Before they have a chance to find Dr. Keller and ask him something that'll lead to your arrest. And you might want to pretend like your tooth is really hurting."

"Maybe you'd like to punch me, you know, get a little realistic jaw swelling to add to the effect."

"You think that'd help?"

"You're insane, you know that, right?" Grace nodded. "Problem is, I'm even crazier for playing along with all this."

"So why are you?

"I told you. Pauley said I should protect you. I guess he meant I should score some narcotics for you, too."

"Don't do it because of Pauley, Julius. The man is evil."

"Then why should I?"

Grace came over and kissed him on the cheek. "Because I asked you. Isn't that enough?" He rolled his eyes and finished putting on his collar. "You look dashing when you dress like a priest, you know that?"

"Yeah, save the ass-kissing for when I stop doing what you ask me, Grace. Which we're getting to pretty quickly, by the way. Anything else besides duct tape and Percocet?"

"When you take breakfast to Parnell, make sure you put the fear of God in him." She smiled at her little joke. "Make sure he knows not to step foot outside his room or else something really, really bad will happen." He nodded. "And one last thing." Grace took her pocket book from the night stand and fished out two tablets. "Here, take these."

"What are these?"

"Roofies."

"You're kidding me. I thought you were joking at dinner. You were really going to use these on me?"

"Of course not, Julius. Probably not, anyway. I was saving them for my Kuwaiti prince, actually. Anyways, Parnell likes his coffee light and sweet. Put both tablets in, you know, stir 'em up. He'll never know."

"I'm not going to kill him, am I?"

"Probably not."

"Great. I'll meet you back here, then. Take Jack for a walk in an hour, okay?"

Julius saw Grace chasing Jack around the commons as he walked back to the dorm from the Georgetown Hotel. He just stood and watched until Jack noticed him and came flouncing over. Grace followed, winded.

"How'd it go, Padre?" Grace asked, dropping onto a bench. Jack lay down at her feet.

Julius held up the bag from the pharmacy. "Tell me again why you used my real name?"

"Real drugs, real patient. No problem."

"But I didn't have a tooth pulled. What happens when they check with that oral surgeon?"

"Why would they do that?"

"They don't check?"

"Doubt it. When the cover script doesn't come over in a couple of weeks, maybe they'll call to find out why. The dentist's office staff will probably just punch one out, fake his signature and send it over. You know how these academic doctors are." Julius just shook his head. "Black duct tape?"

"Check."

"How's our hostage?"

Julius sat down on the bench beside her. "Bouncing off the walls, in fear of his life. He's a nut job."

"Not completely."

"You really know him?"

"Like I said before, it was another life. What did he say?"

"Said Pauley flew out to see him in Salt Lake. Pauley told him his life was in danger because of his presentation, that if he didn't come back to Washington with him he'd be dead by next week. Only Pauley never showed for the plane."

"Did he say what he did with his stuff, his documentation?" Julius shook his head. "Did you give him the Roofies?"

"Yeah, watched him drink the entire cup. Hope he's not dead."

"His type don't die. Let's get Jack home. We've got stuff to do."

"Stuff?"

"You'll see."

"I've got class this afternoon, at three."

"You'll make it."

They dropped off Jack and headed over to the hotel. "What room is Parnell in?" Grace asked as she and Julius approached the lobby.

"324"

"Registered under his name or yours?"

"Mine."

151

"Smart move, Julius. Kudos. Your key?"

"Shit," Julius said, looking embarrassed. "Left it in the room, with Parnell. Oops."

Grace shook her head. "I take back the kudos comment." She stepped up to the clerk at the desk. "Hi, I'm Grace Zimmerman, 324. My key card isn't working, sorry. I had it next to my phone. I should've known better."

The clerk gave a nod of recognition to Julius, then turned back to Grace and smiled indulgently. "Happens all the time, Mrs. Zimmerman. Just a second." He returned a minute later with a keycard. "There you go."

She smiled. "Thank you. Won't happen again."

"No problem. Have a good day."

"Yeah, I'll try." She walked over to where Julius was already holding an elevator.

"Who are you, anyway?" Julius asked, shaking his head and smiling.

"Truth?" Julius nodded. "Used to be a thief, for a while. But that was—"

"—another life. Yeah, I know. You can stop saying that, Grace."

She shrugged and the elevator doors opened onto the third floor. Grace opened the door to 324 with her new key. Inside, Parnell was asleep in a chair.

"Shit, he couldn't just lay down in the bed?" Grace asked. "Help me get him in bed, will you, Julius?"

"Why?"

"Because it'll be a lot easier to get his clothes off him in bed, that's why."

"Oh. Of course."

They managed to half drag, half carry Parnell into the bed. Thankfully, he was a rather slight man. Julius helped Grace take off the man's clothes.

"I'm sorry, silly question. Why are we taking off his clothes?" Julius asked.

"Interrogation 101, Julius. Didn't you go through SERE? People feel weak when they're naked. Or so I'm told. And because no one believes they're dead if they're still dressed in the same clothes they had on yesterday, Julius."

"Oh."

They got Parnell stripped naked. Grace started going through his pants pockets.

"Shit, shit, shit," she said. "Nothing."

"What are you looking for?"

"A locker key, a coat check, something to tell us where he stashed his stuff. Dammit!" Grace went to the desk and grabbed the roll of duct tape they had brought with them. "Gonna have to do this the hard way after all. Fuck me sideways."

"Can I help?"

"You mean here, right now? You didn't seem too interested, before."

"I meant help with the interrogation, Grace."

"Oh. Well, that's embarrassing. Yeah, unplug the phones, okay? And all the lamps except the one on the desk."

Julius started doing what she had asked. Meanwhile, he watched as Grace closed the blackout curtain and sealed the sides with duct tape. That completed, she grabbed two glasses from the bathroom and filled one with four fingers of whiskey. She took a sip.

"Nice. Good job, Julius."

"Thanks. You won't mind if I don't join you, do you?"

"Actually, it's not for you. It's for him."

"Don't think he's in any shape for whiskey." Julius watched as Grace took out six tablets of Percocet from their vial and crushed the pills on the desk with the other glass. She slid the powder off the side of the desk and dumped it into the whiskey, stirring it with her finger. She licked her finger. Julius looked aghast. "You're going to kill him."

"Probably not. Hope not. Maybe." Parnell started to stir in the bed. Grace looked over, then started to pull her shirt over her head. "Time for you to go, Julius."

Julius gaped at her as she slid out of her jeans. She kicked her clothes under the bed. "What are you doing?"

"Told you. It's a commonly held belief that people don't wear clothes when they're dead. White togas with wings would be great, but we don't have time for costumes."

"You really think—"

"Oh, yeah. You don't know Chuck like I do. He opens his eyes and sees me, I won't have to say a word." She made a whisking motion with her hand, dismissing him. "Time to go, Julius. You got a class to teach."

He smiled at her and sat in the desk chair. "Actually, I think I have some time. I'll just sit and watch."

"Yeah, in your dreams, Padre. You had your chance, Julius. And you don't look dead enough."

"Had?"

"We live in hope, Father." She made the whisking motion again and Julius rose, shaking his head. Grace stashed her bra under the bed as Julius walked to the door.

"Good luck, Grace," he said, turning and giving her a smile. He closed the door as he left, still smiling and shaking his head.

Grace turned out all the lights except the desk lamp. She took off the lampshade and tossed it in the bathroom. Then she carefully positioned the bare bulb so it would be exactly behind her as she sat in the chair at the foot of the bed. She stepped out of her underwear and sat, waiting for Parnell to wake up.

She had to wait another ten minutes. Finally, Parnell's eyes fluttered open. He was looking right at Grace, but it was a minute before his eyes managed to focus on her. When he did, he uttered a short scream and scrambled back against the headboard.

"Helena?" he gasped. Grace said nothing, nodding slightly. "Ohmygod, ohmygod, ohmygod," Chuck slurred, struggling to keep his eyes open. Grace stood and, careful to keep the light behind her, brought the glass over to Chuck. Chuck took it and drank, staring at her. He winced, and blinked, but he drank most of the glass before coughing and handing it back. Grace took the glass and set it down on the nightstand next to Parnell. She sat back down on the desk chair and just stared at Parnell. He stared back at her, agape. His eyelids drooped.

"Helena?" Parnell said again, trying to focus on her. "Am I..." He couldn't finish the question, only mostly because of the drugs coursing through his veins. Grace nodded solemnly. "Ohmygod," Parnell whispered again, and then he passed out.

Grace crossed to the bed again and felt Parnell's pulse, pleased to find he still had one. She knelt next to the bed and brought her face next to his. "Chuck," she whispered into his ear, without response. She repeated it louder, but he only turned away from her in his drugged stupor. She reached down and gave his testicles a squeeze. His eyes came open with a moan. "Chuck," she repeated, even louder. He stared about, unable to focus on where her voice was coming from. "Where did you put it? Where is Gabe's stuff?" He shook his head weakly but said nothing. She gave him another little squeeze.

Parnell twisted around to look at her, her face close to his. "I hide to had it. I hid it," he slurred.

"Where, Chuck? Where did you hide it? At the airport?"

"It's safe, Lena. Safe," he said, falling back asleep.

She gave his shoulder a shake. "It's not safe, Chuck. We need to get it, bring it here. Where is it? Where did you hide it?"

"Locker," he whispered, eyes closed.

"Where's the key, Chuck? The key to the locker, where is it?"

"Hid it. Hide the key, safe."

"Where, Chuck? Where did you hide the key?" She shook him again until he opened his eyes. His pupils were pinpoint, unfocused.

"Bathroom. Tired, Lena. Go to sleep now," weakly, eyes closing and head lolling back off the pillow.

Grace straightened up and went into the bathroom. She got down on her hands and knees and looked under the sink, running her hands along under the cabinets, finding nothing. She stood up and looked around the little bathroom. Grace pulled the top off the toilet tank—empty. She replaced the porcelain top. She felt along the top of the door without result. Finally, she felt in the bathtub spout with two fingers. "Bingo," she said out loud, carefully reaching in and grabbing it. The key was obviously to a locker, the plastic tag numbered 42. Grace quickly dressed and pocketed the key. She turned out the light and left, Parnell breathing noisily in the dark behind her as she pulled the door shut.

Zimmerman sat at the desk, scanning the classroom. It looked like a few students were missing. His cellphone on the desk said 3:05. Chu was one of the missing students, he noticed.

"Mr. Kasperski," Julius said to the man sitting in the back row. "Would you mind shutting the door? I think we've been more than patient. Thank you." He waited until the man returned to his seat. "Anyone know where Chu and the others are?"

Sanchez gave a short laugh. "Chu said you bought her an all expense paid vacation in Manhattan. Couple of the others are in Boston, I think."

"Oh." Julius wondered if he was going to have to excuse their absences, in addition to the promise of extra credit. Probably, he thought. He walked to the board and erased the definition of miracles. Picking up the chalk, he wrote "The Afterlife," and sat back down at his desk.

Zimmerman looked around the room at the expectant, intelligent faces. "How many of you believe that there is some form of existence after we die?" he asked of his young audience. All of the students before him raised their hands. "No, I mean which of you really, really believe? Who in this room knows beyond a shadow of a doubt, with their whole heart and certainty of mind, that there is something for them after death?" Everyone dropped their hands except one—Ms. Lightley. She looked about self-consciously. "Thank you, Ms. Lightley. You may also lower your hand now."

"What's up, Father Zimmerman?" Sanchez asked. "The readings were Nietzsche, *Beyond Good and Evil*. Nothing 'bout the afterlife."

"Don't panic, Mr. Sanchez," Zimmerman replied. "Just going off on a bit of a tangent for a bit." He walked along the windows, thinking. "Consider the following hypothetical, please: I present to you today irrefutable scientific evidence that your soul, your consciousness, will exist in some continuing form after your death. Your thoughts." He stood at the window, looking at them.

"Everyone?" one of the students asked. He nodded.

"You mean, like born again as another person?" another student volunteered. Julius shrugged.

"Whatever. Back to this existence, continuing on in heaven. Whatever," Julius said, looking about the room.

"Even if you're like, really bad?" He nodded.

"Even if you don't accept Christ or get baptized or confess your sins or anything?" He nodded.

"Jews, too?"

"Yeah, Jews, too," Zimmerman said with mock exasperation.

"Well, Father," Sanchez said, smiling. "That changes everything, don't it?"

"Doesn't it," Julius corrected.

"It sure do," Sanchez replied, smiling more broadly.

"What changes?" Julius asked of his class.

"Like he said, Father," Steponowicz said. "Everything." The other students were all nodding. "The entire perspective, the world. Everything."

"Why?" he asked her, puzzled. He didn't understand, didn't really understand it when Grace had said the same thing.

"Are you kidding, Father?" Steponowicz asked. He shook his head. She shrugged. "If there's more than this, then maybe there's something better, you know?" Nods all around at that.

" 'Specially for those that don't have it so good in this life, you know? They need to know that there's more waiting for them," another student added.

"So what if there is?" Julius asked.

"Then maybe I want to be there," Sanchez said. "And maybe, Father," he winked at Julius, "I raise a little hell on my way, you know?"

"Not for me, Father Zimmerman." It was Lightley, turning her head to give Sanchez a malevolent stare and then looking back to Julius. "I agree with you."

"I didn't express an opinion, Ms. Lightley," Zimmerman said. "We're having a discussion. Why doesn't it change anything for you?"

"Because I know my Savior will welcome me when I die. I knew that since the day I was reborn, so nothing changes. I still have my life to live here first, a duty to do God's work here on Earth before going to my reward."

"Father just said it wasn't a reward, Cheryl," Sanchez said. "He said it was a physical inevitability, like falling off a cliff. Do your duty or don't do your duty, you're ending up in heaven or some such. Changes everything." He shook his head.

"But that's not fair," Lightley said, looking imploringly at Julius.

"So you say," a voice from the back of the room responded. Julius had missed who had spoken.

"I'm sorry, who was that?" Julius asked.

"I did, Father. It's Christensen."

"I know who you are, Mr. Christensen. You respectfully disagree with Ms. Lightley?"

"Yeah, respectfully. She doesn't get to decide what's fair or not. Maybe it's fair that everyone gets to go. Makes more sense to me, anyway."

"It's not me, it's God," Lightley protested. "It says in the Bible."

Julius raised his hand. "You'll recall, Ms. Lightley, that I asked we refrain from referencing the Bible as an authoritative source. It is problematic. State your argument from a different vantage, please."

Lightley sighed, exasperated. "I don't think using the Bible to support an argument is problematic, Father, and I don't think you of all people should be saying such things." He raised his eyebrows but said nothing. "Fine, then," she continued. "It doesn't make sense his way. Not just everybody can go to heaven. It can't work that way."

"Why not?" Christensen asked from the back of the class.

"Because there would be no punishment for evil, that's why. You can't have Hitler up in heaven, obviously."

"Really, Ms. Lightley?" Julius said. *"Reductio ad Hitlerium?* That's your argument?"

"Well, yeah," she responded. "I mean, he was evil, you know?"

"You can't even say that," Sanchez interjected. "I mean, Hitler didn't think he was evil. He claimed to be a Christian, said he was doing God's work, you know."

"He was not a Christian!" Lightley said.

"I said, he thought he was. Didn't you ever read *Mein Kampf?* You know what it said on the belt buckles of the SS officers?" Lightley shook her head. *"Gott mit uns,"* Sanchez responded. "God with us!"

"But he was evil," Steponowicz said. "I mean, just looking at the Holocaust and all."

"But you can't even say that," Sanchez said. "Maybe you can't even define genocide as evil, not if what Father says is true. Just because Hitler killed millions of people? Even that's not totally evil, not if he's sending them to someplace better, you know? How can you judge him then, if every one of them still enjoys an afterlife? Murder kinda loses its stigma, you know?"

Julius leaned against the windows as this brought an angry rejoinder about intent and The Golden Rule. Zimmerman listened as the discussion swirled more passionately around the room, voices rising as his students argued whether good and evil—morality itself—can exist in a world with the unconditional promise of life ongoing after death. As Julius listened, he realized that Grace was right. It changed everything—and not for the better. Far from it.

CHAPTER 20

Julius was surprised when Grace came into the classroom as the students streamed out, still arguing between themselves. She looked around at them as they gave her acknowledging nods but kept up their vigorous discussions. Grace dropped into the chair in front of Julius's desk as he put away his papers.

"Sounds like a helluva class, Father," she said.

He looked up and smiled broadly. "Back from the dead so soon?" She smiled back and nodded. "It was a helluva class. One of my best ever, I think."

"Really? They all stayed awake, proving that there really are miracles? What'd you talk about?"

"What you were talking about, before. What happens if everyone finds out there's something after death," Julius said.

"They're kids, they don't give a shit. They're all gonna live forever."

"No, they were serious. I think you might be right."

"Yeah, well, get back to me when you're sure, Julius. Listen, I don't have time to discuss metaphysical philosophy right now. I gotta go. I found where Parnell stashed the stuff."

"Really? He bought the whole 'died and in Purgatory with Grace' gambit?"

"Oh, yeah? Seeing me naked is now some kind of Purgatory? Is that what you're saying, Zimmerman?"

Zimmerman blushed. "No, that's not what I meant..." he stammered.

She smiled at his embarrassment. "You're probably right, Julius. The drugs and the whiskey were probably more effective than seeing my tits. Didn't hurt, though, you gotta admit."

He nodded, smiling sheepishly, still blushing. "I'm sure it didn't hurt, Grace."

"Damn straight, Father." She stood up. "Gotta go. I just came by to say goodbye and let you know I didn't have time to walk Jack. Sorry." She stood on tiptoe to give him a kiss.

"Wait, what do you mean?" he said, recovering from the kiss and glancing about to be sure no one was watching. "What do you mean, goodbye? The stuff's gotta be at the airport, right?"

She nodded. "Yeah, I think so. In a locker. I got the key."

"I'll go with you."

"Why, Julius?"

He paused, feeling like he'd been kicked in the stomach. "What if there's trouble?" he asked, weakly.

Grace shook her head, smiling at him sadly. "There won't be any trouble, Julius. Nobody else knows where it is. Thanks, buddy. I'll be fine."

"What will you do with it?"

"I don't know. Get rid of it somehow. Probably dump it in the ocean. I gotta go, Julius."

"What about after? Where will you go?"

"I gotta go back, Julius."

"How?"

"I'll find a way. Don't worry about me, Julius. Dying's the easy part. You take care of yourself." She kissed him again, and this time he kissed her back.

"Bye, Grace." He pretended to put stuff back in his satchel as she headed for the door. He looked up just as she left. "Hey, Grace." She poked her head back in the door, questioning. "For the record, I think it probably was your tits." She smiled and winked at him, then disappeared out the door. A student came in right behind her.

"She does have a nice set, doesn't she, Father?" the student asked, stepping into the room.

"I'm sorry," Zimmerman said, reddening. "Can I help you?"

"Oh, sorry, Father. Just delivering a message," the young man said, smiling broadly. "Father Pauley asked if you'd come by his office as soon as you're free."

Zimmerman nodded. "Is there anything else?" Zimmerman asked.

The student was still smiling. "She's not really a nun, is she, Father?"

"Thank you for delivering your message. If you see Father Pauley, tell him I'll be right over." He glared at the student. The boy left, still smiling.

Zimmerman headed across campus to his dorm room. He didn't feel like facing Pauley just yet. He was confused and upset. Pretty damn confused, but mostly upset. He was having a hard time dealing with Grace just suddenly leaving like that. His reaction was upsetting him more than her actual leaving, he realized. As he walked, he forced himself to get a grip on his emotions. Julius tried to think about what was going on, tried to focus on the events of the last several days, but couldn't get his head around any of it. Zimmerman had kept a lot of his questions at bay while he was with her—she had that effect on him, he now realized. Grace never actually lied to him—at least he thought that was the case— but she hadn't been making much sense, either. Now that she was gone, and he tried to sort out what had just happened, he realized he couldn't.

What was going on? Why was Pauley back, and where had he been? What should he do about Parnell? Who was Grace, and how had she just appeared in his life like that—and now was gone, just as fast? Who was after her? He shook his head and unlocked the door to his room. Jack walked up to him, tail wagging. He wore a card tied around his neck. Julius pulled it off and opened it: "Don't be sad, Julius. Come find me after. When we're dead, we won't be wearing any clothes. Of course, we're all pretty incorporeal. And there's no sex either. Sorry we missed out. Love, Grace." He smiled and patted Jack on the head. Julius looked around the room. Every trace of Grace was gone. He could almost believe it had been a dream. Zimmerman looked at the card again, just to be sure, and shook his head.

"Let's go for a walk, Jack."

Grace headed for Union Station. She still had enough money left to grab the shuttle to BWI airport. Not much more, though. She felt the key in her pocket. Other than that, she had only the clothes on her back. That was okay, she thought. Once she had Parnell's stuff, it shouldn't be hard to find a way to throw it into the Chesapeake. After that—well, she'd worry about that after. She sighed softly as she realized that she was going to miss her new friend. She was going to miss him a lot.

Zimmerman stood at the open door of Pauley's office, watching the man working at his desk. He knocked and Pauley looked up, smiling.

"Julius, you got my message. Come in, sit down." Zimmerman took a chair in front of the desk, staring. "What's wrong, Julius? Why the sad face?" Zimmerman said nothing, only stared at the older man, shaking his head. "I know it hurts, Julius. Believe me, I know. At least she didn't kill you." Pauley gave the other man a humorless smile.

"I don't understand what's happened," Julius said in measured tones.

"Of course you don't," Pauley said. "I'm sorry, Julius. I know that this has been hard for you. But I need your help, Julius."

Zimmerman shook his head. "She's gone, Peter."

"I know, Julius. I need you to get her back." Zimmerman felt his heart had stopped for an instant—he looked at the other man, surprised. He wanted to get her back—badly, he realized with a stab of guilt.

"Why?"

"She's in danger, Julius."

Julius snorted derisively. "That's what you said the last time, Peter. I nearly got my head blown off. She's not the one in danger. She's pretty good at taking care of herself."

"I know it seems that way, Julius, but you don't understand what's going on."

"No shit, Peter. I don't understand a goddamn bit of it. I just know she told me not to believe anything you said. And she said she doesn't need my help. So no, Peter. I don't think I can help you."

"You have to, Julius. If you care for her at all, you have to."

"Or what? Or she'll die? That's her plan, Peter. To go back from wherever she came from, before she fell in my lap. She doesn't need my help with that—yours, either."

"It's not that simple."

"Seems pretty simple to me. But of course, I don't really understand what the fuck is going on, anyway."

"It's not as simple as just dying, Julius. She has to go back in a particular manner, or she'll be lost."

"I don't know what you're talking about. Grace seemed to think it was going to be pretty simple. 'Dying's the simple part,' she said."

"She was just trying to spare your feelings, Julius. She cares for you."

"What the hell do you know about it, Peter?"

Pauley sighed and leaned forward in his chair. He spread his palms on the desk, speaking carefully. "Grace came here to accomplish a particular task. She knew that she was responsible for leaving behind something that was very dangerous, so she came back to destroy it."

"I know about that, Peter," Julius said with exasperation. "I know about the recording, that Parnell's lecture wasn't complete bullshit. I got that part."

"Okay, just listen. I don't know what you know, or what you actually believe, so bear with me. If you understand that, then you know where Grace comes from, about what happens after—"

"Yeah, Peter. I think I get it. There's an afterlife, and she was there. I don't understand why everyone feels I should be having such a hard time with the concept. It is, you know, what we Christians believe." Pauley stared at him, questioning. "Really, I get it. What I don't get, Peter, is the coming back part. I thought that was reserved for, you know, Jesus Christ. Our Savior. At least, that's what I thought."

"Yeah, that's the problem."

"I thought so."

"As it turns out, Julius—and I know you might find this a bit heretical or something—it's not that terribly difficult." Julius raised his eyebrows. "Oh, it probably was in His time," Pauley continued, "back when our Lord did it. But things have changed, I'm afraid."

"So, He is the Son of God, then? I mean, we got that part right, didn't we?"

"Can I get back to you on that? It's not really germane to what we're dealing with right now."

"It isn't?" Pauley shook his head. "Seems like it'd be pretty important."

"I'm sure it is, Julius. Just not right now. The problem we're dealing with is that the world has changed. Forces have broken down the barriers between this world and the afterlife."

"Forces? What kind of forces? The devil?"

"No, not the devil. Nothing so biblical, I'm afraid. It's more architectural than ecclesiastical."

"Architectural? You're losing me, Peter."

"Yeah, I'm not surprised. Just listen. There were probably natural channels between our world and the others, dating back to antiquity. They must have been rare, though. Rare enough so that coming back from the dead was almost impossible. Rare enough so that our Lord could make a real show of it, you know?" Julius just shook his head. "No matter. During the last century, however, Wright began designing buildings with a particular characteristic. These structures possessed the ability to channel souls between worlds, between this world and the worlds after death."

"Frank Lloyd Wright?" Pauley nodded. "How?"

"I'm not sure. We just know that his later work began to exhibit this ability, the ability to channel souls. Are you familiar with Wright?"

"A little. I visited one of his houses when I was a kid, with my folks."

"Do you know about the fire? About his mistress?" Julius shook his head. "Short version: Wright was married to a woman named Catherine for many years, with whom he had several children. Catherine was befriended by an enigmatic woman named Martha 'Mamah' Borthwick, a rich socialite. Wright was commissioned to build a home for Borthwick and her wealthy husband. During this time, Wright and Martha began a torrid affair, leaving their respective spouses and traveling together through Europe. This was in 1910, and when they returned to the States, their open affair was scandalous. Anyway, Wright's career had been a shambles before the European trip, but when he returned, he was a changed man. He was hailed as brilliant, a genius. His designs were transcendent—literally. His reputation, and his commissions, took off.

"Borthwick, as I said, was something of an enigma, but brilliant in her own right. She was a feminist, and a spiritualist. She was a writer and translator, a free spirit in a time when there really wasn't any such thing. Maybe a mystic of some fashion. She completely transformed Wright, personally and artistically. Suddenly his work, dating from that period onward, possessed the unique ability to transport souls between worlds."

"What was she, some sort of devil?"

Pauley shook his head. "What is it with you, with this devil nonsense? I don't know what she was—she was a woman, and that's satanic enough for me, Julius."

"What do you mean?"

"Forget it. You may be right, I don't know. Not the devil, but maybe a devil—I don't know. There have been certain—special—individuals through the ages. Judas, Rasputin, Goebbels. Maybe Mamah Borthwick, too. I don't know. I have my theories, that's all."

"What happened to her?"

"She was living in Wisconsin at Taliesin, with Wright and her children. Wright was away supervising a project when one of the workers at Taliesin murdered Borthwick, her two children, and four others. He set Taliesin ablaze, and as it burned he hacked the seven people to death with an axe."

"My God! Who was he?" Julius asked.

Pauley shrugged. "Nobody, really. A domestic worker. The newspapers described him as criminally insane." He paused. Pauley stood up and came around the desk, closing the door behind Zimmerman. He came back and sat back down in his chair.

"That's why Grace was trying to get back into the Robert Llewellyn house," Zimmerman said.

Pauley nodded. "That's how she got here. When things went wrong, she tried to get back. I told you, that wasn't going to work."

"Why not? Who were those people? Why are they trying to stop her?"

"I'm not entirely certain," Pauley said, shaking his head. "I have my suspicions, but I'd prefer not to speculate just now."

"I still don't understand, Peter. If all she wants is to get back, why does she have to get back into the house? Why can't she just die, like before?"

"It's not that easy, no matter what she told you."

"Not that easy to die?"

"Oh, it's plenty easy to die. That's not the problem. But Grace doesn't want to just die. She wants to get back."

"Back where?"

"Back to the world she left, back to her husband and sister, I suppose. And that's not easy, not easy at all."

"So there are other worlds, then?" Julius asked, confused. "Not just one here, and one there?"

"That's right. Too many worlds. Infinite possibilities, and an infinity of worlds, on this side and the other. Worlds enough to be lost in forever, Julius. That's not what Grace wants, what any of us want. We want our world, the world we create with our life, the world we die into when our life here ends. We want to be with the ones we love, the ones we know from this world."

"And the Wright houses?"

"They make that possible. Instead of the randomness of death, the Wright devices somehow act to transport between distinct worlds. Without them, she'd be lost, almost certainly dying into another world, where nothing is the same. Worse than dying, Julius, like I told you. Lost in strange worlds without the people we love."

"You were saying this before. I didn't understand. I still don't understand. About why we're celibate."

Pauley nodded sadly. "Yes, that's what I was referring to, though I was rambling a bit, I guess. I was—not myself."

"You said we were celibate so that we could be God's soldiers."

"Did I? I guess I did. Soldiers, sacrificial lambs. Lost souls. Whatever you want to call it, the point's the same. When the time comes, Julius, we must be ready. Not just to die—like you keep saying, dying's the easy part—but to be lost, utterly and eternally. That is our duty, if need be."

Julius sat, considering. He wasn't certain how much he understood, or how much he actually believed. He looked up and saw Pauley staring at him. "You're like her?"

"What do you mean, Julius?"

"You were dead. You came back here?"

"I told you."

"Tell me again."

"I was dead. Like her. And I came back."

"Why?"

"That's complicated. I can't explain it all just yet. I'm sorry." The older man rubbed his right hand as if it ached.

Julius sighed and looked past the other man, out the window at the shaking trees outside. "I'm not convinced," Zimmerman said.

"I'm not surprised," Pauley responded. He stared at Zimmerman for a moment, considering. Finally, he slid a book across his desk to the other man.

"What's this?" Zimmerman asked, reaching for the book. He looked at the title: *The Problem of God*. "No thanks, Peter. I already own it."

Pauley shook his head. "Take a closer look."

Zimmerman took the book and hefted it. "What is it, a new edition? It's a lot thicker than mine, that's true. Nicer cover, too. Why the Guggenheim picture?" He started to thumb through the pages.

"Don't," Pauley admonished. Zimmerman looked up at him. "Just turn to the page marked, by the bookmark there. Read that."

Zimmerman turned to the marked page and read aloud, "What is it, a new edition? It's a lot thicker than mine, that's true. Nicer cover, too. Why the Guggenheim picture?" Zimmerman looked back up at Pauley, astonished. "What the hell, Peter?" He started to thumb through the pages again.

"Stop!" Pauley commanded. "Don't do that, Julius. Please." Zimmerman looked up at him again. "It is a very new edition, Julius. A recent edition, you could say."

"How is this possible?"

"I can't say. It's not important, Julius."

"Not important?" Julius started reading at random from a page closer to the front of the book: "Give me two seconds of grief, Padre, and I'll start screaming rape at the top of my lungs. Believe me, buddy, the way we look right now, nobody's gonna doubt it for a second." Julius remembered clearly when Grace had said that, in the hospital. How could such a thing get into a book?

"Stop it," Pauley demanded. "You can't do that, Julius."

Zimmerman flushed, both with anger and embarrassment. "What kind of trick is this, Pauley? What the hell is going on here?"

Pauley shook his head and reached out for the book. Zimmerman reluctantly let him take it back. Pauley carefully turned the pages, until he found the passage he needed. He started to hand it back to Zimmerman but pulled it away from the other man momentarily. "It's very important that you just read this page. I can't let you read anything else, Julius. It's important."

"Why?" Pauley shook his head. "Fine, Peter." He took the book and read the indicated page to himself:

Grace opened the locker and, looking about to be sure no one was watching, withdrew the leather duffle. She closed the locker and, leaving the locker room, strode quickly down the hall with her prize. It was surprisingly heavy, she noticed. She looked around and saw the women's restroom ahead. She picked up her pace and headed for it. She glanced about and, seeing no one who appeared interested in her, went in. Once inside, she found an empty toilet stall and closed the door behind her. Sitting down, she set the bag on her lap. She unzipped the—

The resulting explosion destroyed the restroom and a sizable portion of this end of the terminal, killing Grace and seventeen others in the blink of an eye.

Zimmerman looked up at the other man, the color draining from his face. "Oh my God, Peter. Has this happened?"

Pauley shook his head. "No, not yet, Julius. But it will, if something isn't done to change it. If you don't help her, she'll die. Along with a lot of other people."

Zimmerman gulped, only partly relieved. "Parnell?"

Pauley nodded. "I think so. I'm not completely sure, but I think that the man's not the buffoon he pretends to be. It's complicated, more complicated than I first realized, I'm afraid."

"How long?"

"Not very long, Julius. We must hurry. You have to stop her somehow. She'll be lost otherwise." Julius nodded. "We'll take my car, it's the fastest way. With luck, she's not even at the airport yet."

Julius looked at the other man. "You're coming?"

"I think it's the only way, with the time we have."

"Let's go then," he said, handing back the book. "We have to stop at my room, so we better hurry."

"What for?"

"To get Jack. She might not stop for me, and she sure as hell won't listen to you, Peter. She'll stop for Jack, though."

Grace stepped off the shuttle at Baltimore-Washington International Airport. Grace went in the terminal and started looking for lockers. She realized with a start that this was the first time in her life that she'd ever been inside a real airport. She warily eyed the other visitors streaming in every direction, most wheeling luggage or jockeying for position in various lines. Too crowded, too much security. She glanced above her and saw cameras at every angle and cringed inwardly. It felt like everyone was looking at her. She hurried ahead, scanning for a bank of lockers.

After scurrying about for almost twenty minutes, she had failed to spot a single bank of lockers. She toyed with the key in her pocket, thinking. Where else could Parnell have gone, a different end of the terminal? She shook her head involuntarily, not able to come up with an answer. She had to get a move on here, she felt exposed. Jeez, she thought to herself, there's security everywhere; it's like a friggin' police state in here. She kept moving, trying to think.

Maybe the key wasn't to a locker, after all. No, Parnell had definitely said locker, she was sure. Of course, he was higher than a kite at the time, but she thought it must be a locker key, why else hide it like that? This was taking way too long, she kept thinking. She didn't want to, but she was going to have to ask for help. She kept walking, scanning, evaluating the security personnel as she strode by. I really should be carrying some type of bag or luggage, she thought, realizing that almost everyone was carrying something. Shit, she'd look suspicious walking up to one of these guys...

"Excuse me," Grace said, approaching the first female security agent she saw. "I'm sorry to bother you, but I doubt those other guys would be much help." The security woman turned from her seat where she was watching the exiting passengers and smiled at Grace. "My daughter forgot to bring any tampons with her and—"

The woman nodded sagely, saying, "Have three of my own, sister, and I can't tell you how many times I've had to send my husband out in the middle of the night. He hates that, too. Right down the hall, opposite the kiosk there," she added, pointing.

"Thanks," Grace replied. "Oh, and are there any lockers in the airport, you know, to rent for an hour or two?"

The security woman looked at her with puzzlement. "Lockers? Are you kidding, lady? Never heard of 9/11? You won't find a locker anywhere. Least not in any airport, anywhere. You gotta be kidding."

"Of course," Grace said, shaking her head with embarrassment. "Stupid of me. Well, thanks." She walked off in the direction indicated by the woman, wondering. No way Parnell would've left the airport to find someplace else to make his stash—the airport was too far outside of town for that. It had to be somewhere here in the airport, but there were no lockers in the airport. What the hell? She kept fingering the key in her pocket, thinking. She pulled up in front of the big airport map, pretending to look for a restaurant or something, thinking. No locker in any airport, anywhere. She was about to turn away, to keep moving, when her eye fell on a couple of good looking young guys walking down the hall towards her, laughing at something. They were some sort of baggage handlers or something, wearing orange reflective vests and with noise suppressing headphones draped around their necks. No lockers, my ass, Grace thought. Where there's employees, there's got to be lockers.

Jack sat between Zimmerman and Pauley, who was driving. Traffic on the Baltimore-Washington Turnpike was light for once and they were making good time. Pauley was shaking his head. "I'm not exactly sure where she's going, Julius. You read something about a locker?"

"Yeah," Julius responded, scratching Jack's head to keep from wringing his hands with worry. He kept expecting the sound of an explosion from somewhere in front of them. "Your magic book said she took the bag out of a locker. And Grace said that she took a locker key from Parnell."

"I do a lot of flying, and I've been in and out of BWI dozens of times. Never saw any lockers anywhere."

"Shit, Peter. You're right. There's no lockers at the airport—they won't even let you step away from your bags for two minutes." They sat quietly, thinking. "I need to look at the book again, Peter."

Pauley shook his head as he watched the road ahead. "I don't think that's a good idea, Julius."

"Doesn't matter what you think, Peter. If we're going to find her, we're going to need a better idea than we got right now. We're running out of time. Let me see it."

Pauley thought about this for a minute, then reached into his breast pocket for the book. "I'm not giving this to you unless you promise to look only at the one page. It's still marked."

"Why, Peter? What is that thing, anyway?"

"It's just a book, Julius."

"I own a copy of that book, Peter. I've read it like half a dozen times. Mine doesn't say anything about me and Grace. And it sucks, by the way."

"When's the last time you looked at it?"

"Last year. Why?"

"Might want to give it another look. Things change, Julius."

"Books change? I don't think so."

"Might want to check, next time you have a chance. I don't know."

"You don't know? You don't know how you got a magic book?"

"I know how I got it."

"So how's it work? How does it know the future?" Julius asked.

"I'd prefer not to say just now."

"Is it like Grace? Does it have to do with being dead?"

"Not sure what you mean," Pauley said.

"Grace could see the future."

Pauley laughed slightly at that. "Oh, you mean that bit about jumping into bed with her and making love? That was precious."

Julius reddened, both out of anger and embarrassment. "Glad you thought so, Peter."

"Sorry, Julius. I don't mean to make you uncomfortable. You shouldn't feel bad—the girl is quite manipulative. But she can't see the future, no more than you or I."

"She can't?"

Pauley shook his head. "No, she was just playing you. She found your lucky quarter in the nightstand while you were out walking Jack. The rest was just a con. She's good at that."

"She knew it'd come up heads."

Pauley shrugged. "Fifty-fifty chance. I'm sure she had something witty ready to say if it came up tails. It's the way she works, Julius. Don't blame yourself. She's not as nice as she seems, I'm afraid."

Zimmerman just stared out the windshield, considering this statement.

"I must say, Julius," Peter continued conversationally. "You've shown great restraint."

"More than you'd expect, I guess," Zimmerman said, looking at the other man. Pauley just stared at the road. "So then how does this book work?" Julius asked.

"I told you, I'm not exactly sure. It's a tool, it was provided to me. I can use a tool without knowing exactly how it functions."

"So why the big deal about looking ahead? Why can't I look to see what's going to happen?"

"It doesn't work like that. I tried, when I first got it. If you try to get too far ahead, read the ending even, it changes. It's always changing. Looking too far ahead only makes things more complicated, more confusing."

"And you have no idea how this magic book works?"

"I have an idea. It's not important right now."

"It seems that a lot of things aren't important right now. Only right now, they all seem pretty fucking important to me."

Pauley sighed and flipped pages, glancing between the book and the road ahead as he drove. He found the page and handed the book over to Julius. "Just look at this page. Scan backwards, see what's going on just before she opens the locker."

It didn't take long for Grace to find the entrance to the employee locker rooms on the lower level. Two doors, one for men and the other for the women's locker room. Great, she thought. Obviously, she was at a bit of a disadvantage here. She watched the doors from a discrete distance. Numbered keypad, not a swipe card. She could deal with that. Being seen in the men's locker room, however, that would be a problem—particularly in this gulag, she thought. She watched for a bit and saw no one enter or leave, then looked at the clock on the wall. Most, if not all, of these guys would be working shifts, she surmised. As long as she got in and out right after the afternoon shift change, she should be okay. She hoped. She headed back upstairs to the food court and grabbed a couple of foil packs of ketchup and two packs of sugar, then headed back down to the men's locker room door. She checked the clock again: 2:10. Looking around, she saw nobody in the hallway. She quickly painted the keypad with a thin coating of ketchup, then dusted the keys lightly with sugar. Grace left to find someplace to kill ninety minutes.

Grace waited for a while with the crowd outside the security area, pretending to be waiting for an arriving relative. Occasionally, she walked through the food court and then back to the waiting area. After two hours, she headed back downstairs. It was now 3:30. She figured that if shift change was at three, the locker room should be empty by now. If shift change was at four, she'd have a few minutes before people started to arrive. She watched for another five minutes, seeing nobody.

Grace walked up to the door and carefully inspected the keypad. The sugar was missing from the one key and the nine key. "Geez," she almost said aloud, "This country is run by fucking morons." She keyed 9-1-1 and opened the door. She walked in, prepared to excuse herself as the janitor if anyone remained inside, but it was empty. Grace scanned the lockers, moving swiftly between the rows until she found locker 42.

Zimmerman looked up from the book. "Employee's locker room, on the lower level. She's got the duffle. We got to hurry, Peter."

Pauley shook his head. "You don't know that, Julius. What you're looking at probably hasn't happened yet. We'll get there."

"I hope you're right. I wouldn't want to show up as she's opening that bag."

Pauley just nodded at that.

Grace opened the locker and, looking about to be sure no one was watching, withdrew the leather duffle. She closed the locker and, leaving the locker room, strode quickly down the hall with her prize. It was surprisingly heavy, she noticed. She looked around and saw the women's restroom ahead. Grace picked up her pace and headed for it. She glanced about and was about to go in—she saw Jack, running down the hallway towards her. Grace scanned the crowd and saw Julius farther back, running after. "What the hell?" she said softly, kneeling as Jack reached her, setting the duffle down. Jack licked her face, tail wagging madly.

"Grace!" Julius yelled, breathing hard as he ran, still down the hall. "Wait!" Grace watched him approach, petting Jack. This isn't right, she thought. He shouldn't even know I'm here, the timing's too perfect. Something's not right. Grace grabbed the duffle and stood up, facing Zimmerman as he approached. Zimmerman arrived, panting. He grabbed for the duffle.

"Don't!" Grace said sternly, staring back at him defiantly. "What the hell are you doing here, Julius?"

"Grace," Zimmerman said. "Don't. It's a bomb. Give it to me." He reached again for the bag.

"Yeah, right," Grace said. Grace stepped forward nonchalantly and grabbed his shirt as if to kiss him, but instead drove her knee into his groin. Zimmerman doubled over and fell to his knees.

"Shit," Pauley whispered to himself, watching the words change in front of his eyes:

Zimmerman doubled over and fell to his knees.

Pauley put the book back in his pocket and came around the corner of the hallway, heading for the security officer that stood between him and the situation unfolding down the hall. He needed to get some help with this.

Grace looked up to see Pauley emerge from the end of the hall. She knelt down next to Zimmerman, holding the bag with her other hand away from him. "I don't know what the fuck you think you're doing, Zimmerman. I told you, don't listen to that man."

"It's a bomb, Grace," Zimmerman managed to gasp, holding his stomach to keep from vomiting.

"It's not a fucking bomb, Julius," she spat. "Look!" She started to unzip the bag.

"Don't!" Zimmerman yelled, reaching out weakly.

Grace shoved the bag under his face. "Look, you fucking moron!" Zimmerman looked in and saw an assortment of clothing, rafts of papers, some manila folders, a hard drive. "I don't know what he told you, Julius. It's all lies, whatever he said. I'm sorry. I got to go. Sorry." She snapped her elbow down onto the back of his head and Julius collapsed facedown onto the cold tile. "Sorry," she repeated in his ear. Grace grabbed the bag back and stood up. She looked up the hallway, then turned and started running as fast as she could in the opposite direction, away from Pauley.

CHAPTER 21

Pauley reached the guard as he saw Grace turn and run. He explained that he had reason to believe that the woman running down the hall—he pointed to Grace, who was knocking people out of her way at a rapid clip—had an explosive device in her bag. She better, Pauley thought to himself, or I'm going to have a hard time talking myself out of a night in jail. The guard watched her run for a full ten seconds, glanced at Pauley's collar, then keyed the mike on the walkie-talkie clipped to his shirt. The guard swallowed hard, then activated a full terminal emergency lockdown. Pauley nodded, resisting the urge to smile; one just had to know what buttons to push, and the system responded. He asked the guard if it would be okay if he went to help his friend, who was still lying facedown on the floor down the hall. He pointed again.

Grace may not have ever been in an airport before, but she was already pretty impressed that the place was a steel and glass trap. Her only thought was to get out as fast as possible. She ran straight for the nearest doors leading outside.

Grace hit the doors just as the sirens started. She immediately slowed to a brisk, businesslike walk. The dog charged through the doors an instant before they clicked shut, running smack into her legs. Grace looked down at him for a split second, then headed quickly to the taxi stand ten steps ahead. A couple was just about to get into the lead taxi. They turned, like everyone else, to see what the siren was about. Grace strode past them and climbed into the open car, Jack jumping in after her. She pre-empted the couple's protest with a sheepish "Sorry," and slammed the door. "Downtown Marriott," she commanded the driver. Must be a Marriott somewhere in downtown Baltimore, she figured. The driver nodded and pulled away from the curb. "Don't know what you were thinking," she said to the dog. "You obviously don't know where I'm going." Jack gave her the tilted head look for a second, then settled his muzzle on her lap.

I thought we were going for pizza.

When Pauley and the guard arrived, Julius had managed to make it up onto his hands and knees. He fought the urge to vomit. The guard leaned down to help him as he called on his radio for medical assistance. Zimmerman opened his mouth to explain that wasn't necessary, but only managed to vomit on the man's shoes instead. He was eventually able to sit, sirens sounding and strobe lights flashing from every wall. People looked about in confusion. A woman's calming recorded voice proclaimed a fire alarm on level one. She apologized for any inconvenience and assured everyone that all would be fine momentarily.

Pauley bent over Julius and handed him a handkerchief to wipe his mouth. "You were really once a Navy SEAL?" Pauley asked him.

"Fuck you, Peter," Zimmerman said, holding the handkerchief against the laceration on the back of his scalp. Pauley shook his head, waiting to hear if security had managed to get the girl. He knew after two minutes of silence from the guard's walkie-talkie that she was gone. Shit, he thought, she's running and we'll be stuck here for hours explaining why I thought the woman had a bomb. Shit.

"You said the Marriott Waterfront, right?" the driver asked, looking at Grace in the rear view mirror.

"That's right," Grace smiled back. She watched the meter tick past twenty dollars and they were still on the expressway. Not that it mattered, she thought to herself, as she had exactly four dollars and ten cents to her name. She smiled at the driver again in the mirror.

"First time in Baltimore?" the man asked her reflection.

She nodded, still smiling at the man. "Is it a nice hotel?" she asked with her Irish brogue in overdrive.

"Oh, yeah. Right on the harbor, you'll love it. Just be careful where you go walking, that's all."

"Really? Where is it I should avoid, would you say?"

"Tell you the truth," he said, no longer smiling, "I wouldn't walk more'n two blocks in any direction, 'specially after dark. Stay close to the harbor, my advice. Nothing to see elsewhere anyways," he said, shaking his head.

"Thanks for the advice," she smiled again. Perfect, she thought to herself. She hoped Jack didn't mind living on the street for a while.

Parnell awoke with a splitting headache. It was pitch black in the room. He sat up, swinging his legs over the side of the bed, swaying with nausea. He was naked, he noticed, but had no recollection of how he got that way or why. And his testicles hurt. He thought he had dreamt of seeing Helena, naked. He smiled at the memory. After a minute, he managed to stand. He tried to turn on some lights, without success. Parnell stumbled into the bathroom in the pitch black, cursing as he stubbed his toe on something. He turned on the bathroom light, which worked. After wondering why the lampshade was on the floor, he felt in the tub spout for the key. Yeah, he thought to himself, must've been her. And he no longer believed he was dead—he felt way too awful for dead.

The taxi pulled up to the hotel. Grace momentarily opened her door on the driver's side and dropped the duffel outside the car. The driver turned and announced the fare to be forty-three dollars as the hotel doorman opened the passenger side back door with a flourish.

"Let me just get my purse and luggage from the boot," Grace said, smiling at the driver.

"Boot? What do you mean, lady?" the driver asked.

Grace gestured behind her. "You know, in the back."

"Ain't nothing in the trunk, lady," he said, shaking his head.

"Of course there is," Grace said with concern. "The man at the airport put it in, I gave him a twenty dollar tip."

The taxi driver shook his head sadly. "You mighta given him twenty bucks, ma'am, but nobody put anything in my trunk. You sure he was working for the airport?"

Grace looked distraught. "Oh, shit," she said, suddenly about to cry. "I just assumed, since he was right there and all. You really think…?" The driver just nodded.

"Listen, lady, I'm sorry. I can't just take you back. It's near the end of my shift, I gotta be getting the car in."

"No, no, of course not. But how will I pay you?"

The elderly driver shook his head. "You got bigger problems than paying me, ma'am." The doorman poked his head in, wondering at how long it was taking. Grace began to cry. Jack licked her face, concerned, as the driver explained the situation to the doorman. The doorman offered to help her contact the police. Grace stopped crying long enough to thank them both. She leaned over the seat to give the driver a kiss on the cheek.

"I am so sorry. Thank you," Grace said, snuffling a little.

"Best tip I got all day, ma'am. Good luck to you."

Grace got out the passenger side door with Jack. "Before we call the police," Grace told the doorman, "I'm going to walk my dog over to the park there." She pointed to the small park at the end of the block. "He was on the plane so long, he's been such a trooper, poor guy." Jack did his best to look like a trooper with a full bladder. The taxi pulled away.

"Course, ma'am," the doorman said. "You just come back and ask for Carl when your dog's done his business, I'll get you all squared away."

"Thanks, again," Grace said. "Everyone in Baltimore is so nice."

" 'Cept for that dude at the airport," Carl said, nodding.

Grace looked crestfallen. "Yes, except for him." She wiped away a tear and gave Carl a brave smile as the doorman turned to greet the next taxi pulling up. Grace nonchalantly gathered up the duffle as she led Jack across the street to Columbus Park. After a few minutes, she looked back and saw Carl was busy attending to newly arriving guests. She slowly walked Jack to the other side of the park and kept walking.

Pauley was pleased to be out of the airport after only two hours of tedious explanation to various security personnel. If it wasn't for the fact that they were both priests, he doubted that the authorities would've so easily accepted his apologetic explanation that they had overheard the young lady speaking very suspiciously on her cellphone. Certainly there was genuine cause for concern, he continued, for when young Julius had tried to keep her from leaving so that Pauley could summon someone from security, the woman had assaulted him. This obviously established who was in the wrong, particularly when everyone who came to interview them couldn't help but notice the impressive hematoma steadily rising on Zimmerman's head. They were asked to sign multiple papers, leave every manner of contact information, and finally were dismissed.

"You okay?" Pauley asked Julius, back in the car and heading towards DC.

"No, Peter. I am not okay."

"I told you, Julius. She's not very nice."

"She's not the one I'm not okay with."

"She hit you pretty hard. I don't blame you for being upset."

"There was no bomb, Peter."

"We don't know that for sure. It may not have gone off, but that might be because we got to her in time, changed things."

"There was no bomb."

"Maybe there wasn't, Julius. I told you, I don't really know."

Julius stared at the other man, driving. "I don't believe you, Peter."

Pauley looked sideways at the other man. "I don't know what she said to you, Julius, but you can't listen to her. She's a dangerous, deceitful creature. Look what she did to you. Again, I might add."

Julius sat, quietly considering. He was still completely lost. He didn't know who was lying to him; perhaps both of them. He touched his scalp and winced. The girl did have a tendency to kick his ass without warning, he had to admit. Pauley looked over at him and smiled sympathetically.

"Where are we going?" Julius asked him.

"I think it's time we had another talk with Dr. Parnell."

Zimmerman knocked on the hotel door. He heard Parnell curse as he tripped over something in the dark. The door swung open to reveal

Parnell, standing in the doorway stark naked. "What the hell kind of shit hole hotel is this you stuck me in, Zimmerman?" he demanded.

Julius could only shake his head. "Can we come in?"

Parnell looked past Zimmerman to see Pauley in the corridor. "Pauley! I figured you were dead." Pauley shrugged at the man and waited. "Fine, come in and make yourselves comfortable. Great hotel," he said, motioning them into the room. "No lights, phone's broken. I was assaulted, I think. All my stuff's gone, my cell phone." He sat heavily on the end of the bed.

Julius went around and plugged in the lamps, turning them on. "Would you like to get some clothes on, Dr. Parnell?" Julius asked the man, seating himself in the desk chair.

"Yeah, Julius. I'd love to get some clothes on. You got my bag? You the one who took the key to the locker?" Julius shook his head. "No, I didn't think so. Not even a robe in this rat trap. Thanks a lot, Julius." Parnell turned to face Pauley, who was still standing next to the desk. "You're pretty quiet there, Father Pauley. Care to explain to me what the hell is going on? I mean, since you're the one who got me here and all." He glared at the older priest.

"I was planning on asking you that very question," Pauley responded quietly.

"Asking me?" Parnell spluttered. "You're the one pulling the strings here, Pauley. 'Come with me back to DC or be dead in a week,' you said. Well, here I am, Father. A couple hours ago I was pretty convinced you were right on the money with that one."

"Not any more?"

"No, not any more, Father. Now I think I'm just being played. And I don't like it one bit. Where's my phone, Julius? I want my phone back."

"It's back in my room. I'll get it for you as soon as I can."

Parnell shook his head. "I can't believe I was stupid enough to even give it to you. I don't know why I thought I could trust you." He shook his head again, still thick with alcohol and narcotics.

Pauley and Zimmerman said nothing. Eventually, Parnell said, "So what's going on? Why weren't you on the plane?"

"I think you know the answer to that," Pauley said evenly.

"I think I don't," Parnell replied. "What the hell is going on here, guys?"

"We were hoping you'd tell us," Pauley said.

"Okay, I'll tell you. I was sitting in my office, minding my own business, when you walked in and scared the crap out of me. Told me I was being watched, told me that if I didn't take your plane ticket and get to DC I'd be killed. Well, I came to DC—and now I'm sitting in this godawful excuse for a hotel, naked, and all my property has been stolen. And I think I'm being held against my will, incommunicado mind you, by you two. That's what the hell is going on here, Pauley. What I want to know, is why."

"You make it sound like you're the victim," Pauley said.

"And you think I'm not?"

"I'm not sure what you are," Pauley said.

"I can't take this," Zimmerman interjected. He had a headache. He got down on his hands and knees, grunting from the pain in his groin. He pulled Parnell's clothes out from under the bed and tossed them on the bed next to him. "Why don't you get dressed and we can continue this conversation?"

Parnell glared at him. "How'd you know my clothes were there?" Parnell stood and began to dress. "You helped her, didn't you? What is this, some sort of conspiracy to get my research? Is that what this is?"

Zimmerman said nothing. Pauley answered for him, saying, "You amaze me, Dr. Parnell. Yesterday, you thought that a recording of a conversation between a dead woman and her husband was the most earth-shaking discovery of civilization. Now you're convinced that the same dead woman walked in here and stole your clothes?"

Parnell finished dressing and looked levelly at Pauley. "Nothing that bitch does would surprise me," Parnell said.

"Amen to that," Pauley whispered.

Grace walked north on the sidewalk along South President Street, Jack following alongside. The dog carefully looked about as they walked, sniffing for danger but smelling mostly the reek of the fisherman's wharf to their left. Grace spotted a guy sleeping on a bench near the wharf, his head not quite covered with a newspaper. Jack growled softly as Grace approached him.

"Move over, buddy," Grace said, smacking his legs and sitting on the bench at the man's feet. She snatched the newspaper off his head. "Whatcha reading?"

The stubble bearded bench resident looked up at Grace. "What's wrong with you? What are you doin'?" He raised his head and watched as Grace started to fold the newspaper on her lap.

"What am I doing? What are you doing?" Grace asked, folding the newspaper intricately. "Cops get to lay down now?"

"Cops? What are you talkin' about, bitch? What's wrong with you?"

"Please," Grace said, "Spare me the down-and-out, man of the street shtick. You suck at it." Grace finished folding the paper. She held it up, admiring the pillbox hat she had fashioned. She hadn't done that since the orphanage.

The man sat up, rubbing his cheeks. He was white, and now that he was sitting up, Grace could see he was something over six foot and built like a linebacker. "I know," he said, rubbing the stubble on his cheeks. "I hate this shit." He offered his hand and Grace shook it. "Name's Bill. Who are you?"

"Narc?"

He shook his head. "Naw, nothing so sexy. Just patrol, keep the Inner Harbor safe for tourists, you know?"

"Well, I do feel safe, Officer Bill. I need someplace for me and my dog to sleep tonight. Someplace where they won't eat him." Jack looked at her with sudden concern, unsure if she was kidding. He did not appreciate her sense of humor.

Bill shook his head. "I'd worry more about yourself than your dog, lady. Closest place is the Helping Up Mission, over on East Baltimore. Just about ten blocks. Doubt they'll let the dog in, though."

"Guess he'll have to sleep outside, then. Thanks, Bill. I'll let you get back to sleep—I mean, work." Jack was pretty sure she was kidding about sleeping outside. Grace put on her hat and stood to leave. She tucked her curly red hair up into the hat.

"Hold it a second," Bill said, standing. "What's going on? Why do you need a shelter?"

Grace shrugged. "Marriott lost my reservation. Why the hell do you think I need a shelter? I'm a homeless waif."

"Nice hat. You don't look homeless," he said, confused.

"Like you would know, Bill." Bill squatted to scratch Jack's head, which Jack permitted as he was pretty sure this guy had a Snickers bar in his pocket. "Don't start being nice to my dog, Bill. You've got to get back to work—I mean, your bench."

Bill looked up at her. "I could walk you guys over to the station, let you talk to the social worker. She could help out."

Grace shook her head. "Gee, thanks, Officer Bill. Spend the next two hours filling out paperwork so she can put us in the same shit hole shelter I could just walk into up the street. No thanks, Bill."

"Shelter's not gonna let you in till six. Lot of bad stuff could happen before then. Why don't you hang out at the station for a while, then you can do whatever you want?"

"You this nice to all the homeless waifs, officer?"

"Just the good looking ones."

"Tell you what, Bill, you being such a charmer, and all. How about you take my friend Jack here home to the wife and kids tonight, give him a nice meal." Jack nodded at that—this sounded much more civilized.

"You don't even know if I'm married."

"You're married. And you got kids. They'll love Jack. Make them share their pizza, though." Jack liked her thinking. He fought the urge to bark. *Screw it*, he thought. He barked. Bill scratched his head between the ears.

"How do you know so much about me? You stalking me or something?"

"In your dreams, Bill. You gonna take care of my dog for the night?"

Bill nodded, still confused over how this strange woman knew so much about him. "What about you?"

"Somehow I don't think your wife would be as thrilled if you brought me home, too, you know?" He smiled at this.

"Got a point. Where you gonna stay?"

"Helping Up Shelter, I guess. Unless the Marriott calls to say they want to put me up in the penthouse, 'cause they feel so bad for losing my reservation. Bring my dog by in the morning, okay? His name's Jack. He likes pizza." Jack liked this woman, a lot. He barked again, just to emphasize the point. Bill didn't seem all that perceptive; how could this guy not know he smelled like 'married with kids?'

"I don't know," Bill said, shaking his head. "Pretty rough area, 'round here. And that shelter's a snake pit. Might not be a good idea."

"Don't worry, Bill. I make friends easy. Just be nice to Jack and bring him around in the morning. You do that for me?" She gave him her Annie face, eyelashes bravely batting back tears.

"Sure, lady. My kids'd love it. I'll let him hang out at the station while I finish my shift. They'll be nice to him till I can take him home."

"You're a dear. I'll see you in the morning, then." She stood on tiptoe to give Bill a kiss on the cheek, causing him to cringe. "Do me another favor and hang onto my bag, too, okay? Probably be stolen in the shelter."

Bill nodded, taking the bag from her. "Nothing in here I need to be worried about, is there?

"You mean, besides the coke? No, nothing to worry about."

Bill smirked at that. "Come on, Jack. Show you how Baltimore's finest live." He slung the bag over his shoulder and turned to Grace before he left. "You going to tell me how you know all that stuff about me?"

"In the morning, when you bring me Jack. Give you a good reason not to steal him."

"Steal him? I'm a cop. I'm not going to steal your dog."

"No, I don't expect you will. Especially once you hear how loud he snores." Jack looked at her, head tilted. *I snore?* "Bring by the wife and kids. You can take me and Jack to breakfast."

"Have to see what the wife has planned, but maybe. I'll see you in the morning, then. Be careful." Bill walked Jack towards the police station on the other side of the harbor. He stopped after half a block and turned to look for the woman, realizing with a shock that he had never gotten her name. She was gone. Some cop I am, he thought. He shook his head, wondering how she had even known he was a cop in the first place. He was supposed to be undercover.

"Don't call her that," Zimmerman said. His head really hurt.

"Call her what—bitch?" Parnell said, zipping the fly on his cream colored suit pants and sitting back down on the end of the bed. "Are you crazy? That's about the nicest thing I can call her right now. And give me a break, Zimmerman. Unless you just fell down a flight of steps, looks like she beat the crap out of you."

"Again," Pauley said, smirking.

"Really?" Parnell asked. "You got a thing for her or something?"

Pauley preempted Zimmerman's reply. "Perhaps it is time for us to be more candid with each other, Dr. Parnell," Pauley said.

"Yeah," Parnell said. "Sounds great. You first, Pauley."

"I believe that I have been quite candid," Pauley said. "I meant what I said when we spoke in Utah."

"You weren't on the plane."

"I didn't say that I'd be on the plane. It was my intention to join you, but I was forced to change my plans, I'm afraid. I'm sorry that I couldn't let you know, but that was the exact problem."

"What was the exact problem?" Parnell said. Zimmerman listened, his head pounding as he looked back and forth between the other two.

"I was being watched, after we parted ways in the park," Pauley continued. "I felt it unwise to lead the surveillance back to you. It would've placed you in further danger. It might have led to you being unable to leave Salt Lake City."

"Quite the conspiracy theorist, aren't you, Pauley?" Parnell replied, smiling sardonically.

"I don't know you very well, Dr. Parnell," Pauley said. "But I feel quite certain that your aloofness is not genuine. Let me recommend again that we be more forthright with each other."

"Yeah? What makes you feel quite certain? I'm a pretty aloof guy, in general."

Zimmerman shook his head at that, which made it hurt worse. "Like hell you are, Parnell. I got you at the airport, remember? I'd say 'panic-stricken' captures it a little more closely. 'Pretty aloof guy,' my ass."

Parnell remained silent.

"Let me begin, then," Pauley said. "Here's what I think. Your comments lead me to believe, Dr. Parnell, that you are quite familiar with the nature of Return. I also believe, therefore, that your enthusiasm for your discovery, that recording, is a charade of some sort. Either a charade, or you're being manipulated in some way. Maybe both." He waited for a response, but got none. "Let me continue then. I also believe, Doctor, that we share a mutual acquaintance, a certain young woman whom we both know to have recently Returned to our world. How am I doing so far?"

"I wouldn't call her young," Parnell said.

"So let us discuss what I don't know," Pauley continued. "I don't know why you are pursuing a course of publicizing that recording. I don't know what you are trying to accomplish. And I don't know why you'd risk your life to do it."

"Seems there's a lot you don't know, Father Pauley," Parnell said.

"Please, Dr. Parnell," Pauley said. "Enlighten us." He sat on the corner of the desk, arms folded across his chest.

"I don't see that as such a great idea."

"I think it is, Dr. Parnell. I meant what I said in Utah. I don't think that you are truly the master of events, as you seem to believe. Unless we do something to alter the balance, you will not survive the week."

"Yeah? You got a crystal ball?"

"He's got a book," Zimmerman said, tired of listening to these two. "Tell him, Peter." Pauley frowned at Zimmerman.

"What kind of book?"

"A book that tells the future—sometimes," Zimmerman said. "That's how he knows that you're going to die. So let's quit the banter. My head hurts. Tell us what's going on, because I, for one, have no fucking clue."

"Let me see the book," Parnell said to Pauley.

Pauley shook his head. "Not just now. I believe that I have been more than forthcoming, Dr. Parnell. Without some reciprocation, I'm afraid we cannot continue. And yes, in that case, my book says that you'll die."

Parnell considered this for a few moments and then shrugged. "Fine. But you're going to show me that book. After."

"We'll see."

"You're right. I am very, very familiar with the woman. We go way back, her and I. You must realize that the recording is real, that her discovery allowed communication with the dead, at least for a few moments. She gave me the technology, left it for me in a manner of speaking. But she was careful to hide from me its deeper implications. It wasn't until I came upon the recording that I realized what she had really accomplished."

Pauley shook his head. "I don't think that you're being completely candid, Dr. Pauley."

"Think what you want, Pauley, I really don't give a shit. Once I realized what the recording was, certain incidents that had come to my attention suddenly made sense. I became aware of a plot, for lack of a better term. Not really a plot—more of a movement, I guess. That doesn't matter. But it's not good, I can tell you that."

"What is it?" Zimmerman asked.

Parnell shook his head. "I'm not prepared to discuss that. Like I said, Julius, I don't trust you very much. Sorry, pal."

Pauley said, "So you figured that if you publicized the recording, you could attract the attention of the inventor?"

Parnell nodded. "I wasn't entirely sure what would happen, to be honest. I just knew that if I didn't do something—well, I'm not sure what would happen then, either. I think it's going to be bad, though. Really bad."

"But publicizing the recording," Zimmerman said, "that in itself will have effects. Terrible effects."

Parnell shrugged. "Can't be helped. Sometimes you just got to play the cards you got in your hand."

"What is this plot that is so awful that it's worth publicizing that recording? And risking your life. What did you find?" Zimmerman asked.

Parnell shook his head.

"Not good enough, Dr. Parnell," Pauley said. "We can't work like this."

"Tough shit," Parnell said, not smiling now. Zimmerman shook his head again, then immediately regretted the gesture. Zimmerman turned to Pauley. "Obviously, you know more about this. What's going on? Who's after Grace? Why won't they let her go back?"

Pauley said nothing.

"I can answer that," Parnell said. "Once she came back, it was an opportunity to discredit me. As long as she's here, the recording's inconsequential. She's not dead."

"Then who's going to kill you?" Zimmerman said.

"News to me. I don't think I get killed," Parnell said, looking between the other two men. "I'm not sure about your magic fairy book, Pauley, but I'm betting that only happens if the girl gets away. If she stays on this side, nobody needs to kill me. I hope."

"Maybe. Maybe you die anyway. There are a lot of possibilities," Pauley answered.

"Some better than others," Parnell pronounced.

Pauley took the book from inside his coat. The other two watched as Pauley carefully turned pages until he found the one he needed. Pauley cleared his throat softly and read aloud: "Parnell ran down the sidewalk, knocking people from his path. He glanced over his shoulder, looking for his pursuers. He saw an alley ahead and headed for it. He made it into the alley and slumped against the brick wall, doubled over panting, hands on knees. As he stayed like that, getting his wind back, Parnell saw two men enter the alley. He turned and ran out the other way. He never saw the black sedan as it swerved, clipping him and spinning him into the path of an oncoming taxi. The taxi struck him and his neck snapped, head lolling. Parnell was paralyzed before he hit the ground. The next car blared its horn as it drove over him." Pauley looked up and closed the book.

Parnell had gone pale. "Not a comedy, then," Parnell managed to say, swallowing hard.

"I've read better prose in Navy repair manuals," Zimmerman said.

Grace walked past the metro station as she turned onto East Baltimore. She walked up the block and saw a group of unkempt men milling in front of an old, red brick building. She looked too clean and well-dressed, Grace knew, but the newspaper hat would help. She faked a limp as she walked across the street, ignoring the traffic. A car honked at her as she shuffled across its path, but she didn't look up. She ignored the others on the sidewalk as she leaned against the wall and slid down onto the cracked cement. She hugged her knees and kept her head down.

Grace could feel the looks of the others passing over her. She rocked a little, this way and that. She kept her head down, staring into her lap, but could see a pair of homeless person shoes coming her way. She started muttering to herself, "If God is for us, who can be against us? If God is for us, who can be against us? If God is for us—"

The shoes stopped in front of her. An old black man squatted in front of her. She looked up but didn't meet his eyes. "You shouldn't be here, Missy," the man said.

Grace looked back down and resumed her rocking, saying softly, "They will soar on wings like eagles, they will run and not grow weary, they will walk and not be faint." The man stood with an effort, his knees popping. He stood in front of her for another moment, then moved off. Grace pretended to sleep, listening to the people milling about her; all men, mostly elderly. This was reassuring: this place catered more to the alcoholic and mentally ill crowd, it seemed, not the hard-core drug abusers. Grace had spent many years in an institutional setting; actually, her entire adolescence. She knew how these places worked.

Most of the people around her were would be regulars, she assumed. These places had a core community, with a loose-knit group of others who would come and go with varying regularity. She would be a stranger to the group. Grace knew, from her own experience, that anyone new was viewed as a potential threat. Her best bet was to be as passive and unthreatening as possible. That would placate most. Most, but not all, she knew. There was always a reigning clique; the gang that thought they were in charge, because once the lights went out, they really were.

She listened for them, eyes closed and pretending to sleep. Grace listened for the louder voices, the ones with the authoritative edge, the sarcastic tone. They would come late, she knew. They didn't have to worry about the shelter filling up. They'd just step up to the front, knowing no one would challenge them. Grace wrapped her arms around her knees, making herself as inconspicuous as she could.

Eventually, she sensed the group shifting, moving to queue up in anticipation of the doors opening. She kept her head down but stood up, flattened against the wall. The mass of malodorous humanity oozed in front of her, forcing her back. This wouldn't do. Grace moved towards the front and got pushed back again. Too passive, she figured. She raised her head and looked to see who had pushed her, a shabbily dressed guy in his thirties, holding a bottle wrapped in a paper bag. A potential weapon, and he held himself erect; he looked too young, too angry. She let him move ahead. When the next guy tried the same, she stared at him bug-eyed and growled at him menacingly. This guy was quite a bit older and shrank away, letting her shuffle in front. That accomplished, she'd get in. The doors swung open and the bedraggled mass shuffled forward.

Grace greeted the screener sitting at the card table with a sweet smile and a vacuous gaze. She answered her questions in a sing-song voice, giving her name as Lily Mamalujo, which Grace spelled differently each time she was asked until the woman finally gave up. Eventually, she was allowed into the dining room, where she ate while staring fixedly at her food. She ignored those around her. Whenever anyone looked like they might engage her in conversation, she started muttering biblical passages to herself. It was amazing how many passages she could recall verbatim from her upbringing in the Catholic orphanages.

Grace finished her chocolate pudding and licked the plastic spoon. She was about to gather up her tray to leave when an African-American man with closely cropped white hair sat down across the table from her. "You shouldn't be here," he said, and Grace recognized his voice as the man who had spoken to her outside the shelter.

Grace looked down at her tray and muttered, "For our light and momentary troubles are achieving for us an eternal glory that far out-weighs them all. So we fix our eyes not on what is seen, but on what is unseen. For what is seen is temporary, but what is unseen is eternal." He was still staring at her. "You will be secure, because there is hope; you will look about you and take your rest in safety. You will lie down, with no one to make you afraid, and many will court your favor."

"Not in this shit hole, Missy. You gotta go." He stared at her. Grace looked up and met the man's gaze. He was disheveled, like everyone else here. He wore a stained hooded sweatshirt. His eyes were rheumy, the pupils milky with cataracts. "Go back home," he said.

Grace was upset that this man wasn't buying the crazy zealot act. It was her least threatening persona, the one she'd planned on getting her through the night. Everyone tolerated the religious crazies, especially if they were the quiet kind. The only people who bothered them were the even crazier ones. Grace figured that explained this guy. She stood to go and picked up her tray, but the man grabbed it.

"You need to leave. You gotta go home," the man said.

Grace put the tray back down and started to leave. The man leaned across the table and grabbed her wrist, whispering, "Gabe's worried about you. Wants you to come back home." Grace froze. She stared at the man; he winked at her. "Too many interested in your business, he says. Says best be careful and come home," the man continued, releasing her.

Grace slowly sat back down. The old man sat watching her with a conspiratorial grin. "How does he want me to do that, exactly?" she asked the man.

The old man gave a little twitch of his head and laughed a little, like he had heard something funny. "Dyin's s'posed to be the easy part, Missy," the old man said, and gave another little twitch.

"Not as easy as it looks, old man."

"I know, I know," the man said, picking at something invisible on his sweatshirt, head twitching. "If it was that easy, I'd do it myself. But not here, not now—no way."

"Where would you, then?" she asked the man.

"Me? I'm dying to get to New York City. Best place for dying; can die nicely there, without even hardly tryin', you know?"

"New York City, huh?" The man nodded. "I'll do my best. Thanks for the advice, old man. Sleep well tonight."

"I will, I will, Missy. If I don't just die in my sleep, maybe tonight." He winked at her again.

"If you do, old man, you say hello to Gabe for me, okay?" Grace said. He nodded at that and shook her hand solemnly, clasping hers with both hands. Grace watched the man get up and shamble away into the crowded dining room. She gathered up her tray and headed for the dormitory.

"Where is she now?" Parnell asked, still obviously shaken by Pauley's reading.

"I don't know," Pauley said.

"She ran off," Zimmerman said. "With my dog, by the way."

"Did she get my stuff? From the locker?" They both nodded. "Aw, shit," Parnell cursed. "You let her run off with my stuff? How could you? I am so screwed." He looked back and forth between them, plaintively. "You know what she's going to do, don't you? She's going to throw my stuff in the ocean. Just like last time. I am so fucked. Again!"

"Maybe not," Pauley said soothingly.

Parnell rounded on him. "Maybe not? You weren't listening there, Father? If she gets away with that recording, with all the records, I've got nothing. No leverage. I'm the loose end. Damn, it sounds painful, too." Parnell leaned forward, his head in his hands. He looked up at Zimmerman. "She took your dog?" Zimmerman nodded. "Why'd she take your dog?"

"She likes the dog," Zimmerman answered, not really sure himself.

"Probably gonna toss it in the ocean, too," Parnell added. Zimmerman hadn't considered that.

"I think we need to focus on more pertinent problems than the fate of the dog," Pauley said. "The woman is gone, and barring some intervention, I don't think it is in our power to prevent her from doing just what you predict, Dr. Parnell."

"If you're talking about an act of God, I wouldn't count on it," Parnell sneered.

"No, either would I," Pauley replied. "So we are again at the particular point that I made earlier. We work together, or we each fall victim to circumstance. Which in your case, Dr. Parnell, sounds very, very painful indeed." Parnell winced.

"We need to order room service," Parnell said abruptly. "I don't think I've eaten since yesterday."

Grace made sure she was one of the first ones into the dormitory when the doors opened. As she was waiting, she heard the obnoxious arrival of the shelter's ruling class. The group sounded like six or seven guys in their early twenties. Loud and profane, they sounded like they had been drinking. She needed to keep a very low profile.

When the doors opened, Grace headed to the far end of the large dormitory, taking a bed against the wall, deep in the corner. She kept her paper hat on, to hide her hair. She needed a weapon, just in case. Grace sat hunched on the bed and went through the paper bag of supplies that sat on the pillow. Somehow she didn't think that the plastic toothette and small bar of soap were going to do much to dissuade a possible attacker. She lay down with her back against the wall, pulling the rough blanket up to her chin.

Grace watched from her cot as the dorm filled up. After a bit, the pack entered, swearing loudly and laughing. She watched as they made their way up and down the rows of beds, shaking down the other indigents for cigarettes, money, or drugs. Most had nothing to be shaken down for, and said as much, but ended up handing over a candy bar or spare change, anything to get the gang to move on.

Grace watched as the group worked their way closer through the large dorm room. She was liking the tactical situation less and less. As she watched, Grace reached under the mattress and worked at pulling one of the metal springs out of the bed frame beneath her. There were six of the guys in the gang, staying together. Even with a weapon, this didn't look good. Grace doubted that the four dollars and change she could offer was going to impress them, not once they realized she was not a guy and not too bad smelling. She might be able to disable two of them, three with luck, before the rest would have her. From that point on, it wouldn't go well, she was quite sure. She got one of the springs free, a cold metal coil about six inches long. As she kept an eye on the gang, she used the corner of the bed frame to straighten out one of the semicircular ends of the spring so it stuck out about two inches. Grace looked at it. Fairly pitiful, she thought, but it would have to do. She watched the gang get closer. Maybe if lights-out came before the pack made it all the way to her side of the dorm, they'd give up. She didn't really think so, though. And when the lights were turned off, the door may be locked. Not good. Not good at all.

"You're in my bed, Missy." Grace looked up to see the man was back, staring down at her. "You shouldn't be here. You should go home."

Grace sat up and hissed at him, still watching the gang working their way towards her. "Yeah, so you told me, old man. Tonight, this is home. Get used to it."

The old black man shook his head. "You're in my bed."

"Maybe this isn't the best time to—"

"I saved you a bed over there," he said, pointing back to the row of beds by the door where she had come in. "Nice bed. Better for you, I think. This is my bed."

Grace looked where the man was pointing. The gang had already worked past that row. This might work, she thought. Only problem was, she had to get over there.

"How 'bout I show you," the man said, pulling his hooded sweatshirt over his head. "Let old Uriel show you, Missy." He held out his sweatshirt to her. He had another on underneath. She nodded and took it.

"I gotta give you this, Earle" Grace said to the man, mistaking his name. She reached in her pocket and pulled out her four dollars. She put it in his hand.

"What am I gonna do with your money?"

"Get yourself a nice new sweatshirt, Earle. And thanks." She pulled the sweatshirt on over her head, gagging on the smell until her head popped out. It came down below her butt. She pulled up the hood.

"Looks better on you, I think," he said, with a gap-toothed smile.

She nodded, smiling back. "You want to show me where my bed is now?"

The man nodded but waited until the gang had worked their way down the row to the farthest end of the dormitory. He walked over slowly with Grace walking, head bowed, on his side away from the gang. They made it to the other bed, and Grace climbed under the thin blanket while the old man sat down heavily next to her, the springs squeaking.

"You don't mind, Missy, old Uriel's gonna rest here for a bit. Get my strength back before I head back to my bed." Grace nodded behind him, realizing he was timing his return to coincide with the gang's pass back towards the back of the dorm. The old man was no fool, she thought to herself. "Might be best if I just wait here till they turn off the lights, now that I think about it."

Grace thought that the man might be planning on shielding her like this until the gang could no longer notice her. "You sure, Earle? Someone might take your bed, while you're waiting."

Uriel shook his head. "Nobody gonna take old Uriel's bed. Ev'rybody know Uriel's got the lice. Nobody ever bother Uriel's bed, no sir."

"Oh. Great." She heard the old man chuckle softly to himself.

Parnell sat on the end of the bed, the room service trolley pulled up close. He pulled the chrome cover off his plate of steak and eggs. "You guys really not hungry?" The other two shook their heads as they watched him eat. This was all going on his tab, Zimmerman realized. "So you think we need to work together, huh, Pauley?" Parnell asked, between bites. Pauley nodded. "How, exactly, do we do that?"

"First, we need to pool our information, I believe," Pauley said.

"I told you what I know, Father," Parnell said.

"Not all of it, I'm sure."

"Enough for now. How about you tell me something. Something besides how I get run over. Twice."

Pauley considered for a bit, then began, "We are also aware of a certain movement."

"Who's we?" Zimmerman asked.

"Certain members of our order," Pauley said, evading Zimmerman's gaze.

"As in, not me," Zimmerman said.

"Not very many, Julius. Don't be offended. By the end of this, you'll be glad you're on the outside."

"Seems a little late for that."

Pauley continued, "We are aware of a number of individuals who have Returned, so to speak. The Church has been monitoring this activity with great concern since it was first noted almost thirty years ago."

Parnell shook his head as he chewed. "Thirty? More like two hundred, you mean."

Pauley looked at the man, confused. "What do mean? Wright's gates came into existence after 1910. We only recently detected their use in any significant numbers."

Parnell looked up from his meal. "What are Wright's gates?"

"The architectural devices that Frank Lloyd Wright incorporated in his work, the devices that permit travel back from—back. You understand, I'm sure, Dr. Parnell."

"Nope. No idea what you're talking about."

"He's talking about people coming back from the dead," Zimmerman said with exasperation.

"Yeah, I got that part. Just not this Wright business."

"That's how Grace got back, isn't it?" Zimmerman asked.

Parnell shrugged. "No clue. Thought she just tapped her ruby slippers three times or something."

"No, that isn't right," Pauley protested. "You admit to being familiar with the fact that there have been a number of Returns." Parnell nodded. "Then you must know they use the Wright structures to effect that Return. That is the mechanism. Are you not aware of that fact?"

"Nope."

"Then how? To what are you referring, Dr. Parnell?"

"Mormons," Parnell said, matter of factly. His spoon punched through the crust of his creme brulee.

"I'm sure I don't understand," Pauley said.

Parnell shrugged. "They really shouldn't be allowed to call this creme brulee," he said, eating it anyway.

Uriel stayed with Grace until the lights went out. They had a nice conversation about the various individuals that spoke to Uriel on a regular basis; individuals that weren't physically present for the conversations. Uriel seemed okay with that. It turned out, though, that Uriel had only yesterday heard from this Gabe fellow for the first time. Seemed nice enough, Uriel said. Seemed pretty damned worried about Grace, had Uriel watching for her since early yesterday.

"He's a worrier," Grace admitted.

"Yeah, well," Uriel replied, "he's probably right to worry. Little girl like you, in a place like this. Not right. You should be getting yourself home, like he says."

"Got something to do first, Earle."

"Gabe says it's not worth losing you over. Says let it be someone else's problem for once." Grace just shook her head. "Yeah, he says you're a stubborn one. Said you probably wouldn't listen." They both watched and listened as the gang of young toughs settled in towards the back of the gymnasium. "Well, guess old Uriel'll be getting over to my own bed now, Missy. Be careful."

"I will, Earle. Thank you for taking such good care of me. Give Gabe my love."

"If I hear from him again, I will do that, Missy. See you in the morning. Sleep tight." He stood and slow walked over in the near dark to his cot on the other side of the dormitory. Grace watched until she lost his huddled shape in the gloom. She pulled the blanket up around her chin and tried to sleep.

Grace woke up hours later to the squeak of the mattress as she felt Uriel sit down, almost on top of her. She opened her eyes but couldn't see much of anything in the darkness.

"What's up, Earle?" she asked the man as she sat up to sit next to him on the side of the bed, both huddled in the dark. Uriel didn't say anything for a minute, then gave his head a twitch the way Grace had seen him do several times earlier.

"My friend Gabe seems to think you're gonna be raped and killed in about five minutes. Least, that what he says. Don't know how he'd know something like that, and it's not a funny thing to say if it's some kind of joke."

Grace shook her head in the darkness. "I'm sure he's not trying to be funny, Earle. What time is it?"

"My Rolex is in the shop right now, sorry. Don't have the time."

"Oh. Right."

"Gabe thinks I should loan you my knife. He seems to think you know how to use it." Grace nodded in the dark next to him. Uriel produced a short knife and offered it to Grace.

"Keep your knife, Earle. I got what I need. Not going to be much good, anyway."

"Take these then," Uriel said, handing Grace a couple of plastic zip ties.

"Thanks, Earle. You're just a regular boy scout, aren't you? They coming yet?"

"Don't think so. Soon, though."

"How many?"

"Enough."

"That door locked?" she asked, nodding at the exit.

"Probably not. Maybe. Yeah." She looked at him. "Thinking of runnin'?" Grace nodded in the darkness. "Won't get to the end of the block, most likely. And in here, they'll have to stick to knives. Outside, they can use their guns and all."

"Good point." Uriel nodded sagely next to her. He chuckled a little to himself.

"What's so funny, Earle?"

"My friend Gabe just talkin' is all. Says it's pretty pathetic when a girl can't even seduce a guy who ain't been laid in over a decade. He's funny."

"Yeah, he's a real card. He's not talking about you, Earle. Sorry."

"Oh." He laughed again. "Still pretty funny, though."

"Tell Gabe he can go fuck himself."

Uriel laughed out loud, head twitching. "I don't think I should tell you what he said."

"Probably just as well. Listen, Earle, sorry to interrupt your little repartee with my dead husband, but I'm thinking we should focus a little on the situation at hand." Uriel nodded more seriously. "We got any friends here, Earle?"

"Got me, Missy. That be about it."

"I got some people coming in the morning. Maybe we can buy some time."

"Your people can identify the body, then."

"I was hoping for a little more optimism from you, Earle."

"Your people the kind of people that carry guns?"

"As a matter of fact, Earle, they are that kind of people."

Uriel smiled in the dark. "Then I'm a little more optimistic, Missy. Uriel's going to go buy us some time, then. Until your people with guns come by."

Grace could hear the muted voices of the gang members approaching from the back of the gymnasium. Somebody laughed. "How do you plan to do that, Earle?"

"No plan, exactly," Uriel said, standing.

"Then maybe you should wait until we—" but Uriel had already started walking towards the sound of the voices. Grace listened as she sat on the side of the bed, gripping her zip ties and the coil spring shiv in her sweatshirt pocket.

"Hey, old man, look where you're going," Grace heard from about ten rows away, then a grunt that sounded like Uriel getting shoved.

"Hey, hey," Uriel said. "You boys know about the girl?" Grace heard the shuffling steps come to a stop.

"Yeah, we heard," a young man's voice said from the darkness. "Gonna check it out right now, old man."

"Going to be a bit disappointed, I'm afraid," Uriel said.

"Yeah, why's that?"

Grace listened, fingering the sharp end of the spring in her pocket.

"Was just talking to her," Uriel said. "Only not really a her, least not all the way, you know?"

"What the fuck are you talking about, old man?"

"She's a he, that's what I'm talking about. Used to be, at least. Now part he, part she."

"Aw, shit," Grace heard from a new voice. "A tranny? Shit."

Grace huddled in the darkness, mildly offended. She wasn't optimistic that her friend was going to buy much more time with this line of reasoning.

"Let's find out what parts she and what parts he." There was mixed assent at this.

"You sure, old man?"

"He's ugly enough, yeah. I believe it." Grace was more offended at this. "Stinks, too. Got lice." That might be true at this point, Grace thought.

"Fuck that shit, man. I'm going back to sleep."

"Not me. I'm gonna check this shit out. Never seen one of those before."

"Not worth it, man. I'm going back to bed, too." Nice job, Earle, Grace thought.

"Darqueze, come on, man. Let's check this shit out."

Grace didn't hear a response, but figured she was expecting two assailants, maybe three, tops. But the odds looked a lot better. A minute later, she saw two figures approaching from out of the gloom. Grace kept huddled on the bed, her hood up. She clutched her pointed steel spring in her hand, hidden in the big pocket on the front of her sweatshirt. The two young men stared down at her for a few moments.

"Hey, bitch," one said, leaning forward to give Grace's head a shove. Grace grabbed the back of man's neck with her left hand and drove the end of her makeshift weapon into the side of his neck with her right. The man went down with a short, guttural cry, holding his hands to his neck, newly slick with dark blood. Still sitting on the bed, Grace brought her boot down on the man's neck and held it there.

"Hey, what the—" the other one managed to say before yelling out in pain as Uriel cut the back of the man's lower thigh from behind, severing his hamstring. The man crumpled on the floor next to his friend. Grace came off the bed and planted her knee in the second man's chest, knocking the wind from him with a grunt. She quickly zip tied the man's wrists together.

"Shut the fuck up, both of you," she whispered in a menacing hiss, bending close to them. "One more sound and I'll do both you mother-fuckers." She waited a few seconds to control her own breathing. "You, asshole, have a hole in your jugular vein. You hold both hands real tight like that and you just might live to make it to hospital. And you," she bounced on her knee, still planted on the other man's chest and elicited another choking grunt, "might walk again someday if I don't fuck you up next. You hear me?" Grace pressed the sharp end of her spring against the second man's neck. She could make out each of them nodding in the semidarkness. The first guy had his hands clamped around his neck, eyes wide with fear. The dark blood seeping between his fingers had nearly stopped. "That's just great. Now we're just going to hang out together, nice and quiet for a little while, until somebody opens that door and says good morning." Grace looked around for Uriel, but he had disappeared back into the gloom.

Grace returned to sitting on the side of the bed, huddled in her sweatshirt with her foot on the second guy's chest. Her situation was, she realized, tenuous at best. It was just a matter of time before one or the other of these guys got more scared of dying from his wounds than of her. She thought that might take a little while, however, as neither had suffered a particularly painful injury. Her other problem, though, was that the rest of the gang might wonder what had happened and come around at some point. That would require some difficult explanations.

After about fifteen minutes, Grace stopped wondering if Earle was going to come back to help out. Probably not, she realized. Grace was calculating her odds of going back to plan A, making a run for the door and hoping it was unlocked. Of course, that guaranteed that the rest of the gang members would come after her. Victim number two under her boot began to mutter something. Despite having his wrists bound, he made a move to grab her foot from his chest. This got Grace to thinking about an alternative. As she thought of it, she twisted her leg away from the guy's grasp and stomped her boot down onto his groin, with the expected result. He gasped, doubled over and curled up on his side, moaning. Grace leaned over and felt the guy's waist for a weapon. She found a small pistol stuck in the waistband above his backside and pulled it out. She checked it over in the dark. It seemed such a worthless piece that she wasn't even sure it would fire. Oh well, this guy probably thought it would.

Grace pushed the barrel of the small weapon against the man's temple and knelt close. "Okay, guys. I'm going to leave now. Just keep in mind that if I hear anything from either one of you, the last thing I'm gonna do is shoot both of you before I go." Grace tensed to sprint for the door, but as she watched, the door opened partially, a sliver of light slicing into the gymnasium towards her. The door stayed like that for a few seconds, but nobody entered. Grace could only hear a snuffling sound. She couldn't see anyone. She stayed crouched, listening, wondering if she should start running when Jack appeared out of the darkness and licked her face.

Grace smiled in relief. "Hey, Jack. Good to see you, boy." Jack didn't like the smells in here. He thought they should go. "We should go," Grace said to him. She added to the other two, "We gotta go now, boys. Best of luck to you both." With that, she sprinted for the door, Jack scrabbling on the hard floor right behind her. Grace bolted through the partially open door and ran straight into Bill, her Baltimore cop friend, nearly knocking him to the ground.

CHAPTER 22

Zimmerman and Pauley waited while Parnell polished off the carafe of coffee. He looked up at the other two. "You guys didn't want any, did you?"

"Would it have mattered if we did?" Zimmerman asked, shaking his head.

"You need to explain, Dr. Parnell," Pauley said. Parnell put down the cup and shrugged. "Listen, Dr. Parnell. Obviously, we are all involved in something of great import, something that involves each of us—"

"Yeah, yeah. Cut the crap, Pauley. I get it. What's pretty obvious is that we don't know shit," Parnell said. "You're talking some nonsense about Wright gates and Returnees. Sounds like you got a different problem, I don't know. Can't help you."

"It sounds like maybe it's just a different side of your problem, Chuck," Zimmerman said. "And I think, if Peter's book is any indication, you could use some help with your problem."

Parnell sat, considering. "I got to get out of this room," Parnell said.

"Where would you like to go?" Pauley asked.

"You need to get me some clothes and stuff, since you two let my bag get stolen. You can take me shopping in Georgetown, get something to

207

wear and some toiletries, since it looks like I'm going to be stuck with you two jokers for a few days."

Pauley shook his head. "You mean, you wear something besides that?" Pauley asked.

"What do you mean?"

Zimmerman preempted Pauley's reply. "We can walk you over to the student bookstore. They'll have everything you need."

"Bookstore?"

Pauley smiled. "Oh, that's a good idea. I'll put it on the department account. My treat, Dr. Parnell."

"Damn right, your treat," Parnell said.

They left the bookstore, Parnell carrying two large plastic bags as he walked between the other two men across campus. "I can't believe I'm going to be living in sweatpants and tee shirts," he said, shaking his head.

"It'll be an improvement," Pauley said. He led them to his office, closing the door before taking his chair behind the desk. Pauley leaned forward on the desk, hands clasped before him. "I must say, Dr. Parnell," Pauley said, "I find you and your faith rather enigmatic."

"The LDS Church?" Parnell asked. Pauley nodded. "Can't argue with you there, Father."

"But you said it was involved with this Return business?" Zimmerman asked, taking his seat on the small couch. Parnell sat in a chair in front of the desk, looking back and forth between the two men. He nodded.

"Yeah, I think so. Enigmatic doesn't get close, guys. I've been in the church for over five years and I still don't get it. I thought I was on the inside there for a while, when I discovered the salmon again—"

"The what?" Zimmerman asked.

Parnell shook his head. "It doesn't matter. Long story. Really long. It's just that I thought I enjoyed a certain amount of respect amongst the elders of the church, that I was part of management, you know? I was at the meetings where decisions were being made. I was at the table with all the big guys, all the time."

"But you weren't? You weren't on the inside?" Pauley asked.

208

"No, not even close. It's impossible to know. I mean, I'm sure I was in with all the important people and all, sometimes. But it's like some Russian novel. Boxes inside of boxes, everything compartmentalized and secret. Nobody really talks to anybody about anything outside their box. It's a little crazy, I got to tell you."

"But you found out something," Pauley insisted.

"Not really," Parnell said, shaking his head. "It's not like I found some locked room full of secret documents or anything. I just started putting some things together, lots of little things that didn't make any sense by themselves, in isolation. That's what they want, to keep everything separated. And then I found Sheehan's stuff, and a lot of shit that didn't make any sense just kind of fell into place."

"Like what stuff?"

"Like a lot of stuff, a lot of stuff everybody knows about us but nobody really thinks about. They just think we're kooks, that's all. The magic underwear, the temples nobody's allowed in. I mean, look at our history."

"What do you mean?" Pauley asked.

"All of it. Look at the earliest history of the Mormons, the Great Migration. How they had to keep pulling up stakes and moving."

"Religious persecution," Zimmerman said. "The Mormons were chased out of Ohio, Illinois, Missouri—"

"They were chased out of everywhere," Parnell said. "But not because of religious persecution. It wasn't that straightforward. It really bothered me, studying the history of the religion when I was doing my early research. It didn't make any sense. Lots of new, crazy religions were springing up in the United States at that time, some a whole lot wackier than Mormonism. And the Mormons weren't immediately persecuted when they settled into a community. I studied the primary records. That's what made the whole thing so pitiful, so awful. They settled in, sometimes for years, became integrated in the towns and societies in which they lived. Then, all of a sudden, the populace turned on them. Their neighbors, their friends and business associates, turned into torch carrying mobs and ran the Mormons out of the state on the threat of death. What causes that kind of behavior? It bothered me, but I couldn't come up with an answer." He looked between the two priests, but they were both blank faced, listening.

"Listen," Parnell continued, "You two have heard of the Mountain Meadows massacre, right?" The other two shook their heads.

"Was that one of the times that townspeople turned on Mormons?" Julius asked.

"No, no. Geez, don't you guys know anything about us?" Parnell sighed expansively. "The Mountain Meadows massacre was just the opposite, when the Mormons slaughtered an entire wagon train of settlers passing through southern Utah, in 1857. The Mormons weren't threatened at all, the settlers were passing through on their way west, completely peaceful. But in a series of attacks led by Mormon elders, the entire party—men, women, children—were slaughtered. Well over a hundred people. Only seventeen children, all younger than age seven, were spared. All the others were killed, their bodies burned and buried. Why would an otherwise peaceful religious community commit such an atrocity? It made no sense to me."

Pauley was shaking his head, confused. "You're making no sense to me, either, Parnell. What did you find out?"

"I didn't find out anything," Parnell said. "I just put it all together. That was my job. I was the historian, that's what I did. I had to, to find where Helena had hidden her salmon—er, the program." He waved his hand at them dismissively. "It doesn't matter, you don't know what I'm talking about. But I figured it out. One day, like an epiphany, like, it just all came together. I figured it out."

"Figured out what, Chuck?" Zimmerman asked, exasperated.

"That's what the Mormons were doing, all the way back in the nineteenth century. Bringing people back. That's what got them run out of town. At some point, people noticed. People will put up with a lot of crazy religious shit, but man, they are not going to let you start having the dead folks come back. No way." The other two stared at him, stunned. "You see? It all just makes sense. That's why they had to kill all those innocent people in the wagon train. Somebody in the Baker-Fancher party—that's what they were called, the emigrants in the wagon train—found out. Maybe a bunch of them. The Mormons weren't going to be run out of Utah by a group of transients, that wasn't the threat. But they couldn't let these people get away and carry their secret out of Utah. They had to be eliminated, all but the very youngest children."

The two priests stared at Parnell, almost not believing him.

"Where's your proof?" Zimmerman finally asked.

"Proof? I don't have any proof. Or what little proof I had you let get stolen. I told you. I just put it all together. There's so much more, so much that didn't make any sense until I got hold of Sheehan's recording. When I listened to that, when I realized what he had done—he made the existence of the afterlife seem so ordinary—all those loose pieces that were rattling around in my head just suddenly snapped together."

They sat in silence, thinking. Finally, Pauley asked, "So do you think they're still doing it?"

"Hell, yeah. I'm sure they are," Parnell said. "Like on an industrial scale."

Bill had to grab Grace's shoulder to keep from being knocked to the ground. Grace grabbed his arm and spun him into an arm bar before she realized who he was.

"Hey," he managed to grunt as Grace doubled him over and removed the gun from his waist band in a swift, smooth motion. She quickly released him. Bill straightened up, rubbing his wrist.

"Oops. Sorry, Officer Bill," she said, smiling at him sheepishly. Jack crashed into her legs, nearly knocking her into him again.

"My gun?" he asked, holding out his hand.

"Oh, yeah. Sorry, thought you were someone else." She handed it back to him carefully.

"Yeah? Who would that be?" The door pounded open and crashed into the wall behind her. The remaining four members of the young gang poured out into the hall where they stood. Jack barked at them.

"That would be these guys," Grace said, gesturing.

Bill quickly assessed the situation, noting the pistol in the hand of one of the gang members. He raised his own weapon and pointed it at the man's face. Grace pointed the gun she had taken off the guy in the shelter at one of the others. "Drop the weapon," Bill barked. As the gun clattered to the ground, he continued, "Face down on the floor, all of you. Now!" The young men complied.

"She killed two brothers in there," one of them said, pointing.

"Shut up," Bill said, kicking the gun back behind him. Bill looked at Grace, questioning. She shrugged. "You, too," he said. Grace pointed at her own chest.

"Really? Me?" she stage whispered. Bill nodded. Grace safed the pistol and slid it on the floor towards him. She sat down on the floor, cross-legged. Jack jumped in her lap and licked her face. "Hope you were nicer to my dog," she said.

Bill pulled out his phone and called the station. Three minutes later, two squad cars squealed to a stop in front of the mission, sirens dying. Bill talked briefly to the other officers and the four gang members were handcuffed and led outside. An ambulance appeared, as well as a third police cruiser. The officers from this car escorted two EMT's into the mission. They waited.

Bill returned to where Grace was still sitting on the floor, Jack lying in her lap. He looked down at them and shook his head as the EMT's passed by, wheeling the two victims out on gurneys.

"Get better soon, boys," Grace said as they passed. The one with the leg wound raised his arms up off the stretcher to give Grace the finger. "See, Bill? They're not even dead." Bill reached down and gave Grace a hand up, shaking his head. "Is it time for breakfast?" she asked.

"A little early yet. It's about five am."

"Really?" She and Jack followed Bill outside to walk to his car. "Came to pick me up so early?"

"My wife's idea. She was pissed I didn't bring you home with the dog, asked what kind of guy let's a girl sleep in a shelter but takes her dog. About an hour ago Jack started barking, woke us both up and wouldn't stop. So she said I should come get you while she made some breakfast." He opened the car door and Jack jumped into the back seat, Grace climbing in the front. Grace saw her bag sitting on the floor.

"She's sweet," Grace said.

"Oh, yeah. Real sweet." He started the car.

"Good thing you didn't bring me home, Bill."

"You got that right." He looked at her as he pulled away from the curb. "Nice sweatshirt. That your blood?"

Grace shook her head. "Naw. Not my sweatshirt, either." She pulled it over her head and threw it out the window. "Whew, that stunk." Bill nodded and drove home.

He parked in front of a well-kept brownstone. When Grace opened the car door, Jack jumped out and ran to the front door. He barked and was admitted by two little girls who screamed with delight when he ran in, bowling them over.

"Two girls?" Grace asked as she followed Bill up the front walk to the small porch. Bill nodded. "You are so screwed, Officer Bill."

"Don't I know it," he said. "Hey, hon! I got her." Bill's wife appeared from the kitchen, wiping her hands on a dishcloth. She smiled at Grace, shaking her head.

"Sorry my husband's such an ass," she said, shaking Grace's hand. "My name's Laura."

Grace smiled back and shook her hand. "He's not so bad. It's very kind of you to have me to your home, Laura. Thank you."

"We love Jack," Laura said.

"Yeah, he's a charmer," Grace said. "Can I help with breakfast?"

Laura wrinkled her nose, shaking her head. She gestured with the spatula in her hand. "Shower's waiting for you at the top of the steps, to the left. Left out a towel and some clean clothes." Grace started to protest, but Laura pointed her spatula threateningly. "Don't even start, girl. And hurry up, breakfast will be ready in about twenty minutes."

Grace came downstairs dressed in the loose sweatshirt and sweat pants Laura had left out for her. Laura immediately took all her dirty clothes and the wet towel and put them in the washer, muttering about how she would've preferred to burn them. The three of them sat down to eggs, waffles, and bacon; the little girls had already eaten and were busy dressing Jack up for a tea party in the den.

"You're very kind, Laura," Grace said after her first bite. "And maybe a tad too trusting. I hope your husband doesn't make a habit of bringing folks home from the shelter."

"No, you're the first. But I had a hard time sleeping last night, thinking of Jack's mom in that awful place."

"Wasn't her you should've been worried about," Bill said softly between bites of waffle.

Grace ignored him. "I hope Jack wasn't too much trouble."

"Trouble? Not a bit. He does like his pizza, though," Laura said, wondering about her husband's comment. "The only trouble will be getting him away from my girls."

"I'm glad he's playing nice. Can't believe anyone got any sleep with his snoring."

Bill couldn't make small talk any more. He turned to face his guest, saying, "You said you'd tell me in the morning. It's officially morning."

"Tell you what?" Grace asked, still eating.

"How you knew I was a cop. I'm supposed to be undercover, but you made me from across the park. How?"

"Don't worry about it, Officer Bill. It's not important."

"Sure it is," Laura interjected. "If he's supposed to be undercover, it's a matter of life and death. Isn't it, hon?"

"Well, I wouldn't say—"

"Please," Laura said.

Grace shrugged and put down her fork. "I presume you've never lived on the street?" Grace asked Bill. Bill shook his head. "Ever spent a night in a shelter?" He shook his head again. "Then I wouldn't try to fake it."

"No, that's not good enough, Miss—gosh, I don't even know your name. Bill, why didn't you tell me her name?"

"Actually, that's another problem," Bill stammered, embarrassed.

"It's Grace," Grace said.

"Grace, then," Laura continued. "If Bill's told to go undercover, he's got no choice. He's got to be better at it, that's all."

"Fine. But you'll never be good at it, believe me."

"You spotted me from across the park, Grace."

"Yeah, true. Here's the thing. We're not homeless people. We're just people—without homes, you know? Sounds trite, I know. But you can't just pretend to be homeless. Who are you pretending to be? Why are you homeless? Are you a junkie, strung out till you find your next hit? Are you a drunk? Some midlevel administrator that got laid off, and now the money's run out? Are you mentally ill, just out of a group home and off your meds? On that bench, you looked like a cop pretending to be homeless."

Both Bill and Laura nodded at that.

"Then, as I looked at you, you stared right back. Nobody on the street does that. When's the last time a guy on the street looked you straight in the eye? Never happen, not unless he's asking for money. And then, only long enough to figure if you're going to give him any."

Bill slurped his coffee. "Makes sense. What else?"

"Like I said, Bill, too much else. Up close, you don't have a chance."

"What? I dressed him up in some pretty shitty clothes, Grace," Laura said, smiling.

"Yeah, doesn't matter. He didn't pass. Those old tennis shoes you were wearing? Laces, nicely tied—in bows! Mostly though, it's the smell. Go step inside the Helping Up Mission, or any other shelter. You don't stink, Bill. Homeless folk don't shower on their way to the bench in the morning, you know?"

"I skipped shaving," Bill said lamely. Laura and Grace laughed.

"Okay, so how'd you know I was married? With kids, you said." Grace pointed to his wedding ring. "No way. I took it off, had it in my pocket."

"Go ahead and take it off." Bill did so. "See? It's still there." Laura looked over and saw the deep crease that remained in his finger.

"And the kids?"

Grace shrugged and reached for the pot to refill her mug. "No reason not to have kids, a guy that's been married long enough to get a dent in his finger. Just a guess."

"Didn't sound like you were guessing."

"Yeah, that's the key."

They sat in silence for a bit, drinking their coffee and listening to the sounds of the tea party from the next room. Laura stared at her guest as she finished her breakfast.

"I don't think you're homeless," Laura said at last.

Grace raised her eyebrows at that, meeting the other woman's gaze. "Oh, I'm homeless all right. Believe me, nobody sleeps in a shelter if they got a choice, Laura."

Laura looked down into her mug. "Sorry. I meant no offense."

"None taken. Thanks again for breakfast. You're too kind. Really. But Jack and I should be going. We've imposed too long already."

Laura shook her head. "I don't think the tea party's over yet. And your stuff isn't dry, either. Why don't you go upstairs and take a nap for a couple of hours? Bill doesn't have to work until the afternoon shift, he can give you a ride back downtown on his way to work if you want."

"Yeah," Bill said. "Didn't look like you spent last night sleeping much."

"What do you mean?" Laura asked him.

"Nothing."

Grace considered the offer. "Sure, Laura. Thanks. Just wake me up whenever, okay?" Laura led her upstairs and let her lie down in the spare bedroom. Before she left, she took Grace's hand.

"Thanks for helping my husband. I worry, otherwise." Grace nodded. "I hope it gets better for you, Grace."

"It already has, Laura. Thanks."

CHAPTER 23

"We need proof," Pauley insisted. "We need to know what's going on."

"Why?" Parnell asked. "Why do you care? I know what's going on. I don't need proof. I don't even want proof."

Zimmerman was wondering the same thing. He waited for Pauley to answer, but there was only silence from the old priest. Zimmerman thought about everything that Pauley had said to him, how he had watched the priest following Grace. He stared at the other man suspiciously. "What's going on, Peter? What is your interest in Grace?" Zimmerman finally asked. "I understand his angle," he said, jerking a thumb towards Parnell, "but where do you come in? Why are you so concerned with her?" Pauley stared at him and shook his head. "Parnell here is caught up with her, I see that. Once he decided to go public with his proof of an afterlife, things got complicated. As long as Grace is running around, he looks like a lunatic, his proof is worthless." Parnell nodded. Zimmerman paused, thinking. "If someone wants to sideline Parnell, all they need to do is keep Grace alive. On the other hand, Grace can die as long as the proof disappears, too." He looked up at Pauley and jabbed a finger at him. "That's what your book said. It said that Grace was blown up by a bomb in the duffle bag. A bomb would destroy the evidence at the same time. Somebody's problem solved. That's what was supposed to happen, wasn't it?"

"You can't say 'supposed to happen.' It didn't happen," Pauley said.

"But it was going to. Somebody, something that's involved here, wanted that to happen."

"Certainly would've solved a big problem for somebody," Parnell agreed, nodding.

"But you had to get me involved," Zimmerman continued, looking at Pauley. "You didn't want that to happen. Or was I supposed to be taken out with Grace and the bag, with the evidence?" Pauley didn't say anything, just stared back at the younger man.

"Gotta admit, Zimmerman," Parnell said, smiling. "You're as big a loose end as I am right now. Welcome to the club."

"Was that it, Peter? Who's pulling the strings here?" Pauley said nothing. "I am sick of being played, Peter. Who's writing the book? What's going on?"

Parnell and Zimmerman stared at Pauley, waiting. Pauley stared down at his hands on the desk in front of him. "Let's just think this through, Julius," Parnell said. "Father Pauley said that your church authorities have been monitoring an increase in Returns, even though they don't know anything about Mormons. So they must be watching some other activity. Maybe they saw Grace come over as part of that other program." Pauley looked up and met his gaze, unblinking. "Now as I see it—I'm just thinking out loud here, mind you—the Roman Catholic Church, the holy guardians of the Christian faith and all—might not be too pleased to see folks coming back from the great beyond. I can see how the Pope and his Pope folk might see this phenomenon as a bit of a threat to the true faith. Yeah, I can see how that might be a problem."

"Not just a threat to the faith," Pauley finally said. "A threat to civilization."

"Civilization?" Parnell said, smiling wryly. "You mean to Catholicism."

"Same thing," Pauley said.

"I can see the threat to the Church," Zimmerman said. "I understand that we lose our influence if we're not the intermediaries to the afterlife anymore, if everyone knew about it and is going there without us. Like any influence at all. I get that."

Pauley nodded.

"Hey, what about this," Parnell said brightly. "What if we get a dead guy to come back with a big splash, full media coverage and all, wearing a robe and sandals? Maybe a beard, long straggly hair, couple of apostle looking dudes with a donkey in the background? How cool would that be?"

"That," Zimmerman said slowly, "might not be such a great idea."

Grace had a nice nap. Laura woke her up and let her get dressed back into her freshly washed clothes, then made her a peanut butter and jelly sandwich, which she ate with the girls. Jack had leftover pizza, which was fine with him as Jack always had a problem with peanut butter. As predicted, Jack's goodbye was a little tearful from the kids, but when Grace explained that they could visit him whenever they wanted just by calling up Father Zimmerman, they were mollified. Jack was just relieved to be out of the dress and makeup he had to wear for the tea party. Bill gave them both a lift back downtown.

"Where am I dropping you?" he asked Grace as he drove.

"Is there an animal shelter downtown?" Grace asked. *I'm sorry*, Jack thought, his ears perking up. *Come again?*

"Uh, yeah. Downtown right near the stadium. Why?"

"You can drop us there, that'd be great." *Why would that be great?* Jack wondered.

"Why would that be great?" Bill asked. "If there's a problem, Jack can stay with us, no problem." *Damn straight*, Jack thought. *Though I am not wearing that stupid pinafore again for no amount of pizza. Shit*, he thought, *who am I kidding? I'd wear the thing for more pizza. And the lipstick.* He went back to listening to the conversation.

"No, it's not a problem. Just drop us there, okay?" Bill just nodded. *No, no*, Jack thought. *Don't just nod, buddy! The woman has obviously lost her mind. Never trusted this girl, not from the very first. Did you know she jumped off a bridge? Almost got me killed. Not reliable. Quirky.*

Bill stopped the car outside the shelter. Grace got out and opened the back door for Jack. Jack didn't budge. "Thanks for everything, Officer

Bill," Grace said, leaning in to help Jack get out. *That's okay, girl*, Jack thought. *I'll just wait for you here.*

"No problem, Grace. Been a pleasure. Anytime you're in the neighborhood, you know."

"Not likely, but thanks."

"You got my cellphone number?"

"Nope. I know where to find you. Stay safe, Bill. Come on, lardass, move it." *I think she's talking to you, Bill*, Jack thought. The dog reluctantly jumped onto the sidewalk. He barked a goodbye and thanks for the pizza to Bill over his shoulder as Grace slammed the door. Jack listened to the car pull away, sniffing at the animal shelter in front of them. This did not smell good. Not good at all. He sat down.

"Come on, Jack." *That's okay, girl, I'll just wait out here.* "Come on. We got to get you straightened away." *Yeah, that what you call it? Not 'going to live on a farm with Grandpa,' huh?* He made the sad sound, but followed the girl in through the door anyway.

Grace got the attention of the worker at the desk. "Excuse me," she said, "I need some help." *'Help me,'* Jack added under his breath. The woman looked up and smiled.

"Yes?"

"I think this dog belongs to someone." *Yeah, you think?* Jack sat down and tried to take deep, calming breaths. "I kinda found him in the park and he's been following me around all day." *Yeah, because that's what I do—follow around the crazy ones in the park. Wonder where Officer Bill went off to? I could probably find that park again. I wonder if they have pizza every day.*

"Ooh, he's a cute one," the woman cooed, coming around the desk to squat in front of Jack and scratch his head.

"No collar, huh?" *She's observant. A veritable shelter professional.* "He looks too good to be a stray. Strange he doesn't have a collar." *Strange you don't have a collar, lady. Oh, that's right. You don't look too good.*

"Maybe he has one of those radio chips," Grace offered.

"I'm sorry?" the lady asked. Jack stared up at the woman with concern. Jack made his sad sound.

"You know, those ID chips some owners have implanted in their pets, under their skin," Grace explained. The woman looked at a loss.

"They do that?" *Oh my god,* Jack thought. *She's in the prison community work program, I'm sure of it. Please get me your supervisor.*

"Do you have a supervisor?" Grace asked pleasantly.

"Sure, just a sec." The woman moved off behind the counter. *All dogs go to heaven, all dogs go to heaven, all dogs—*

"Can I help you?" the supervisor asked, coming around the counter to stare down at Jack.

"I was just wondering if you could check if this dog had an implanted ID tag," Grace explained.

"Just leave him with us," the woman said. *No, no, no. Not a good idea. Maybe the supervisor has a supervisor?*

"No, I don't want to do that. I'll leave him if you tell me he has a chip and you can call his owner," Grace said, arms folded. *How about you don't leave him at all? Huh? How about that, girlfriend? Exactly what did I do to piss you off, anyway? Not my fault you chose to skip the pizza and ended up in the slumber party from Hell, you know. Which you still smell like, by the way.*

The supervisor shrugged and turned back to the counter. "Bring him over here, then." Jack reluctantly followed Grace over to the counter. The woman bent over him with her scanner. Her eyebrows went up as she looked at the monitor. "Huh." *What exactly does she mean by that, do you think? Let's use our words, now.* "Hmm." *I am so screwed. Last meal was pizza, though. Can't ask for more than that, can we?* "He's from DC, from Georgetown University. Wonder how he got all the way here." *Somebody here has never gotten to ride in a car. Probably travels by broom.*

"Really?" Grace said. *Really? We're doing method acting here? We could show some emotion, wouldn't kill you. Wish I hadn't thought that.* "Is there a phone number?"

The woman nodded. "Yeah, he's registered to a Father Julius Zimmerman. There's a number." *Yeah, I heard of him. Call the number, lady.* "You'll have to leave him with us. We'll contact the owner." *Don't leave me here, please don't leave me here. Please, do not leave me with Nurse Ratched here.*

"I'll just wait here, then."

"Why would you do that? It may be quite a while. Could be tomorrow." *Maybe because she's not the cruel, crazy bitch I have her pegged for. And I can call her "bitch" because I'm a dog, and that's just how we talk. I can do that.*

"Might be a reward. I'll wait." *No, she is such a bitch. All about the Benjamins, huh? Why don't you just ship him one of my ears? You know, proof of life. Wish I hadn't thought of that.*

"Well, he can't wait here. I'll have to take him to the back." *Here we go—Dead Man Walking. The Long Green Mile. Cue the music.* Grace shrugged and took a seat on one of the plastic chairs in the waiting room. *That's it? That's all you got? A shrug? Love the minimalist approach. Very DeNiro. Hold on a second, let me take a bite out of the bitch's shin before I go. It's been swell. Hope you die in that chair.* The supervisor came back around the counter and put a rope leash around Jack's neck. *Oh, really? Hanging now instead of lethal injection? Where are we, Texas?* She led him through the swinging door to the back.

No tears, no tears. Look tough, head up, now. I am nobody's bitch, no sirree. Hell, who am I kidding? An hour ago I was wearing a pinafore and lipstick. Jack took in the smells and tried not to listen to the chorus of barking dogs in the cages on either side as he was led to the back of the pound. *Hey, Martini, how's it hanging? Oh look, there's Ruckly. Wish I'd never watched "Cuckoo's Nest" with Father JZ...*

"I got to know, Peter," Zimmerman said. "What side are we on with this? What side are you on?"

"We're on the same side, Julius," Pauley said patiently.

"Which is what, exactly?"

"There is no exactly. We're trying to contain a situation. It is important that this not become public knowledge. It is of the utmost important to the church."

"Important enough to kill?"

"Nobody's killing anyone, Julius," Pauley said, shaking his head. "I told you, we can't take the book at face value. It changes."

"You specifically used it to get me to help you get to Grace."

"That's not what happened and you know it," Pauley said. Zimmerman shook his head, not really knowing what he believed at this point.

Pauley continued, "Look, a lot of this is murky, I admit. But we can all agree on principles. There are people Returning, maybe more than the Church even appreciated. Maybe by multiple channels, I don't know. But the reality of it can't be disputed. It can only be contained. We have a duty to manage this situation, to do everything we can to maintain its secrecy. Everything we can."

"Maybe that's your duty, Pauley," Parnell said. "I'm not interested."

"Your life depends on you being interested," Pauley said, glaring at him.

"So you keep saying. Tell you the truth, I'm starting to lose faith in your magic book there."

"Grace is trying to destroy the recording," Zimmerman said to the two of them. "I say we let her. That solves the problem."

"It solves your problem," Parnell said. "Not mine. And if I'm right, it leads to a much bigger problem, down the road."

"Which is what?" Pauley asked.

"You're not going to believe me," Parnell said.

"We're listening."

Zimmerman's phone began buzzing in his pocket. He stood and walked out to the hallway, looking at the number. It was a Baltimore area code, a number he didn't recognize. He closed the office door behind him as he answered.

Pauley watched the door close behind Zimmerman. He turned back to Parnell. "What do you think is going on? Why are you trying to publicize this?"

"To stop them," Parnell said.

"Stop who from doing what?" Pauley asked.

"My people. Mormons. From fucking it all up." Pauley waited for the other man to continue. "I think they're trying to start the Rapture," Parnell said.

"Really?"

"No shit. Really."

Zimmerman came bursting back into the room. "I need to borrow your car, Peter."

"What? Why?"

"I'll bring it right back. They have Jack at a shelter. I have to go pick him up. I'll be right back."

"Really? Is the girl with him?"

"It's a pound, Peter. They got him in a cage. What do you think?" Pauley tossed him the keys. "Thanks. I'll find you when I get back." He left.

Pauley turned back to Parnell. "Really? The Rapture?"

Parnell nodded and looked at his watch. "I'll tell you about it over an early dinner. Let's drop the bags at my hotel and then walk over to the Tombs. We'll beat the crowd. What do you say, Father Pauley?" Pauley had a pretty good idea who'd be picking up the check.

Jack stood in his cage, watching the supervisor approach. *So this is it,* he thought. *So young, so young. Get busy living or get busy dying. Never got started on that tunnel. Red never got me that little hammer; probably couldn't use it anyway, no thumbs...*

The supervisor opened the cage and slipped the rope leash over his neck. She walked Jack past the cages on either side, every dog in the place barking at him. *Tell the warden I got a secret copy of the books, tell 'em I'm taking him down with me!* The big swinging door opened and Jack walked through. He saw Julius at the counter and tried to run to him, only to be brought up short by the leash with a yelp. *Dammit, Red! You made it! Hope can set you free!* Julius came forward and, kneeling, pulled off the rope leash. Jack kissed Julius on the lips.

"Hey, Jack, relax," Julius said, wiping his face with the back of his hand. "Good to see you, too." Zimmerman signed the necessary papers and turned to leave. Jack, however, ran around the corner of the waiting room to where Grace was still sitting, curled up asleep in her chair. *Give me a second here, Padre. I just gotta pee on this bitch's leg before we go home.* Julius turned to see where Jack had gone and saw Grace. He ran over and shook her awake.

"Hey, Grace! Grace! Hey, wake up." *No, just give me a second. I got a full bladder here, this'll be great.* Grace's eyes fluttered open and she smiled up at Julius.

"Hey there yourself, Padre." *Damn! Okay, guys, let's take this outside. Gotta find a tree or something.* The three of them walked in silence to Pauley's car. Jack took a minute to relieve himself along the way.

They sat in the car, not saying anything.

"You gonna start this thing?" Grace finally asked. Instead, Julius leaned over and kissed her. "Wow," Grace said, after. "Glad to see you, too, Julius."

Julius looked at her, grinning. "I didn't think I was ever going to see you again. I really didn't."

"Yeah, well, that was kind of the plan, a while back. Your dog's a pain in the ass, like you said. How're your balls?"

"Recovered, thanks for asking."

"And your head?"

"Still sore."

"Oh."

"Good to see you, Grace."

"Yeah, Julius. You, too." They sat in the car for a few more minutes, quiet. *Anybody else feel like going for pizza?*

"We just going to sit here, then?" Grace asked. Julius started the car, still grinning. "Where are we going, Julius?"

His smile faded. "I don't know," he said, and turned off the car. "I told Pauley I'd bring his car right back. But I didn't know I'd find you. I'm not sure going back to Georgetown is such a good idea."

"I'm not going back to Georgetown, Julius." She gently touched the knot on the top his head. "Sorry I clopped you so hard."

"It's okay. You meant well."

"Not really."

"Oh."

"I was kinda pissed at the time, tell you the truth," Grace said.

"I can understand that."

"What were you and Pauley doing there? How'd you even find me?"

Zimmerman tried to explain to her about Pauley's book, and their conversations with Parnell, though it was clear that Julius was pretty lost in the whole situation. He finished, shaking his head and looking over at her. Jack had fallen asleep on her lap. "So, you're saying that somebody wants me dead?" Grace said. "But not in any way that I want to be dead. Maybe you, too? But somebody else might want to keep me from dying, so that I can be living proof that Parnell is an idiot. And everybody feels that this," here she kicked at the duffle at her feet, "needs to be at the bottom of the ocean. Except Chuck, who thinks it might be the only thing keeping him alive." Julius nodded again. "Yeah, Julius, way too complicated. Not going back to DC. Bottom line."

"So where to, then?"

"I can't tell you where to go, Julius. But I'm heading for New York."

"Oh, so now New York's a good idea? Not such great advice when I said it, you know, just before people started shooting at us. What changed?"

"Old man in the shelter suggested it. He seemed to know what he was talking about," Grace said.

"Oh. Well, yeah. I can see how that would be a hard thing to argue with, old guy living in a shelter."

"It's not that random, Julius. His name is Earle and he was very kind to me."

"Earle."

"Yes, Earle. And if you must know, he was channeling my dead husband, Gabe, who also said that I should go to New York. Well, he actually didn't say it in so many words, but Earle implied that Gabe felt pretty strongly that I should go there as soon as I can."

Julius looked across the car at her, frowning. "Are you listening to anything you're saying?"

"Not really, no. I'm sorry, hon. I know you're kind of lost in all this." Grace leaned over and laid her head on his shoulder. Julius put his arm around her. Jack snored loudly.

"Not a problem, Grace. New York, then." She nodded on his shoulder. "We could steal Pauley's car. I got a little under half a tank."

"Tempting. Probably not a great idea, though. Between Pauley being such a dick and that magic all-seeing textbook you told me about, probably get pulled over before I make Delaware, even if I switch the plates and all."

"Okay, ditch the car idea. How much money you got?"

"Not that much."

"About how much is that?"

"Zip."

"Zilch?"

"Nada. How about you?"

"Got about fifty bucks, give or take," Zimmerman said.

"Not enough for the train, then."

"Or a plane."

"I don't do planes."

"Or a bus."

"Hate buses."

"Just as well, then."

Grace snuggled closer. "We could just stay here for a while, Julius."

"Yeah, this is great. Not getting us any closer to New York, though."

"Us?" Grace asked.

"Yeah, I think I might have an idea on how to get you to New York. But I don't think you can do it on your own."

"Oh, so now I need you, is that what you're saying, Zimmerman?"

"Yeah," Julius said, smiling down at her and giving her shoulder a hug. "I think you need me."

"You just keep thinking that, Julius. I'm going to take a little nap."

Julius started the car.

Parnell looked up from his menu. He knew what he was going to order, same thing as last time when Zimmerman was buying. He looked over at Pauley who was holding his menu in front of his face.

"You seem to be missing a finger there, Father."

Pauley lowered the menu. "Actually, I stopped missing it a long time ago. Nice of you to notice, though." He went back to scanning the menu.

"What happened? Accident?"

"You know another way to lose a finger?" Pauley said, not looking up from the menu.

"Not really." The waitress came and took their order. "What kind of accident?" Parnell continued, once she had left with their menus.

"Got too friendly with a stray dog."

"Really? Ouch. What kind of dog? I was bitten by a Chihuahua once, when I was a kid."

"Just a mongrel bitch, Dr. Parnell. The kind that you think would be more appreciative, you know?"

Parnell nodded, but wasn't sure he was following. He felt he should change the subject. "You know, Peter—I can call you Peter, right?" The other man nodded, taking a sip of his water. "You know, I haven't always been with the LDS church."

"So I gather."

"Before, I worked for the government. I was with the National Security Agency." Pauley nodded politely. "I was an electrical engineer by training. I was good at it. Did you know that I helped invent the mind reading technology, Insight Technologies?"

"No, I didn't know that. I thought that was Sheehan, the girl's husband. And that entrepeneur, I forget his name."

"Schlessel, Arthur Schlessel. He really had nothing to do with it, just made a ton of money off the whole thing. No, it was really me and Sheehan, together." Parnell finished off his martini, on the rocks with five olives, then signaled the waiter for another by holding up the ice filled glass and shaking it at him. "Anyways, I bring all this up so you understand that I'm not a religious zealot or anything, so you know where I'm coming from." Pauley listened. "You know what else I'm good at? Patterns. It's part of what I do, I guess, part of the stuff I did at NSA and Insight Technologies. I can recognize patterns, see things in the way events lay out. That sort of thing. You following me here, Peter?"

"I think so, Dr. Parnell." Parnell's drink arrived and the waiter took the empty glass away.

"Thanks a lot, asshole," Parnell said to the back of the retreating waiter. "Only two olives. I specifically told him five, I'm sure. Anyway, I see patterns. That's how I was able to reinterpret the Mormon scriptures. In less than five years, I was the leading authority on Mormon history, scripture, commentary—the whole thing. Nobody even came close to what I did. Ever."

"I'm sure that's a great accomplishment, Dr. Parnell."

"You should call me Chuck."

"Chuck, then."

"Not my real name, you know."

"I know."

"Really, you knew that?" Pauley nodded.

"You were talking about your ability to see patterns."

"Oh, yeah. Just as a way of introduction, just so you understand where I'm coming from. Because I think you're full of shit, Peter." The waiter arrived with their meal. They each paused in their conversation to eat for a bit. "I mean, I understand why you were playing things close to your chest when the kid was around—"

"The kid?"

"Zimmerman."

"Oh, yes. Of course. He's probably not much younger than you, actually."

"I think I'm way older, probably. In all the ways that count."

"If you say so. You were saying I was full of shit."

"Yeah. I mean, between us, we can be honest, can't we? You were pretty much spewing bullcrap back there in your office, about the church and all. I can read the tea leaves, like I was saying. You've known about the Returns longer than I have, you guys know a lot more about what's going on than you're pretending."

"I'm not sure I follow."

"Stop it, Peter. You'll ruin my appetite."

"Not sure that's possible, unless I tell you that I'm not picking up the tab." He smiled at Parnell.

"I'm technically still your guest, you know."

"Of course you are. Even if you do claim I'm full of shit."

"Yeah. I was raised Catholic. Kind of. Ephesians 6:12, the Church Militant, *Ecclesia Militans.*"

"No need to start speaking Latin, just to impress the priest, Chuck."

"The church on earth who are the living, fighting the good fight against sin, the devil, and 'against spiritual wickedness in high places.' "

"You know your bible, I see."

"And then there's the Church Triumphant, the guys on the other side."

"With Jesus Christ, you mean."

"Yeah, right. Him, too. The whole holy administration calling the shots from the penthouse suite, the corner offices in Heaven. Them folks."

"We've kind of moved away from that concept in the modern catechism. That's pretty much all last century, Chuck."

"No, you stopped talking about it, out loud at least. Now that the barriers are breaking down, you got to throw up some curtains, keep the masses from noticing. Can't have them seeing who's really pulling the strings." Pauley shrugged as he ate. "That magic book of yours, that's what I'm talking about right there," Parnell said, gesturing with a fork-ful of steak at the other man's breast pocket. "That's an instrument of *Ecclesia Triumphans.* That's exactly what I'm talking about."

"Back to Latin, huh? One way of looking at it, I guess. I'm not sure I'm getting your point, Chuck."

"You're not just investigating some police action involving twentieth century Prairie home architecture. This isn't about 'a recent increase in Returns,' or whatever crap you said back there. There's something much bigger, much older going on. And you know it."

"Perhaps you give me too much credit, Chuck."

"Perhaps you're just lying through your teeth."

Pauley finished his salad and laid down his fork. "What is it you wish me to say, Chuck?"

"You know about the Mormons, don't you?"

"Honestly? No, I don't think we do. We have some suspicions, of course. Like you said before, there have been hints. Nobody bought the explanation about why they were secretly baptizing all those Holocaust victims without anyone's permission. But we don't have much in the way of hard information, I'm afraid. Yours is an effectively secretive organization, as you said."

"What, then? If not us, then who else? Besides you, I mean."

"What do you mean?"

"Well, I'm sure your organization isn't just monitoring the whole thing, are you? You're a pretty sophisticated, highly capable organization, a couple of hundred years—"

"Thousands, actually."

"Yeah, thousand years in the business of souls and all. I'm sure you guys have your own methods, your own gates or some such." Pauley said nothing, signaling the waiter for the check by catching the man's eye and pretending to write on his palm. "What are you doing? We haven't had dessert yet."

"We should be getting back."

"Why? I've got no place I gotta be."

"Julius may be trying to find us."

"He can't just call your cell?"

"I have work to do, Chuck. I'll walk you back to the hotel."

"Gotta check in with the higher-ups, huh?"

"Cute."

"Maybe consult the magic book, get your new mission, if you choose to accept it?"

"Something like that, I'm sure. Are you finished?" he asked, having finished signing the check. Parnell chugged the last of his martini and popped both olives in his mouth, nodding.

"Hope you didn't tip that guy," Parnell said between chews, his mouth full. "Screwed up with the olives."

"You know, Chuck," Pauley said as he stood from the table, "you forgot about *Ecclesia Penitens.*"

"Who are they?" Parnell asked, following Pauley up the stairs and out of the restaurant.

"You must know. The Church Suffering. Those who don't make it to heaven."

"That's a real thing?"

"It's in the Book."

Uriel sat down on the park bench next to Bill, who was in the process of tying his shoelaces into knots.

"Man, what are you doing?" Uriel asked him. Bill straightened up.

"Nothing."

Uriel shook his head. "We should just switch jobs or something. You keep trying to be a bum and I got to go all commando helping that girl. I coulda gotten myself hurt."

"Don't think my wife would go along with it, tell you the truth, Earle."

"You don't take a shower once in a while, you're not gonna have a wife," Uriel said.

"I'm under cover, Earle."

"Cop, you're about as convincing at being homeless as I am at being sane."

"That's what the girl said. You seem pretty sane, Earle."

"Well, I'm not. You're no judge, that's all."

"You say so, Earle."

"She get away okay?" Bill nodded, wiping his nose on his sleeve.

"Will you please stop that? Homeless people don't do that. That's just poor upbringing, that's what that is."

"Sorry. My nose is stuffy when I don't shower in the morning," Bill said.

"Where is she off to?"

"Not sure. She didn't say."

"She sure as shit better be heading to New York. You give her some money?" Bill shook his head. "You didn't give her any money? What is wrong with you? What kind of Christian turns a girl out on the street with no money?"

"She didn't ask for money. Wife and I fed her pretty well, let her catch up on her sleep a little bit. Laura washed her clothes."

"You're pathetic. What did you feed her?"

"I think she had peanut butter and jelly sandwiches with my girls," Bill said.

"You are a sorry excuse, you know that, right?"

"Well, I'm sorry we didn't take her out to a nice steakhouse, Earle. Her dog pretty much ate up our pizza budget the night before."

"Fuck that dog," Uriel said. "Sounded like he was cursing me out the whole time I was rowing him back to Georgetown. Dog's got an attitude." Uriel shook his head, remembering. "How the hell is that little girl supposed to get to New York with no money? Huh?"

Bill shrugged. "Honestly, Earle, I'm not too worried. She seems to know how to take care of herself. You see what she did to your two homies?"

Uriel nodded. "Yeah, you got a point. Could've given her bus fare, at least."

"You should be more worried about where she's headed than how she's getting there, I think."

"Why? Where'd you drop her?"

"Animal shelter down by the stadium."

"No shit? Well that makes no fuckin' sense."

Bill shrugged again. "Not my problem anymore, Earle. Did what I could."

"You know what you need, Bill?"

"What's that, Earle?"

"You need a more altruistic attitude, that's what you need."

"Don't we all, Earle. I gotta go."

"What's the only thing folks got, Bill?"

"Each other, Earle."

"Damn right."

"I gotta go, Earle. Got work to do."

"Like what you do is work." He spat on the ground between his feet. "Give me fifty bucks," Uriel demanded, holding out his hand.

"What? Why? I don't have fifty bucks."

"Yes, you do. Give it to me."

"How do you know I have fifty bucks?"

"Because you're a shitty liar. Because you got the shifty eyes. Because it was the third thing you said. Because I can see through you like glass. Now give me my money so I can get to DC. I got stuff to do."

"I'll give you twenty," Bill said, shaking his head and standing. He fished the bills from his wallet. "I need the rest. Can't you just do crazy homeless shit right here, save us both a lot of money? Why does a crazy homeless person need to go to DC all the time, anyway?"

"Saving this sorry world, that's what." Uriel took the bills from him and stuffed them in his pants pocket. "Saving your cheap sorry ass, that's for damn sure." Bill stared at the decrepit old man, confused. "Don't think so much, Bill. It's not healthy." Bill turned to leave, still shaking his head. "Stay safe, Bill," Uriel said. Bill waved absently as he pretended to amble drunkenly across the park. "Dammit, Bill. Straighten up and walk right. Drunks don't walk like that. You look like a constipated undercover cop."

Grace woke up when she felt the car stop. Julius turned off the engine. Jack kept snoring in her lap, which was now damp with drool.

233

"Shit."

"What?" Julius asked.

"Damn dog's drooling all over me."

"Yeah, he does that. Sleep okay?"

She nodded. "Where are we?"

"Baltimore Yacht Club."

"Oh, cool. Didn't know you belonged."

"I don't. Not yet." He tossed her the keys. "Need you to go shopping."

Grace caught the keys and pushed Jack off her lap onto the floor. His snoring caught for a brief moment, then resumed with a schnorgel. "I can do that. What do we need?"

"Groceries," he said, fishing the money from his wallet and giving it all to Grace. "Enough for us to eat for about three days, just to be on the safe side. And dog food, the dry kind."

"Got it. Anything else? How about some duct tape?"

"What is it with you and duct tape?" Julius asked.

"I love the stuff. Duct tape can save your life."

"You say so. Sure, get some duct tape. And there's something else."

"What else? We're pushing up against the budget here."

"You told me once that you used to be a thief, right?"

Grace squinted at him, suspiciously. "When did I tell you that?"

"Can you hotwire a car?"

"No—what are you talking about? There's no such thing as hotwiring cars anymore. I told you, we can't steal a car for this."

"How about an old car, like from the eighties?"

"What are we going to do, steal a Delorean and travel back to when I could hot wire a real car? There's no chance."

"What did you need, back when you could?"

"Not much. Just a pair of diag's. Used to be able to get a car going in under a minute, back in my youth. In a pinch, you can do it with just your teeth."

"Why am I not surprised? Pick up a pair of diag's then, whatever they are. Get two pair if you need 'em. And a flashlight. With batteries. And a crowbar."

"A crowbar?" He nodded. "You're just making this shit up, aren't you, Zimmerman?"

"No, I'm not. I'm going to get you to New York. I'll be here, doing some recon. Laying the groundwork, as it were. Get back as soon as you can, okay?"

"Do I have to take your dog? Again?"

"Yeah. Just leave him in the car. Probably sleep through the whole thing."

Pauley walked Parnell back to the hotel in the middle of campus and continued on to his office. He spent a few minutes, as he walked on alone, wondering about what the other man's plans might be. He was even less informed now after their conversations, and also less inclined to care. Parnell obviously possessed information that he did not, but was just as obviously not the threat that Pauley had feared. He gave a mental shrug and moved his thoughts to other matters. It seemed that Zimmerman had been gone long enough to retrieve his dog; he should be back by now. He'd give him a call if he didn't get his keys back in an hour or two.

Pauley unlocked the door to his office and sat heavily behind his desk. He heaved an old man's sigh, tired of intrigue. He took his copy of *The Problem of God* out of his coat pocket and laid it on the desk in front of him, staring at it. It always looked the same from the outside, a picture of the interior of the Guggenheim museum on the cover, clouds seen through the skylight. Strange he had never wondered about that picture before, not until Julius had brought it up. A tool of the Church Triumphant, Parnell had called it. A nice turn of phrase, Pauley thought. Though the man acted a buffoon, Parnell seemed strangely insightful in some ways. 'Older in all the ways that count,' he had said; whatever that meant. Pauley hoped his dealings with the man were done. He drummed his fingers on the desk, hesitating. Pauley was reluctant to open the book, to see what new lines were written since yesterday. He feared reading them, because he knew they must concern the girl. He hated the girl.

Instead of opening the book, Pauley stood up and walked around the desk to the sideboard that held his liquor. He poured out a short tumbler of Irish whiskey and knocked it back. He smacked the heavy glass back down and refilled it, his hand shaking. He carried the bottle and glass back to his desk and sat down again. Another gulp of whiskey, and then he opened the book to the page he had marked with the small, squarish yellowing carapace that he used to indicate his current point in the book. But instead of reading the page, he stared at the small bookmark, fondling it between the fingers of his left hand, the hand with all five fingers, remembering back to a past life. He thought about the day he lost his finger, the index finger of his right hand. He remembered the agony and shock he had felt when the girl had bitten it right off, the revulsion on her twelve year old face, her mouth bloody, as she spat the amputated thing at him, staring at him defiantly. He hated the girl. The surgeon who informed him that reimplantation would not be possible—the tissues had been too macerated, he explained—had given him the fingernail as a token. Something to remember it by, he had said, just before tossing the bloody digit in the trash. Pauley remembered, all right. He remembered every day. Pauley rubbed the nail between his thumb and only index finger, remembering. He placed the milky yellow nail down on the desk and finally looked at the book.

Pauley gaped with shock at the page before him. In the middle of the page, one word stood alone:

excision

He stared at it, incredulous. "Dear Mother of God," he whispered softly. He turned back through previous pages, reading and rereading. "Excision," he said softly, pronouncing the word as a test of whether it was really what the letters in front of him represented. "Jesus, Mary, and Joseph." Pauley finished the glass of whiskey before him in a couple of gulps. The bookmark was brushed to the floor, unnoticed.

Grace drove to the large home supply store she had passed on the way to the grocery store, after she left Julius at the yacht club. She shook her head and smiled, amused at the thought of him doing 'recon and laying the groundwork.' Grace looked at Jack sitting on the passenger seat, staring ahead out the window. She scratched the dog's head. "Your roommate is a piece of work, Jack."

Don't even get me started, Quirky Girl. Wanted to room with Steve, the Party Priest. No such luck. Steve has pizza every Friday. Of course, my guy's got a girl rooming in. How many priests got that going on, huh?

Grace pulled into the Home Depot parking lot. She looked up at the exterior cameras and evaluated their field of vision. It seemed they were mostly covering the two main entrances, so she pulled up to the curb close to the contractor's entrance. She stopped the engine and lit the four-way flashers.

"Listen, Jack. Wait here while I do a little more shopping."

No, problem. Pretty sure I smell steak in those grocery bags back there. Take your time.

"You touch the groceries while I'm gone and I'm gonna lock you in the trunk. And I'm pretty sure we're ditching the car after this."

You're bluffing. Father Yawn wouldn't let you get away with it. I'm University property you know.

"And by ditch, I mean let it roll into the Chesapeake Bay. Think about it." She glared at the dog.

Fine, you convinced me. I don't like the visual. Hurry up, then.

This would be a lot easier, Grace thought, if she hadn't spent all their money on the groceries. But as she had rolled her cart up and down the grocery store aisles, shopping for the two of them, she realized that there was no way she was going to eat Ramen noodles for what may well be her last three days alive. No way. The steaks had been expensive, as well as the wine, and cheese, and fruit. Two bags of Snickers. One bag of Twizzlers.

Grace intensely preferred the afterlife to this one. She ached for it, actually, missed it with her whole being. But, she had to admit, this world did have its attributes. Unlike the next, this world was physical, corporeal, tangible. You couldn't get a good steak in the next world. Or get laid. She hadn't missed any of that when she was there, of course; things were so different, ethereal. But now that she was back, her appetite was extraordinary. She bought a lot of steaks.

As a result, she had blown their wad, completely. Grace had to put back the dog food, even. Hell, she thought, Jack deserves steak. Who needs dog food? She still had to get the diagonal pliers, though, and some duct tape, of course. So she parked her car just outside the door. Nobody tows a car with a dog in it, anyhow.

Grace grabbed a shopping cart and strode at ramming speed up and down the aisles of the huge store. She loved these places so much it seemed almost pornographic. She threw a nice canvas tool bag in the cart without breaking stride, then stopped to get two pair of diagonals (Julius had said two, after all), one small and one large, just in case. Grace had just thrown the short wrecking bar in the cart when she spied the battery powered mini-Sawzall and almost swooned with desire. Power tools beat hand tools any day. She threw the Sawzall in the cart, barely noticing that it was over a hundred dollars. The great thing about not having any money, she thought, is that it doesn't matter how much things cost. Flashlight and batteries. Grace slalomed her shopping cart over to the paint department and tossed two roles of duct tape—one black, one grey—into the cart. Then she headed over two aisles and had to take a few minutes surveying the paints, finally picking up a six ounce can of blood red. Hope so, she thought. Oh, shit, Grace realized, then rapidly backpedaled her cart back to the tool aisle to pick up a small screwdriver and a razor knife. She threw in some other odds and ends at random, lots of nuts and bolts and a couple more tools, just for show.

Okay, she thought, showtime. Grace shook up the paint can and took off the top with the screwdriver, then set the can carefully back in the cart. She slowly approached the checkout area, surveying the personnel, the setup, glancing up at the ceiling to locate the cameras. Every one of these places was identical, Grace knew. She'd spent a lot of her last life browsing these stores, like everybody else in this level of existence. Grace pulled up short of the self-checkout area and studied the employee who was manning the station. Young guy, looked to be in his early twenties. Perfect, she thought. Probably working part time as he gets his degree in art history. Hopefully, he was the kind that passed out easily; most guys were, she'd found. She approached the checkout lane farthest from the young man's station. Grace removed the tags from the tool satchel and put in the stuff she really wanted; the wrecking bar, the Sawzall, both rolls of duct tape, both diags, flashlight with batteries. She tossed in the screwdriver as an afterthought.

Grace began scanning in a bunch of other stuff she didn't really care about and placing it in the plastic bag on the side of the scanner. She stole a glance over her shoulder and saw the attendant helping another customer. Grace took the small pot of blood red paint from the basket and drizzled it generously over the checkout station, trailing a small puddle onto the floor. Then she hid the paint can behind the machine. She took the razor knife from the shopping cart. This was the part she hated. Taking a deep breath, she drew the blade across the back of her hand, cutting the web between her thumb and index finger, then tossed the knife back in the toolbag.

"Yeow!" she screamed, not entirely acting. "Aw, fucking son of a bitch!" She let some blood run over her hand and up her arm, glancing back to see the young attendant heading over. She squeezed her hand and hopped up and down. "Shit, shit, shit, shit. Shit!"

"Something wrong, ma'am?" the young man said as he came up to Grace, a look of helpful concern on his face.

"Yeah, there's something wrong," Grace said, pointing to the checkout station covered in red, "I sliced my hand open on that fucking thing."

The man looked at the blood all over the floor and the machine and visibly blanched. "Oh my god," the man said. "Are you hurt bad?"

"Yeah, I'm hurt bad," Grace replied. Guy looks pale enough to pass out, Grace thought to herself. "Look!" She shoved her cut hand into the guy's face and released the pressure from the other hand, blood spurting onto the young man's shirt.

"Hey!" he said, flinching.

"I'm think I'm gonna pass out," Grace said. Might as well plant the idea in the poor guy's head.

"Just squeeze it like this," the man said, showing her how to hold pressure on the wound. "Keep it above your heart." He smiled at her.

"What are you, the Home Depot house doctor?" Grace asked, irritated that the guy wasn't passed out on the floor by now.

"No," he said, still smiling broadly as he helped her hold pressure on the cut. "I'm an EMT."

Aw, shit, Grace thought. What are the odds? "Well, lucky me." This guy's thinking of asking me out after this, I just know it, she thought.

"Not a licensed EMT, actually, not yet. I'm still in training. Listen, just sit here for a second—"

"Hey, buddy, I appreciate that you're almost a fully trained surgeon and all, but I gotta get to an emergency room, I think. This thing's pretty deep."

"Just sit for a second, I'll run and get my bag. I got some bandages and stuff. You can't go to the ER bleeding all over like that."

"Fine. Go. Thanks. I'm going to sit down, I'm not feeling so good." She sat down on the check out counter, being careful to avoid the paint.

"I got to just get my supervisor to cover my station, one sec." She watched him sprint over to where his supervisor was standing, then point over to where she was sitting. Grace reached into the toolbag with her two hands, still holding pressure to keep from bleeding all over, and got out a roll of duct tape. She watched as the young man started sprinting towards his locker to get his medical bag, the supervisor sauntering over slowly, obviously not too anxious to get involved. She liked his attitude. Time to go, she thought. She tore off a short piece of duct tape and applied it to the wound like a butterfly bandage, staunching the bleeding. "I love this stuff," she said softly. She grabbed up the toolbag and headed for the exit.

"Hey!" the supervisor yelled, quickening his pace. "Where you going, lady?"

"I'm bleeding," Grace yelled back, holding up her bloody arm; the one not holding the bag. She pointed to the stuff at the checkout. "I gotta just leave it. I'm sorry, I made a big mess. I gotta get to hospital."

The supervisor was just a few yards away now. "But Billy went to get his bag, so he can fix you up."

"Tell him thanks," Grace said, waving with her bloody hand as she kept walking steadily towards the door. She took a glance over her shoulder and saw the supervisor had stopped following, hands on hips and shaking his head. The alarm buzzer sounded as she exited (sure that Saw-zall must have an RFID tag, Grace thought) but she just kept moving. She tossed the bag in the back seat and climbed into the car. Jack lifted his muzzle from his paws where he had been resting on the front seat.

What the hell? You look like Day-Lewis at the end of that Gangs of New York movie. You bring a weed whacker to a knife fight or something?

"You better not have eaten those steaks, Jack."

Good thing I didn't. Smelling you, I'd probably vomit if I did. I'm thinking maybe I should drive.

"Shit," she said aloud, fishing the car keys from her pocket with a wince, "wish you could drive. Hand's killing me." She killed the flashers and pulled away, heading out of the parking lot just under the speed that says, 'I just shoplifted a ton of shit from your store.'

Grace found her way back to the yacht club without much difficulty. As she approached the entrance to the club, Julius flagged her down from the side of the road. She pulled over to him and stopped.

"Jeez, took you long enough," Julius said, heaving Jack into the back seat so he could sit down. "Holy shit," he said, looking at her. "What happened to you?"

"Shopping was brutal. Sorry I took so long. There was a problem at the checkout."

"Oh. Are you okay?" He looked at her blood covered arm with concern.

"Yeah, it's just a scratch, really."

"You look like Liam Neeson at the end of Rob Roy."

"Yeah, yeah. I know. What are we doing here on the side of the road, partner?"

"Waiting."

"For what?"

"Till it gets a little later. About half an hour, I figure."

"Why? What happens then?"

"Then we leave for New York. You get everything?" She nodded. "What do you want to do for half an hour?"

She smiled at him seductively. "I got Twizzlers."

Pauley wrestled with what he had just read. He was familiar with the concept of excision, but only in the abstract. It occupied a place in his training somewhere alongside exorcism, or interpreting images of the blessed virgin on toasted muffins. He never really considered the possible veracity of the concept. He thought long and hard, considering, while it grew twilight outside the windows of his office. Eventually, he decided that he owed Parnell some semblance of explanation, if he could provide it. While he disliked the man on many levels, the implications of what he had read required that he warn him, if only out of common decency. Pauley put on his suit coat and walked back across the campus to the hotel.

Parnell answered the knock on his hotel room door dressed in George-town sweatpants and sweatshirt. "Pauley," he said, obviously surprised. "You taking me for ice cream and a movie?"

"Not exactly. May I come in?" Pauley asked.

"Sure, sure," Parnell said, standing aside to admit the priest. "Not like you're interrupting anything. You want a coke or something?"

"No, thank you." Pauley removed his coat and draped it over the desk chair, then sat down. Parnell sat in the only remaining chair in the room.

"To what do I owe the pleasure, Peter?"

"There's been a development. I have become aware of some information that I feel I should share with you."

"Really? Why? Because, so far, I didn't have you pegged as the shar-ing type. No offense."

Pauley shifted uncomfortably in his chair. "This is somewhat differ-ent than our earlier conversations, Dr. Parnell. I feel compelled to make you aware of what's in store for our mutual acquaintance."

"The girl, you mean." Pauley nodded. "Must be horribly awful, Peter. You started calling me Dr. Parnell again."

"Sorry. Chuck. Not so horribly—well, I shouldn't judge. I feel com-pelled to share this information with you, but not because of its implica-tions for the girl. Far from it. It is only right, I feel, to tell you, because of the inevitable effects upon yourself, personally."

"You're going to kill both of us? Shit, Pauley!" Parnell half rose from his chair.

Pauley waved him back. "No, Chuck. Nothing so dramatic. You are not in danger, I assure you."

"You said me personally."

"Yes, I did. Please, allow me to explain. It is rather difficult. Truth be known, I'm certain that I was not meant to share this with you at all." He stared at the other man, reconsidering. Parnell sat back down.

"Fine. Shoot." He smiled at his little joke.

"The girl is to be excised." Pauley stared at the other man and waited for a response. Parnell just stared back at him and finally shrugged.

"No idea what you're talking about."

Pauley sighed. "Excision," he explained softly, "is the process of removing an individual completely. She is to be removed. Completely." He flushed with the thought.

"Killed, you mean."

"No," Pauley said, shaking his head. "You're not understanding. She's already died."

"But she's not dead now. She's alive, running around like you and me."

"Quite. For the time being. Not for much longer."

"So you're going to kill her."

"No. It's not killing."

"She's going to kill herself, anyways. I'm sure of it. She did it before. No big deal, Peter. I really don't care if you guys kill her. Really."

"She won't be killed, Chuck. That's what I'm telling you. She will be excised. Not like before. Not like dying, then or ever again."

"What do you mean? What is it then?"

"It will be as if she never was. Not in the last life, not in the afterlife, not in this one. She'll be gone, completely. Past, present, and future."

"You can do that?" Pauley nodded. "But that's murder. I mean, really murder. Like killing her completely, and like—forever."

Pauley shook his head vigorously. "It is not murder," he insisted.

"Sure it is. You just said. You're going to kill her, forever."

"It's not murder, Dr. Parnell," Pauley insisted, "because she will never have lived. She will vanish, that's all."

"It's murder."

"No, it isn't!" Pauley said, more emphatically than he intended. He realized that he was clutching at the arms of the chair tightly. He forced himself to relax. "Would you have any whiskey?"

"No, sorry." They stared at one another. "Why are you telling me this, Peter?"

"Because it affects you. You have a connection to the girl, I know."

"So?"

"So, she'll be gone. Like I said, it will be as if she never existed."

"In this life, you mean."

"No," Pauley said, shaking his head again. "In any life, in all her times. Her presence will be erased from your own life, as a consequence."

"But, but," Parnell stammered, "we worked together for years and years! She was the reason that Sheehan and I discovered the whole mind reading concept. Her work on mental illness! Everything?" He looked plaintively at the priest. "What will happen to everything we worked on?"

"I honestly don't know," Parnell replied. "I'm sorry. You have to be prepared, though, for the possibility that some portion of your work may disappear with her excision."

"But that's my life! That's my life, too, you're talking about. Not just the mind reading. All the work we're doing with the church, the progress we've made with caring for the mentally ill as a result—"

"You must accept the possibility that it will be altered to some degree."

"Altered to some degree? You sound like a fucking lawyer, Pauley. You can't do this. This is murder, plain and simple. Worse than murder! You're destroying her soul—and my life's work. You can't do this."

"It is not murder. It is not the same thing at all. She will have never been, so she cannot have been killed."

"Sophistry! Bullshit and sophistry. You bastard."

"It is not murder. The church does not commit murder."

Parnell sat, seething as he stared at the other man. "You know what it is, Pauley. You came here because you know." He stared at the priest, but Pauley couldn't meet his gaze. The priest stared down at his lap, his hands folded. "How about you, Peter?" Parnell asked, more controlled. "You have some past with her, I'm sure. What's this excision going to do to you?"

Pauley looked up at that, meeting the other man's accusatory gaze. "Me?" He rubbed his hand and didn't smile. "I believe I may get my finger back."

"Your finger? But you said—you're a bastard, Pauley."

Pauley stood and shrugged on his coat. "Good night, Dr. Parnell."

Grace and Julius walked Jack up the rural road, sharing a bag of candy between them. "So what's the plan?" Grace asked as they walked.

Julius looked up at the sky to judge how much time remained until sunset. "In about twenty minutes, I think we should head back to the car. We'll drive to the club and load our stuff in the boat."

"Won't be dark by then."

"No, we don't want to wait until it's really dark. That'd look suspicious. And I don't think we could get the boat into open water in the dark. Too risky."

"Won't it look a little suspicious, our loading stuff onto a boat that's not ours in broad daylight?"

"Groundwork, Grace. We're all set."

"Groundwork, huh? What'd you tell them?"

He smiled, proud of himself. "You just have to know a little bit about how these rich guy yacht clubs work, that's all."

"And you know?"

"Yeah. We never actually belonged, back in Chicago. But I spent a lot of summers crewing, hanging out with my rich guy friends. They're all the same. You know, like Mumsy and Pops." He winked at her.

"No, Julius, I don't know. I told you before, you need to stop making assumptions about me and let that go. You don't know shit about me."

"No, Grace, I don't. Why don't you tell me?"

"Maybe later," she said, holding out her hand for the bag of Twizzlers. They had eaten half the bag already.

"You're going to make yourself sick."

"Probably be sick any way, going on a boat."

"You get seasick?"

"Don't know."

"You never been on a boat?"

"Once. But not a little boat. Commercial freighter, like the size of a small town. Couldn't even tell when we left the dock." They walked back towards the car. "So what'd you tell them? The rich guys at the club?"

"Oh," he said, smiling again. "Did some checking before I talked to them, asked around the docks. Found a nice boat that's owned by a fat-ass law firm. Every one of these clubs have a couple of 'em, you know. Law firms, lobbyist groups, multinational corporations and the like—they love to own the big, expensive boats. And they hardly ever use them."

"So you found one?"

He nodded. "Yeah, nice boat that gets taken out only once or twice a month. Just sits there, mostly."

"So we're just going to take it?"

"Yeah, no problem."

"No problem?"

"Yeah. I told them we'd be taking it out for a long weekend. For the kids," Julius said.

"The kids?"

"Yeah, the orphans. Told them the firm was donating time on the boat for the diocese to take a bunch of orphans out for a spiritual sailing experience. They loved it. I implied that the orphans were of the minority type. They love that, you know."

"I'm sure. Until somebody makes some phone calls. Which they've probably been doing while we have our little stroll here." Grace ate another Twizzler.

"Exactly. Had to give them time to get comfortable with the idea, not make it look like we're just buzzing off all suspicious like." Grace looked at him quizzically. "Gave them Steve's number, as a reference."

"Father Steve? Your next door neighbor Steve?"

"Yeah, hunky Steve. He loves this kind of shit."

"They'll call the firm."

"I called first, told her I was a consultant, out of the Washington office. Secretary could care less. She never gets invited on the boat. She'll forward the call to Steve. At the orphanage."

"Not bad. Might work."

"It'll work. Of course it'll work. I'm a priest."

"You told these guys you're a priest? You used your real name?"

"Sure did. Had to. Even wore the collar." He pulled it out of his pocket and waggled it at her.

"You are so screwed, Julius. You shouldn't have done that."

"Hey, had to. Worked for the narcotics, didn't it? Everybody trusts a priest, you know."

"I don't."

"I know. It's one of the reasons I love you, Grace."

Grace abruptly stopped walking. Julius and Jack stopped a couple of steps later. Both turned to look back at her, puzzled. Grace was bright red, her hands balled into fists at her sides. "What?" he asked.

"Don't do that, Julius." He walked back to her. He took her hand and gently unfolded her fist, smoothing her palm with his thumbs. She stood stock still, rigid and flushed red as a stop sign. "Don't do this," she repeated, more softly. "In a few days, Julius, I won't be here. I'll be gone. Dead and gone."

"I know."

"Then stop."

"Too late." He bent to kiss her, but she shook her head dismissively and pushed him away. She stalked quickly ahead to the car, Jack and Julius following. As she walked, she dropped the bag of Twizzlers onto the road.

Quirky.

Pauley walked across the dark campus from the hotel, hands thrust deeply in his pockets. His right hand ached, preventing him from thinking about anything else but the girl. He didn't care what Parnell called it, or what the man thought. Pauley regretted even telling him. So much for trying to do the decent thing.

The more Pauley considered the prospect of the girl's excision, the more appropriate it seemed. She was, to his mind, a perfect candidate for this solution. She was almost isolated, recently dead. In her past life, she was orphaned, her parents unknown. Her only relative, her twin sister, had died as a child. He felt a sharp pain in his chest as he recalled that fact, but pretended it was just the whiskey revisiting him. The girl had been married, of course. But she had no children; her husband, too, was dead. She was indeed a perfect candidate for excision. Pauley was careful not to analyze his feelings too closely, but the more he considered the girl's fate, the more comfortable he was.

Pauley was initially headed to his small apartment on campus, but detoured toward his office. He remembered that he had no whiskey left at home and thought it best to stop at the office to pick up the half-empty bottle he had left there. Pauley labored up the steps to the floor of his office and, starting down the hallway, noticed light spilling from the doorway at the end of the hall. He paused, considering. Odd, he thought, I'm sure I locked that door. Perhaps not, though, what with being so distracted and all. He was uncomfortable, however, as he approached the open door. Pauley peered in cautiously and saw a disheveled black man sitting in the chair across from his desk. He watched the man for a minute, but it seemed that the man was just staring at his empty desk chair. The bottle of whiskey sat on the desk in front of him. Pauley considered turning to leave. He could always buy another bottle of whiskey.

"Come for your friend here, Pauley?" the man asked. "Don't just stand there in the hall, Peter. Come have a drink with your only friend in the world."

Pauley took a step into the room, looking at the man. The man stank to high heaven, Pauley noticed. "I don't think I know you, friend," Pauley said amiably.

"Not me, you murderous, child raping bastard. I was referring to this fine bottle of whiskey here, the only true friend you've ever had."

Pauley clenched his fists in his pockets and seethed. "Who are you? How did you get in here?" he demanded.

The man turned to face Pauley. "How the hell did you get in here, Pauley? Murdering rector molestor, Professor drunkard—how'd you ever get in here? Sit your ass down, Pauley, before I sit it down for you."

"I'll call security. Get out of my office!"

"Sit your ass down or I'll bite off one of your other fingers, you self-loathing scum!" Pauley was stunned, deflated, his legs suddenly weak beneath him. Pauley reached for the desk to keep from folding to the ground, barely managing to drop into the desk chair across from the stranger. "Security, my granny's ass. Any security ever found out who the fuck you really are, Pauley, probably have you crucified or something," the man muttered, almost to himself. They stared at one another.

"I don't know who you are," Pauley said, afraid of the man for some reason that he couldn't identify. The man looked ancient, white haired and lean—hardly threatening in his appearance.

"Well, tough shit. I know who you are. I know you well, you miserable maggot of a man. I know you very well, indeed. And I know what you and yours are fixing to do."

"I don't understand—"

"Shut up," the man said with a menacing crack of his palm on the desk. The bottle of whiskey rocked, threatening to fall over. "Shut up, shut up, shut up! Got no time for the likes of you. You understand me fine, I'm sure. You got a question when we're done here, you can read your little magicky book," he continued, pointing a boney finger at Pauley's chest.

"Who are you?"

"Uriel."

"Earle?"

"Close enough."

"Earle who? How do I know you?"

"No who, no how. You wouldn't know me if you did, not in this world or any other. You're not fit to smell my stink, you lowlife vermin." Pauley gaped at the man, reeling from both the man's vehemence and his odor. "Yeah, you don't know me. Truth is, I know you and I know what you think you can do, but you can't. You can't and you won't. You think, woo-hoo, girl gonna be excised, girl gonna be cut out of the fabric of my life, gone, gone, gone for good, and she'll never have been, so I never raped her skinny twelve year old ass all those times, over and over, while she screamed bloody murder. Oh, and oh, murder never happened either, since she being cut out of the universe, maybe I never killed her little sister, sweet sister, either, on that cold, grey winter day. Cold day in hell, I say. All gone and now Pauley's a new man, a clean man, a sweet sanctimonious clergy man. No, no, no! Not going to happen, Pauley. Not going to happen! You are what you are. You hear me?" the man snarled with broken teeth at him, half rising from his chair, Pauley cowering. The crazy old black man grabbed the bottle of whiskey and smashed it on the desk, shards of glass flying and yellow liquid spraying, a pool running off the desk onto Pauley's lap. The man pointed the broken neck of the bottle at Pauley's nose. "Not going to happen," he said again. He continued in a hoarse whisper:

"Line in nature is not found,
Unit and universe are round,
In vain produced, all rays return,
Evil will bless, and ice will burn."

"You know what I'm saying, Pauley?" Pauley could only shake his head, clutching the desk before him as an anchor. He felt dizzy, nauseated. Pauley thought he felt a deep rumbling from outside the windows of the office, thought he heard the windows rattle around him. "I'm saying, Father Pauley, that if any harm comes to the girl, I come for you. The universe is round, Pauley, a spiral up and down, you see? You think it's straight? It ain't straight. No straight lines, Pauley. It turns and it's turning. And when next it turns—next turn, next turn—I will find you. I will find you, Pauley! Do you hear me?"

At this, Pauley could only nod.

"Good," the man said, standing. Pauley flinched as the old man flung the glass shard onto the desk. And then the strange man left.

Julius and Jack caught up to Grace as she climbed into the car's passenger seat. She didn't say anything as Julius started the car, Jack settling down in the back seat. Julius drove them back to the yacht club. He drove slowly along the access road to the row of docks, coming to a stop at the farthest slip. It was a beautiful late afternoon, but there seemed to be no one about. He turned off the engine.

"What do you think?" Julius asked, turning to look at Grace.

"Think of what?" she asked, stirred from her reverie and looking at him, sad and confused. Julius was grinning like a six year old on Christmas morning. He nodded at the boat docked in the slip. She looked over and stared in disbelief. "You gotta be shittin' me. That?" He nodded, still smiling broadly. "No way. Are you crazy?"

"Come on," Julius said, opening the door and climbing out. He came around and pulled Grace out of the car, leading her by the hand onto the dock. Jack decided to stay with the groceries.

"Nice, huh?" Julius asked, enjoying her astonishment as he led her up onto the dock to where the boat was tied alongside. "Swan 60, racing rigged, with all the bells and whistles." Grace came to a stop at the edge of the dock.

"You're crazy. We can't steal that."

"Sure we can. It's all set. For the kids, you know." Grace stood stock still, arms crossed, shaking her head.

"Hey, Father!" Julius and Grace turned to see a young man jogging toward them from the other end of the dock.

"Oh, shit," Grace said. "Sure, he says, 'we can steal that,' he says. What am I supposed to do, club him on the head with the crowbar? That what the crowbar's for, Julius?"

Julius was still smiling, turning now to the young man approaching at a trot. "Won't be necessary," Julius said softly.

"Hey, Father," the young man repeated, slowing to a walk as he met them. "Didn't think to see you until tomorrow. Thought you said tomorrow, Father."

"Hey, Mark," Julius said casually.

"Haven't finished with her yet, Father," the young man continued, embarrassed. "Just got her fueled and watered. Her Zodiac is still out for service. Sorry, you said you weren't leaving 'til tomorrow."

"No, Mark, don't worry about it," Julius said. "Just brought some supplies to drop off, so we wouldn't be trying to do too much once we got all the kids with us."

"Oh. Okay." Mark turned to Grace and offered his hand. "Hi. I'm Mark."

"Grace," Grace said, smiling and shaking the man's hand.

"Nice to meet you. Pretty, isn't she?"

"She is that, Mark," Grace said.

"So we're set for first thing in the morning then, Mark?" Julius asked.

Mark nodded. "Yeah, I was just going to tidy her up a little for you. Been almost six weeks since she's been out, I think. Everything's working, though. I'll get the Zodiac back in her garage first thing in the morning."

Julius shook his head. "That'll be great, Mark. Sister Grace and I are just going to lay in some provisions for the morning. We'll straighten her up a little. Thanks." They both stared, smiling, at the young man.

"Well, okay then," Mark said. "Nice to meet you, Sister. Have a nice cruise."

Julius and Grace watched the man trot off back down the dock.

"He seems nice," Grace said, turning back to Julius.

"Yeah. Too nice to hit over the head with a crowbar, I think."

"So, maybe he won't even notice when the boat's gone in the morning."

"Maybe not."

Grace went back to staring at the boat. It was, she thought, the most beautiful machine she'd ever seen; it looked to her like something out of a Hollywood movie, a sixty foot long racing sailboat, graceful grey fiberglass curves, black mast, machined fittings dotted about a grey teak deck. It reminded Grace of the Gulfstream jet she had ridden in once, but much larger, gently rocking before her. She shook her head and whistled softly.

"Come on," Julius said, smiling that he had managed to impress her. He took her hand and helped her aboard.

Grace stepped into the cockpit and looked about at the instruments, the huge, paired black steering wheels, each almost as tall as she, colored rigging lines stretching like tapestry up to the carbon mast towering ahead of her. "Wow," was all she could manage to say, looking about.

"Damn right, wow," Julius said. "I crewed in high school on a smaller version of this boat, raced it all over Lake Michigan. This boat, though—this is something special."

"Maybe we should be stealing something a little less special, Julius."

"Nah. What fun would that be? Why steal a Honda when you can take the Porsche, right?" He winked at her. Grace rolled her eyes.

"What about when they notice that we're gone before morning?"

"I was going to wait until morning. We can sleep on board tonight. Nobody'll notice if we're quiet."

Grace shook her head. "Don't think we should wait. I got a bad feeling."

Julius considered this as he glanced about at the ship. "That's a problem, then. Going to be tough enough sailing her, just the two of us. She's meant for a crew of at least three or four. And that's three or four who know what they're doing. No offense. Pushing off tonight, without time to check her out, check the weather and all...I don't know, Grace."

"Then let's just take something smaller, Julius. Really, we don't need the Porsche this time around." She smiled indulgently at him, but he shook his head, frowning.

"Actually, we do. Even though she's a big boat, she's got all the extras that'll make sailing her a lot easier, especially short-handed. Instead of me having to fly all over hauling on lines, this boat lets me control everything from here. No, this is the only way. But you might be right—we should get moving tonight. We can do this."

"We can?"

"Sure," he said, decided. "You get the provisions stowed away. I've got a lot to do."

Grace moved the car closer to the dock. She carried the groceries and the stuff she had stolen from the hardware store on board in a couple of trips. Jack followed the bag with the steaks without a pause as he jumped the short gap from the dock onto the boat's deck.

"Shit," she heard Julius curse from below deck. Grace followed the cursing down the stairway into the cabin. She whistled softly as she looked around. Everywhere she looked was polished to brilliance; tan leather, white cotton duck, brushed metal fittings, polished teak. Grace came down the last step and walked over to the desk. Julius was seated in front of a console with a bank of gauges and displays, all dark. He looked worried as he pulled at the various drawers and cabinets. All were locked.

"Problem, Captain Kirk?" He looked over at her.

"Yeah, problem."

"Can't find the switch that turns her on?"

"Something like that." He pointed at the plexiglass cover over the electrical panel on the bulkhead. "It's locked. So's the drawer. And I don't see the laptop."

"Laptop? As in computer?"

"Yeah."

"You need a computer to sail this thing?"

"Yeah, Grace, we need a computer. Check weather, lay in our course, work our position. A dozen things."

"Can't sail without it, huh?" He shook his head. "Then it's got to be here, somewhere. Probably in the drawer."

"That's what I'm hoping. Since the boat's taken out by different people in the firm all the time, makes sense to just leave it locked up on board."

"Sure."

"Key phrase, pardon the pun, is locked up."

"I'll get the wrecking bar. Just take a minute."

Julius looked at her aghast. "What, are you crazy? We're not going to bust open the console."

"Why not?"

He just shook his head. "We need to pick the lock or something."

Grace laughed at that. "Yeah, right. You don't want to do it the hard way? Fine. Key's probably here, too. Is there a fridge on board?"

"Sure there is."

"You look in the fridge?" she asked. He shook his head. "Check." Julius got up out of the director's chair and walked back past her to the galley. He opened the refrigerator door. After a minute, he pulled his head out, smiling. He held up the key to her. "Egg drawer."

She nodded. "This sailing thing ain't so hard."

Julius came back and unlocked the drawer. He pulled out the laptop stowed there. "Bingo. We're in business. Listen, Grace, I've got some work to do before we can get underway. Can you stow all the provisions there in the galley?" he said.

"What about the car?" she asked.

"Don't think it'll fit."

"We have to ditch it. When they find Pauley's car here, they'll know we stole the boat."

"Yeah, so?"

"So they'll come after us, that's what."

"By then, it won't matter."

"It won't?" He shook his head. "You sure? Because I can roll it into the water. Might be fun."

"Not necessary. And somebody might notice, car in the water and all. Why don't you just park it somewhere inconspicuous. Not in the water, though."

"You sure?" He nodded. "Maybe I should just switch the plates, though. Just in case. Won't take a minute."

"Whatever you think, Grace. I got to do some stuff here, okay?"

"Sure. You lay in our course, Mr. Sulu. I'll just take care of the car and all. Don't mind me."

Grace went back up on deck. Jack was stretched out in the sun, sleeping. Grace stepped over him, carrying the groceries down into the cabin. She stowed their supplies and provisions.

"Hey, Julius," she called over. "Sorry to interrupt, but the fridge isn't cold. Steaks'll go bad."

He didn't look up from the computer, but said, "Don't worry about it. It'll cool down when we get the diesel fired up. Steaks?" he asked, looking up over the laptop screen.

"Diesel? I thought this was a sailboat."

"You're kidding, right?" She shook her head. "This is going to be a problem."

"What's going to be a problem?" He shook his head and bent to squint at the laptop screen again. "Going to ditch the car now, hon." Julius waved, still squinting at the screen.

Grace stepped over the dog on her way out to the dock. She started the car and drove it over to the only other car in the lot. She didn't like doing this in daylight, but didn't think she had a choice. Julius was right, it might look a little funny just driving the car into the water. People might notice.

Grace fished the screwdriver out of her stolen tool bag. She squatted behind the car and nonchalantly switched plates with the other car. No one seemed to notice. Actually, no one seemed around at all. She drove the car to the rear of the yacht club, parking behind the clubhouse next to the dumpster. Might take them a while to notice the car back here, she thought. When they went looking for a car fitting Pauley's description, they'd see that the plates didn't match the car they were looking for and hopefully just move on. No reason for them to actually run the plates and find out that the plates were registered to an entirely different make and model. Hopefully. Grace locked up the car and dropped the keys into the tool bag, then walked with her bag at a leisurely, yacht club-like pace back up towards the docks.

When Grace got back on board their boat (she smiled as she thought of it as 'their boat'), she saw Julius purposefully moving about the deck, muttering to himself as he pulled open hatches and peered into various lockers. She watched as Jack followed him about the deck with his stubby tail wagging, helping Julius coil ropes and following lines in various directions, then returning to the cockpit where Grace stood, watching. The lights were on around the cabin now, she noticed.

"Found the switch to turn the boat on, huh?" she asked.

"Yeah, the same key unlocked the breaker panel. But we're just on battery. Still got to fire up the diesel."

"Okay, Cap'n Crunch. Let's fire her up, then. Gotta get those steaks cold, you know."

"Yeah. This might be a problem."

"How so? Where's the ignition?"

"There isn't."

"Oh. Easy then."

"Maybe." Julius moved over to the starboard side of the cockpit and ran his hand over the bank of switches relating to the engine. "Here we go." He flipped a switch and then jammed the red button next to it. Nothing happened.

"Pretty quiet for a diesel," Grace said.

"Shit. That's what I was afraid of."

"Which is what, exactly?"

"Kill switch," Julius said.

"Where?"

"Don't know. Could be hidden in about a hundred places."

"Should we look in the fridge again?"

"Not in the fridge."

"The bathroom?"

"The head."

"Whose head? What?"

"Doesn't matter. We don't have time to go looking for it. We gotta get moving, before it gets dark."

"Okay. Show me where this diesel is hidden. It's not under water, is it?" He led her down the steps into the cabin. He pulled her into the galley. "It's in the fridge?"

"No, it isn't in the fridge. Just step over here for a second." Julius pulled two latches and raised the stairway, pointing into the engine compartment.

"Oh. Cool." Grace peered into the space for a couple of minutes. "Need my tools."

Julius had to lower the steps back down to let Grace back up on deck. She came back down with her stolen tool bag of stolen tools. Julius raised the steps again. Grace peered about, pulling herself halfway into the tight compartment. "Hand me the torch," she called back to Julius, holding her hand back behind her.

"Torch? What are you, nuts? You'll blow us up."

"What are you, an idiot? Just give me the light thing, whatever you call it."

"The flashlight?"

"Yeah, that thing. Give it to me." He handed her the flashlight from the bag. She hummed to herself as she crawled further into the compartment.

"Can you hotwire it? Is that possible?" Julius asked, trying to get his head into the small compartment.

"Don't think it'll be necessary," he heard, muffled by the engine compartment. "Diags," she called back, extending her hand behind her again.

"What are they?"

"Look like pliers, kind of."

"Oh. Got it. Here." He handed her the smaller pair of diagonals.

After two minutes of grunting, interspersed with a steady stream of cursing and complaints about whether they could make this compartment any fucking smaller, Grace climbed back out, her face and arms smeared with grease. "Try it now."

"Really?"

She nodded. "Think so. Give it a shot."

They replaced the stairway and went topside again.

"Here we go," Julius said, briefly crossing himself. He punched the red button again. The diesel fired up at once. They smiled at one another and Julius gave her a high five. "Nice! What'd you do?"

"Found a couple of wires that looked like it was probably going off to that kill switch of yours. Just shorted across them."

"Can we leave it like that? Is it safe?"

"Should be. Don't see why not."

"Just to let you know, Grace: Fire on a boat—not good."

"It'll be okay. Probably. Pretty sure."

Julius was about to comment further when he noticed the police cruiser. "Hey, Grace." She looked up.

"Aww, shit."

"You believe in coincidences?"

"Never."

"Yeah, neither do I," he said as they watched the cruiser slowly track through the nearly empty parking lot. "Guess Pauley got tired of waiting for me to return his car."

"Didn't take very long to find us here. How is that possible?" she asked, watching the police car as she stood next to Julius, hands on hips.

"Told you—his book. He pretty much knows everything we do, sometimes before we do it."

Grace shook her head. "That's not possible." He shrugged at her and nodded pointedly at the police car, now moving farther away towards the clubhouse.

"We should probably be going," he deadpanned.

"Couldn't agree more, Captain Picard. Let's push off or whatever you call it—oh, fuck me!" She was looking about the deck, suddenly looking very upset.

"What?"

"Did you bring the bag from the car?"

"What bag?"

"Parnell's duffle, you idiot! Did you bring it on board?"

"No, Grace. You were bringing the stuff from the car, remember? That was your job." She turned bright red as they watched the police car.

"Don't get snippy with me, Julius. A simple 'no' would've been fine. I gotta go back to the car."

"No way, Grace. They're heading straight for it."

"Can't leave the bag, Julius. I'll be right back. Shit!"

"What now?"

"Need the keys." She jumped down the companionway to retrieve the keys from the tool bag.

Julius watched the police car disappear around the back of the clubhouse. "Don't want to sound snippy or anything," he called down to her, "but you're not going to make it, Grace." Grace pounded up the steps two at a time and went running past Julius and jumped back onto the dock without breaking stride.

"Prepare to dive, Cap'n Nemo," she called back to him as she sprinted back to the car.

Grace ran around the far side of the clubhouse and crouched in the bushes. The police car had come to a stop about ten feet behind Pauley's car, flashers now lit. From what she could see, there was just one cop inside the car. Grace thought about waiting him out, to see if he'd leave since the plates didn't match the car he was looking for. If she gave him too much time, though, and he decided to run the plates, she'd be screwed. She walked quickly over to the police car and knocked on the door. The cop lowered the window.

"Hey, officer," she said, smiling at him. "Is there a problem?"

"Who are you?" He wasn't smiling back.

Grace pointed at the back of the clubhouse. "I'm Liz. I work in the kitchen."

"That your car?"

She shook her head. "No, it belongs to the cook. Just need to get his bag out of the car, okay?" She jangled the keys at him.

"What's the cook's name?"

"Pete. But we call him Cookie. Why?"

"Just checking. Go ahead," he added, gesturing at the car.

Grace unlocked the car and retrieved the bag. She gave a wave to the cop as she carried the bag into the clubhouse through the back door. Once the door closed behind her, Grace went running, bag over her shoulder, through the hallway and out the front door. She ran back across the parking lot towards the docks. Grace was running flat out as she saw Julius standing on the deck, watching her. She gestured frantically as she ran, shouting, "Go, Go, Go!" She threw the bag on board and jumped from the dock into the cockpit. "Go!" she yelled at him again.

"You're kidding, right?"

"No," she said, "not," she gasped, "kidding! Go!" she said weakly, out of breath and waving at him as she stood bent double, trying to catch her breath.

"Okay, then," Julius said. "Here we go!" He took his position behind the wheel. "Cast off fore and aft!" he yelled. Grace just stood looking at him, her chest still heaving. "Cast off fore and aft," he said to her again. "Grace!"

"Yeah?"

"Cast off."

"What exactly are you talking about, Julius?" She stood with hands on hips, having recovered her breath. She was looking past Julius, waiting to see the police cruiser appear from behind the clubhouse.

"The lines, cast off the lines!" Julius turned to look where she was staring and saw the police car, lights flashing, swing around from behind the clubhouse. It was moving slowly, however, obviously not sure where Grace had run off to. "Shit!" Julius said, stepping up on deck.

"Agreed," Grace said, sitting down in the cockpit out of sight. She watched as Julius ran to the front of the boat and untied the mooring line from the dock. He jumped aft and was repeating the process as Grace watched the police car slowly progressing down the line of docks toward them. "Might want to make haste, Captain Morgan."

"Yeah, well, I could use a little help here, Grace. This isn't a one man show, you know."

"Well, if you want me to help, then you can't be doing your Captain Blye imitation, matey. Next time try, 'Hey, Grace, untie those two ropes that are holding the boat to the dock.' And a 'please' thrown in once in a while wouldn't hurt, either." He paused as he took the wheel and looked at her.

"Really?"

She pointed at the cruiser, now only one row of docks away. She hunkered down behind the gunnel and yelled, "Gun it, Captain Jack!"

"Here we go!" he yelled back. Julius pushed the throttle to full ahead. "Yee ha! Hold on, Grace!" The boat slowly eased away from the dock.

Grace watched, incredulous. "You're kidding, right?" They were barely two feet from the dock, moving at a crawl. "That's it?"

Julius nodded. "Yeah, Buttercup. Some getaway, huh?"

"Julius, I can walk faster than this. Give it some gas, will you? He's almost here!"

"I see that," Julius said. He waved at the cop as the cruiser pulled up to the dock. "This is flat out, Princess. Stay down."

"You think?" She shook her head. "Maybe I should lean forward, get us some momentum."

"Shut up or I'll make you start rowing."

"Probably go faster."

Julius smiled as the cop waved back. It wasn't clear if the cop was trying to get him to stop; actually, Julius was pretty sure that was exactly what the cop was indicating, but chose to just wave back and smile. "Goodbye, sucker. Have a nice day!" he muttered. Julius turned back to the wheel and concentrated on getting the huge vessel into the offing without hitting anything. He didn't look back. "What's he doing?"

"Nothing. Just shaking his head. Looks like he's heading back to the clubhouse."

"Great."

Grace sat up on the bench now that the police cruiser had headed back up the parking lot. "You think they can stop us? Blow us out of the water or something?" She looked ahead as Julius guided the boat out into the bay.

"If they really want to, sure. He can call the Coast Guard, bottle us up here in the bay, if he wants. Wouldn't worry about it much."

"No?"

Julius shook his head as he stood at the big wheel, smiling. He was obviously enjoying himself immensely. "No, don't think it's a problem. What's he going to tell them? You gotta have a damn good reason to mobilize the Coast Guard to commandeer a private boat. He didn't see you, can't be sure you're even aboard. He's not even that interested in getting ahold of you, even if he does figure out you're aboard this boat. Not like you killed anyone or anything."

"There you go again, making assumptions about me." He laughed at that briefly, then stopped as he glanced at her and realized that she wasn't joking.

"Oh. Well, I think we're okay, anyway."

"You say so, Captain Ahab." Grace settled into the seat next to him, arms behind her head, and watched as Julius brought the big sailboat out into the open water of Chesapeake Bay, blue sky starting to turn orange with the sunset off to their right. She heaved a relieved sigh and relaxed.

CHAPTER 24

Parnell spent the night seething over what Pauley had told him. He tried to work through the complex facets of his current situation, trying to understand the angles being played by all the individuals involved. He just didn't have enough information, not nearly enough to make a rational decision as to how to proceed. Worse yet, Parnell thought that he probably had a better understanding of the situation than any of the other people involved. The only thing that Parnell was certain of was that large, opposing forces were lumbering toward some form of confrontation. It seemed to him that the impending conflict was somehow focused on Helena, or Grace, or whoever she really was. Her excision, as Pauley described it, could only be a disaster.

Pauley was right about a few things, though. Chuck was certain that the priest was correct when he said that the rate of Returns had increased dramatically. Parnell had lived many times himself, as many different individuals. Despite his accumulated centuries of experience, Parnell had never before encountered a Returnee. Yet now he was caught up in the machinations of at least two others he was aware of. Something was definitely going on—something fundamentally had changed to make such a thing not just possible, but common place. What really scared Parnell, as he paced about his little hotel room muttering to himself, is that he had very little insight into what exactly that something was. He was being manipulated, buffeted by outside forces, shunted by the will of others with their own intentions, other goals—he had to make some move, get out of this whirlpool that had him trapped in this hotel room, powerless and vulnerable.

He needed more information in order to act, Parnell thought. Pauley may have his magic book, but Parnell had no such resource. He was on his own. Chuck realized that he was going to have to take some action, force events in some way, in order to even get the information he needed. His first move would have to be a blind one. On the face of it, the easiest and most straightforward action would be to get the girl killed. It was simple, and it had the benefit of being already set in motion. Parnell needed her dead. Obviously, the girl was trying for the same thing: momentum was on his side. Her death would serve his original plan: his plan to publicly expose those manipulating the afterlife. Now that he realized how many and powerful were the forces involved, however, this first plan seemed pretty naive. 'No battle plan survives the first shot,' it was always said. Parnell realized that his was already out the window, even before the battle had begun. No, he couldn't just let events take their course. If Pauley and his Church managed to excise the girl, or even if she managed to destroy his evidence before she died, his leverage was lost. He didn't think he'd survive very long after that eventuality. As Parnell paced in tightening circles in the room, he realized he was alone, his hand far too weak. Hell, he didn't even have the proof in his possession at this point. Parnell knew that he'd have to take the initiative, somehow. He'd have to ally with one of the other, more powerful, forces in play. But which one, and how to do it? He sat down on the side of the bed, thinking. His options, Parnell realized, were few. He'd just have to play the few cards he held, as weak as they were. Parnell was pretty good at bluffing, and he was always at his best when he made the big, risky play. Parnell nodded to himself in the mirror, decided. He felt in his pockets for his cellphone, now that he knew what to do. "Damn it," he said sullenly. "That dumb bastard never even gave me my phone back."

Pauley remained seated at his desk, watching whiskey drip onto his lap. The stench of the other man still hung in the air, mixing with the pungent smell of alcohol. Pauley was having a hard time catching his breath. His head was pounding, his chest ached. For a few minutes, he could think of nothing to do but breathe. Finally, and with an effort, he brought out the book and found his page. He scanned for a bit, backwards and ahead, but there was nothing to tell him how to proceed. He leaned on the desk, recoiling with a curse as a glass shard pierced his elbow. He brushed it off and replaced the book inside his coat pocket. With a resigned sigh, Pauley heaved himself up out of his chair. He brushed debris from his lap and walked, pieces of glass crunching beneath his shoes, from his office. Whatever he was going to do, he thought, it would have to wait until morning. Tonight he was too tired, and too old. He went home.

Julius stood with one hand on the big wheel of the boat as they smoothly motored down the middle of the bay. He hadn't stopped beaming since gaining the main channel without incident. It had occurred to him how much more fun this was than rowing. Julius still didn't know what the hell was going on, what he gotten himself into, but he felt reinvigorated, the excitement of his former self rushing back. He ran his free hand through his hair and looked about. Jack was still sprawled asleep in front of him on the main deck, the teak darkening around him with drool. Grace smiled back at Julius from where she lay along side in the cockpit, propped up on a cushion so she could look about. The water was smooth and there was a pleasant breeze blowing across the deck, trailing her cloud of red hair behind her.

"So this is sailing," Grace said.

Julius shook his head. "No, it isn't. But I don't think I can sail this in the bay without getting us into trouble. At least, I don't want to try, particularly since it's going to be dark soon."

"What kind of trouble?"

"Crashing into something trouble."

"Oh." She watched the water and the birds and the shore drift by as the sky deepened slowly to purple.

"Make a wish," Julius said, pointing with his free hand at a star off the left side of the bow.

"I wish we don't crash into something." Julius nodded at this, wishing for the same thing. "So we stop when it gets dark?" Grace asked.

Julius shook his head. "We can't. We have to make it out of the bay and into open water before they figure out we stole their boat."

"Isn't that kind of dangerous? Do we have headlights?"

Julius laughed at this and shook his head. "No, Grace. No headlights. Come over here, I'll show you." Grace got up and walked over to stand next to him. Julius pointed out the displays on the cantilevered instrument pod in front of them. "This is the GPS, and this is us. That line is our course, pretty much down the middle of Chesapeake Bay. And this," he said, tapping the next display over, "is the radar. This and this is the shore on either side of us. Any other boats ahead should show up on the display."

"Looks easy enough," she said, sitting down next to him behind the wheel.

"It is. Right up until it isn't." Grace nodded, knowing exactly what he meant.

"Where are we going?" she asked, tapping the large, black domed compass on the console in front of them. "I'm no sailor, but from what I remember, New York used to be north of Baltimore. Looks like we're heading south, Captain Sparrow."

Julius chuckled. "You already used that one."

"No, I didn't."

"Yes, you did. You called me Captain Jack, back in dock. Captain Jack Sparrow."

"I meant a different Captain Jack," Grace said.

"There is no other Captain Jack."

"There must be another Captain Jack," she said. "Billy Joel song."

"Doesn't count," Julius said, shaking his head.

"Fine," she said, "have it your way, Captain Corrigan. We're going the wrong way."

"No, we're not. Your captain is a brilliant seaman. You need to appreciate that."

"Oh, really? We taking the southern route, going round the horn, are we, Captain Aubrey? Hey, that's another Jack. Lucky Jack Aubrey, of His Majesty's Royal Navy."

Julius shook his head. "I think it was John Aubrey. And he wasn't a real captain. You want to bring up the laptop, I could show you."

Grace was enjoying the sunset too much to move. "I'll take your word for it. Just tell me. And I got news for you—there was never a real Jack Sparrow, either, genius."

He chose to ignore this. "So everybody knows we're going to New York, right?" Grace nodded. "Well, like you said, New York is north. Anybody sailing Baltimore to New York takes the C and D canal, cuts east into the Delaware River and then it's a straight shot up the coast."

"Anybody who knows how to navigate, you mean."

"Exactly. You could make the whole run up the Intercoastal Waterway, just like driving on the parkway. Probably make it in less than twenty-four hours."

"Doesn't sound like much fun."

"It isn't. And too dangerous, for us at least. Too easy to find us, we could be stopped anywhere along the way."

"So we're going exactly where, instead?"

"South, like you noticed. Clear the Chesapeake Bay and head out into open ocean. Probably even head a little farther south, just to be sure we're clear."

"Really? Open ocean? Is that going to be fun?"

"Depends. You get seasick?"

"I don't know. Feel fine so far."

"Yeah. This doesn't count. But I think we're going to be okay. The only thing that really matters is the weather, and it looks like we're going to get lucky with the weather."

Grace was about to comment on her usual experience with luck when Jack appeared and stood staring up at Grace. Grace stared back. "I think he needs to go out, if you know what I mean."

"That could be a problem."

Parnell dressed the next morning in his white suit. It was wrinkled, which upset him, but it was still better than wearing Georgetown athletic gear for what he had to do today. Parnell didn't bother to check out, seeing as he had no luggage anyway. He just gave a nod to the desk clerk as he crossed the lobby to the entrance. He ducked into a waiting taxi.

"Mormon temple, please, on the Beltway."

The driver turned around to look at him. "Visitor center? Not open yet, I think."

"Not the visitor center. The temple."

The driver shook his head. "They don't let nobody in the temple. Just the visitor center."

"Yeah, thanks for the information. Can we go now?"

"Why do you want to go there if they're not gonna let you in?"

Parnell sighed with exasperation. "They'll let me in, don't worry about it, okay? Can you just drive me there? You are a taxi driver, right? That is what you do?"

The driver shrugged as he turned forward and started the car. "No need to get snippy, now. Just trying to save you some money and a wasted trip, is all. Hey, suit yourself." He pulled away from the hotel. Parnell gritted his teeth, waiting for the inevitable. "So, you're one of them, then, are you?"

Here we go, Parnell thought. He considered pretending that he hadn't heard the question, but the driver was staring intently at him through the rear view mirror. Hell, he thought, if I don't answer this guy it looks like he's never going to look where he's going. "Yeah, I'm a member of the Church of Latter-Day Saints, if that's what you're asking."

"That what you call yourselves? Saints, huh?" Parnell nodded at the man. "Is it true that you folks believe that Jesus was a space alien and you all are going to be a god on your own private planet after you die?"

"That's right." Parnell had heard a great many misconceptions about his adopted religion in his travels. He had long ago assumed the approach of agreeing with whatever twisted, crazed misinterpretation with which he was confronted. It had proven much easier than trying to explain his religion, much of which was fairly inexplicable. Also, just as effective.

"Huh." The driver seemed to be digesting this admission as he drove on, considering his next question. "Is it true that you have to wear special underwear?" Parnell nodded as he looked out the window at DC streets passing by. They always asked about the underwear. "Really? You wearin' 'em right now?"

"Sure am," Parnell lied.

"Ain't that something. What's so special 'bout them underwear, anyway?"

"Really, really comfortable. Silk, actually."

"That's it? Comfortable?"

"We believe that a man cannot be truly spiritual if his nuts are all twisted, you understand me?"

The driver nodded appreciatively while looking at Parnell in the mirror, trying to tell if he was joking. "I see," he said gravely, shifting in his seat as he merged his taxi onto the highway.

"They also serve as kind of a suit for traveling between worlds," Parnell added.

"Seriously?" Parnell nodded gravely at the man looking at him in the mirror. "Other worlds, huh?"

"Seriously. Lots of other worlds. In the afterlife, you see. We have to be prepared at all times to make the journey."

"No shit?"

At that moment—they were making good time, the Belt Parkway being unusually devoid of traffic—Parnell saw the gold-tipped spires of the Mormon Temple loom ahead through the windshield, bright godly white in the morning sun. It was an inspirational sight. In the next instant, Parnell saw the span of a green railway bridge crossing over the expressway, perfectly aligned below the temple. In tall black letters across the bridge, it said, "Surrender, Dorothy!"

Parnell looked at the driver in the mirror. "Did you see that?" he demanded of the driver.

"See what?" the driver said, looking again at the traffic ahead as they sped under the bridge.

"On the bridge. It said, 'Surrender, Dorothy.' Did you see?"

"Oh, that. Ain't nothing. Always says that."

"It does?" Parnell asked.

"Yup. They keep painting it over, and it keeps coming back," the driver explained.

"It does? For how long?"

"Oh, years. Gotta be more'n forty years, since before I started driving this taxi."

"No. Really?" The driver nodded. "Who's doing it? What does it mean?"

"Nobody knows. Just there, is all."

"That's crazy," Parnell muttered, almost to himself.

"You say so. Ask me, not much crazier than wearing spacesuit underwear all the time."

But Parnell hadn't heard this last comment. He was lost in his own thoughts, because Parnell was suddenly and completely convinced that the message on the bridge was for him. He knew in a flash of certainty that the girl—the girl he knew as Helena for most of his life, that Zimmerman kept calling Grace—was his Dorothy. Parnell had watched the Wizard of Oz every birthday as a child, always in the company of his mother, and he loved that movie. During his childhood, he had been terribly frightened by the scene where the Wicked Witch writes that very phrase in the sky over Oz, suddenly shattering the peace and happiness that his heroes had finally found in the Emerald City. Forty-something years the driver had said, and Parnell knew that someone had been writing that phrase over and over in anticipation of this exact moment, when he would come over the rise to see that bridge, with his temple, shining in the sunlight—a message for him in particular.

The girl was Dorothy, trapped in a strange world and trying to get back home, Parnell believed. He himself was a player in this story, was responsible in some way for her plight, he felt certain. Parnell didn't know, however, what exactly his role was, what he was supposed to do; he knew, however, that he was supposed to somehow help her get home. He stared ahead at the approaching temple spires and pictured it as his Oz, his drama unfolding. Looking at it, he was seized with the impression that the temple really did look remarkably like the castle from the movie. Parnell stared ahead in amazement. He would play his part. He would have to protect her, somehow; protect her, and help her get home. Not to Kansas, but back home to her own world. Parnell shook his head; suddenly it all seemed so black and white.

The taxi pulled up to the temple and Parnell paid his fare. He walked past the visitor's center and entered the temple proper. He was immediately greeted by the temple matron, a stout, middle-aged woman dressed in white. She approached Parnell with a smile worthy of a tax auditor.

"Can I help you?" she asked.

"You certainly can, Matron," Parnell said, offering his hand. "I am Dr. Charles Parnell, Elder of the Church and President of the Council of Seventy."

The woman gave Parnell a cursory handshake.

"How can I help you?" she asked again.

"I wish to avail myself of the temple's resources this morning, Matron."

"You wish to what?"

"I need to enter." She looked at him suspiciously, pointedly eyeing his wrinkled suit and unpolished shoes. "Really," Parnell added.

"I'll need to see your Recommend," she said, fixing him with a steely gaze, arms crossed over her ample bosom.

"You're not serious. I told you who I am."

"Well, I'm sorry, Doctor, President, whoever. You will not enter the temple until I see your Recommend."

Parnell fished his wallet out of his back pocket and pawed through the contents. "Haven't been asked for my Recommend in over five years, woman."

"Well, maybe you should go to temple a little more often, Doctor."

"That's not what I meant," he said, handing over his dog-eared card. She eyed it closely for much longer than what was obviously necessary. "I had hair then," Parnell added, trying to be pleasant.

The matron handed back his card and turned her back to walk into the temple. Parnell followed the woman into her office. He took a seat across from her desk, careful to wait until the woman had seated herself. She stared at him.

Parnell cleared his throat. "As I was saying, I am on church business. Actually, this is something of an emergency. I will need to communicate with our home temple."

"Will you?" the woman asked. Parnell nodded, adding a weak smile. "Just how do you plan on doing that, Mr. President? I'm sorry, Doctor President. Elder Parnell."

"I'll need to use one of your offices."

"By whose authority?"

"Why, by yours, of course," Parnell said, smiling.

"Indeed." She didn't smile, however. Instead, she made a dismissive motion with her hand and continued, "Have a seat outside while I figure out exactly what you are."

Parnell nodded and headed back to the lobby. He didn't expect to wait long.

Pauley gathered his wits sufficiently to begin sending several messages. He arranged for one of the other priests to take over Zimmerman's class, suspecting that Zimmerman was not going to be back for a while; maybe never. And as he would not be around for a while himself, Pauley asked one of the other senior Jesuit faculty to assume his responsibilities as rector 'for an indefinite period.' Without even consulting his book, Pauley felt confident that 'an indefinite period' was pretty accurate. Finally, he arranged for transportation and a room in the archdiocese in New York. He thought about contacting the Cardinal's office to inform them of his impending arrival, but thought better of it; more than likely, he thought, they already knew.

Pauley kept fingering the book in front of him on the desk, riffling the pages but making no attempt to read any. He was concerned that he had let too many in on this particular secret. At the time, he had no other way to get Zimmerman to help him; he felt he had no choice. But Zimmerman was right—the book had been entirely wrong about the bomb. Why? Had there been a bomb, but something they did changed events sufficiently to make it disappear? Was the bomb passage just a device to accomplish his goal of goading Zimmerman? Pauley didn't know, and not knowing disturbed him. The book, at times, seemed to have a mind of its own, maybe even its own agenda in the events unfolding.

If there ever was a bomb, certainly Parnell must have put it there. No one else had access to the bag. It would make sense: Parnell needed the girl dead, or his proof of an afterlife was trashed, his leverage lost. Parnell didn't seem like the type to be planting bombs, but the only thing that Pauley was sure of was that Parnell was not the man he appeared to be. He had said as much: "Not my real name, you know." Obviously. But what was his real name, who was he really? If there was a bomb, what had they done to make it disappear? The more Pauley thought about it, the less likely it seemed that there ever was a bomb; how could a bomb be inside a bag that Parnell had carried on a plane? No bomb then, just the idea of a bomb.

Zimmerman had told Parnell about the book. That was a problem. Pauley hadn't intended to reveal the book's existence to Parnell, didn't think it would be necessary in order to scare the man sufficiently to go along. He was again tempted to open the book, to read ahead for some hint at what was to come, some insight into all these mysteries, but refrained. He knew it would do no good.

And then Pauley thought about the worst thing that was bothering him. It should have been the idea of the girl's excision, that should be the most horrific thing imaginable, but it wasn't. The crazy old black man was right, perfectly right: Pauley loved the idea. After living with the pain and guilt of everything he had done, trying to repent for his unrepentable acts every day of his life and then some, having almost reconciled himself to the purgatory of his unforgivable sins, here suddenly was a way out, a way of cleansing himself completely. It was the most desirable thing he had ever contemplated. It was so much better than forgiveness—it was absolution. But there was so much in the way. Earle, whoever he was, scared him. He didn't know why, but the man scared him down to his very soul. And this Earle, he knew about the book. And Zimmerman. And Parnell. So many people knew, and their knowing was dangerous. It was dangerous because Pauley was pretty sure that if any of them were to get a hold of a copy of *The Problem of God*, they would have full access to the only real advantage he held all this time. He didn't know everything about how the book worked, but he knew enough to know that his wasn't the only copy undergoing changes, that every copy reflected these same alterations. What if one of the others involved stopped by a bookstore and picked up a copy? Not much chance of that, he hoped. He stood up to pack.

Julius spent the night slowly motoring the yacht down the Chesapeake Bay, Grace sleeping intermittently on the cushioned bench alongside the cockpit. With a little coaching, Jack had mastered a technique of standing along the storm rail, raising his leg and peeing overboard. Julius was impressed until Grace pointed out that she doubted the dog was acrobatic enough to poop over the side without falling overboard. They would cross that bridge when the time came.

Shortly after midnight, Grace awoke and watched Julius quietly steering the boat. It was perfectly quiet, save for the muffled drone of the diesel and the sound of water sluicing along the boat's sides, the occasional hoot of an owl, hunting. It was a warm night, and Grace watched the stars as they were eclipsed by Julius's dark silhouette. It was beautiful, and peaceful.

"How're we doing, Cap'n Kangaroo?" she asked quietly.

"We're doing just fine, shipmate. Haven't hit anything yet."

Grace nodded in the dark. "How about I take the wheel for a bit, let you get a couple hours sleep?"

"Thought you didn't know anything about sailing."

"I don't, but it doesn't look too tough. Keep the little dot thing in the middle of the great big bay thing."

"What if you come up on another boat?"

"In the middle of the night? Have you seen any other boats?"

"Nope. Could happen, though."

"Then I'll go around, Julius. Unless there's like a horn I can blow, get 'em to move out of the way. You'll be sleeping right here, I'll let you know if I see anything."

"Fine." He showed her their position on the instruments and let her take the wheel. Julius sat on the bench and watched her steer for a bit.

"Go to sleep."

"You'll wake me if you see anything, a light up ahead or anything on the radar?"

"I'll call you, Julius. Go to sleep."

Julius lay down on the bench. "Wake me up in two hours, tops. Okay?"

"Aye, aye, Captain Courageous. Sweet dreams."

"Dr. Parnell," the matron called to him. "If you please." He hadn't waited long. Parnell rose and approached the matron, smiling. She smiled back. "You might've told me that you were a celebrity, Dr. Parnell."

"Am I?" He followed her back into the temple and past her reception desk.

"It appears so, Dr. Parnell." She gestured him through an open door into the temple president's office. He raised his eyebrows, questioningly.

"Am I waiting for someone?"

"You said that you were in need of the temple's offices. This is an office."

"Yes, I see that."

"Please have a seat. I believe someone will be with you momentarily."

"Really?" She nodded. "Okay, then." The matron gestured to the desk inside. Parnell sat down at the desk.

"Please let me know if you need anything else, Dr. Parnell," the matron said as she left, then closed the door before Parnell had a chance to thank her.

Parnell looked at the desk, looked about the office. There was a computer, the keyboard housed in a shallow drawer, a large flat screen monitor just to the side. Parnell was wondering how he was going to contact anyone in Salt Lake City when the monitor came to life. A man appeared, smiling at him.

"Charles! Great to see you!" Parnell gaped at the screen. He recognized the President of the LDS Church. It took him a moment to respond.

"Prophet! Best wishes to you, Prophet. How—"

"Oh, no need to be so formal, Charles. We're so relieved to hear from you. We were worried."

"You were?"

The man nodded emphatically on the screen, and now Parnell noticed the shadow of someone next to him. "Of course we were, Charles. You just disappeared, without a word. Is everything okay?"

"Yes, yes, just fine, sir. I'm sorry that you were worried, I—"

"So you're in DC. That's great, just great. Listen, Charles, we're just thrilled that you're okay. You need to just sit tight and we'll make arrangements for your return to Salt Lake City this afternoon."

"This afternoon?"

"Sure, won't be any trouble. We're looking forward to talking with you here."

"About what?" Parnell asked.

The other man seemed puzzled at the question and took a moment to respond. "Why, about whatever it is that you want to talk about, Charles."

"We do need to talk, Prophet. But it can't wait until I get back, I'm afraid." Parnell watched as the man on the screen leaned slightly to the side, apparently listening to another man off camera. Parnell couldn't hear what was said.

"It'll only be a few hours, Charles. It might be best to speak when we're together."

"No," Parnell said, shaking his head, "I don't think it can wait, Prophet. It is a matter of great urgency."

"It can't wait, Charles?" The Prophet looked concerned. Parnell shook his head. Parnell saw the shadow on screen lean closer to the Prophet. "What is it that's so important?"

"I have been abducted by the Jesuits here. They are the ones responsible for taking me away from Salt Lake City."

"Abducted? By Jesuits? Why would anyone do such a thing, Charles?"

"They know, Prophet. They know what the Church is doing."

"What are you talking about, Charles? What do they know? What church?"

"Our church, Prophet. They know our secret."

"I'm sure I don't understand what you're talking about, Charles." Parnell saw the shadow of someone gesture sharply off camera.

"Is everything okay, Prophet?"

"Yes, of course. You can speak freely, Charles. This is outrageous, the Jesuits abducting you? But why?"

"The Jesuits here at Georgetown know about Granite Mountain, Prophet."

The Prophet blanched briefly on the screen, an expression of one who had just eaten a bad oyster passing over him. He quickly recovered himself, half smiling and saying, "I'm not surprised, Charles. The Granite Mountain vault is hardly a secret. Of course the Catholics know about our genealogy project, though they're not as upset about it as the Jewish people, you know—"

"Not the genealogy project, Prophet. The other project at Granite Mountain."

A hand appeared on the Prophet's shoulder and he leaned off camera momentarily. When he returned, his face was flushed, his expression stern. "Charles, there is no other project at Granite Mountain. You should know, you spent quite a bit of time there. Our archives, our genealogical records and all. That's all, Charles."

Parnell shook his head forcefully. He could see the shadows of several people moving about quickly at the rear of the room in Salt Lake City.

"You're right, Prophet. I've spent a lot of time at the Granite Mountain facility. I know about the other project. That's not important. What you have to realize, Prophet, is that the activities there are no longer secret. The Catholics, at least the Jesuits here, know. I think they know quite a bit. And they have a project of their own, as well."

The Prophet stared intently at Parnell through the screen, leaning closer to the camera. "What sort of project do they have, Charles?"

"A program of Return, Prophet. A highly sophisticated and established program of crossing back."

"Are you sure?" Parnell nodded. Parnell had indeed spent over two years utilizing the Granite Mountain Facility for his own research into the history of the LDS Church. The facility was enormous, carved like a nuclear bunker into the depths of the mountain range. Publicly, the facility was used to permanently house the genealogical records of the church. But as he rose in rank within the church, and was granted higher levels of freedom within the facility as part of his research, he had come upon large sections of the giant facility that were inaccessible, apparently dedicated to another purpose entirely. Parnell had never been able to directly ascertain what that purpose was, but over the last few months he had made an educated guess.

The other man paused on screen, leaning back in his chair. "In that case, Dr. Parnell," the man said gravely, "it is all the more important that you are back with us as soon as possible. It is important that we discuss all you know on this subject."

Parnell shook his head again. "I'm sorry, Prophet. I can't do that yet. There's something else."

"Something else?"

"Yes, Prophet. Just as important, I believe. Maybe more so, because time is short. It concerns the girl, Helena Fianna."

The other man looked puzzled. "I'm sorry, Charles. Helena something? Should I recognize that name?"

Parnell was impressed with how lousy his president was at lying. "Yes, Prophet. Helena Fianna—the woman was instrumental in the discovery of the techniques the Church utilizes in caring for the mentally ill. She was responsible for gifting the techniques to us. You remember."

"Of course," the Prophet said, now nodding sagely. "I'm sorry. But she's been dead some years now. Am I correct?"

"Yes, Prophet. She died several years ago. It seems, however, that she has Returned." Parnell was certain that he was telling the Prophet nothing he didn't already know.

"Returned? What do you mean?"

Parnell tried not to sigh in exasperation. How long was the man going to play this game? Oh well, it wasn't important. "I mean that she's alive, Prophet. She's alive and in DC." The Prophet made a show of looking confused and surprised. Parnell sighed for real this time. "No matter," Parnell continued. "Here is the important thing, Prophet. The Catholic Church intends to perform an excision upon her. To excise her completely."

At this, Parnell could hear angry, but unintelligible, utterances from the other room, then heard a chair knocked over. The Prophet went nearly apoplectic. He began to stammer something, but was caught by the arm and suddenly leaned out of the camera's view. Parnell saw two men cross behind the Prophet's chair, moving quickly out of sight. He had finally gotten their full attention, Parnell thought.

"I'm not entirely clear on what it is they mean by this excision, Prophet," Parnell continued after a while, having let the commotion on the other end settle somewhat. "But from what I understand, that if they are successful in excising Ms. Fianna as a soul, it might have significant effects upon the Church and our work. I thought it was important that I tell you as soon as I learned of this plan."

"Yes, yes, Charles," the Prophet said, composing himself. "You were right to let us know right away." He looked off camera for a moment, then nodded his head. "Of course, it's all the more important now that we get you back here as fast as possible."

"But I thought that I might better help if I were to stay here, in DC."

"No, no," the Prophet said, shaking his head vigorously. "We'll make arrangements. Where are you staying?" He paused as he listened to the off-camera voice again. "No, it doesn't matter. Just stay at the temple, Charles. That'd be best. Safest and best, I'm sure. We'll make arrangements."

"But, I'm sure—"

"Nothing more to talk about, Charles. Good work. Great work, really. I'll see you tomorrow, then. Here, first thing in the morning. Goodbye, Charles." And with that the screen went white. Parnell leaned back in the big office chair and let out a deep breath. That, he thought, should get the pot boiling. Of course, he was sitting in that pot.

Grace sat, steering the sleek ship with her foot on the big wheel in front of her. She was bored. Julius lay on the bench beside her, his snoring in perfect syncopation with the snoring coming from Jack on the deck in front of her. Surround sound. Exactly nothing had happened during the four hours she captained the vessel. It seemed no one else was into midnight sailing on the Chesapeake tonight. She wondered what Gabriel, her husband, was up to. She wondered if he was keeping an eye on her. She looked up and smiled, just in case.

Grace looked back down at the duffle bag at her feet, dark on the floor of the cockpit. She laughed at herself, remembering how she had almost left it behind, the whole reason she had come back. Gabriel had tried hard to talk her out of returning. They were happy, together again. It wasn't her concern, he had insisted. But it was. What she had done, what she had made possible, had been wrong; foolish and self-serving. She hadn't thought it through, hadn't seen past the goal of getting back her sister without losing her husband. She had been selfish, she realized.

In truth, she hadn't really thought it would work, despite all her efforts. Grace had underestimated her husband in so many ways, expected too much from him in the end. She should have known that Gabriel wouldn't rest until he had figured out what she had done, why she had left him. But in the end, she had asked too much of the man.

Grace pushed at the duffle with the toe of her other foot. She felt relieved. All she had to do, Grace thought, was toss the thing over the side, and it would be done. Better to wait until they were further out to sea, she figured. And then the real fun will start, Grace thought. Then she had to find a way back to her Gabe, and her sister.

Julius cried out in his sleep, jerked, and fell off the bench, thrashing.

"Hey," Grace called, bending down to shake him awake, one hand on the wheel. His eyes opened and he sat up, hitting his head on the wheel.

"Ow, shit," he cursed, holding his head, still sore from the blow he had taken from Grace's elbow. "Everything okay?"

"You tell me, Captain America."

Julius stood, rubbing his head. "I got it," he said to her.

"You got what, Julius?" she said. "Trust me, I got this. It's not that hard. Why don't you go downstairs, throw some water on your face. Maybe grab some juice or something. Then you can assume command, Dread Pirate Roberts." He nodded and went below.

Julius returned, looking better. He took the wheel and Grace sat back down next to him. "Anything?" he asked.

"Not a thing. Smooth sailing, Skipper."

"Why don't you go below yourself, get some sleep?"

"In a little bit." She lay back on the padded bench, hands behind her head. She watched him as he stood at the wheel, sailing. "You want to tell me about it?"

"About what?"

"About why sleeping next to you is like going ten rounds with Joltin' Joe Frazier."

"Who's Joe Frazier?"

"I'm thinking your nightmares have something to do with why you left your SEAL job a little early. That's what I'm thinking."

"Great. I'm sailing with Doctor Faustus as my First Mate."

"Your only mate, you mean."

"Yeah. Even better." They watched the bay slip past quietly for a few minutes, the stars disappearing on their left as the sky gradually lightened. She waited. Julius took a deep breath and sighed, but still said nothing.

"Gonna be on this boat for a while, you know," Grace said, her smile apparent in the thin dawn.

"Not gonna let it go, huh?" Grace shook her head. He sighed again and leaned both hands on the big wheel. "What the hell," he said softly, looking ahead. "You're going to be dead soon, anyway. Right?"

"Hope so," she said, giving him an encouraging nod. She waited for him to begin.

"My first tour was Helmand Province," Julius began. "In Afghanistan. Heard of it?"

"Nope. Should I?"

"Probably not. You were probably dead at the time. Nastiest corner of a very nasty country. A lot of people with guns, none of them too thrilled that we were there. Anyway, I had been in-country for six weeks with my team, mostly doing bullshit recon stuff; just strutting around, letting 'em know we were there, you know. Couple of firefights, little stuff. Learning the lay of the land.

"Six weeks in, we get a real mission. Recon and rescue, they told us. Bullshit—we knew that from the start."

"Rescue? Rescue who?"

"Exactly. We were the only friendlies in the whole valley. Some HVT. Check him out, see if he needs evac, they tell us."

"What's an HVT?"

"High value target. Only you don't rescue targets, you know? You kill or capture. Which pretty much means kill. Rescue, my ass. We knew it was FUBAR from the get-go." She looked at him. "Fucked up beyond all recognition."

"Of course."

"So the squad loads into our armored personnel carrier and we go rolling into the badlands. Stinks the whole way. No air support, not even any eyes overhead. Just us."

"So why'd you go, if you knew it was fucked—I mean FUBAR?"

Julius shrugged. "Hey, Grace, we're SEALs. It's what we do. Besides, I was just a kid, a whole two months out of training. I had no idea why we were fucked—just knew we were. I could see what the other guys, the guys who knew the score, were acting like, what they were saying. Get in the bus and let's take a ride, boys, they said. So we went for a ride. One way trip, straight to Hell."

"What happened?"

"Less than a quarter mile from the HVT's village, we get popped. One second we're on a Sunday drive, the next second we're taking RPG rounds and automatic weapons fire from two sides. The second after that, our APC rolls over something that goes boom."

Grace waited for Julius to continue, but he didn't.

"So what happened then?" she finally asked. The sky was brightening now and she could see his expression in profile. He continued to look ahead at the bow slicing through the soft swells of the bay. The sun, broad and orange in the morning haze of the Chesapeake wetlands, peeked up over the horizon behind him. He shrugged.

"No, really, Julius. What happened then?"

"Nothing happened then, Grace. Everybody died."

"Except you."

"Yeah, Grace. Except me."

"But what happened? How'd you get back?"

"I don't know."

"What do you mean, you don't know?"

"I don't know. I don't remember anything after the explosion. Somehow, I must've walked back to the base and stood outside the wall until somebody saw me on the security cam and let me back in. End of story."

"Shit, Julius. No wonder you're fucked up. Sorry."

He shook his head again. "That's not the part that fucked me up, Grace," he said softly, briefly looking over at her before he turned again to face forward. In that brief moment, she saw the pain on his face, shadowed by the sunrise. Julius swallowed. "They told me about it two days later, while I was still in the hospital at Kandahar. They sent a heavy patrol to recover the rest of the team, to bring back the squad. And to check out the village, and the HVT."

"And they got jumped, too?"

"No," Julius said, shaking his head. "Not at all. Found our wrecked APC, retrieved the bodies of my squad mates. But the village..." He trailed off, shaking his head.

"What?"

"They were dead, too."

"The entire village?" Grace asked, shocked.

"No, not all. There were nine of them. Dead."

"Civilians, you mean?" He nodded. "How did they die?" Julius said nothing. "I don't understand, Julius," she said softly.

He didn't look at her, but she could see the pain rise in him, in the way he held himself up by holding onto the wheel, his shoulders stiffening. "A family, they said. Nine people, dead. Two men, three women, four children. Dead."

"How? From the explosion?"

"They didn't know. One family, they said."

"What about the guy you were after? The HVT guy?"

Julius shook his head. "They did a full investigation, because of the civilian dead. Flew in a full JAG team."

"What did they find?"

"Nothing," Julius said.

"What do you mean, nothing?"

"Nothing. Just the dead family. It was like the HVT never existed. They never even could find our orders or anything. They kept asking me what I was doing out there, like I had just decided to take my squad out for a drive or something."

"But that makes no sense, Julius. What about the guy?"

"I'm telling you, Grace. Like he never existed. They interviewed everyone alive in that village, no one had ever even heard of the guy. No one knew anything."

"But a family was dead?" He nodded. The sunrise was making his eyes water. "How did they die, Julius?" she asked, softly. Julius shook his head, not looking at her. "It wasn't you, Julius. You didn't kill them.

He shrugged again at this. "I don't care if you don't remember anything, Julius. You didn't do it. Shit, Julius, they can tell if you discharged your weapon. They can tell from ballistics and all, that it wasn't your gun. Dammit, Julius, say something."

He looked over at her at that. "No, Grace. It wasn't my gun. I never fired my weapon. But there wasn't any ballistics. It wasn't like that." She saw that he was clutching hard to the wheel, muscles knotted.

"What do you mean, Julius?"

"They hadn't been shot, Grace. They had been killed by hand, choked to death or something. Asphyxiated, the JAG said. No ballistics."

"All of them?"

Julius nodded. "Yeah. All of them. Five adults. Two men. Three women. Four children. They made me look at the pictures, while I was in the hospital. Three little girls, and a baby. A baby boy." Tears streamed down his cheeks. He blinked against the sunshine.

"You didn't do that, Julius."

"I don't know, Grace. I don't remember."

Parnell looked up from the computer to see the old black man leaning against the doorway. Parnell startled and looked at the man.

"Zowee, Chuckie. Now you've done it," the old man said, shaking his head.

"Who are you?" Parnell asked. "Don't call me that."

"Why not, Chuckie?"

"That's not my name."

"I know your name, just as well as you."

"Then don't call me that. Who are you? How'd you get in here?"

"Maybe I'm a good member of the church, Chuckles. Or am I too black for that? Not Nephite enough for you, Chester?" Parnell squeezed the armrests of his chair. The man scared him. He shouldn't be here.

"You know my name?"

"I know all your names, Charlie."

"I don't know what you mean."

"Hell you don't, Parnell. You want me to start the list? Huh, Madame Borthwick?" Parnell narrowed his eyes at the man, confused. "You don't remember me? Maybe this'll jog your memory..." The old man strode purposefully into the room, crossing to the desk while making clownish chopping motions with his arm, his face a crazed, smiling mask. Parnell cowered in his chair behind the desk. Uriel leaned over the desk, palms flat. "Remember me now, Mamah?"

"Julian? The gardener?" Parnell pushed back in the chair, away from the strange man.

"So you remember me now, huh, Boss Lady?" Parnell nodded nervously.

"How? What are you doing here?"

"Not gardenin' no more, Boss! Come to hang with you Mormons, yessir!" He came around the desk and sat on the corner, swinging his legs and staring down on Parnell.

"You're crazy," Parnell said.

"I'm crazy? You're the crazy one," Uriel said, more seriously. "I don't think you know what you're doing. That's what I think."

Parnell took a deep breath and sat up straighter in his chair. "I know what I'm doing."

"You do? Okay, Chumpster, you know what you're doing. Should we go, then?"

"What do you mean?"

"Let's leave."

"Where?" Parnell asked.

"Don't matter. You want to leave, right?" Parnell nodded. "Okay, then. Show me how you leave." Parnell got up from the chair and walked out of the office, Uriel following close behind. They turned the corner in the hallway and nearly walked into the temple matron.

"Can I help you, Dr. Parnell?" she asked, ignoring the other man.

"No, Matron, thank you. Thank you for arranging my talk with the President. I'll be going now."

The matron looked uncomfortable. She smiled at Parnell unconvincingly. "It's my understanding that a car has been arranged, Dr. Parnell. If you'd like to wait in the office, I'd be happy to let you know when it arrives. I'm sure it won't be too long. Would you like something to drink while you wait?"

"That'd be nice," Uriel said from behind Parnell, but the woman ignored him. Parnell ignored him also, though he was surprised that the matron was doing so. The man stunk to high heaven. Parnell couldn't believe she had even let him in the door.

"Thank you, no," Parnell continued. "Actually, I won't be waiting for the car, either. Thanks anyway, but I'll be going now. A pleasure, Matron." He started forward but the matron stepped in front of him and gently put a hand on his chest.

"My instructions, Dr. Parnell, are to make sure you're comfortable while you wait for your car," she said, less pleasantly. "Surely you don't want to get me in any trouble, Dr. Parnell."

"Trouble? No, of course not. But I can't wait for your car—"

"She's not gonna let you go, Chicklit-Nuts," Uriel said from behind him. "They got you now, boy. You're being shipped back to Salt Lake fucking City, Chuckster."

"Quit calling me that," Parnell said. He watched with amazement as Uriel shrugged and walked past the woman. She stood in front of Parnell and didn't say anything. Uriel kept shambling down the hall. "Hey," Parnell called to him. Uriel stopped and looked back.

"What?" Uriel said.

"What am I supposed to do?" Parnell asked him.

"I told you," the woman said less pleasantly, "just have a seat and I'll get you something to drink while you wait."

"Bet it's poison," Uriel said, smiling back at Parnell.

"Julian!" Parnell pleaded. The matron looked at him, confused.

Uriel shrugged again. "You know what you're doin', you said. Good luck, boss lady."

"Julian, I'm serious. Help me out here."

"My name isn't Jillian, Dr. Parnell," the matron said, offended.

"You do me a little favor then? After?" Uriel asked. Parnell nodded. He watched as Uriel slowly walked back up the corridor to stand behind the matron. Uriel bent down and took off his shoe. Parnell gasped as Uriel whacked the woman on the head with the heel of his old shoe. She went down in a heap.

"What the hell—" Parnell started to say.

"You coming?" Uriel said, putting his shoe back on. He turned and started walking back up the hall to the door. Parnell stepped over the woman and followed him. "And quit calling me Julian, Chuckle-Putz. Julian died. Starved myself to death, in prison."

"Maybe I should drive for a while," Grace said, sitting up. She put a hand on Julius's arm.

"No, thanks. I like to drive," he said, smiling at her weakly. He rubbed the wetness from his cheeks with the heel of his hand and looked back out over the bay ahead. "Should make the ocean in another couple of hours. Get some sleep."

"You sure?"

"Yeah, I'm sure. Maybe you should take Jack for a walk before you turn in, though." Jack opened one eye when he heard his name. Grace took him for a couple of turns around the deck, Jack stopping to raise his leg and pee over the side at one point.

"Good boy," Grace said, scratching his head. "Can't wait to see how you poop over the side." Jack looked at her quizzically. They walked back to the cockpit. Jack lay down again on the deck in front of Julius. Grace gave Julius a peck on the cheek before she went below to sleep in one of the smaller aft cabins.

Two hours later, Jack picked his head up. He smelled eggs and bacon. The dog jumped below to find Grace in the galley, cooking breakfast. Jack followed on her heels as Grace carried two plates of food up to the cockpit, handing one to Julius. He smiled at her, taking the plate and sitting down to eat.

"Thought you had to drive," Grace said, gesturing to the wheel as she forked a bite of scrambled eggs into her mouth.

"Autopilot," he said, pointing to the console. "What about Jack's breakfast?"

"He ate downstairs," she said.

"Below."

"Yeah, whatever. You feeling okay? You didn't sleep very well."

"I'm fine, thanks. I'm used to not sleeping very well, you know."

"Yeah, I know. I've been thinking about that," Grace said.

"Wish you wouldn't." He looked out over the water. It was a bright blue morning now, gentle swells on the bay and still too early for other boats. Reedy wetlands drifted by on either side, buzzing with insects and laden with heavy white mist. Jack stared past at the ocean, a darker shade of blue in front of them.

"It doesn't make any sense, Julius." He ate, not looking at her. "Did they court martial you?"

"No," he said. "No. They wanted to bring charges. They tried. The JAG was some gung-ho, just out of law school asshole trying to make a name for herself or something, tried really hard to make a case."

"So what happened?"

"There was nothing. No evidence, no records, no witnesses. Just nine dead people. She couldn't get her case together. Eventually, they had to drop it." He put his fork down and stared out.

"But they threw you out."

"Yeah. 'Discharge other than honorable,' they call it. Shortest active duty career in the history of the SEALs."

"Ouch." He shrugged again, eating. "So you joined the seminary."

"Not right away. Wasn't my first choice, to be honest. Fucked up my marriage first. Tried some other stuff for a while, but with a discharge like that, well it's not a great thing to have on your resumè, you know?" Grace nodded and took the empty plate from him, heading back down the steps.

She turned to look at him before she went below, saw Julius take the wheel again and bend down to disconnect the autopilot. He straightened, and she watched him at the wheel, back in the present, the captain of the ship. "Their loss," she said. He turned and gave her a smile. "You're a helluva priest, Julius."

"Helluva priest, huh? You're one to judge, Grace."

"Damn straight, Julius. I am just the one."

Uriel sat across from Parnell on the late morning Amtrak train to New York. The train was nearly empty. Parnell wrinkled his nose. He could smell the man from here. "So this is the little favor you needed?" Parnell asked him.

"What?" Uriel turned from the window to look at Parnell.

"This. I bought your ticket."

"So what?"

"You said I'd owe you a little favor, you said. Back at the temple."

"Damn right."

"So?"

"So this ain't it, Chuckie. Nice try."

"Don't call me that, Julian."

"Don't call me that, Chuckie."

Parnell rolled his eyes in exasperation. "What should I call you then?"

"Uriel."

"Earle?"

"Close enough. I know who you are, Chuckles. I know who you've been. Shit, I know who you'll be. Maybe. What name you want me to use, asshole?"

"You don't have to be so nasty."

"You don't have to be such a dick. Oh, right. You do. Because you're a dick."

"Why did you kill me?"

"Haven't killed you yet."

Parnell winced. "I meant, before."

"Oh, sorry. You were fucking things up. I mean, literally fucking things up. You had to be stopped. Only sorry I didn't do you before you and Wright left for Europe. Bad timing."

"So you're planning on killing me again?"

"Probably. Maybe not. Depends."

"On what?"

"If you fuck things up again, asshole. Actually, you've pretty much fucked it up already, back at that Temple of Doom of yours. Not sure what you were thinking, saying those things. Not gonna kill you, though. Not yet. 'Cause I'm hoping you can unfuck it." The old man looked into Parnell's eyes, questioning. "Rasputin, right? Still don't get how you did that."

"Did what?" But Parnell was smiling a little.

"Two people, two different lives. Living between Russia and the States. You pissed off a lot of people as Grigori, too. Lot of people."

"Hold it. You didn't..." Parnell stammered. Uriel smiled back, nodding. "The first time, with the knife?" Parnell asked. Uriel nodded again. "Shit, Earle. You left me with my guts hanging out all over the floor."

"Yeah, I know. But you didn't die, did you, asshole? Pretty damn impressive, that. And going back and forth like that, flashin' between Mamah the Powerbitch and Crazy Ivan. You must've been one busy muthafucka." Parnell shrugged sheepishly at the man.

"A person does what a person must. And the second time?"

"Yeah. Had to make sure you stayed dead that time."

"You did that, Earle. You did that." Parnell looked out the window at the passing countryside, thinking back. That time he had been poisoned, shot four times, stabbed too many times to count, and beaten with an iron rod. Then they had burned his body. He shuddered, remembering. Of course, being axed to death and burned as Bothwick wasn't much fun, either. Earle seemed a bit of a zealot, Parnell thought. The man had a thing for burning people up. Well, maybe not people in general, but certainly him personally.

"And before that?" Uriel asked, interrupting Parnell's reverie.

"I thought you said you knew, Earle." He smiled at the man again. Uriel frowned back. "Taliesin," Parnell said.

"You're a right sentimental bastard, aren't you? Making Frank pay homage to your former self? Shit, Wright kept naming stuff after you over and over, even when it made no sense. But there was a long while between. What were you doing, in between?"

"Wasn't fair, Earle. Nobody remembered poor Taliesin. What was I doing in between? Nobody you know. Nobody important."

"Everybody's important, Charles. Every body."

"You say so, Earle."

Uriel thought about this for a bit. "I know about the gate in Wisconsin. You had Frank build it, after all. But you must've had one in Russia, too, so you could bounce back and forth."

Parnell nodded. "Natural gate, in the Monastery of the Caves, Kiev Pechersk Lavra."

Uriel looked surprised. He tapped a finger against his lips. "Huh. Is it still there?"

"Must be. Church is still there," Parnell said.

"Oh, really? Well, that answers that, I guess. And the him/her flipping? That ain't natural."

"Oh, Earle. You can't expect me to tell you all my secrets. That's not fair."

Father Pauley sat in the ornate anteroom of the Cardinal's office. He had taken a cab straight from LaGuardia to the archdiocese on First Avenue. Dressed in his collar and black suit, his bag sat next to him on the floor. He waited. Pauley wished he had taken the time to eat something before coming. He knew he could be waiting a very long time. He took out his book.

Pauley had spent the short flight reading his copy of *The Problem of God*. He was impressed by Julius's devotion to the girl, as well as his resourcefulness. A boat to New York! Who would've thought? Pauley hoped that Julius wouldn't be too much in the way when this ended, wouldn't be hurt too badly. Zimmerman would, of course, be hurt. He was too involved with the girl now not to be, when it happened. As for Parnell, he had proven true to Pauley's suspicions. The man was much more than he seemed. The truly worrisome part, besides the obvious fact that Parnell was aggressively maneuvering powerful forces with a great deal of skill and audacity, was that the man's motivations remained an enigma. Recent events revealed that Parnell was not truly allied with the Mormons, certainly not in any position of power within the organization. What was his goal in lighting such a fire under the leadership in Salt Lake City? What did he hope to accomplish? The man was playing a very dangerous game, narrowly running a path between powerful opposing sides, but to what goal? The book didn't help in this matter. Pauley had even taken the imprudent step of reading ahead, trying to glean some insight. It was obvious, however, that the situation was so confused, so fluid, that the story became nearly unintelligible and ridiculous just a couple of pages beyond his current position. He couldn't believe any of it. Pauley thought about all he had read, where he stood, what might come; he closed the book with a resigned shake of his head, and waited.

Uriel shook his head and muttered something under his breath. "What?" Parnell asked.

"Wasn't talking to you," Uriel said, scowling at the other man.

"I'm the only one here, Earle," Parnell said.

"How do you know?"

"You're pretty weird, Earle."

"Look who's talking. You're dressed like Colonel Saunders."

"Who?"

"Doesn't matter." Uriel scratched at the scraggly beard on the side of his face. "I just don't get it."

"Get what? Or are you talking to someone else?"

"Don't get wise, Chump. I'm trying to figure out if you're even stupider than you look, or if maybe there's something more to you." He stared at Parnell.

"Why do you say I'm stupid?"

" 'Cause of what you told that guy on the TV in the Temple. Stupid. Or crazy. Or...I don't know."

"You don't like not knowing, do you, Earle?" Parnell was smiling again.

Uriel squinted at him sharply. "I don't think you know what you're playing at, Mamah. I don't think you know. Because if you knew, I don't think you'd be pulling the shit you're playing at. And you sure as shit wouldn't be smiling, asshole."

"I was stuck, Earle. Had to play a card. And don't call me Mamah. My ex-husband called me that."

"I can guess what you were thinking to do, Chuck. But what you did, makes no sense."

"How so?"

"Tellin' 'em about the plans of the Catholics. That was crazy."

"What, about the excision? I had to."

Uriel shook his head, slowly. "No, Chester. Tellin' 'em about the girl, I get that. Though they know all about her, of course. You knew that. No harm telling 'em what they already know, already working to fix." Parnell nodded. "But given what's happened, telling them about the excision? Excessive, Chuckles. Over the top. Fuckin' off the rails, man."

"Why is that?"

"You don't know, then?" Uriel asked.

"Know what? About excision? Pauley explained—"

"Oh, Pauley explained? So you know about the excisions, right? Before?"

"No. Not really. It's been done before?"

"Oh, boy. You are out of your depth, son. For an Old Soul..." He shook his head.

"What?"

Uriel took a deep breath and puffed it out slowly, looking out the window. The window fogged with his breath for a moment. "Yeah, they've done it before. On more than one occasion, believe me. And most recently, well—that's what's got your Mormon friends' knickers all good and twisted right about now."

"Tell me."

Earle leaned forward, a waft of body odor washing over Parnell. "I will tell you, Gregori. I'll tell you. Now you know what they—your LDS pals, the guys you been working for all this time—you know what they're up to, right? The End Game?"

"I think so. I know what's going on at Granite Mountain, at least. Well, I have my suspicions," Parnell said.

"Granite Mountain's a big part of it, sure. The big underground 'genealogy project.' More genes than genealogy, you know, if you know what I mean."

"I know."

"So you know that for over twenty years they've been working on the whole Apocalypse thing. They think it's about here, you know, so they think they gotta get prepared. Divine Will and Providence. The Rapture! They've been moving a lot of traffic back and forth, but mostly back. A lot of 'coming back' going on under that mountain, and I ain't just talking about the six million Jewish folks, neither."

"I suspected as much."

"Yeah, well, what I guess you didn't suspect was the whole missing Messiah thing."

"What do you mean?" Parnell asked.

"I don't know all the details. I know that there was a man, or maybe not a man, I don't know. He appeared, and was starting to make something of a name for himself. Which was pretty impressive, because he was in the middle of fucking nowhere."

"Where?"

"Afghanistan," Uriel said.

"No shit?"

Uriel shook his head. "Inconvenient. Your Mormon supreme leaders had a lead on the guy, were very much impressed. Unfortunately, that part of the world is one of the few little corners where LDS has no boots on the ground. Maybe not a coincidence, I don't know."

"This was during the war?" Parnell asked.

"Yeah, like I said—inconvenient. Or part of somebody's grand plan, I don't know. The Dude seemed pretty fucking important, though."

"Like messianic, important?"

"Mormons thought maybe so. I don't know. You gotta realize, those folks are looking at the world through Revelations-tinted glasses. Every little earthquake is seen in Salt Lake City like another Holy Harbinger, you know?" Uriel said, making crazy jazz hands. "They see four guys riding horseback at the Preakness, it's Armageddon Time. I don't know if they were convinced, but they were more than a little interested. It fit their world view. Time for Act Two, *comprendere?* So they were just starting to move on him, but didn't have any smiling, white shirted Brownshirts in the neighborhood. Had to work by proxy, through their government connections and all. No Marriott in Kandahar."

"So what does this all have to do with the Catholic Church?" Parnell asked.

"I'm getting to that. Mormons just cozying up to the idea that the guy in the desert was just maybe, possibly, the Real Deal when our Catholic brethren decide the Dude is not good for our world. And not just our world, you understand?"

"They didn't!"

"Oh yes they did, *mon frere*. RCC excised the motherfucker. Zap! Poof!" Uriel made an explosive gesture with both hands.

"They killed the Messiah?"

"Who the fuck knows? Can't kill the Messiah. Don't think so, at least. If there is one, Dude should be bulletproof, my opinion. But whoever he was, he got cut out. He isn't, wasn't, won't be. Completely. And the Mormon folks who knew about him—oh baby, they were big-time pissed off. Big time."

"But Pauley said that when someone gets excised, it's like they never even existed. They wouldn't know what they had known. You know what I'm saying?"

"That ineffably evil, inebriated, child murdering, redhead raping, rat bastard, Pauley? He's so full of shit. Besides the fact, he doesn't know shit about shit, either. But he knows more than he was telling you, that's for sure. 'Excision' sounds so nice and neat, so surgical. Makes the Pope feel better about it. Like cutting out a tumorous growth or something. Not that simple cutting out a soul, completely. It's messy. Everyone touches someone else, you know? Children and relatives, friends and acquaintances; they don't all just disappear. It's pretty fucking messy."

"So the Prophet, the leaders of the LDS—"

"Yeah. They remember. And they're crazy apeshit pissed off about it. Still, this many years later."

"I should think. Just cutting out the guy who might be the Messiah," Parnell said, shaking his head in disbelief.

"Maybe. First or Second Coming. Depending," Uriel said.

"Right. Doesn't matter. First or Second, that's got to be a bad thing."

"Gotta be," Uriel agreed.

"I didn't know," Parnell said wistfully. "I may have said a bad thing..."

"Yeah, maybe. You think?"

Pauley stood as the door at the far end of the anteroom opened. He was stiff, having sat for over two hours, waiting. The Cardinal of New York strode heavily across the room, arm extended in welcome.

"Father Pauley," he boomed, smiling. "Very good to see you, Father." Pauley stooped to kiss the man's ring.

"Your Eminence," Pauley said, straightening and smiling back. "You are looking well."

"I'm looking old, Peter, because I am. But I wax larger, while my time is waning. I am like the moon! Please, come in." He turned and led Pauley back through the door and down the narrow hallway to his office, settling into his chair behind a massive, wooden desk. "Please, Peter, sit down." Pauley sat down across from the Cardinal and waited while the man attended to some papers on his desk for several minutes. The Cardinal eventually looked up and smiled again. "So good to see you, Peter," he repeated. Pauley nodded. Pauley noticed a copy of *The Problem Of God* on the desk, close at hand. The Cardinal noticed his glance. "I take it you're here regarding this matter," he said, tapping the book.

"I am, your Eminence," Pauley nodded. He waited, the Cardinal appearing slightly uncomfortable.

"I am sorry that you are involved in this matter, Peter. I counseled against it," the Cardinal said. "It must be difficult for you."

"It is a difficult business, your Eminence."

"Indeed. But a necessary one."

"No doubt," Pauley said.

"Is this a courtesy visit then, Peter?"

"Not entirely, your Eminence. I do have some concerns regarding the matter."

"Concerns? It is my understanding that the matter is very close to being resolved."

"Yes, that is my understanding as well, your Eminence. Regarding the disposition of the matter, however—"

"I am aware of the disposition."

"Of course you are, your Eminence. It's just that—"

"I should think that the disposition would be a great relief to you, personally. A very great relief. Not to mention, a physical restoration, as well as a spiritual one." He nodded at Pauley's hand, folded in his lap.

"Yes, your Eminence."

"What is your concern, then?"

"I had a visitor, just before I left Georgetown. A very disturbing episode that—"

"I am aware of your 'disturbing episode,' Peter," the Cardinal said, picking up the tattered book and tossing it back down on the desk in front of him. "I'm sorry that it disturbs you, but there's nothing for it."

"It led me to consider—"

"There's nothing for you to consider, Peter. Your concerns, your visitor, your disturbing episode—they count for nothing. The matter will be dealt with soon, and then it will not have been."

"I just wish to convey my reservations, that perhaps you may relay them—"

"Your reservations?" the Cardinal asked heatedly. "You want me to relay 'your reservations?' To whom? To the Holy See? Should I offer up prayer on your reservations, Peter? What would you have me do? That's not the way our organization works, is it? Not a 'bottom-up' kind of decision-making process, is it? You think that your 'special insight' into this matter, your 'disturbing episode,' should change the disposition, is that what you're suggesting?" The Cardinal didn't wait for Pauley to answer. "You come into my office and suggest that I 'express concerns?' Do you know where this type of disposition is initiated? You've got a book, do you not? Are you oblivious to its authorship? Do you have any sense of the rank audacity you exhibit in coming here and speaking of such things? Do you?"

"I realize, your Eminence, that—"

"No, Pauley, I don't think you do. I don't think you have any idea what you're talking about. Of the forces involved. I don't care how disturbing your little episode was. This is a matter so far above you, above all of us for that matter, that it's not worth the breath required to dismiss your childish concerns."

"But the girl; so much will be affected by her—"

The cardinal raised his hand, cutting him off. "Don't speak of it. I will not hear any more of this. She doesn't exist. She never existed."

Pauley looked plaintive, desperate. "I'm only saying, that if there was any other way—"

"Enough, Peter!" The Cardinal took a deep breath, obviously trying to calm himself. "You've said enough. Too much, actually. You overstep. I knew this would be a problem. I told them that you would have difficulty in this matter. Be that as it may, there is no excuse for this. You will do what you must. It is your duty, your part to play." He sighed, and heaved himself up out of his chair. The Cardinal came around the desk as Pauley stood. The Cardinal took Pauley's deformed right hand in his and held it up before him. "Accept what is given to you, Peter. Few are given such an opportunity for," he paused, considering his words, "for restoration."

Pauley swallowed what he wanted to say and simply nodded. Restoration or redemption? he wondered. The Cardinal allowed him to kiss his ring again and Pauley bowed slightly, taking his leave. That, Pauley thought, hadn't gone at all well. He wasn't surprised.

Parnell and Uriel sat silently for the last part of the train's journey, each looking out the window at the warm New England morning passing outside in a blur. Occasionally, Uriel muttered something, apparently to himself. Parnell couldn't make it out. Occasionally, Parnell shook his head, considering.

"I'm trying to figure this out, Earle." Uriel ignored him. "Earle. Quit talking to yourself. I'm trying to get a handle on this."

Uriel looked at him. "You fucked up."

"Yeah, I got that. But I'm trying to figure out what's going to happen now."

"Wouldn't have been too hard, you kept your mouth shut. Catholics have shown their hand, nothing going to change about that."

"I know that, Earle. Not talking about the Catholics."

"Worried about your team, huh?" Parnell nodded. "Not your team any more. 'Nuff said."

"No, I don't think it's just that simple. There are factors in play here, Earle."

"Well, I'm assuming they've known for a while that you were on to them, to the 'big secret' and all. Prime motivation would've been to neutralize you as a threat to their secret project."

"You mean, kill me?"

"No, they don't work like that, Chippy. They're God-fearing Christians, by God. No, they would just make sure you were discredited, inconsequential. All they have to do is keep the girl from going through, keep her from going back to being dead and all. Long as she's alive and here, you look like an idiot. Look more like an idiot than usual, I mean."

"Thanks for clarifying that, Earle."

"No problem."

"So you think they'll leave me alone, just work to keep Helena alive?"

"That was their plan, know that for a fact. You shoulda seen the resources they put into trying to grab her back in Bethesda. They were just trying to get a little more control over her, reel her in so's they didn't have to keep spending so much keeping her on this side and publicly available. Like what they were fixing to do to you, back in the temple there."

Parnell nodded. "Now it's a little more complicated, though," Parnell said.

"Damn right, it's more complicated. Mormons feel strongly about the technique of excision, very strongly. Even beyond the whole recent business with the Afghani Muhammed Maybe-Messiah guy, whatever he was. It's against their whole belief structure."

"I realize that, Earle. I'm one of them, remember?"

"Course you are, Chuckles. Course you are. You understand the whole concept of prebirth existence of the soul, continuity of the soul after death and all. Excision is anathema to the entire Mormon belief system, like denying the godliness of Christ. Worse, probably," Uriel said.

"That's what I'm realizing. But I can't figure what effect the threat of excision to Helena might have on them. It's not exactly clear."

"No, it isn't. Which is why we're fucked. Before you opened your mouth, I knew the Catholics were moving to excise the girl, the Mormons were hoping to keep her good and alive. Left us a better'n even chance of getting through all this without calamitous consequences. Now, Dr. Fuck-up, you've bent the balance-beam but good. Now, Mormons don't have to keep the girl alive to keep their secret, keep you neutralized. They have a fallback position, now."

"What's that?" Parnell asked.

"Let the Catholics go ahead and excise her. She's out of the picture, their secret's golden. You're just an idiot. Which they're right about, by the way," Uriel said.

"But you just said, they hate the idea of excisions," Parnell protested.

"Yeah, I did. And they do. But how much do they hate it? As much as the world finding out that their church is pursuing a secret plan to hit the play button on the End Times? Do that calculation real quick in your head, Einstein."

"I see your point."

"Oh, great. That's a relief. Well, think about this, too, then. What relatively easy third path exists between spending all the resources for who knows how long making sure the girl doesn't cross over, and the unsavory thought of just letting the Catholics do their little snip?"

"I'm not sure. You lost me," Parnell said.

"Just getting rid of you, Sherlock."

"Oh. Right. But they don't do that sort of thing."

Uriel shrugged. "Every rule got an exception. Now you disappeared on 'em again, might be you're looking pretty exceptional."

Eventually, the train arrived at Grand Central Station. They both sat as the few other passengers disembarked. Finally, Uriel stood and started for the door. Parnell followed, catching up to the other man as they crossed into the busy station.

"Where are we going?" Parnell asked him.

"Hotel," Uriel said, not turning to look at him. "I need a nice hot shower."

Hell yes, Parnell thought to himself. Once outside, he stood next to Uriel, a sufficient distance from the man to avoid being assaulted by his odor, as Uriel whistled for a taxi. Parnell climbed in after him and lowered the window.

"Surrey Hotel," Uriel announced.

"Why there?" Parnell asked as the cabbie nodded and pulled away from the curb.

"I like their beds, that's why. You got a better idea, lunchbucket? You want maybe we should hole up in the Times Square Marriott Marquis, wake up in a box being shipped to Utah? That where you want to stay?"

Parnell shook his head. "Surrey sounds nice. Is it expensive?"

Uriel smiled at him. "We're in New York, aren't we?"

The taxi halted in front of a small boutique hotel on the upper East side. Uriel got out, leaving Parnell to pay the driver. Parnell caught up to Uriel at the front desk. Uriel turned to Parnell as he arrived.

"Give this man a hundred dollars, Parnell," Uriel said, gesturing to the uniformed desk clerk. "He don't like my looks." The clerk frowned.

Parnell fished out five twenties from his wallet and slid them across the desk to the clerk. The man's scowl was immediately replaced by a look of professional amiability.

"How long will you two gentlemen be staying with us?" he asked, typing into his computer.

Parnell opened his mouth to answer but Uriel was already saying, "Two, three nights, probably. Two rooms. He snores like a leaf blower." Parnell opened his mouth to protest but the clerk just nodded, smiling, as Uriel continued. "Don't have to be adjoining. Better not, actually. Snores like a street cleaner. Better put him on a separate floor. I'll need a bottle of Jameson Black in my room, don't fuck that up. He don't drink, he's Mormon." The clerk kept nodding as he typed. "And you got somebody to run an errand?"

"Of course, sir. What errand would that be?"

"There's a bespoke tailor on the corner of Lex and Fifty-third, name of Antonio. Tell him Uriel needs a two-piece, grey silk; he's got my measurements. And a couple of shirts, socks, underwear. And pajamas, I'll need some pajamas." Uriel was watching as the clerk wrote this on his pad. "No, not 'Earle.' U-r-i-e-l. Nobody listens anymore. Have him come by with the clothes this afternoon, after three. Gonna need a nap, first. Parnell, he's going to need some plastic." Parnell looked at him, not understanding. "Parnell, what's wrong with you? Give the man a credit card. Shit man, you look like a cow, standing there with your mouth open like that."

Parnell recovered and slid his credit card to the clerk. "So this is the 'little favor,' huh? Pretty damn expensive little favor."

Uriel took his room key from the clerk and winked at Parnell. "This ain't the favor, Chicklet." He turned and walked to the elevators. Uriel punched the call button and called back to Parnell. "I'll come get you for dinner at seven." He disappeared into the elevator. "Well," Parnell said to the clerk as he accepted his own key, "at least he's taking me to dinner."

Grace finished cleaning up breakfast and came up on deck. She looked around, not seeing Julius at the wheel, not anywhere in the cockpit. She spun around, panicked. "Julius!"

"Over here, Grace," he said, smiling at her. He had never seen her scared before, would've bet up to that moment that it never happened. She scowled at him, coming forward to where Julius was working on the rigging. "Thought I left you?"

"Thought the captain was supposed to be driving," she said, recovering her composure. She looked around, taking in the beauty of the warm, sunny morning. They were leaving the mouth of the bay, several other sailboats now scattered about, each under broad white triangles of sail. Ahead of them lay the expansive royal blue of the Atlantic Ocean. Grace looked at it, considering. She never felt so small as she did at that moment, seeing the vastness of the ocean extending across the entire horizon before her. Jack was standing farther forward, also staring at the deeper blue sea ahead.

"We're back on autopilot for a bit," Julius explained.

Grace took a deep, shuddering breath and turned back to watch Julius working the rigging. "What're you doing?"

"Sailor stuff. Preparing the sails, stuff like that."

"You okay for a bit if I go back downstairs?"

"Below."

"Yeah, whatever. I was thinking of taking a shower."

"Go ahead. We're good. You know how to work it?"

"I've used a bathroom before. I'll figure it out."

"Head."

"Head where?" Julius shook his head. "So, I'm heading for the bathroom. Be careful, okay?"

He smiled at that. Julius had this girl figured out—she was deeply out of her element. "Don't worry, Grace. I promise not to fall overboard. Which reminds me, actually. When you come back up, we need to go over some emergency procedures."

"What kind of emergencies?" She looked worried again.

"Nothing to worry too much about. Standard boating stuff; where the life preservers are stowed, how to use a lifeline, the radio, that sort of thing."

"Yeah, let's not bother with that shit."

"We have to—"

"No, Julius. We don't have to. Quit trying to scare me."

"I'm not trying to scare you."

"Then stop it. I don't need to know where the fucking life preservers are. I'm not wearing one. I don't need a life-line. I'm going to be dead in a day or two. No life-lines."

Julius felt like she had kicked him in the stomach. He forced a weak smile and turned back to the carbon black mast, adjusting the rigging. "Guess I'll just show Jack, then."

"Yeah, good idea. You do that. I'm going to go take a shower." With that, she went below. Jack kept staring ahead at all that water.

Sink like a bowling ball, he said. Wish he hadn't said that.

Grace took her time exploring the beautifully appointed cabin. Below deck, the boat was a finely crafted Chinese puzzle box, every nook and cranny utilized. Teak and tan leather covered every surface, every compartment and cabinet secured with a polished fitting or a hidden latch. It reminded her of how much she loved to strip down her motorcycle when she was in her late teens, the hundreds of finely machined parts fitting back in place so perfectly; but this was a machine that she could live inside of. Grace tried to feel secure, despite the constant motion of the floor.

She explored the master's cabin in the very front of the boat and sat, bouncing for a minute on the big bed. She pulled off her shoes and socks and went into the adjoining bathroom—the "head" she corrected herself—and figured out how to work the shower. She took a long, steamy shower. Grace could almost enjoy the strange new sensation of the gentle rolling beneath her, standing beneath the piercing spray of hot water.

Relaxed now and refreshed, Grace stepped from the shower and wrapped herself in the thick bath towel she found rolled neatly in a compartment above the sink. The whole room felt like a five star hotel suite, set afloat. She could get used to this, she thought. Her smile vanished as Grace looked down at the clothes she had been wearing, still heaped on the floor. She didn't feel much like putting those back on. Wrapped in her towel, she explored the master's cabin. Maybe the rich attorneys brought their wives with them. Or, more likely, she thought, someone other than their wives. She didn't care, long as they kept some clothes on board. She pushed at the various panels without success, then discovered the cleverly concealed master latch. Which was locked. She went forward and found the key Julius had used to open the desk. Grace cursed when the lock didn't respond. Of course not, she thought. The stuff in here was probably private, only used by the big boss. Other, lesser mortals who used the boat probably had to make do with what they brought on board. She hadn't brought anything on board except...

Grace skipped up to the deck wrapped in her towel. Julius looked at her quizzically, worrying at the controls in the cockpit. She gave him a smile and grabbed her bag from next to where he was standing, holding the towel about her with her other hand and headed back below.

Julius shook his head as he watched her disappear. "Come down here, next to me, Jack," Julius said to the dog. Jack jumped down from the main deck into the cockpit. "I think this is going to work, but better be down here, just in case."

The dog stood next to his leg, tilting his head back to look up at Julius.

And what if it doesn't?

"Here goes nothing, boy." Julius crossed himself just before activating the electric winch to raise the main sail. Suddenly, there was a high-pitched screeling sound from the front of the boat. Julius stopped the winch. "Holy shit. What was that?"

That doesn't sound so good, Captain Smith. Iceberg, dead ahead! Where'd you say they keep the life preservers on this tub, Ed?

Grace put down the Sawzall, having neatly sawn through the hasp on the cabinet lock. She gently blew the metal shavings away and swung open the compartment. "Jackpot," she said softly, smiling. She stood up and went through the neatly organized contents, women's wear on one side, men's on the other. Small drawers and cubbies held an assortment of underwear, bathing suits, suntan oil, toiletries. She checked the sizes. "Close enough," she said, and began to pick out an outfit. "Wonder if Jezebel keeps any makeup on board?"

Grace dressed in shorts and a blouse she was forced to tie at her mid-riff—Jezebel must've been damn tall. Grace was applying the makeup she found, using a little mirror that slid out from next to the bed, when suddenly the entire room turned on its side. "Holy Fucking Hell!" she yelled as the lipstick smeared up her cheek and nearly put out her eye. She grabbed onto the cabinet as the boat lurched sideways beneath her. "Shit! Fuck! Shit, fuck, shit, shit, shit!" Grace chanted aloud as she swung around in panic and, clutching onto one handhold after another, staggered swearing her way back through the tilted state room and up the steps to the main deck, emerging back out into the sunshine. She stared wild-eyed at Julius at the wheel. "Where the fuck's those life preservers?" she yelled at him.

"What?" Julius asked, staring at her, confused.

Screw you, bitch, me first. You didn't even want one, remember?

"The fucking life preservers! Where?" she yelled, holding on as the boat pitched again, still tilted on its side.

"Why? What's wrong?" he asked, suddenly concerned. The broad smile he had worn a brief moment ago vanished as he looked about, scanning for trouble. "Is there a problem down below?"

"Down below? What's wrong with you?" She tried to gesture at the whole general situation while still clutching to a stanchion in front of Julius. "We're going over!"

"Going over?" His smile returned, even more broadly than the few minutes before when he had successfully deployed the main sheet and trimmed it home, the boat coming under way in the steady ten knot breeze, close hauled. "This is sailing, Grace. We're fine."

Grace opened her mouth to say something, but snapped it closed again. She straightened up and, still holding on for dear life, turned to look forward. She stood next to Julius at the wheel. Ahead of her, the sharply angled deck was now shadowed by an expanse of wine colored sail, towering over them in the bright sunshine. She looked about at the wide horizon of the ocean, deep blue and ticked with long white lines of waves on either side. The bow was throwing a crystalline spray back along the side of the ship, breaking into thousands of tiny rainbows just ahead of her. Grace smiled and turned to look at Julius at the wheel, who turned to look at her for just a moment, before returning to scanning the sea and the set of the sail.

"So this is sailing?" she asked.

"Yeah, Grace. This is sailing." He turned to look at her again. "What do you think?"

Grace stood straighter and felt the steady, warm wind against her face and neck, her red hair tugging behind. She felt the rhythmic lift and heave, lift and heave of the boat, not like a machine at all now, but rather more like a giant thoroughbred beneath her, seeming to gallop in slow motion, up and forward with each oncoming swell, then smoothly nosing down to slice the wave ahead and rise up once more; a living thing. She looked up and saw the huge pyramid of the colored sail, a taut purple curve against the brilliant deep blue of the sky, felt the warmth of the sunshine on her face. She looked at Julius and, letting go of the stanchion, took his free hand and gave it a squeeze. "It's nice," she said. He nodded, smiling.

So where's my life preserver?

Father Pauley walked up First Avenue, enjoying the warmth of the late morning sun. He had secured a room for his stay in the archdiocese and thought he'd take lunch back in the building with the other visiting priests. First, though, he needed to find a liquor shop. He walked the crowded sidewalk slowly, distracted by his thoughts. All that is required of me, he thought to himself, all that is expected—is a touch. That's what they had told him; just a brief touch, a casual embrace would be more than sufficient to trigger the excision. So little was expected of him.

Pauley found himself shying away from the other pedestrians as he walked, unconsciously fearful of even a momentary brush. Certainly he could do something so easy, so trivial. Besides, he must admit at least to himself, he wanted to do it. No, that wasn't right, he thought, jerking out of the way of a child who almost touched his leg as she passed, she didn't look to be more than ten or eleven years old...

No, that wasn't right. He didn't want to do it—he wanted it to be done, desperately wanted more than anything for it to be done, but not by him. He had done so much to the girl already—so much to the child, her sister, caused so much pain for so many years, so many years of suffering...

Father Pauley pulled up short on the sidewalk, arms clutched tightly about him, afraid to move, people giving him stares briefly but continuing to stream past on either side, in both directions. He grunted and turned as a stroller struck hard into his Achilles' heel.

"Sorry," the mother muttered as she maneuvered the stroller around him. Pauley stared into it, horrified that the small baby inside might suddenly disappear into a mist, the pastel blankets puddling into nothing; but no, of course not, the baby was fine as it wheeled rapidly past him, that's not how this works...

Pauley looked up, turning, breathing raggedly and sweating in the middle of the sidewalk, turning in place until he saw that across the street was a liquor shop, its window sign inviting refuge, succor. He shuddered, gathered himself and crossed. He would do it, he knew. He would have to.

Uriel pounded on Parnell's hotel room door in a steady roll until it finally opened. Parnell stood inside the door and looked at him, bleary eyed. "Can I help you?" Parnell asked.

"Can you help me? Hell no, you can't help me. What's wrong with you, jackass?"

Parnell gaped at the other man as Uriel pushed past him into the room. Parnell hadn't recognized him. Uriel was clean-shaven, dressed in a perfect grey silk suit and striped red tie. He smelled of an expensive cologne Parnell didn't recognize. Instead of his prior slumped, shambling gait, Uriel stood erect, moving with intrepidity. He sounded the same, though.

Uriel stared disapprovingly at the other man's attire. "You sleep in that?"

"I took a nap, just like you said," Parnell answered defensively. He looked at himself in the room's mirror. His white suit was indeed even more rumpled than earlier.

"Damn, sucker. Never heard of sending a suit out to be pressed? What'd your father ever teach you, anyway?"

"I was a bastard."

"Explains so much."

"You wearing Bulgari?" Parnell asked, sniffing.

Uriel nodded. "You got a good nose, Parnell. Means you got one sense, at least. You ready? We're leaving." He strode past Parnell again out the door. Parnell grabbed his room key from the console and followed. He caught up at the elevator.

"Where you taking me to dinner, Earle?"

Uriel laughed and shook his head at that. Parnell had to hurry to keep up with the reinvigorated old man as they crossed the lobby. Doors were held open as he strode past the bellmen with a nod. A black-capped chauffeur held the door of a limousine open as Uriel slid without pause into the back seat. Parnell followed.

"Nice," Parnell said, admiring the interior of the car. "I hope you're not expecting too much on our first date, Earle, going to all this trouble to impress me."

"You're a funny guy, Chuck."

"Not too gracious of you, Earle. You didn't tip the bellman." The car pulled away from the hotel.

"Not necessary, Chuck. You already did."

"I did?" Uriel nodded, straightening his shirt cuff and adjusting the jewel-encrusted cufflink. Parnell winced. "We could've taken a taxi," he said, just now realizing who was picking up the tab for the limousine.

"Tough to get a cab at night where we're going. Best to have a car waiting."

"Of course. Bad neighborhood, huh?"

"Worst in the world, Dr. Parnell. Good food, though."

"Oh, well. That it makes it all worthwhile, I guess."

The black car eventually glided past the bronze bull on Wall Street, coming to rest in front of Delmonico's Steakhouse. The car door was opened and they passed more attended doors into the elegant restaurant. The elderly, portly *maître de* hurried forward to clasp Uriel's hand with a welcoming smile. "Mr. Earle, so good to see you again, sir. So good to see you looking so well." Uriel shook the man's hand and slapped him on the back.

"You still in charge of this shithole, Bobby? Thought you would've had the good grace to die and let someone younger run the place."

"Not quite yet, Mr. Earle, and not today, either. I have your table all ready. Right this way, please." The man led them toward the back of the restaurant, to a small, private alcove with a table set for two.

As they followed, Parnell stage whispered to Uriel, "I suppose I've already tipped him, too?"

Uriel nodded. "You've been very generous, Dr. Parnell. You already took care of the tab, too, so please feel free to enjoy dinner without giving it another thought."

"I'll try not to think about it too much, Earle."

They sat quietly for a bit, enjoying their drink; a Bombay Sapphire martini with caper berries for Uriel, the same for Parnell, but with half a dozen olives instead of the berries. A waiter brought over a small dish filled with more olives. He stood patiently. Parnell was spending a long time looking at the menu.

"You should stop doing that, Charles," Uriel finally told him.

"Pricey."

"Worth every penny. Close the menu, Doctor. Just order what's on the sign on the door. You won't be sorry."

They enjoyed their steaks in relative silence, broken occasionally by various bartenders and wait staff, all appearing in their late fifties or sixties, coming over to say hello to Uriel. Uriel greeted each warmly by name.

"Pretty impressive, Earle. You are quite a people person," Parnell said. "Get here a lot, huh?"

"Don't believe I've dined here in over ten years. Great restaurant, great service. Always has been, since they invented the idea in 1827. Invented that steak you're eating, invented the Baked Alaska we're having for dessert. Shit, these motherfuckers invented class. Everybody else just followed after."

"You know how to live, Earle."

"How is the easy part, Charles. It's the 'why' that's hard to figure out sometimes. Enjoy your meal, you're paying for it."

"Can't enjoy it if you keep reminding me of that, Earle."

"Just money, Chuck."

"Just my money, you mean."

"Was never really yours, Chuck. You're just borrowing it until it slips through your hands, might as well enjoy the slipping away part."

"Yeah, well, looks like someone let slip a good ten grand for that suit of yours," Parnell said, pointing at him with his steak knife.

Uriel looked shocked. "Antonio wasn't supposed to post the bill to the room until we were leaving. What a stupid bastard," Uriel said, shaking his head as he angrily slashed at his steak.

Parnell looked up from his plate. "What, really? I was just kidding."

"Oh. Good. Antonio's a great guy, great fucking tailor. How's your steak?"

"No, really? I bought you a ten thousand dollar suit? That's ridiculous."

"No, it's not. It's a nice suit. What's ridiculous is three hundred dollars for a pair of pajamas. That's ridiculous. Think Antonio was taking advantage of you there, my friend. So it goes." He shrugged and ate.

"Some little favor," Parnell mumbled.

"This ain't the favor," Uriel said. He ordered another bottle of wine.

Eventually, they finished the wine, the coffee, the Baked Alaska. They were shown to a sitting room, the walls lined with bookshelves. They sat in burgundy leather chairs with brandy and cigars.

"I'm just making a wild guess here, Earle," Parnell said, "but I'm betting that this isn't it, either." Uriel nodded, tilted his head back and blew a ring of smoke into the air. It wavered above his head for a few brief seconds before dissolving.

"Nope. Good brandy, though."

"If you say so. I'll have to take your word for it. All this stuff tastes like paint thinner to me," Parnell said.

"Shame."

Parnell sucked on the end of the cigar after dipping the end in the brandy. "So, Earle. You seem to know a lot about me."

"A bit."

"I don't know much of anything about you."

"Nothing to know. Just a broken down, crazy old Negro." The waiter standing across from them narrowed his eyes at Earle, then shook his head with a hint of a grin. Uriel winked at the man.

"You're too modest, Earle," Parnell said.

"Not possible." Uriel eyed Parnell through the smoky haze of his cigar. "Still don't have the full handle on you, neither."

Chuck shrugged and took a swig of his drink. "Just a man, like you, Earle."

"You're trying to be funny?"

"You know who I am, who I've been. Shit, Earle, you've killed me enough times to be an expert."

"I know some, sure. Don't know the why."

"You don't know why you keep killing me? I hoped you had a good reason."

"Oh, I know why I killed you. Told you on the train. You were fucking things up, each and every time."

"Your opinion."

"Only one that counts." Parnell didn't bother to argue.

"Wait, what do you mean, 'every time?' There were more?" Parnell said.

"Not entirely sure. You told me back to Taliesin. That wasn't the first you either, was it?" Parnell shook his head. "Damn, you're old."

"You're no spring chicken, Earle."

"That's true. Can't figure the why of you, Charles. Why do you keep doing this?"

"Doing what? Let you keep killing me or letting you spend all my money?" Parnell smiled.

"Why you keep comin' back. Nobody does that, nobody wants to do that." Parnell stopped smiling at that.

"You do, Earle."

"No, that's not true. Haven't left yet. Not nearly old enough." Parnell laughed aloud, nearly choking on his drink. "You though, Chuckster. You make a bad habit out of dying and coming back. You keep dying, and dying, and dying again. Why is that?"

"Because you keep killing me, I guess."

"You're just dancing with me, Parnell. What are you playing at?"

"Not playing at anything, Earle. Just a guy—or a gal," Parnell said, winking at the other man, "just doing a job."

"Any job makes you die over and over like that has got to suck. You need to get yourself a new job, brother."

Parnell shook his head, setting down his drink. "It is what it is."

"That doesn't mean anything."

"So you say."

"I do say," Uriel said.

Parnell spoke softly, almost wistfully, remembering. "I was made a promise, Earle. I pledged to do the work that was needed, to make good on that promise. That's all."

"The only man I know who was granted that promise lived a very, very long time ago," Earle said. Parnell nodded slowly at that. " 'John, my beloved, what desirest thou?' " Uriel waited for the other man's response, studying him.

Parnell's eyes closed, remembering, " 'And I say unto you, Lord, give unto me power over death, that I may live and bring souls unto thee.' "

Earle shook his head, whistling softly. "Damn, you are *old*."

Parnell stubbed out his cigar in the glass with a hiss. He coughed, and cleared his throat, shifted in his winged chair. "Probably not as old as you, Earle. Not nearly so old as you. So what's this 'little favor,' you keep talking about?"

"I said maybe. Might not need your favor. We'll see when we see."

"That doesn't mean anything, Earle. What favor do you need?"

"We'll see if I need you to kill the girl," Uriel said. The color drained from Parnell's face. He picked up his glass again, looked at the stub of cigar sticking out of it, set it back down on the table.

"Some fucking favor." Parnell sat for a moment in thought, slowly shaking his head. "I'm not the man for that job, Earle. Seems more your specialty."

"Not for her. You, maybe. But not her."

"I could use another brandy."

Julius and Grace sailed south by east the entire day. Julius set a course for nowhere in particular, and they made good time. The day remained brightly sunny, the westerly wind steady, the boat in easy rhythm beneath them. They napped on deck in the sun, Jack nestled between them on the cushions. The dog awoke to the smell of broiled steak, discovered Grace still asleep, but Julius gone. He followed the scent to find Julius setting out lunch on the topside table.

"Hey, Jack," Julius said. "Smelled lunch, huh? Looks like your friend bought enough for you, too, buddy. She's got a strange idea of dog food. Go tell her lunch is ready." Jack padded forward to where Grace was still asleep. Jack knew why the priest had asked him to do this—guy didn't trust the dog enough to leave the steaks and do it himself. *Bastard knows me like a book.* He knelt down and licked Grace's face. Her eyes opened.

"Jack." She rubbed the dog spittle from her face. "Thought you were Julius." She sat up and smelled steak. Grace walked aft to find three plates set out. "You're one lucky dog, Jack." Julius came up from the galley with a bottle of wine and two glasses. *Not lucky enough for the guy to bring another glass, I bet.*

Julius shook his head at Grace, sitting at the table with Jack at her side. "Didn't think I gave you that much money. You're some shopper, Grace."

She curtsied from the waist. "A lady must know how to make do." They ate lunch, Jack settling for water, which he slurped from a tumbler that Grace held at an angle for him. As they ate, Julius explained the workings of the sailboat. He tried to teach her nautical terminology as well, but the woman insisted on left and right, front and back. *Quirky. But a great little shopper. I think I'll keep her.*

Grace's eyes lit up as she looked at the mast, trying to understand the rigging and set that Julius was explaining. "You mean," she said with delighted disbelief, "that we can go faster?"

"Oh, yeah. Much faster."

"How? The wind is only blowing so hard."

"Yeah, but we can catch a lot more of it, for one thing. There are other ways as well, but the most important is just make more sail."

"I'm not sewing anything, Julius. You got the wrong gal."

"No," he said, laughing at her. "We have a lot more sails. I'll show you after we eat. We'll set the jib. Hell, maybe even the spinnaker. I saw they have a spinnaker in the sail locker. You'd like that, and the wind's great for it. And it's not like we have to worry about our point of sail, we're not going anywhere in particular."

"Where are we going?"

"For now? East and south."

"New York is north, remember? We discussed this."

"I know. Just not heading there yet." She tilted her head, giving him a considering look. He put up his hands in surrender. "I know. We'll get there. We shouldn't rush to our own funeral, Grace."

"It's my funeral, Julius. But no, dear. There's no rush." She leaned over Jack and kissed Julius on the cheek. Jack seized the opportunity to finish the last of the steak from Grace's plate.

"He who doesn't cook, cleans," Julius said, standing.

"I cooked breakfast and cleaned up. What happened there, Captain?"

"You screwed up, squib. Now you know. I'll get the sails ready. You can help me set 'em when you're done."

They spent the afternoon setting the new sails together. Grace ran about the deck at Julius's direction, Jack chasing and barking at her heels. Julius steered from the cockpit as he directed her to tally the jib, then watched as Grace stood, hands on hips with her piercing emerald stare until he apologized, then more graciously asked her to please pull the corner of the sail towards the back of the boat. This dance was repeated several times until he called her aft—"Come on and stand by me, please?"—and they watched as the spinnaker blossomed ahead. Grace cheered as the brightly colored bubble snapped open with the wind, a multicolored balloon taking flight right in front in them, dancing about for a minute before settling down a few feet above the bow. Grace lunged to grab onto a stanchion, the ship suddenly surging up and forward with the added thrust, the bow wave now coming the entire length of the boat. Julius held to the wheel, stealing glances at his friend's delighted expression between careful scrutiny of the sea and the set of the sails. The weather remained warm and the wind friendly, the seas calm. Julius was careful not to try anything so impressive that it might get them in trouble, keeping a course more designed to maintain his trim than get them anywhere in particular. Julius fought the urge to show Grace what maneuvering at speed felt like, just to see her reaction.

He wasn't that smitten, he hoped. He was smiling an insane amount, though, he realized.

They ran a nonsensical course for several hours, designed only to keep the passengers entertained. Jack initially was somewhat thrown off by the new movement of the ship, continuously dancing in little to and fro steps to keep his balance. By late afternoon, however, Jack had gained his sea legs, now standing proudly at the point of the bow like a lookout, staring unblinking at the sea ahead, head up and ears raked back by the wind. He was a seafaring dog.

They struck the spinnaker as evening came on, the winds having grown more variable. Julius didn't want to push his luck. In truth, he kept reminding himself, he was really soloing on this cruise. If there was trouble and something needed doing in a hurry, he'd have to do it himself. The colors of the billowing spinnaker were replaced by those of the sunset, an evolving display of yellow, orange, and finally red as the boat slowed to a more restful rhythm. They reset the jib, another triangle of wine colored sail in front of the mainsail, the boat now slicing smoothly ahead at a more stately pace.

The crew enjoyed a light evening snack and drank another bottle of wine. Jack settled for water, again. All three watched night advance across the inverted dome above them. A shaker of salted stars slowly spilled across the darkening sky. The wind kept dropping, and the night remained pleasantly warm. They stretched out on the cushions again as they had that afternoon, not napping now but looking up at the black purple sky, pricked by constellations, no moon to be seen yet.

"It's beautiful," Grace said softly, hands behind her head. Jack hadn't started snoring yet, but they knew it was coming. "More stars than what I've seen camping. A lot more."

"We're a lot farther from civilization out here. No lights. Until the moon comes up; it's almost full. It'll be as bright as a searchlight." They waited for the moon to come up. Jack began to snore.

"How does this work, tonight?" Grace asked, later. The moon had risen and was indeed almost full, as predicted. They could clearly see each other, the boat, the waves glowing in motion around them.

"What do you mean? There are three bunks below."

She squinted at him. "That's not what I was asking. Is it like last night, we have to take turns steering? Keep a watch?"

"No, we just keep doing this. Let the autopilot take us somewhere while we sleep."

"But somebody has to stay upstairs—"

"On deck."

"Whatever."

"No, they don't," Julius said.

"What if there's another boat? Or something goes wrong with the sails or something? Or something breaks?"

Julius shook his head. "You said you used to go camping? Well, when you went to sleep in your tent in the middle of the woods, did you stay awake listening for a truck to come crashing out of the trees, worrying you might be run over? Out here, there's even less chance of running into anything than that, believe me. It's a big ocean, Grace. A really big ocean."

"What about the other stuff?" she asked, not convinced.

"Really, Grace. We don't have to sleep in life preservers or anything. There's alarms in the stateroom. I'll have the radar set, the autopilot set—if anything happens, we'll know right away, before anything bad happens." She nodded at that. She trusted technology, up to a point. "Besides," he continued, still trying to reassure his friend, "there's the transponder. We show up on radar for over twenty miles. No way anybody could accidentally hit us."

Grace stiffened next to him. "Say that again."

"A transponder. It projects a signal so—oh, shit."

"Fuck yeah, 'oh, shit.' You want to fix that, Captain Notorious?"

"I'll be right back," Julius said. He jumped down to the command console, Grace following. Jack padded behind. Grace continued on past to the master cabin to find her tools. When she came back, Julius looked chagrined. "That was incredibly stupid. Incredibly, fucking stupid. Sorry. We're good, now. It's off."

"Show me." He pointed to the electronic device set in the face of the cabinet. Grace hoisted the Sawzall.

"Whoa, Grace. That's not necessary. It's off, see?" Julius pointed to the darkened face of the instrument, the switch set to off. "It's not a prob—" He was cut off by the screeling sound of the machine chewing through the front of the cabinet, sparks flying. "Holy shit, Grace!" Julius yelled over the horrifying noise, "you're going to fuck up the electronics. You can't—" Grace ignored him, continuing to work the heavy saw around the instrument, smoke now added to the occasional spark and flash. Julius thought about grabbing her arm, trying to stop her as he watched her destroying the teak face of the electronics cabinet, but hesitated as he got a vision of the saw slicing neatly through an arm, probably his. He fell back to cursing loudly at her as she continued. "Shit, Grace, are you fucking crazy? Enough, stop!" She finished and set the saw down. Julius looked at the ugly tool sitting on his chart table, the hot blade smoking and beginning to cause the chart beneath it to smolder. He moved the saw so that the blade was hanging in the air off the side of the table to cool. He smothered the map with his palm as he watched Grace wrenching at the transponder device until it was out of the cabinet and hanging by its wires.

"Excuse me," she said, brushing past him to go back to the cabin. She came back with the diags, the big pair. She snipped all the wires, one at a time, the last one sparking for a second, the lights in the cabin dimming briefly. Julius looked about, worried. He shook his head as Grace finally wrestled the device free. "Fucking crazy," he said again.

She looked at him, dropping the diags on the desk. "Don't call me that, Julius. I'll be right back." She headed up the stairs with the transponder, trailing wires behind her.

"Where are you going?"

"To throw the fucking thing in the ocean." Which she did. Jack and Julius waited below, both shaking their heads.

Girl really likes to use a saw.

They both watched her come back down the stairs, rubbing her hands clean and smiling now. "There," Grace said. "All better." Julius stared at her, mouth agape. "I think I'll get ready for bed," she continued pleasantly. "You coming, then?"

Julius closed his mouth and studied the mangled hole in the cabinet. "In a few minutes. I just have to check some things, ready the boat for the night." He ran his hand through his hair. "You go ahead."

Julius prepared the boat for easy sailing under the autopilot. He checked to make sure that the rest of the electronics were still functioning, since Grace had lobotomized the command console. Luckily, everything looked okay. He checked the radar and set alarms. He checked the weather. He rechecked their position, their heading. He checked his charts, though they were well out to sea, with nothing anywhere close or potentially close, even if the winds increased dramatically overnight, which they weren't predicted to do, and which would set off another alarm if they did, besides the fact that he was sure he would feel it while down below, in bed. In bed with Grace. He swallowed hard, and decided to go through everything again, just in case. He came below after another hour, hoping to find Grace asleep in the big bed. She was still in the bathroom. Incredible, he thought to himself. Julius considered going back topside to maybe check on things one more time. Jack lay at the foot of the bed, eyeing him. *I think Winston said it best: "We have before us an ordeal of the most grievous kind." Of course, he was talking about the Nazis.* For just a second, Julius thought the dog had winked. *Just leave the saw on her pillow.* Julius sighed. He looked through the closet to find something suitable to wear. He doubted there was anything adequately protective, though he fingered the foul weather gear, tempted.

Grace eventually stepped from the bathroom, naked. She stood just outside the door, her pose not coincidentally exactly that of the statue of Venus de Milo. Grace knew, however, that she looked even better than the statue—she had arms, which she held in a perfectly flattering, sensuous position at her sides. She also knew she had much better abs—Venus had that little bump, obviously had never done the thousands of crunches Grace had done in her previous life. The light poured from the open bathroom door, bathing her slightly oiled skin from the side and above, the soft shadows emphasizing and flattering her curves. She knew this was true, because she had experimented with the lighting twenty minutes earlier, to make sure it was just right. She stood, looking down on Julius sitting in the bed, her facial expression a practiced mix of Madonna purity, the enigmatic smile of Mona Lisa, the come-hitherness head tilt of Marilyn Monroe. It was an expression born of hours of labor in front of a mirror in her youth, an expression appreciated by more than a few men, particularly her late husband. Men had died for that look. Julius, however, was staring down at the glowing screen of the computer on his lap. She softly cleared her throat.

Julius looked up and saw her, his mouth involuntarily making a little surprised "Oh" as his breath visibly caught in his chest. Grace smiled gently at him, internally giving herself a high five.

"Grace," he said softly, staring at her, entranced by how her red curls tumbled over her shoulders and breasts. It had taken her the last fifteen minutes getting it to do that, her hair usually being a self-possessed beast that thrashed about her head with a will of its own. "You're beautiful."

"Thank you, Julius," Grace breathed. She looked down at him, the bluish glow of the open laptop computer bathing his face in a most unflattering light. "What are you doing?"

He looked down at the computer. "Oh, this? Just checking the weather for tomorrow. It looks like it'll be—"

"Lose the laptop."

"—really nice. I just have to—" he cut off and looked back up at her. She had folded her arms across her chest now. Somehow, it made her seem more naked to him. "Okay." He closed the computer and let it drop with a thunk on the floor next to the bed. Julius looked back up at her, smiling. She wasn't smiling back.

"Are you cold?" she asked. He looked down at himself. He was wearing the cotton pajamas he had found in the closet.

"Not really, no." She arched an eyebrow. Julius reluctantly got out of bed and stood. He tediously unbuttoned and removed his top, looked back at her, saw her eyebrow still arched, her arms still folded. He stepped out of the pajama bottoms. He was wearing boxers. "Oh, Jesus, Mary, and Joseph," she cursed quietly in her brogue.

"I believe, Grace," he said, still standing on his side of the bed, "that you have blasphemed."

"The boxers, Julius," she said matter-of-factly. He raised his eyebrows and now crossed his own arms across his chest. Something about the way she stood changed slightly, the tilt of her pelvis or something; now subtly more threatening. "Lose the boxers or I throw your dog overboard."

The dog's head came up off his paws at that. Jack looked back and forth between the other two as Julius bent to comply. Jack stood and stretched, mildly relieved. He padded out of the room. There were other beds on this boat, the dog remembered.

Grace watched as Julius bent to step out of his shorts. She noticed the small dark tattoo at the top of his hip, but couldn't make it out from where she stood; lettering of some kind. She sincerely hoped it wasn't the name of his ex-wife.

"Come hold me, Julius." Julius slowly came around the bed and stood in front of her, then embraced her tentatively. She hugged him back as he kissed her gently. They stood together like that, holding each other. He felt somewhat unengaged to her—unengaged, and definitely unaroused. Grace considered the distinct possibility of an unfortunate war injury. She sighed and released him. Grace turned to turn off the light from the bathroom as Julius walked to his side of the bed. She hesitated before hitting the switch, taking a moment to note the dimples on either side of the man's angular buttocks. Her Gabriel had dimples like that, when they were young, she remembered. These buttocks appeared distinctly more muscular, as she recalled. Must be all the rowing.

The bathroom light was replaced by pale moonlight spilling in through the portal over the bed. Grace stood, giving him the look again, allowing enough time for their eyes to adjust, just so he could appreciate the look this time. Then she poured herself into the bed as a mountain stream pours over rocks smoothed by a thousand years of pouring just this way; a silky, sensuous descent that was, she felt strongly, her signature move. Gabriel loved that move, sometimes made her get out of bed just to see her repeat it, sometimes two or three times. Or at least that's how she remembered it; it had been quite some time, of course.

Julius lay on his back, propped on a pillow as she poured herself into the bed next to him. Grace hugged him and laid her head on his chest, exhaling warmly. He kissed the top of her head and fondled her hair, merlot in the moonlight, in a mildly annoying way.

"What did you say your husband's name was?"

"I'm not sure I did," she muttered into his chest through clenched teeth.

"I was just wondering…" he began, then let the statement trail into silence.

Grace waited with her head on his chest, but he didn't continue. Finally, she pushed herself bolt upright next to him, facing him, face flushing as red as her hair, which he had, thankfully, stopped fondling for the moment. "What?" Grace demanded. "You were wondering what, Julius?" He couldn't meet her gaze. He sensed that she might be getting upset. Julius said nothing, looking down at his hands in his lap. She stared at him and crossed her arms again, fixing him with a glare, eyes opalescent in the moonlight. "What? You're wondering if I'd really fling Jack overboard? You're wondering if I'll make you pancakes for breakfast? What, Julius? Just trying to figure out how you're going to sneak away in the morning while I'm still asleep since, oh that's right, we're on a fucking boat? Is that what you're wondering? Huh?"

He looked up and met her gaze. "I'm wondering if he can see us, Grace."

"Oh, fuck me sideways." Grace flopped back against the pillow next to him. She pulled the sheet up to her chin and stared at the ceiling, blowing a ringlet of hair off her forehead with a huff. Julius said nothing more. Grace practiced her yoga breathing for a bit, watching the stars slowly waltz through the portal above them. This was not going well.

"I'm sorry," he began, but stopped as she shook her head just enough to cut him off.

"Stop, Julius. I see where this is going. Or not going." She tried not to sigh but wasn't entirely successful. Grace swung her legs over the side of the bed, sitting up away from him. Julius watched her back as she pulled on the pajama bottoms, then the shirt, buttoning it to the collar. She lay back down, curled up in a tight comma facing away from him.

"Could you hand me my boxers?"

"No. I can't."

CHAPTER 25

Pauley awoke with a start. He looked around, frightened and confused. He sat up in the darkness, trying to breathe, trying to remember. Moonlight from the small window reflected off the crucifix on the wall at the foot of his bed and it came to him; he was on Earth—in New York, he remembered now. Pauley reached up and turned on the lamp on the small table by his bed. He picked up his watch and checked the time. Three in the morning. He must have had a nightmare or something. Pauley picked up the book from the little table and opened it, checking. A great deal had happened since yesterday, he noted. He wanted a drink—he tried not to, but reflexively looked across the room to where the half-empty bottle stood on the dresser. He shook his head and told himself that it wasn't even morning yet, kept shaking his head as he poured the drink anyway.

He sat in the one chair in the sparse room, book in one hand, drink in the other, reading. It wasn't long before he realized that today was not going to be the day. At the rate they were going, he wondered when, if ever, they would get to New York. What if the girl didn't come at all? he wondered for the first time. What if she wasn't excised? Pauley didn't know, he realized, because he didn't know why the poor girl was to be excised at all. For the first time since reading the word in this book, he wondered why. Pauley thought it likely he would never know. 'Not that kind of organization, is it?' he could hear the Cardinal saying. He finished the drink and closed the book. He fell asleep in the chair, wondering what the girl had done to deserve this.

Grace awoke alone in the big bed. She had slept well. She hadn't expected to sleep, since she was angry. Angry and frustrated. But she had slept anyway, slept deeply and dreamlessly, lulled by the motion of the boat gentling her through the night. In spite of the sleep, she awoke grumpy. Grumpy and frazzled-feeling. Grumpy and frazzled and, she thought to herself, utterly unfucked. Grace sat up on the side of the bed and rubbed her eyes. She stumbled sleepily up on deck to find Julius, where else, but at the wheel of the ship.

Julius turned to see her standing there and couldn't help but smile. Grace was dressed in men's pajamas that were so big on her that the sleeves fell past her hands like flippers, the legs of the pants trailing behind her. Her hair was a flock of cardinals flapping crazily about her head in the wind, over her shoulders, across her face. She brushed her hair back from her face and rubbed her eyes with her fists like a child. She looked at him, blinking. She was, he thought at that moment, even more beautiful than the night before.

"What?" she asked.

"Nothing, Grace. Sleep, okay?"

She nodded. "Guess so. Everything shipshape, Captain Cockblocker?" He winced inwardly but nodded, his smile a bit less enthusiastic.

"I don't think that even makes sense," he said.

"My thoughts exactly," she said, "I'm going to—" She cut off, staring hard at the black dome of the big compass in front of them. She spun on him, suddenly vibrating with anger, flushing redly above the collar of her pajamas. "What the fuck, Julius?" she demanded.

"What?"

"What? You know what, jackass. You're still heading us south. New York, jackoff—New fucking north York! That's what. What is it you don't understand about getting my ass to New York so that I can JUST FUCKING DIE!" She stood there, trembling.

Julius faced her, bile rising in the back of his throat, feeling the heat rise in his face. He clenched his jaw, fought down what he wanted to say, instead turning away from her to look forward at the impassive sea ahead.

"Turn the fucking boat, Julius!"

Julius felt his chest tighten, he couldn't inhale, suddenly felt like he was going to vomit. The boat lurched in the swell as he held tight to the wheel. Julius faced her again and couldn't stop himself this time. "You can be a real cunt, Grace," he said levelly.

"Oh, slay me with irony!" she said, throwing up her arms, sleeves flapping as she turned to go back down the stairway. "Get us to New York, Julius! I got a date. I'm going to take a shower." She stomped down the stairs.

Julius stared steadily ahead, but Jack watched her go. *My advice? Throw that fucking saw overboard while she's in the bathroom, buddy. And the knives.* Jack slumped onto the deck and laid his muzzle on his paws. *Feel like that damn cat in* Alien. *You know, at the end? Not a good feeling. And you, buddy,* Jack looked over at Julius, still clutching to the wheel, *are no Sigourney Weaver. Just saying.*

Grace stood under the hot needle spray of the shower, her hands braced on either side, head down with her forehead pressed against the wall. It was her third shower in the less than twenty-four hours she had spent on this boat. All she did was take showers. She sucked in at the billowing steam that filled the tiny stall and felt the rolling of the ship with her whole self. She felt trapped. In her entire life, she had never felt this way. She had spent a lifetime running, escaping—but always in control, always the one driving. I've made a terrible mistake, she thought. I'm on this fucking boat, in the middle of the fucking ocean, and I don't know shit about boats, or oceans. She couldn't believe that she had been so stupid as to let herself be trapped like this. No control, no way out. Completely at the mercy of a man who...who, what? What was he? A fucking crazy mass murderer, that's what he was. He was obsessed with her, she thought to herself. He kept showing up whenever she ran from him; now he had trapped her, holding her hostage on this boat. She smacked her forehead against the wall. No—she stopped herself, that's bullshit and she knew it, he hadn't murdered anyone. Whatever had happened, that wasn't Julius. And no, he wasn't obsessed with her. She wanted to use that word, to make him sound in the wrong, deranged. But he wasn't deranged; he was just in love, she knew. It wasn't fair, it wasn't what she wanted, but that was the truth of it, and she was at fault, at least in good part. She had to admit that—she knew Julius cared for her, despite her protests; she had known. She had known and she had used him. She had used him, and when she tried to stop using him, he had reappeared, and saved her again, so she used him again. Suddenly, the boat lurched in a sideways corkscrew motion that caused Grace's body to smack wetly against the glass door, as above her Julius threw the boat into the turn she had demanded. She steadied herself in the little stall and deeply inhaled the steam, tried to fill herself with steam. He wanted to keep her here, keep her in this little world out to sea, keep her for what? Maybe he loved her, but he wouldn't make love to her. He couldn't get past what he wanted, refused to see that she had to leave him, so he was afraid. The man was a coward, she thought to herself, and she couldn't stand it. She didn't give a shit about looks (though she had to admit Julius had looked pretty impressive by moonlight), her Gabe hadn't been a looker by a long shot, but her Gabriel had a spine, damn it. This guy needed a stout piece of pine strapped to his back—he needed stiffening. Julius wasn't strong enough, couldn't commit to the moment because he was afraid of what was to come. He was weak, and afraid.

Her Gabe had been strong. Grace had put Gabe through hell, she knew. She had forced her husband to watch her die, made him witness her death without benefit of any warning or explanation. But he had stood the test. Gabe had survived. Hell, more than survived; Gabe had turned into a man on a mission, as she knew he would—had taken up the challenge and never wavered, fighting through his grief and solving her stupid puzzles and knocking down everything in his way to find her and save her and make everything okay. That's what her Gabriel had done. This guy couldn't do her, couldn't do anything for her—this guy was a coward.

Grace breathed, and felt the ship settling into a new rolling rhythm, now on its new course—north. She might be crying, she realized, she wasn't sure, since the water from the shower was spraying hotly over her

326

head and face. She was crying, though—crying because she knew that no, her Julius wasn't really a coward, that this was her lying to herself, too. He had been brave, foolishly brave, just to save her. Brave enough to save her over and over again; pull her out of the river, get her out of that hospital, to almost get himself killed when she insisted on that crazy stunt at the Wright house—despite knowing it was crazy he had come through to help her. Over and over he had been more than brave. He had crossed the line for her, again and again, and why? Her Gabe was brave because he loved her, had spent a lifetime with her—but this guy? This guy stood up before he even knew her name. Stood up even though—and here she inwardly had to wince, remembering—she had beaten the shit of him (twice), had cursed him six ways from Sunday and given him every kind of grief. No, she admitted to herself, Zimmerman was not a coward. Not at all. Her Julius was broken. He was hollow on the inside. He had no inner strength left, had been through hell, had the marrow sucked whole from him and she had used what little strength he had left, taken the fragile shell that remained and almost snapped it; not on purpose, but because she hadn't seen what she was doing to him, hadn't wanted to see because, in truth, she admitted finally to herself as her tears mixed with the water that was now turning cold as it sprayed over her, she had to admit that she did need him, had needed him then and still needed him or she was completely fucked, completely lost, with no chance, no chance to get back to where she needed to be, back to her Gabriel and her sister and the place she belonged. Without Julius, she would've been lost already, utterly. And what had she done to show her thanks, her appreciation, she asked herself. She slid down the wall of the tiny shower and sat, back against the wall and hugging her knees to her chest, and let her head sag as the water now sprayed icy cold needles into her. She had tortured the man, tried to get him to violate his vows—the vows that were probably the only thing holding the thin eggshell of his self-esteem together, his priestliness like encircling threads. Grace kept picking at those threads, and torturing him for resisting, for trying to hold onto the one thing he needed to survive. She shook her head and forced herself to stop crying, struggled and finally managed it, letting the cold water wash the tears away. She reached up and turned off the water, then let her head thunk back against the wall. Why was there never enough hot water? The steam was gone. She was cried out. She had fucked the guy, she concluded. Just not in the way she had intended. She hoped there was another dry towel in the cabinet.

Parnell and Uriel sat side by side in the limousine on the ride back to the hotel. Traffic was light. Each looked out their side window, watching the lights of the city glide by.

"Well, Earle," Parnell said, "I have to thank you for spending my money. I've had a particularly pleasant night." Uriel nodded and made a perfunctory sound as he continued to look out the window. "I'm still confused, though—"

"Not surprised."

"No, really. It seems that big things are in motion and I am still at a loss here. There are a lot of moving pieces."

Uriel nodded in the darkness of the car. "You should be worried."

"I am worried, that's what I'm saying. I don't even know where you stand in all this."

"Told you what I might need."

"I know that, Earle, but I don't know why you asked me that. What are you hoping to gain?"

"It's not like that. Not in this for any angle, John. Just trying to make sure everything works out."

"That doesn't tell me anything. I need to know—"

"It's late," Uriel said as the car pulled up to the front of the hotel. The door was opened and they entered the lobby.

"We need to talk about this," Parnell said, struggling to keep abreast of the older man. They came to a stop in front of the elevators. "What if Helena shows up in New York tomorrow?"

Uriel shook his head as he repeatedly stabbed the call button. "Not coming tomorrow."

"How do you know?"

"I know. It's late. I'm tired of talking to you."

"But—" The elevator doors opened.

"Tomorrow. Good night, Gregori."

"Breakfast?" Parnell asked between the closing doors.

"No. Not breakfast," Uriel said as the doors kissed closed between them. Parnell headed to the bar. He wasn't too tired to talk to someone. Anyone would do.

Grace came up the steps to the deck. She had dressed in a pair of knicker length sweats and a workout top that she'd found in the closet. As soon as she set foot on deck, she could feel the change. Literally, the wind had changed, now coming abeam, causing the deck to angle more steeply. She could see the change in the way Julius stood at the wheel, in his rigid posture, saw it in the way he looked her over for the briefest moment, not quite meeting her eyes before turning again to look ahead. She saw it in the way Jack, lying on his side on the deck, opened one eye to look at her without moving a muscle.

Ripley! The Alien, it's back! Don't let it eat me!

Grace stepped up beside Julius, who clung to the wheel. After a bit, he finally acknowledged her.

"What?" he asked.

"We need to talk, Julius."

"Nothing to discuss. We're heading north. Look." He tapped the compass in front of them.

"Put it in park, Captain Picard. We need to palaver. Now."

"What if I don't want to talk?"

"Then I jump over the side." Julius looked at her with a smirk. "With the dog." Jack raised his head.

Why always 'Or I'll kill the dog,' huh? Does that make sense to anyone?

Julius rolled his eyes. "Fine. Give me a minute to get this thing in park."

"Take your time. I'll make pancakes."

I love pancakes.

That kid at the yacht club had really done a job, Grace thought. Pancake mix, eggs, bacons, syrup, orange juice, coffee had all been stocked; enough for a week at sea, at least. Of course, he thought he was stocking for more than two people. Grace remembered that Julius had told him that they were taking out a boatload of orphans for the weekend or something and felt guilty. But only for a moment, then she was over it. She could only feel guilty about one thing at a time.

As Grace started to cook, she felt the boat come almost level. That's better, she thought, as she had been wondering how she was going to manage cooking breakfast with the boat halfway on its side. Twenty minutes later, Julius and Jack followed the smell of cooked bacon below deck. They found breakfast laid out in the dining area.

"Looks great, Grace. Let's take it topside. It's too beautiful to eat down here." He grabbed the plates for himself and Jack. "I cannot believe you made a plate for Jack. You're out of your mind."

I will not have you speak of this beautiful, kindly, young woman in that manner! How dare you, sir? How dare you?

It took two trips to lay out the breakfast at the table on deck. The three sat to eat. Jack waited until the others began, looking back from the other dishes to his own.

Really, scrambled for the dog? You guys get sunny-side up and the dog gets scrambled? Will someone please explain why there is a general belief aboard that the dog prefers his food in the fashion of a common cafeteria? Anyone?

The day was unseasonably warm, the air already balmy this early in the morning. Julius had brought the boat to an easterly heading to allow it to run before the wind and therefore close to level, also resulting in very little wind across the table to disturb their meal. The sun shone brilliantly in a bowl of cloudless blue from horizon to horizon, interrupted only by the stark purple triangles of the sharply trimmed sails. Despite being pissed as hell and emotionally miserable in general, the three ate in pleasant companionship.

They ate in silence, each looking up frequently from the table to take in the changing scene around them. A broad winged sea bird appeared from nowhere, swooping in over the stern, wheeled above the shipmates once and disappeared astern again, each of them twisting their head to watch it go. The sea remained cooperative, now a series of broad rollers that the graceful boat rode with a slow, soothing sway. Jack finished first as the others continued to eat in silence.

Jack gazed fixedly at Grace's plate. She saw the dog staring. Grace scraped her remaining egg and bacon onto Jack's plate.

"Sorry, Jack. You must be starving. Here."

"You are going to kill that dog," Julius said, shaking his head.

"So I've said. A couple of times now," Grace said, trying a smile.

Jack ate the new portion and continued to lick the traces of yolk from the plate. *This gal has the greatest sense of humor. Love this woman.*

Grace stood to clear but Julius stopped her. "Don't. Sit. You cooked, remember?" Julius said, rising to gather the empty plates and glasses. "I'll bring up the pot of coffee. Then we'll talk."

Grace and Jack waited while Julius did the dishes, laying back to soak up the sun. When Julius returned, they were both flat on their backs, eyes closed. Jack's legs were splayed straight up in the air. Julius stopped in the cockpit to check their course, scan the radar. He trimmed the sail with a few toggles of the electric winches. He made no attempt to turn them north. Not yet, he thought. Let's see what the talk is about. They continued eastward, out to sea.

As Julius sat back down at the table with the pot, Grace stretched, cat-like, and sat up. Jack didn't. She accepted a mug from Julius with a nod.

"I'm sorry I called you a cu—called you that," Julius said. "I didn't mean—"

"Yes, you did mean. You're right. Don't apologize."

"I am?" Grace nodded, cradling her mug with both hands. "You know," he continued, "you did say yesterday that there was no hurry, and I thought—"

"Shut up, Julius," Grace said. "I said we need to talk. That means that I talk, you listen. I'm surprised you don't know that, you having been married once before."

"It's been a long time. I'm out of practice."

"I forgive you." She took a deep breath. Jack began to snore. Grace rolled him off the cushion and he thumped onto the deck, shook himself, and padded to the bow where he settled down in the sunshine. "I'm sorry, Julius. You were right. I have been a—what you said I was. I'm stopping now."

"Grace, I didn't—" she gave him a look and Julius closed his mouth. He sipped his coffee instead.

"First," she said, "I'm sorry. I have been unkind to you. No, actually, the truth is closer to what you said. In many, many ways. I don't know why I've treated you like that, but I'm sorry." She paused.

"Apology accepted."

"Shut up, Julius."

"You paused there for a bit. I thought it was okay to let you know that—"

"Jesus, Julius, just shut the fuck up for a couple of minutes, will you? I'm not good at this shit as it is." He nodded, chastised, as Grace desperately drank coffee. Her hand was shaking, he noticed. "So, I'm sorry. We won't speak of it again." She paused and stared at him, eyebrow arched. He smiled back, not speaking. "Second, thank you. From the bottom of my heart, thank you."

"You're welcome."

"Don't push it, Julius."

"Okay. Are we done? Because there's something I'd like to discuss, if you're done."

"For now. What is it you want to discuss?"

Julius sat, not sure how to begin. "This morning, when you came on deck and saw the compass heading—"

"I said I'm sorry, Julius."

He shook his head. Suddenly, he looked like an embarrassed little boy, staring at the tabletop between them. "No, that's not it. You were right. I was still heading south because I thought that..." He trailed off. When he looked up and met her gaze, he looked so sad that Grace felt her heart sink. She took his hand and gave him a weak smile. As she watched him, however, she could see his mind suddenly shift gears. Julius pulled his hand away, sitting up taller. "Grace," he stopped, started again, "Grace, why are you here? Why did you come back?"

"I told you. I had to come back to destroy the work Gabriel left behind. The work I made him leave behind." He nodded, looking straight at her now, challenging. "I told you that, Julius."

"But you haven't done it, Grace. We've had it on board since we left. It's sitting right back there, in the cabin." Grace turned away, face reddening. "That's what you're here for, right? You said you had to destroy it, to fling it in the ocean. Why haven't you? This is it, Grace," Julius said, gesturing around them expansively. "It doesn't get any more ocean than this." She shook her head, not looking at him. "Because once it's done, you have no reason to stay. Toss it overboard, Grace. Get rid of it, and there's nothing keeping you here. Do it now."

She looked over then and met his gaze, her eyes moist. "You think I should?" He nodded. "You said you wanted to say something—"

"After." She stared at him, searching for some opening, some softening, but there was none, so she rubbed her eyes and stood. Julius nodded. Grace went below. She returned with the bag. She set it down on the table between them and sat down again, looking for a sign he would relent, would let her kick the bag under the table, at least for a while, not to have to do this just now.

"Now?" Grace asked. He nodded. Grace stood and grabbed the handles, lifting the bag.

Julius grabbed her arm. "Whoa, there," he said. "Wait a second."

She sat back down. She smiled at him, relieved. "You said?"

"Well, you can't just toss it overboard."

"You just told me to toss it overboard, Julius."

"You can't just toss it without opening it up, checking what's in there. How do you know that's it?"

"It damn well better be, dipshit."

"No, I know it is. But you gotta look. To be sure."

Grace shrugged and let the bag drop back on the table. She sat back down and unzipped the duffle. Grace began pulling out Parnell's clothes, then manila envelopes thick with papers, and finally a computer hard drive. She rummaged through the duffle to make sure it was empty. "Happy now, Father? Maybe I should—what the hell?"

"What?"

"That crazy motherfucker! I'll kill him, the little fucker!" Grace pulled out a ring that was rolling loose in the bottom of the bag. She stared at it in disbelief.

Julius looked over at her. "It's a ring."

Grace shook her head. "No, Julius, it's not a ring. It was Gabe's. I gave it to him as a wedding gift."

"A wedding ring."

Grace looked at him sharply. "No. Not a wedding ring. It is not a fucking wedding ring."

Julius shrugged, confused. "Okay. It must've been in with your husband's belongings when—   "When that fucking cocksucking motherfucker stole it."

"Yeah, that's what I was going to say. Sort of." Grace rubbed the ring tenderly in her hands. "Can I see it?" Hesitantly, she handed it over to him. "It's a Claddagh. Never saw any like this. It's massive. Is it old?" Grace nodded, watching him hold it, inspecting it. Without knowing why, without thinking, Grace took the ring back. She took Julius's hand in hers and put the ring on his right hand, careful to point the apex of the heart towards him as she slid it on. He looked at it there on his hand, then looked up to meet her eyes. Grace burst into tears. Julius slid next to her and held her as she began to sob uncontrollably. Grace cried, Julius holding her and rocking her, trying to console her. After a while, her crying diminished and she snuffled on his shoulder, but made no effort to raise her head. Julius looked past her at the ring there on his finger, his arms wrapped about her.

Without a word, Grace straightened up. Julius released her as she bent forward and flung the hard drive into the ocean. She stood up and threw the envelopes, the clothes, and finally the bag itself over the side. She dropped back down on the seat. She looked at Julius, who was looking at the ring on his finger.

"Why?" he asked. She shrugged and gave him a feeble smile.

"It fits," she said. He nodded. Grace turned to watch the clothes and bag floating astern. The folders and drive had already sunk. "Now, what were you going to say?" she asked, still sniffling slightly.

Julius blushed. He frowned at the ring and twisted it on his finger. He shook his head. "I don't think I can say it now."

"I threw the shit overboard."

"I know."

"You know what goes over next?"

"Jack." She nodded. Julius put his palms flat on the table and tried not to look at the ring, tried to meet her flint green eyes but couldn't quite force his gaze higher than her chin. "This morning, I was heading south, because I thought you might...I was going to ask you if you might consider..."

"Consider what?"

"Just think about maybe heading down to the Caribbean for a little bit. Just a few days. Or even a couple of weeks, maybe." She looked at him, not quite understanding. "I've sailed around the Caribbean a lot, Grace. It wouldn't be a problem. I know places we could put in for stores and fuel, no questions asked. I could secure a copy of my passport, get a line of credit in Grand Cayman. I know people there." He stopped, looking at her. "You'd love it, I'm sure." He was afraid he was sounding pathetic.

Grace took his hand. She twisted the ring so that it faced correctly and rubbed his hand. "That sounds nice, Julius." He smiled, relieved. "I don't know, Julius. I don't know. I'm sorry." Julius nodded.

"You'll think about it, though?"

"Sure, Julius. I'll think about it. How far are we from New York?"

"Two days sailing easy. Day and a half if I push her."

Grace leaned back against the cushion and let her head fall back, closing her eyes in the sun. "It's so beautiful," she said. "Can we just park here for a bit?" She thought she was kidding.

Julius beamed. "Sure, Grace. I can do even better than that. Just hang out here for a while."

Grace watched as he headed back to the cockpit. She couldn't tell what he was up to, so she just lay back and felt the warm sun on her face. She could get used to this, she thought, feeling the easy roll of the boat beneath her. She fell asleep.

When she opened her eyes, Julius was gently shaking her. She shaded her eyes against the dazzlingly bright sunshine. The day had turned hot. She didn't understand why it was so sunny until she realized that Julius had taken in the sails. She blinked at him. He had changed into swimming trunks. He smiled at her.

"How long did I sleep?" she asked, shading her eyes.

"About an hour. Who cares? Listen, I gotta take Jack for a walk. You go below and see if you can find something to swim in. You can swim, right?"

"A little."

"Doesn't matter, don't worry. We'll be wearing life vests anyway. Go!"

Grace went down to the cabin and pawed through the drawers. She found a drawer full of women's swimsuits, all bikinis. She cursed. She tried on a bright orange one, thinking that it would be easier for Julius to recover her body when she drowned. She had never gone swimming in her life. The bottoms fit. The top was another story. Her previous suspicions were correct, she realized. Any woman with boobs this artificially huge must be the concubine. She tossed it aside and put on a white tee shirt she tied at her midriff before going back on deck. Grace watched Julius working at the back of the boat as he made fast two safety lines. Then he turned to her and said, "You're not going to believe this," as he pushed a button. With a whirring sound, a swimming platform lowered from the stern into the water. "Pretty cool, huh?" he asked. She nodded. She watched the waves lap over the platform. Grace was thinking that maybe the middle of the ocean wasn't the best place to learn to swim.

She watched as Julius snapped a shortened line to Jack's collar.

"Really?" she asked, "he's going swimming, too?" Somehow, she found this reassuring.

Are you crazy? No fucking way. You're all going to die.

"No way," Julius said. "I just want to make sure Jack's still in the boat when we're done."

"Oh."

"Come on over here, I'll get you set." She came over to him and he fitted her with a life vest, a snug and reassuring fit. Then he secured the lifeline to the vest. "See? No worries." He donned his own vest and secured himself to the boat. "Wait a sec," he said. He went to the cockpit and rechecked the radar and the instruments, made sure the autopilot was set to make a gentle circle in the water. "Okay, Grace. We're all set."

"Listen, Julius, this looks like fun and all, but—"

"Oh, it'll be great, you'll see. Not like the Caribbean, though. Down there, it's like swimming in a bathtub. Great for skinny dipping." He winked at her, then blushed.

"Sounds nice, but I thought maybe I'd just sit and dangle my legs in for a bit, okay?"

He shook his head. "Not gonna work, Grace. We do this the SEAL way. I'll show you."

"SEAL way? Listen, Julius, why can't I just..."

"You'll see. Here." She let Julius maneuver her to stand upright on the back corner of the deck. He stepped up next to her. "On three, okay?" He put his arms around her. She didn't nod or anything. "One, two," on two he jumped powerfully with her in his embrace and they landed on his back with a splash to the side of the boat. If Julius hadn't been cradling her tightly in his bear hug, Grace would've panicked. The startling cold of the water struck her like a sharp slap. She was about to scream, despite being under water, when Julius gave a forceful scissors kick and they broke the surface into the sunshine.

Grace still wanted to scream but couldn't, her chest clenched tight with an icy iron band. Julius still held her for a bit, now releasing her except for a hand gently on one arm as they bobbed in the life vests.

"Holy FUCK!" was all she could finally manage to yell. Julius laughed.

"Yeah, it's a little colder than the Caribbean, that's for sure." Grace tried to control her breathing, forced herself to try to relax a little, at least to push down the panic. "That's great, Grace, breathing is good. The cold will go away in a little bit."

"It's not going away!" she screamed at him.

"You'll get used to it. Give it a minute."

"I'm not getting used to it, Julius," she said. "SO fucking cold, SO fucking cold, SO fucking cold, COLD, COLD!" she chanted through violently chattering teeth. She caught sight of the boat. Jack was standing on the deck, watching them.

You won't get used to it. You're going to die.

"You'll get used to it faster if you swim. Let's swim to the platform."

"I can't swim." Her lips were blue, she was sure.

"You said—"

"I lied, Julius."

"Oh. Well, fine time, middle of the ocean, Grace. Just roll onto your back, like this." Julius showed her the rescue position, which she was keen to master. "Now just kick." He showed her this, too. He helped steer her around the stern towards the platform. "Okay, we're good. Turn around and grab on, Grace."

She turned and was never so relieved as to see the platform in front of her face. She grabbed on desperately, noticing that her fingernails were indeed blue. Actually, purple. Jack looked down at them.

Hypothermia. You're all going to die. I'll die, too, but I'll be eating a lot of steak before that happens, won't be so bad...might even get picked up before I finish it all. Worked out okay the last time this joker left me in a boat on my own...

"That was great, Julius," she said. "I'm getting out now." Though as she bobbed beside the platform, she realized that she had no idea how she was going to do that.

"No, Grace. Give it another minute. You'll get—"

"Yeah, I know, I'll get used to it. I'm not fucking getting used to anything, Julius, I'm getting..." She trailed off, still holding on to the platform, realizing that she had no idea how she was going to get up on the thing, then realizing that she really didn't feel nearly as cold. Her teeth had stopped chattering. Actually, it was pretty refreshing, after sitting in the hot sun on deck. Julius swam over to look at her.

"See? You're hardly blue at all now." They looked around, enjoying the view, the vastness of the ocean completely overwhelming from this vantage. Grace felt the swell of the ocean buoy her up, then gently lower her again. She had to admit, this was pretty great. She wasn't cold at all any more.

"Can you teach me to swim?"

"We can try."

Julius spent the next twenty minutes teaching her the basics of a crawl stroke, as best he could with both of them in vests and periodically getting entangled in the lifelines. Grace would never be a natural swimmer, he could tell, but she was athletic and coachable. She was starting to think that she was getting the hang of it when Julius came up along side her and grabbed onto her vest.

"Let's get back to the boat," he said, propelling her with a powerful stroke back to the platform.

"Damn, Julius," she said. "You can swim."

"Yeah, Grace. I used to do it for a living, remember? Get up on the platform, like this." He showed her how to raise herself up with both hands on the platform as he propelled her out of the water with a powerful shove on her buttocks. Grace landed on the platform, legs dangling. Julius surfaced up next to her with a sharp kick and plopped down beside her, the platform rocking. She wasn't cold or shivering at all, she realized, amazed, feeling the sun on her. "Look," he said, pointing into the water. The water was a deep azure, surprisingly clear, but she couldn't see anything.

"Look at what?" she asked, and then she saw the flash of white beneath them for a split second. "Oh, wow. Look at the size of that fish!" He nodded. "That's incredible, it looked as big as me."

"Yeah, pretty much. You okay?"

"Yeah, great. Why?" He just smiled. "Hold it, that wasn't a fish, was it?" He shook his head. "Shit, Julius!"

"Yeah, we should be getting back aboard." They climbed back aboard and raised the swimming platform. Julius undid the lines so they could get out of the vests. Jack, they noticed, was asleep in the sunshine. It looked like a good idea. Julius untied him and they all lay in the hot sun for most of the afternoon.

After, Julius spent a lot of time puttering around with the set of the sails and other nautical matters that he addressed with great solemnity. It seemed to Grace, as she occasionally stole glances at him busy in the cockpit or scurrying around the deck, as just a half step above 'boys with their toys.' She even followed him about for an hour, trying to get a handle on how to drive this bus. Julius loved it, launching immediately into Professor of the Sea mode, but he kept lapsing into nautical speak and losing her. The only thing she was sure of was that driving the Ferrari was a lot easier. Oh, and if Julius fell overboard, they would all just die.

As the day fell, Grace left Julius to his job of captaining the boat while she went below to explore the galley and assess their stores in more detail. She loved this part, because it seemed to combine the best of wilderness camping with staying in a luxury hotel. The camping part was the simplicity of their existence, just like hiking or climbing, where all one had to think about was waking up, washing up, doing some cool outdoor shit, what to eat, where to sleep. She loved that; it was therapy for her. Especially when she was thinking about what to eat, since instead of considering what kind of freeze dried crap she was going to heat up in a pot of water over a stupid little camp stove the size of her palm, she had a full kitchen, with a microwave and a refrigerator and spice racks, every manner of tool and spatula and bowl—everything stowed in neat little compartments and secured by some latch doodad. She sang something in Irish as she put together a menu for tonight's dinner. No steak tonight, she decided. Except for Jack, that was his dog food, Grace remembered.

The essence of camping, only in luxury. And without the strenuousness, the sweating part. Grace needed to do something about that, she couldn't just keep sunbathing all day. Sunbathing and showering, she reminded herself, her two major activities since she'd come aboard. Maybe she could try swimming again tomorrow—the way she swam (she put little mental quotation marks around that word) was certainly a workout. It was so damn cold, though, she had to admit the only way that was going to happen was if the boat sprung a leak. She'd have to find another activity. She doubted she could do wind sprints on the deck with any success. Maybe she could ask Julius if it would be okay if she climbed the mast. That would be awesome, she suddenly thought, smiling to herself.

She stopped smiling and her singing faltered as she cooked, her mind having stumbled past the practicalities of making dinner to the inescapable prospect of going to bed, eventually. She tried to concentrate on her cooking, trying to not contemplate the inevitable awkwardness that was to come. Of course, Julius might just pretend that the captain was needed on deck all night, after all. Actually, she thought as she violently chopped fresh carrots for a salad, I bet that what's going happen. She sighed. That would be the best thing. Every other possibility portended disaster. Again. She was okay with the 'captain needed on deck' gambit.

Grace brought up two plates of chopped salad with shrimp to the table on deck, drawing Julius and Jack in her wake.

"A salad," Julius enthused, taking a seat, "with shrimp! Where'd the shrimp come from?"

"Fridge. Hope you weren't expecting more steak."

I was expecting more steak.

"I was afraid it was going to be all steak, all the time, on this cruise," Julius said.

Yeah, that sounds like the cruise I signed up for, guys...

Grace said, "I was going to make some macaroni and cheese to go with it. That guy at the dock must've thought you were taking an entire troop of boy scouts out to sea or something, there's enough mac and cheese to survive being marooned on an island for a year." She sat down to eat.

"No, no way, Grace," Julius said. "Leave some room for dessert. Maybe we can make Smores later, with wine. I saw you got a few more bottles."

Jack jumped up on the cushion next to Grace and stared at her as she began to eat.

Listen, girl, I have not been squeezing my sphincter like a nutcracker the last two days just so I can graze on what you think is a healthy alternative to food—

Grace turned to meet the dog's unblinking gaze. "Did you just growl at me?" She turned to Julius, who was eating. "I think he just growled at me."

"Probably. Jack doesn't really like salads."

"Your steak is cooking, Jack. It isn't ready yet."

—have a mind to let fly right now with over two days worth of poop, see how you like them apples, which, by the way, I ate a couple of crab apples outside the pound; remember the pound, honey? I sure as hell do, still having nightmares every time I close my—I'm sorry, I didn't quite catch that last bit. Did you say, steak?

"Jeez, Julius, your dog is skeezing me out here, just staring at me like that."

"Jack isn't good at blinking."

"I'll go get his dinner. Watch my plate, don't let him touch it."

Oh yeah, I'm jumping on that, right. Wouldn't worry about it, really. And don't worry if that steak's not too cooked, I'm okay with that. You kinda killed that last one, you know, yesterday. Just saying.

Jack watched Grace walk back below, then stared fixedly at the passageway until she reappeared with his plate. She had cut up the steak into little pieces for him. Grace set the plate on the table in front of Jack, who didn't wait for Grace to sit down again before beginning his own dinner.

"The dog is going to expect to eat at the table when we get back," Julius said, shaking his head.

"Not going to be my problem," Grace said before thinking. She blushed. "Oh, shit," she murmured. "Sorry, Julius. I'm being a...that wasn't nice. I'm sorry." He looked up from his plate at her. "And no, Julius, I'm sorry. I haven't really decided about your offer."

He looked relieved. "That's okay. I was afraid for a second there you were about to say that you decided against it. Just think about it, okay?"

Grace nodded. "It sounds nice, Julius." Julius beamed, and spent the rest of the dinner telling of his sailing adventures around the Caribbean, which Grace found surprisingly entertaining. She enjoyed hearing him talk about a part of his life when he had been genuinely happy. His stories made sailing around the Caribbean sound idyllic. It sounded like something she could really enjoy, she realized, smiling back at Julius as he went on about some drunken party in the Caymans where he ended up cartwheeling a Hobie Cat with three people aboard, none of whom could swim. She had no idea what a Hobie Cat was, but she laughed to hear him tell it. As he talked, Grace found herself staring at the ring on his finger. Julius noticed.

He stopped in mid story. "I can give it back, Grace. I wouldn't mind." Grace looked up at him, surprised. She shook her head. "Well, then I could take it off. Maybe keep it on a keychain, if you think that would be more—I don't know, appropriate."

She shook her head vehemently. "No, Julius. Wear it. Promise me you'll wear it, even after I'm—even after. Especially after."

He squinted at her. "Why? I mean, sure, Grace. Of course I will. But I don't understand why you even put it on me. What's up?"

She took his hand across the table and played with the ring. Jack had finished his dinner and excused himself, dropping back on deck to lie at their feet. "I'm not exactly sure, to tell you the truth. It just suddenly seemed like something I should do. And it feels important." He still looked confused, looking between her and the ring. "It's not about Gabe. It doesn't feel like his anymore. It's just..."

"What?"

Grace let go of his hand and laid back against the cushions, watching the sunset, now almost touching the ocean, royal blue streaked with blood orange. "When you die," she said, "there isn't just one place, you know? I'm not sure if I should even talk about this, I don't want to get you upset."

"It doesn't upset me, Grace. I want to hear about it. Pauley was saying something like that, that we're celibate because we have to be willing to be lost when we die, not be tied to anyone. I thought he was talking nonsense."

"No, that kind of makes sense, now that you put it that way. It's complicated, the universe, you know. So much more than anybody thinks. I mean, I'm no expert, I don't understand anything about—"

"Seems you're one of the leading experts alive today, actually."

"Yeah, I guess you're right. But I don't understand most of it, believe me. I mean, when I died, I didn't do anything special, but I ended up with my sister. And because I had screwed so many things up, Gabe died and—"

"You killed Gabe? Your husband?"

"No, I didn't really 'kill him,' kill him. It's complicated, and, to be honest, I don't know exactly what I did. Basically, I fucked up his place in this world to the tipping point. Sort of. Kind of a long story."

"We're just going nowhere in the middle of the ocean, Grace. We got time for a few long stories."

"Yeah, well. Maybe some other time. It's just that, when Gabe died, he was with me again. And when I was dead, I just knew that was going to happen. So it didn't even bother me that I was dead, or he was going to die—"

"—because of you, you mean."

"No, shut up. I'm thinking through this. Like Pauley was telling you, you could be lost. The universe is big, and you don't go to one big Heaven."

"You don't?"

"Sorry to burst your bubble, Father. Maybe I shouldn't be talking about all this, except I'm trying to make a point. I think. I mean, everyone dreams that when they die, they'll be with their loved ones, you know? And when the people they leave behind die, they'll come and join them. And I think that's true, at least in my experience."

"What about others? Were you with others, or just Gabe and your sister?"

"Oh no, I was in a whole world of other people, and they seem to feel the same way. I mean, it just seemed to be a given, nobody worried about it or did anything special. It just seemed to be the way things are."

"But. It sounds like there's a 'but' coming there."

"Yeah. Sitting on this side, it doesn't feel that way. It's scary. It feels like if I screw up, I'm a goner, like I might never be with them again. I can't just die. I don't know what would happen, but I'm pretty sure it would be bad. Really, bad. Like, really, eternally, bad."

"That's why you have to get to one of the special gates? That way you get straight back to Gabe?"

She nodded. "Yeah. There's a trick to it that I don't understand. Gabe knows a lot more about it than I do, tried to talk me out of even coming back. He said it was way too dangerous."

"So why did you?"

"Because I had to. I fucked up, Julius. I was the one responsible, so I have to fix it. It was going to be bad, really bad on this side, otherwise. I couldn't handle that. Gabe wanted to do it, wanted to come back instead of me. He said he had a better chance of fixing it, since he's the one who did all the work and all. That was bullshit, though."

"He sounds a pretty decent guy."

"He's a good man. I'm lucky that way. My one piece of luck."

"You only need one."

"You're right about that, Julius." She looked at him, feeling suddenly guilty, and sad for him. "I'm sorry yours hasn't come yet."

"Maybe it has, Grace."

She didn't want to go there again, so she steered the conversation back to what she was trying to sort out in her mind. She started thinking out loud again, saying, "Gabe found out about the Wright gates. It's not hard or anything. But if I don't go through one of those gates, it'll be bad."

"Why? You said when you died the first time, you didn't use a gate. Or Gabe, or your sister. Maybe that's just how it is."

"The first time, yes. But coming back is—not natural. It's not the same at all. Somehow, when we live in this world, we get bound to people, certain people, and you end up on the other side in a world with those people. But when you do what I've done, when you come back, I'm not sure the bonds apply anymore. You need a trick, to go through a gate, to get back to where you came from."

"The Mormons talk about binding. It's the basis for their baptism. In the baptismal right that imbues the person with the Holy Spirit, that's supposed to bind them in their family forever, right into the next life."

"Learn that in seminary, did you?"

"Studied a lot about other religions. It's what we learn."

"So you can be sure that you're right and they're wrong."

"Not entirely. That's part of it, though."

"Well, I got news for you, honey." He raised his eyebrows. She shook her head. "I better not."

"That's why the Mormons used to believe in polygamy, you know," Julius said.

"Not for the sex you mean?"

"Maybe that, too. But primarily, or at least by teaching, it is a means of binding everyone in an extended family through eternity, so a family stays together in the afterlife."

"Yeah," Grace said, "probably works fine in the next life. Not so much on this side of the river. Still think they're trying to maximize the guy's chances of getting laid every night. One woman marrying multiple men makes much more sense to me."

Julius considered this for a bit.

"Seems like they got some things right that we don't even know about," Julius said.

Grace nodded. "True. There's a good reason for that."

"Yeah? What's that?

"I'm not going to talk about it right now, Julius. I don't want to insult your church or anything. I know I haven't been acting like it, but I really respect who you are, what you've done with your life."

"Wouldn't be too certain just now, Grace."

"Don't say that Julius. You've been dealt a shitty hand. Actually, it sounds like about three shitty hands in a row. But you didn't just lay down and give up. I've seen you in that classroom with those kids. You're a good man. I think you're a great priest."

"Thank you, Grace. That means something, to hear you say that."

"It should. More than you could ever imagine, Julius."

"What did Pauley mean—"

"I'm not going to talk about that, Julius."

"Okay." There was an awkward silence for a bit, briefly interrupted by Jack belching. They both looked at the dog and laughed.

What? Be thankful it wasn't the other end. Which at some point, you know, is going to be an issue.

Julius looked back at Grace, saying, "So then tell me what you were thinking about the ring."

"Oh, yeah. I'm not sure, I might be just making this shit up. I don't know. It's just that the Claddagh is such an old, storied kind of ring design. It's been popular for hundreds of years, but nobody knows why."

"Maybe just because it's old."

"Maybe. There are all sorts of legends, fables about the design. All of them obvious bullshit. No one has an explanation for that design. I mean, look at it: two hands holding a crowned heart. There's no other icon in the world with a motif that's even close. What does it mean, do you think?"

Julius looked at the thing on his finger. "You think it represents the same sort of binding we're talking about?"

Grace nodded. "Yeah, I do. It just occurred to me, is all. I mean, I have no evidence at all for thinking that. It just looks like it. It feels like it. I don't know."

"It makes sense, in a way. So you think, maybe, if I keep wearing this, we'll be bound together? In the next life?" Grace looked at him, and barely nodded. "That would be nice, Grace. Thank you."

"Don't say thank you, Julius. It's probably bullshit. I just made it up."

"I hope it's true, Grace. But even if it isn't, thank you." He leaned over the table and kissed her, Grace turning so he kissed her cheek. "Thank you. If you're right, I hope Gabe isn't the jealous type."

Grace shook her head. "It doesn't work that way, Julius. I wouldn't worry about that."

"No? How does it work?"

"I don't really want to talk about that stuff anymore, okay? What do you mean, make some Smores? You said before, fire on a boat is a bad idea. You're not talking about microwaving them, are you? Because that's just wrong."

"No, there's a barbecue."

"You're kidding."

"No, I found it while rummaging through the deck lockers. Just a little thing that hangs off the side of the boat, runs on propane. Do we have the ingredients?"

"Yeah, I told you. That guy stocked us like we were going on a Boy Scout jamboree."

"I kind of steered him in that general direction. Great. If we're going to do this, though, we got to get it going before it gets dark."

"If we don't end up burning up the boat, tomorrow we can barbecue the steaks." Jack's ears perked up at that.

CHAPTER 26

When Pauley awoke again, it was because his back and neck were in spasm from sleeping in the chair. He barely managed to straighten up and stand. His head was pounding, pain radiating down his neck and back. He felt old.

It was light out now. He had missed morning service. He'd just have to make evening mass, he told himself. Pauley dragged himself into the shower, trying to clear his head from the alcohol. Why did the girl have to be excised? he kept wondering. He needed to know. He needed to know, because he knew that he was going to go through with it. He was going to do it. But he had to know why.

Pauley had no idea how he would find the answer to that question. He wasn't even certain the Cardinal knew the answer, had gotten the impression from yesterday's audience that the man neither knew nor cared. Who then? Who wanted her excised, and why? What had she done to the church to deserve such a fate? He shook his head as he dressed. If the Cardinal didn't know, he couldn't think of anyone in the archdiocese who might know. Hell, Pauley thought, the Pope himself might not know. Not that kind of organization.

Dressed again in coat and collar, Pauley crossed the room to check his book. As he opened it, the thought struck him that the book itself might be the answer. This book, this strange device that he had been given back in Georgetown, was a tool to help him with the mission of finding the girl. It had helped him find her, and now would allow him to complete the task, to be the instrument of her excision. This book—where had it come from? It had just arrived one day at his office, he didn't even know how it was delivered. Pauley had actually ignored the thing for months, left it lying on a table. It was a book he was well familiar with, had never actually liked very much. It was only once the Cardinal had contacted him and told him he needed to find the girl that the book had come to his attention. He had been shocked to learn of the girl's Return, at a loss as to how to locate her until the Cardinal had asked whether he had received the book. The Cardinal had sent it, then. Pauley remembered, the Cardinal had his own copy as well. The book was his answer. If he could find out who was writing the book, and to what end, he might know why the girl was doomed to be excised.

Pauley walked down to the dining room, absently returning the greetings of the other priests he encountered on the way, lost in thought. The Cardinal had referenced the book in their meeting yesterday, had implied that it was exceptional. "Are you oblivious to its authorship?" the man had said. Such a strange question. Yes, he was completely oblivious. He didn't have a clue.

Pauley ate alone, thinking. The Cardinal might know. It seemed he knew something about it, at least. Maybe not specifics, but certainly more than Pauley. As he considered this, though, he doubted that he could get the Cardinal to share his insights. Not that kind of organization. Who else, then? It was then that Pauley remembered the visitor at his office. The crazy old black man who had threatened him, that guy who had smashed his bottle of whiskey and smelled like offal—he had made a reference to his "magicky book." Pauley was sure of it. He didn't know who the man was, was certain that the man scared him to his core for some reason that he couldn't even understand, but this man knew about the book. How? He knew how to find out. He knew where the man was, just uptown from where he was sitting now. The man was in his book.

Uriel cursed in response to the knocking on his hotel room door. He looked at the clock on the nightstand. Ten in the morning. He was still in his pajamas. He cursed again.

"Dammit, Parnell, you're a fucking blood-sucking leech, you know that?" He swung the door open to see Pauley standing there. He closed the door without a word and went back to bed, ignoring the repeated knocking on the door.

When he came downstairs for lunch three hours later, Uriel wasn't surprised to find Pauley sitting next to Parnell in the hotel restaurant. He was also not surprised that Parnell was still wearing his rumpled white suit. Uriel shook his head in disgust. He joined them at the table. Obviously, they had been waiting for him.

Uriel pointed to the drink in front of Pauley. "Betting that's not your first one today, Pauley. Sure you want to do this?" Pauley said nothing as the waiter arrived to distribute menus. "Didn't know you were treating the whole party, Parnell. Can't wait till Zimmerman and the girl show up. Hope you got some room on that credit card, sucker."

Parnell opened his mouth to protest, but then decided to look at the menu instead. They ordered. "You look very different from the last time we met," Pauley said to Uriel. He picked up his drink but put it back down, untouched.

"So do you. Even worse. Look like a man who's gonna die soon. Again."

"Listen, Earle," Parnell said, placating. "Father Pauley and I were talking, before you came down." He waited for Uriel to say something in response, but Uriel just kept carefully buttering his roll. "Father Pauley needs to—"

"Father Pauley needs to die," Uriel interrupted. "Father Pauley is a child-raping, child-murdering, alcoholic, lowlife maggot who shouldn't be here using up our oxygen. Did you know that, Chuck?" The other two men just stared. "Why don't you tell Dr. Parnell about your past dealings with the lady, Father Pauley? Isn't that why you're here, to bring us up to speed on your plans to cleanse your soul? To make your little redheaded guilt bitch go up in smoke? That why you're ruining an otherwise pleasant lunch, making me sick by just being this close and still breathing?"

Pauley reddened, obviously struggling to control himself. Appetizers arrived. "Pauley was telling me that he doesn't really want to perform the excision," Parnell said. "He says—"

"Then he's a lying scumbag, on top of everything else. He can't wait to do this, get his whole hand back. Get his God-fearing soul back." Parnell watched Pauley rub his injured hand self-consciously. Uriel allowed the waiter to grind pepper on his salad before he began to eat. "Which, it gives me great pleasure to point out," Uriel said between bites of salad, "will never be accomplished. Not in this universe, leastwise. I promise you that. I'll make sure of that, like I told you in your office."

"I'm afraid he's serious," Parnell pointed out, now also beginning to eat. "In my experience, Earle's a very persistent person, at least in regards to that sort of thing."

Pauley finally recovered himself enough to speak. The bitterness in the back of his throat prevented him from picking up his spoon to begin his soup, however. He cleared his throat with difficulty and took a sip of water. "I believe you, whoever you are. I don't know who you are, or how you are involved in this matter." He waited for Uriel to respond, to explain himself, but the other man went on eating. "You know about my book. You called it a 'magic book." Uriel kept eating. Parnell watched both men, waiting and eating.

"Zimmerman told me about the book," Parnell interjected, conversationally.

"Who gives a fuck?" Uriel said, finishing his salad. "You gonna eat that? It's getting cold." Pauley shook his head. Uriel took the man's bowl of soup, moving his empty salad plate to the side. He reached over to take the spoon. "Wasted on the likes of you, anyways." Uriel ate the soup.

"I was given the book," Pauley started again, "to help me with this task. It is obviously tied to this process, somehow."

" 'This task, this process.' You just dancing around, Peter. Just dancing. Raping a twelve year old girl not enough dancing for you, throwing the girl's sister off a building to her death not 'process' enough for you? Now you get to murder the girl's soul. Murder her soul, motherfucker! Let's call a spade a spade here, Peter."

"I need to know why," Pauley said softly, looking down at the space where his soup had been. Uriel tilted the bowl to mop the last of the soup with a portion of his roll. "Why the girl is to be excised. I have to know."

"No you don't, Pauley. You want to do it, period. You can't even claim you're just following orders, *kleine* Himler. You'd love following this order. Shit man, if his Eminence told you today that the deal's off, you'd still want to do it."

Pauley shook his head, meeting Uriel's gaze. "I have to know. Nobody in the Church is going to explain to me why this has to be done."

"You're sure as shit right about that."

"But you know why," Pauley said. "You know about the book. They're connected."

"You're right, Pauley. I know why. I know about the book. Sure, I know they're connected. I know about you and I know what you are."

"Tell me. Please."

"No, Pauley. I won't. And not just because I take a great deal of pleasure in anything that makes your existence even more miserable, you putrid rat excrescence. Not just that. If I tell you why your fascist organization wants this girl destroyed, you think maybe it'll be justified, maybe you feel a little better about yourself. I wouldn't give you the satisfaction, motherfucker. But I will say this: If I told you why, you'd hate yourself even more, because they want this done for all the worst reasons. But you're going to try to do it anyways. And when you do, even when you fail, I'll find you. Even if you die in the process, I will find you. I promise you that. Oh, look, here's our lunch."

"Who is writing the book? Tell me that much."

"Why should I?" Pauley blinked at the other man. "You know what, Pauley? I'm going to give you an honest answer to that question. I won't fuck with you on this. Just to show how sincere I am when I say that, if you give that girl the touch, if you go ahead with this, I will come down on you like a building falling from the sky. Okay?"

Pauley nodded, eyes pleading.

"I don't know."

Pauley deflated. Uriel ate his lunch. Parnell looked between them, also eating. With effort, Pauley stood and left the restaurant without another word.

"Hate it when people don't eat what they order," Uriel said.

"You really don't know?" Parnell asked.

"Not specifically, no."

"Who in general, then?"

"Some dead guy. Gotta be. Probably some dead church functionary, charged with monitoring the situation and updating the stupid thing. That's the way this shit works."

"You know how they're doing the book?" Parnell asked, incredulous.

"You need to close your mouth and swallow before you speak, Parnell. Raised without manners. I know, I know—bastard, right? Bastard, my ass. No excuse." Uriel pushed his empty plate aside, then continued, "Yes, I know. It's just a cheap parlor trick. The girl even used it, had it figured out even before she died."

"She did? Helena?"

Uriel nodded, now having started on the lunch that Pauley had abandoned. "You should know, Parnell. That's how she got you hooked into this whole thing."

"What? Me? How?"

"And you should call her Grace. That's her real name."

"She never had a real name, just kept taking—"

"Grace is her real name," Uriel interjected passionately. "You're in no position to speak of her that way."

"I'm just saying, when I knew her, she—"

"Shut up about that. You don't know shit. I'm trying to enjoy my lunch."

"You did enjoy your lunch. Now you're enjoying Pauley's lunch."

"Not as much as I would if you just shut the fuck up."

"Grace, then. What did she do for me?"

"That's how she pulled the trick with the Book of Mormon, how she got you back that precious program so you could save the crazy people of the world. Make you all famous and pious. Elevate the Church to something above a self-absorbed bullshit machine. She timeshifted the Book of Mormon back, had a new one made to replace the original. Actually, pretty impressive for someone who'd never even been dead before. Not entirely sure how she figured that all out, ahead of time. Someone dead must've been talking to her; probably her sister, I suppose."

"I'm not sure I get it."

"Don't really give a rat's ass."

"So the book doesn't predict the future? It doesn't tell him what's going to happen?"

"No, of course not. That's crazy shit. It says what's already happened. Of course, everything's just about already happened when it's actually happening, so it's pretty much real time. But you look ahead, just starts sounding like nonsense. It's gotta, cause it hasn't happened yet. Until stuff happens, it's just nonsense."

"Oh, I see."

Uriel looked up from his plate to stare at Parnell. "You do?"

"Yeah, I think so."

"Hmmph. Praise the Man Jesus." Uriel finished up his second lunch. He gestured to the whiskey neat still sitting at Pauley's place. "He touch that to his lips?"

"No, it arrived just before you sat down."

"Oh, good." Uriel sipped at the whiskey and nodded approvingly. "Connemara. Nice."

Grace and Julius enjoyed their Smores as it grew dark again. Jack was asleep in the bow, the sound of his contented breathing mixing with the splash of the boat parting the sea ahead. They had enjoyed a quiet silence for quite a while, each lost in thought. Both looked out past the stern as the darkness deepened, the boat's wake an iridescent glow curving away in the moonlight. Grace lay back on the cushions, licking chocolate from her fingers, watching the huge triangle of the ship's sails eclipse the night's stars as they slid forward like a huge scythe.

"Why is it always Hershey's chocolate?" Grace asked. "You noticed that? Nobody ever uses Cadbury, or anything."

"True. I don't know. Cadbury is English, isn't it? Wouldn't be right."

"There's plenty of shitty American chocolate. How'd Hershey get to be the official candy bar of sickeningly sweet, carcinogenically burnt marshmallow and graham cracker camping convention?" Julius shrugged.

"Marketing?" Julius ventured.

"Bet it has something to do with the *sub rosa* influence of the Masons on the Boy Scouts of America through the centuries. Masons probably hid some kind of mind controlling chemical in the Hershey bars, secretly influence the future leaders of industry and government. You should check the wrappers for the all-seeing eye thing, probably hidden in the logo."

"It is common knowledge amongst the Illuminati that Hershey Chocolate Company was founded by the only remaining caste of the Knights Templar, when they fled to America, Grace. When they escaped the referendum of Pope Clement, in 1311. Haven't you ever seen Hershey Park? From above, the layout mimics a contractor's compass. That's why you never see any Saracens in Pennsylvania. That, and marketing."

"Now that you mention it, it does seem rather obvious."

"Of course." Julius lay down on the cushions next to Grace, head to foot, and also watched as the stars pirouetted about the mast. "It's all in the Book of Mormon."

Grace smacked Julius in the stomach at that, eliciting a grunt.

"Nice. You want to be wearing semidigested Smores?"

"Don't make fun of my Book. I helped write that book, you know."

"Of course you did. You and Molay, the martyred Captain of the Knights Templar, took turns dictating it to Joseph Smith in his sleep."

She hit him again. "I'm not kidding. Don't make fun."

"You're nuts."

"No, I'm not." Grace spent the next half hour explaining her work with Charlie the goldsmith from Salt Lake City, her prank on Parnell, how she had arranged for the book to be buried in upstate New York by her Hispanic friend Jesus, then shifted it back in time once she died. "I'm the one who got Smith to finally dig up the plates. Otherwise, who knows?"

Julius was shaking his head in the deepening evening. "So you're the one who dictated the Book of Mormon to Smith, eh?"

"No, I didn't say that. I just got him to dig it up. Somebody else must've been whispering to him for the translation."

"Yeah? Like who?" Grace shrugged. "I'm sorry, I missed that. Who?"

"No idea, Julius. Somebody dead, obviously. I mean, when you read the book, it's pretty obvious that somebody with perspective was talking to the guy. An awful lot of it is pretty dead on, you know. A lot closer than your Books, anyway. More up to date, at least."

"You expect me to actually believe any of that? Let's go back to Masonic One World Order conspiracy theories, more believable."

"No, it's all true. I wonder how Jesus is doing. He owns those restaurants in Chicago you were telling me about, you know. Must be him."

"But you rewrote the Book of Mormon?"

"No, not the whole thing. I just modified it a little, switched it for the original."

"No shit? Hold it—explain how this works. The time shift thing."

"You wouldn't understand. It's a 'next life' thing."

"Somebody has to start telling me something. All I get from you and Pauley is 'it's not important,' or 'you wouldn't understand.' Well, it is important and I don't understand, so somebody better start explaining this shit."

"So ask Pauley."

"I'm asking you. Don't expect to ever see Pauley again, to tell you the truth."

Grace snorted at that. "Don't think we're going to be that lucky, Julius."

"Why do you say that?"

"Because he's stalking me or something. Too much of a coincidence, otherwise."

"I was wondering what was going on."

"I don't know what's going on. But it can't just be bad luck that both of us end up in Georgetown at the same time. No cosmic fuck-up is that fucked up."

"Maybe it's me. I have a penchant for being in the middle of cosmic fuck-ups, you know."

"You might be right. It's probably you."

"I was just kidding, Grace."

"Oh, sorry."

"Why would Pauley be stalking you? It doesn't make any sense. He's been at Georgetown for years, before I arrived. Just waiting for you?"

Grace shook her head in the dark. "You still don't get it. The time thing is pretty meaningless."

"That doesn't make any sense."

"Look, it's an afterlife thing."

"Then tell me."

"It's hard."

"Try."

Grace paused for a minute. "You know how heaven is always talked about like it's above here? Well, that's kind of right, in a sense. Only it's not heaven—it's a higher plane of existence, but not completely disconnected. A higher dimension."

"So when you're dead, you're looking down on us, here?"

"Not down, exactly. Everything here is flattened, kind of. It's like you're looking at a picture, or I guess it would be more like a movie, kind of. The only depth to it is time, since we're above time, too."

"I don't get it."

"No, I don't really know how to explain it any better. Like I was telling Gabe, before he died, it's like you were looking down on a chessboard or something. Everything is flat, like the squares on the board, but you're moving through time. And since we're above time, it's like we can move pieces through time, back in time. But you can't move the squares on the board, you can't even look around them to get a better view or anything."

"I think I get that. So you can see some things, but not everything. Like in a movie, if the camera isn't pointing in that direction."

"Yeah, I guess that's a pretty good analogy. Like a movie. We can't manipulate anything physically. That'd be like you trying to move the squares on the chessboard. The only way we can move things is in your time—like sliding pieces on the board, but through time, not space. But that's not the important thing." She shook her head in the dark.

"So what's the important thing?"

"The important thing is nobody really cares, Julius."

"What do you mean, nobody cares?"

"Nobody there cares about this place. They've moved on. Like when you asked if Gabe could see us, last night. I mean, if he wanted to, he could probably see us lying here now, but I'm sure he isn't. He just wouldn't. Even if he did, he wouldn't care."

"Why not?" Julius asked, looking up at the stars and wondering if Gabriel was looking back.

"It's just not important, Julius. Nobody there spends any time looking down here, or is particularly interested."

"I thought you said there wasn't any time there."

"There is a kind of time, but it's not our time. I mean, there has to be another kind of time, there, or else everything would be happening at once, right? But it's different from our time here. I'm sorry, I'm not making much sense, I know."

"So why wouldn't Gabe be watching us? He's worried about you, I'm sure."

"No, I don't think so. Either I'm back with him, or I'm lost. He didn't want me to come back, to leave him. Now that I left, it seems like I'm spending time here, with you. But not there. He can't help me, or fix it if I fuck up."

"Oh. I'm sorry to hear that. I was kind of hoping that he was on our side."

"Honestly, Julius—I don't think anyone is on our side."

Uriel finished the whiskey and dabbed his mouth with the linen napkin. He started to push back from the table.

"Wait," Parnell said. "Where are you going?"

"Doesn't matter to you."

"Why not?"

"Because I'm doing it without you, that's why. You are going to buy yourself some clothes. Buy some clothes and burn that shit you've been wearing for the past week."

"Maybe I'll just have this cleaned, like you said."

"No. Don't have it cleaned. Have it burned. Stuff it down the incinerator chute. I'm not kidding Parnell. If I see you wearing that shit this evening, I'm not letting you in the limo."

"We're taking a limo again? Where to?"

"Where do you think? Dinner. Be out front at seven-thirty. Now that I think of it, though, if you show up in those clothes, I think that'll be reason enough to kill you, right then and there."

"Maybe I could get Antonio to make me a suit."

"No chance. Just get something off the rack somewhere. This is fucking New York, for chrissakes. But get something nice, I don't want to embarrass my friends again. Not brown. Or plaid. You pull that shit, I don't think they'll let you in the front door this time."

"We're going back to Delmonico's?"

"You got a better place in mind?" Parnell shook his head. "Didn't think so. And besides, I don't think we'll have a lot more dinners this trip."

"She's coming to New York?"

"Yeah, I think so. Even if she doesn't know it quite yet."

"Hold it. How—"

Uriel cut him off with a wave of his hand as he stood from the table. "Seven-thirty. No white suit, or it'll be covered in blood."

Eventually, Grace sat up and watched Julius as he stood at the wheel in the moonlight. She walked back to the cockpit and put a hand on his arm. "I'm going to bed, Julius." He nodded. She stood on tiptoes to give him a kiss on the cheek. He smiled at her.

"Night, Grace."

Grace went below and showered, briefly this time. She dressed in another pair of men's pajamas from the closet, buttoned to the collar. After considering for a bit, she chose one of the smaller cabins. She found a book in the stateroom on sailing technique and propped herself up in bed, reading.

Grace was surprised that the book was making sense to her, probably because of the instruction that Julius had given her earlier; that, and the fact that she was pretty much immersed in the whole deal. She was so engrossed in the book she didn't notice Julius enter the cabin until he sat down on the side of the bed. She looked up to see him, sitting in his boxers again. She blushed, flustered.

"Whatcha reading?" he asked her.

"Idiot's guide to sailing for morons. Listen, Julius," she said, meeting his eyes for the first time since he entered the small cabin. "You don't have to do this."

She saw him swallow hard. "I don't?" Grace shook her head. "Last night...it seemed that, you know..."

"No, Julius. I was wrong. You don't have to. I don't want you to."

"You don't?" She shook her head. "Well. Okay, then, Grace." He stood and walked out of the little cabin. Grace watched him leave and sighed softly to herself. Maybe not entirely to herself, she realized. She raised the book from her lap and tried to find the spot she had left off, the spot where Julius had come in. In his boxers. She was having a hard time finding the exact spot to start reading again, the print blurry and swimming before her eyes, when he came back in the room. Julius sat carefully back down on the side of the bed next to her. "Just seems kind of silly to read a book like that when I can teach you all about sailing, Grace." He took the book from her and closed it gently, setting it aside on the cabinet. "I should explain about points of sail. Did I teach you about the points of sail earlier?" She shook her head, watching him. Julius reached over to turn off the small reading light. Moonlight filled the cabin. "Well, you can't go sailing until you understand the points of sail." Julius began to quietly lecture her on the points of sailing, the terminology of wind direction in relation to the boat, how the sail should be set at each point to maximize the thrust of the wind...

Grace tried to listen in the moonlight, but was having a hard time focusing on what Julius was saying. As he quietly lectured, Julius began to slowly unbutton her pajama top, starting at the collar. He kept lecturing softly about sailing, and winds, and points of sail, as he lingered over each button, fingering each like it was a bead on a rosary. Grace couldn't make out the words, was hearing only a steady roaring in her ears, mixed with the sonorous tone of Julius going on and on as she realized that she wasn't breathing, she really should be breathing, but she seemed to have forgotten the trick of it, the part that made it automatic, so she found that she had to actually think about breathing in, and then out, and then in again...

Grace was still trying to breathe as she wondered just how many goddamned buttons were on this stupid shirt, anyway, he must've undone at least twenty as he droned on, Grace letting her eyes close and her head drop back against the headboard as she forgot to breath again, had to take a deep breath as she realized that must be the last one, since she couldn't breathe at all now, because he was kissing her...

Evidently, Grace's concerns about an unfortunate war injury were unfounded. The boat, however, was another matter. Grace wasn't used to boats. Early on, and at the most inopportune moment, a gust of wind caused the boat to heel over sharply. Julius felt it coming, having been in this position more than once before, and automatically braced them with an arm against the bulkhead, but the sudden lee lurch caused Grace to cry out, which caught Julius up short, concerned, as the boat rolled back, the gust passing. All of which would have been just fine, a momentary pause of intimate momentum, if only Grace hadn't then burst into laughter. Laughter was one thing Julius hadn't previously experienced at this particular point in a relationship, and had to wait, watching Grace laugh until she was crying, eventually controlling herself to the point where he could get her to explain exactly what was so funny, but all Grace could tell him was that she finally figured out what was meant by her favorite curse. This made no sense to Julius at all. It wasn't until quite a bit later in the evening when, at another completely inappropriate moment, he recalled, unbidden, her epithet from the night before and, despite trying hard to concentrate on the task at hand, he in turn burst into a fit of giggles, followed by a full blown gale of laughter, eliciting the same response once again from Grace.

At one point during the night, Jack padded unnoticed into the room and settled down on the floor. After a short while, however, the dog decided it would be best to sleep topside for the evening. It was a warm night, after all.

Grace cradled her head in her hand as she lay on her side. She fell asleep as she watched Julius sleep. When she awoke, moonlight had given way to the thin grey of morning, and she could make out the lettering there on his hip quite clearly now; "Salome," it read, in small script letters. His ex-wife, no doubt; he was that kind of a guy, she realized, the kind who felt an obligation, even after the woman leaves. Just that kind of guy. She silently walked from the room, leaving him asleep, to go take her shower. She wondered if he'd get another tattoo for the other hip, after she left him.

CHAPTER 27

Steaks again, at Delmonico's, with a couple bottles of wine. Parnell realized that his credit had no chance of recovering from this little escapade, not in this lifetime at least. Might as well enjoy it while it lasted. Chuck was dressed in a navy pinstripe suit he'd purchased at a small men's shop around the corner from the hotel. The sleeves were too short.

"But you know what's going on?" Parnell asked, for the third time that evening.

"Of course I know what's going on," Uriel answered irritably. "You think I'd be hanging with you if I didn't have to?"

"I'm picking up the tab, Earle."

"Still not worth it, Chuck. You are a tedious dinner companion; you know that, right?"

Parnell decided not to argue the point. He knew by now Earle's technique for steering conversations away from subjects he'd rather avoid. "I'm not talking about the magic book. I get the book thing, I think. But why so much attention on the girl? Why is she so important?"

"Why did you think she was so important? You spent a good part of your life tagging along with her and Sheehan." Parnell shrugged. "Don't give me that shit, Parnell. Remember who you're talking to here."

"I really don't know who I'm talking to, Earle."

"True. But I know you and what you've been doing. Just about this whole life you been focused on the girl and her work. Even after she died. Especially after she died. Now you got the whole LDS church caught up in the mix."

"Didn't mean to."

"Sure you did, you crazy motherfucker. Sure you did. You know what's happening here. You dragged them in by the scruff of their collective, Jesus lovin' necks. First you sold them on the 'save the crazies of the world' program, then you made that little play back in the temple that really set the pot to boiling. Don't bullshit me. You got an agenda. I don't know where you get your information, how you cut that 'untouched by death' deal you got. But I can see that you're in the loop on this shit. You're workin' it hard, mi amigo."

"I know what she's done and the harm it could cause. It affects what I do, what I'm supposed to do."

"Managing souls, you mean?" Uriel asked, eating.

"Yeah, in broad strokes. This technology, the widespread knowledge of 'the what happens after,' it could cause great damage."

"It has caused great damage, Parnell. And you saw it coming from a long way back, I know. You answered your own question."

"What question?"

"Why the girl's a problem. Why the forces are arrayed against her. Why she's the target of the church's excisioners. She will piss off a lot of very, very important people."

"But it's not really her fault, is it? I mean, she's done a lot of good..."

"Nobody cares 'bout that shit. Look what's going on around here, now. All these Returnees, the gates you got Wright to build, all that shit the Mormons are doing. The wheels are comin' off the bus here, Parnell. Not quite yet, not quite here. But it's coming and they know it. They're ahead of this game, you know."

"I *don't* know, Earle. That's my disadvantage, I guess. Never been on the other side."

"Never? What happens, then? When you die?"

"You mean when you kill me?"

"I haven't killed you every time. Don't start whining here, Chuck. I'll have Tony move you to the table by the bathroom. What happens when you die? No time off at all? No vacation in limbo or anything before getting back to work?"

Parnell shook his head, saying, "No, don't think so. Never remember anything like that. Just get born again, start all over."

"As a baby, like normal folk?" Parnell nodded. "What a pain in the ass. You get to pick, at least?" Parnell shook his head, refilling his glass of wine.

"No, actually seems pretty random. Maybe there's some sort of predestination or something, nobody really explained it to me. I just do the best I can with what I'm given."

"But you remember what came before, right?" Uriel asked.

"Not right away, no. It comes back to me, slowly. Not all at once."

"Weird. No wonder you're always getting used."

"It is what I am, I guess. I'm not the only one, you know."

"Really? How do you know that? You run into others like you?"

"No. That would be cool, though. No, I found out when I was researching. It's in the Book of Mormon. Three Nepthi were given the promise of everlasting life. Three of us."

"You believe that shit, huh?"

"Oh, yeah. Most of it, at least."

"So who are the other two?"

"Well, I'm sure the Dalai Lama is one."

Uriel nodded as he finished his wine. He noticed that Parnell had polished off the bottle. He motioned for the sommelier, who just nodded and retreated to the cellar for another bottle. "Sure, that makes sense. Everyone always running around trying to find the new baby Lama. Who's the other?"

"I don't know."

"You don't know? All this time kicking around on this rock, never occurred to you to find out the third member of your trio?"

"Just found out there was a trio."

"Seems like it might be important, to know."

"Yeah, it might be. I don't know."

"Fuckin' lot you don't know, Parnell. Seems like you don't know a lot of stuff, but you got yourself a pretty intense plan, all the same. You made some waves, motherfucker."

"Never really my intention, Earle."

"Bullshit. Who's callin' the plays? Who gives you the mission, should you choose to accept it?"

"Doesn't work that way, I'm telling you," Parnell said, shaking his head. "No voices in my head, no burning bush talking to me from the side of the road."

"You just makin' this shit up as you go along?"

"Yeah, pretty much."

"You're not playing me here, are you, Chuck?"

"No, Earle. Why would I lie? Like I've been saying, I'm pretty much doing what I think is right."

"And getting Wright to build portals for the dead, that just seemed like the right thing at the time? How'd you get that idea?"

"It's complicated."

"Oh, I'm sure it is. I don't buy it. Somebody's playing you, Parnell. Just like you're trying to play me, now."

"No, Earle. Nobody's playing anybody. There was a need, that's all. At the time. It was a different time, and it had to be done. But it was supposed to be just once, that's all. And he was supposed to tear it down, after. It got out of hand. Frank just stopped listening..." Parnell seemed to get a little distraught, remembering.

"Hmmph. Like I said, Parnell. You got used. You know why Frank stopped listening? Cause he started listening to someone else, that's why. Once they used you to plant the seed—they couldn't do that from where they're sitting. But once they got the ball rolling, had you balling the little architect and delivered the seed for them, then they got to take over."

"But maybe it was you, then. You killed me, and I couldn't—"

"No, wasn't me. I was trying to stop you, but I was too late. No way to know that at the time. Same with the Rasputin thing. Tried to stop you from fucking everything up then, too. But you wouldn't just die. I'm sure there was some sort of intervention there, too. No way you should've survived that cut I gave you."

"The first time, you mean."

"Yeah, the first time. By the time I finally did you, damage had been done."

"What damage? What did I do?"

"It's complicated. Don't worry about it," Uriel said, approving the new bottle of wine for the sommelier and setting his glass back down to be filled. "That's very nice, Sheryl."

"No, what happened?" Parnell insisted.

"Just a little thing, don't sweat it."

"What little thing?"

"World War Two. Hitler. The whole Holocaust thing."

"You're kidding," Parnell said. Uriel shook his head, finishing his steak. "Gee. I feel terrible."

"Yeah, can't blame you there. Well, what's done is done. And now your church is busy bringing 'em all back. Ironic, huh?"

"Yeah, I guess." Parnell shook his head, trying to clear it. "But what is Grace doing, then? Who do you think is behind her excision? Who do you think was manipulating me?"

"Forces, Parnell. Forces in the universe. You know how it is."

"No. I don't. What forces are you talking about?"

"Come on, Chuck. You know it's not a level playing field here. You must've noticed that, been around all these millennia and all. All kind of forces in the here and now, in the ever after; shit, even in the before the here and now. You're a Mormon, you know."

"I think I know what you're referring to, but I'm not sure what forces. You mean God?"

Uriel spluttered his sip of wine. He wiped his mouth as he shook his head. "Hell, no. Never said anything 'bout any god, did I?"

"Then who? What forces do you mean?"

"Shit, Parnell. I got to tell you how the world works? How the whole fucking universe works? Every day, every where, and every how, things getting played here, you know that. You think Einstein just wakes up one morning, thinks to himself, 'I think I'll write a letter to the President of the United States, tell him about nuclear bombs and shit?' That how you think it works? You think Picasso wasn't shown a picture of Guernica from whenever folks really started liking that kind of shit, somebody tell him 'you really should paint this kinda stuff, Pablo, screw that Blue crap, that's not you, this is the shit make you be famous someday?' You think he just came up with that on his own? On what basis? No fucking way. You think Fosbury one day just decides to flop over the high bar like that on his own, when every other motherfucker since sport began has been jumpin' frontwise? No fuckin' way. I don't believe you. Maybe somebody else might not see it, but you? Who tells Oswald, 'Don't worry too, too much about actually aiming, motherfucker, just take the shot, we got the rest covered?' You think the Supreme Court of the United States just decides to skip the flipping a coin part, go straight to crowning the crazy-ass one so's he can invade Babylonia? And that's after the entire state of Florida votes into a dead-even tie? Are you kidding me? Shit, man, there are a lot of perfectly normal folk, folk living only one life, you know, they know better. They know it's rigged. You probably the only one who don't. Idiot."

"But who, then? Who are these forces?"

"Who? Who isn't in on it? Everybody got an angle, Mamah, ev-er-y bo-dy. Folks without bodies, mostly, you know what I'm saying? Both sides of the Styx, working in kahoots. Come on, buddy. Read your history. You think the Popes and Cardinals just retire when they're dead, not going to keep fuckin' with folks? Read about those Rosey Cross folk—"

"The Rosicrucians? They exist?"

"You're serious? You were there, you tell me. Think the Knights Templar were fighting for the Popish good will? For what? What Grail you been drinkin' from? The Great White Fraternity, the Masons, Sacred Sects of Isis? One World Order? General Electric? Pick one, mother-fucker. Hell, pick half a dozen, don't matter. Plenty to go around."

"I'm lost."

"First factual thing you've said all evening."

"No, I don't get any of it."

"Just get this: It doesn't matter what you get. Just keep doing your thing, Parnell."

"I don't even know what that is anymore."

"Truth is, seems you never did."

"Maybe not. We getting dessert?" Parnell asked.

"Sure. Why the hell not? Not as if we're getting a lot more dinners like this, not in this life, at least."

"You can be pretty depressing, you know that, Earle?"

Uriel squinted across the table at the other man. "Yeah, Chuck. I know that."

Grace made breakfast while Julius showered and went back to sailing the boat. She had to squint as she brought the plates on deck, as it was another perfectly sunny morning, steady winds with moderate seas. Julius and Jack joined her at the table as she made her second trip up, bringing orange juice and Jack's plate.

"Just so you know, Grace," Julius said, sitting down. "It's not always this perfect. Sometimes, it rains."

"I like it this way. Don't let it rain."

"I'll do my best. No pancakes? Jack'll be disappointed."

No pancakes? Jack took his seat at the table next to Grace. *Oh, steak and eggs. And hash browns. I'm good.*

"Had to make hash browns when I saw that you had saved the bacon grease in that little jar under the sink."

"What are you talking about? What little jar?" he asked, eating. "Delicious."

Delicious.

"Under the sink, in the kitchen."

"Galley."

"Where you left it," Grace said.

"I didn't leave anything. Probably a jar of hydraulic fluid."

"You think? Really?" Nobody stopped eating.

I'm okay with it.

"No, just kidding," Julius said, smiling.

"Oh."

They ate in silence for a bit, Jack finishing his breakfast in a matter of a few minutes. He excused himself and dropped back on deck to sit in the bow. He had taken to sitting far up in the very apex of the boat, the breeze blowing back his ears. He'd sit like that for over an hour sometimes, staring out over the sea, when he wasn't sleeping on deck in the sun.

Julius looked up from his empty plate to watch the dog, sitting in the bow. He shook his head, saying, "I have no idea what goes on in that dog's head. Sometimes, I swear he thinks he's in charge, you know?"

I'm telling you, Winston. Yalta is not going to be fun and games. Stalin's no rube, you know. And you can't expect Roosevelt to be any help, the guy's got no guts for this sort of thing. He's a thinker, not a leader like you. Can't expect him to stand up to Stalin. Ha! I made a little joke there, Winston, get it? Let me tell you how I think we're going to have to play this...

"I'm sure he thinks he's in charge. We'd probably be better off," Grace said, looking up at the dog. She lapsed back into silence, pushing the food around on her plate.

"You haven't eaten much, Grace," Julius said, turning back to the table. "You feeling okay?"

"Tell you the truth, Julius? No. Out of sorts, kind of."

"I'm sorry, Grace, I shouldn't have—" He cut off as she looked up at him sharply.

"Shouldn't have what?" she demanded. He just shook his head. "Is that what you think it is? You're an idiot, Zimmerman, you know that? Were you always an idiot, or did they teach you to be an idiot when you became a priest?" Julius chose not to answer, so Grace continued, "What is it with you guys and sex, anyway? Why did you have to pick one of the two, really great bodily functions to completely fuck up? It's sex, Julius! It was great—shit, I thought it was great, who the hell knows what you were thinking. You just kept giggling the whole time. You shouldn't have? Really? Here I thought it was the best thing we've had since you fished me out of that river. I mean, the Ferrari was a pretty close second, maybe even a toss-up if you really want to go there. But you don't have a whole liturgy against the joys of downshifting, do you? Why couldn't you guys have picked some other bodily function to fuck up with your massive guilt trips, huh? You're always harping on the two best things we do on this planet, eat and screw. Why couldn't you have picked, I don't know, farting or something. Let the Pope pontificate on how breaking wind in public will get your sorry ass condemned to eternal damnation. Now that would make the world a better place. But no, you have to go and fuck with the screwing. It's just too nice, too damn perfectly fine; is that it? You shouldn't have? I think you're wrong, Julius. I'm sorry if you feel differently." She went back to pushing her food around on her plate. Finally, she put the plate down on the deck. "Hey, Jack! You still hungry?"

Give me a moment, Winston. My aide-de-camp, bless her. Be right back.

Jack sauntered back to finish Grace's breakfast.

Julius started to say something several times, each time thinking better of it. Finally, he said, "I'm not sorry, Grace. I didn't mean that. It was better than the Ferrari. In some ways. Slightly."

Grace sighed and put her head in her hands. "I'm sorry, Julius. I'm just messing with you here, I guess. Out of sorts, like I said. But not because of that. In spite of that. For the first time since I came back, I feel some real happiness. I am sorry, though, Julius. I didn't mean to make you—I don't know, compromise yourself like that. Your vows and all, I'm sorry. I know it's important to you."

"My vows? After everything that's going on, after what I've seen Pauley and the others doing, after his explanation about why we're celibate? Fuck that, Grace. Fuck chastity."

"Okay, unless Chastity is the secret pet love name you've given me since last night, that statement just made no sense. It's oxymoronic."

"You're oxymoronic," Julius said.

"You're a fucking oxymoron."

Julius decided to demonstrate just how unconcerned he was with resuming his vows, just to further make his point in a more direct, nonverbal manner. Grace was willing to concede to the argument, as a matter of being agreeable, particularly since she wasn't the one who had to start on the dishes.

Ahem. Jack stood at the side of the cushions and tried to get the couple's attention. *Sorry, don't mean to be 'that guy' or anything. Just that, it seems that bacon grease, while being delicious and all, is a fairly effective laxative. I mean, who knew, right? And, in case you hadn't been keeping track, today is day three since Jack had a movement of any kind. And did I mention the crab apples?*

Grace opened her eyes from where she was lying on the cushions, sensing something distracting. Her eyes met Jack's.

"Uh, Julius," she said, extricating herself. "I think Jack is trying to tell us something."

"Oh, yeah?" Julius asked, straightening up to also look at the dog. "What would that be?"

"I think he needs to go out," Grace said.

"I walked him this morning. He peed over the side."

"I think it's time for number two."

"Oh. I see. Well, I thought of that. I got a plan."

Grace said, "Well, time to put your plan in motion. Sorry, Jack, bad pun. I'll do the dishes, then. You initiate Operation Pooper Without a Scooper, Captain Crapper. Good luck with that."

"No problem. I got this." Julius stood up and ran a hand through his hair. "Come on, Jack. Time to go out for a walk."

Grace finished stowing the dishes and came back on deck. When she looked around, she couldn't see any sign of Julius or Jack. "Hey, Julius!" she yelled. "Where are you?"

"Back here, Grace. Just taking Jack out for a walk." Grace followed his voice to the stern. There she found Julius and Jack ankle deep in the ocean, standing on the swimming platform. Julius held a rope leash he had fashioned for the dog. Jack did not look happy. Grace couldn't help bursting into laughter when she saw them.

Oh, you laugh, girl. Glad you find this entertaining. We're gonna be here a while, compadres. Ever try to relax the old sphincters when you're standing up to your knees in the middle of the freakin' freezing Atlantic Ocean? Not happening...

Grace leaned over the rail and finally stopped laughing at the dog's expression. "Geez, Julius. Aren't you worried about that shark coming back?".

Shark? Okay—done.

"Pretty smart, huh?" Julius said. "Just like being outside—oh, look. I think he's done."

Yeah, done. All done. Time to go in, now. Here we go. Walk's over.

Julius lifted the dog back aboard the boat and followed him on deck. Julius raised the platform.

"Whatta good dog, Jack!" Grace enthused.

Yeah, great. I can't feel my fucking feet, girl.

Parnell finished his Baked Alaska as Uriel sipped coffee. "The more I think about this, Earle," Parnell said, pushing the plate back, "the more I think we're in a bad position here. I mean, Pauley has that book. It's all he needs to be wherever he needs to be to perform the excision." Uriel nodded. "So how do we stop him? We don't even know where Grace is going."

"We know. Don't know exactly when, but we know where."

"Where?" Parnell asked.

"She's gotta go to the Guggenheim, right? I mean, she needs a Wright gate to get where she's trying to go. Museum's gonna be the place."

"I guess you're right. Still don't know how we stop Pauley."

Uriel said, "I've been thinking about that. Since you notified your LDS friends of the situation, I'm hoping they'll be dedicating some resources to the matter. They already got an army of whiteshirts on her case. They almost got her in Bethesda, then at the train station in DC. You've given 'em enough information, hope they flood the Guggenheim when the time comes."

"I'm not sure that's much better."

"Better the girl's alive with the Mormons than excised, that's for sure," Uriel said.

"So maybe we're okay, then. If the missionaries run interference, maybe Grace can get away. So you won't need my favor or anything."

"Maybe. But if it looks like Pauley is even close to doing whatever he's going to try to do, we gotta take her out. Better she take her chances being dead again then being excised, Chuck. Maybe she finds her way back, eventually. Not a chance if Pauley is able to touch her, though. Everything comes undone if Pauley gets her excised."

Parnell said, "Well, maybe you should just get Pauley out of the picture."

Uriel shook his head. "Not an option."

"Why not? You never had a problem killing me."

"Not the same thing at all. Chances are, we might not be able to stop him. That's why you have to be prepared to kill her, if all else fails. Because all else just might fail, Chuck. Just might, I'm telling you."

"I don't get it. Pauley doesn't look all that tough, you know."

"I told you, Chuck. There are forces at work, forces that aren't obvious, not right now. But they're in play, and they'll be pretty fuckin' evident in that museum, believe me."

"Why can't you kill her then? Why does it have to be me?"

"Just does, that's all."

"Never tell me anything, do you?"

"Look, I'm going to try. I hope it doesn't come down to you. Believe me, if we're down to you doing her, we're pretty much in the shitter. They know me, and they'll be playing for me plenty hard. You, I hope, not so much. You're a bit of a wild card, so you might have a chance to get it done."

"I still don't know what Grace did that's so terrible that all this is even happening."

"She hasn't done it yet, not all of it. She's just got it rolling."

"What did she get started, then? And when does whatever she does actually happen?"

"It happens, will happen, in the next life. Lot of very powerful folk don't want to see that actually happen. They couldn't even stop it, so it's happened already."

"Doesn't make any sense, all those tenses you're mixing up. Why now, then? What changed?"

"Because she came back. This is their chance to undo it, to cut her out. They couldn't touch her, otherwise. Once she came back, though— they're not going to let this pass. Way too important to make her never was. Too important."

"Too important, why? What does Grace do?"

"You believe in free will, Chuck?"

"Sure."

"Well, you shouldn't. Pretty much an illusion, for the most part. Some of it, though, some of it's for real. Original sin and all that."

"You lost me," Parnell said.

"Yeah, well, don't sweat it. Just that, if they succeed in getting the girl excised, not going to be any such thing as free will anymore. Or ever.

How you like them apples, buddy? No bite of the apple, no fall from grace, no Grace at all, you get it?"

"No, I don't get it. Is that a bad thing, then?"

"Oh, yeah, Chuck. Trust me on this. That would not be good. Not good at all."

"No free will, huh? Not even a little?"

"Not even a little. Not ever. Just God's plan, right down the line. Nobody ever even know the game's been changed."

Parnell thought about this. "I don't know. Maybe that's better."

"You're an idiot, Chuck. I thought you said you were some kind of a Mormon scholar."

"I am."

"Then you should know who proposed that approach. Before God decided to go with plan B? It's in your Mormon Book, buddy."

"Oh, yeah. Right. That was Lucifer's idea, right? Bring every soul along with perfect grace, no earthly trial."

"Bingo. No Grace, no grace. No earthly existence. Not a good idea. That Lucifer's a dick, believe me."

"Wow. This is pretty important, then."

"Yeah, Chuck. Pretty goddamn important. Not sure things get any more important, you know?"

"We better not fuck this up, then," Parnell said.

"Good plan, amigo."

CHAPTER 28

"Spinnaker flying? What's that?" Grace asked.

"You'll see. It's fun. You said you wanted some exercise."

"I still don't see why you won't let me just climb the mast a few times. It looks like fun."

Julius shook his head emphatically. "Even if you didn't fall and slice yourself in half on one of the stays, I think you'd screw up the boat. Can't let you do it."

"I think you're making this up."

"Yeah, well, we're not going to try and find out. You want exercise, this is about all I got to offer."

"Not sure I like the part where I have to put on the life vest again. No swimming, I said."

"If this goes right, no swimming."

"And if it doesn't go right?" Grace asked.

"Then you'll be glad you wore a life vest, believe me."

"Fine, I'm game. Mostly because I'm a little bored. And out of sorts. What do I do?"

Julius pointed to the small bosen's chair he had placed in the bow. "Have a seat."

"On that? It looks like a seat from a swing set."

"Yeah, swing set. Just sit down. I'm going to be back in the cockpit. Did I mention the part about holding on really, really tight?"

"Yeah, about thirty times. I'm good at that."

"We'll see." Grace took a seat on the little chair sitting on the deck. She grabbed onto the shrouds to either side and waited as Julius stood at the wheel in the cockpit. Nothing happened. She watched him working at the wheel.

"Whee."

"You ready?" he shouted.

"Oh, this isn't it then?" At that, Julius cranked on a windlass that pulled up the sock covering the spinnaker, releasing the brightly colored sail. Grace looked up at it over her head and smiled.

"Pretty, but not very ex—" Suddenly, the spinnaker snapped open, filling with wind and ballooning up and forward as it had before, this time sharply catapulting Grace in the little swingset chair straight up off the deck like a rocket. She screamed. She continued to scream as the spinnaker rose and fell on the wind. Julius used the position of the eclipsing mainsail to keep Grace from being flung about too violently. She held on for dear life as the tiny seat rollercoastered up and down, at times skimming so low that her legs dragged in the water, then suddenly jetting up over twenty feet into the air. After a few minutes, Grace had stopped screaming and was mostly laughing. Occasionally, however, she still screamed out a few well-chosen epithets as Julius brought her plummeting toward the ocean, causing her bottom to staccato through the foam of breaking waves.

After another twenty minutes, Julius brought the boat about to allow Grace to swing gently over the waves, just off the side of the boat.

"Having fun?" Julius yelled at her. He saw she was grinning madly and nodding. "Want to jump?" At this, her smile disappeared.

"NO!"

"It's tradition, you know."

"Screw your tradition, Julius! I'm not jumping in the ocean! Not unless you're there to catch me, at least."

"Okay, hold on then." Julius maneuvered the boat so that Grace swung back over the bow. He winched the sock back down, collapsing the spinnaker slowly so Grace was able to touch down onto the deck. He ran forward and caught her as she swung, grabbing the safety line from her vest and pulling her off the chair. "Got you, Grace."

She clung to him wetly and gave him a hug. "That was a blast!"

"Glad you liked it."

"Can I climb the mast now?"

"No."

"Then can I do the sail thing again? Please?"

"Really?" She nodded enthusiastically. "Sure, if you want."

Uriel led Parnell out of the restaurant to the waiting limousine.

"Still don't know if I can do it, Earle."

"You probably can't, Chuck. Take this anyways," Uriel said, getting into the car beside Parnell and carefully handing Chuck a knife. Parnell took it reluctantly, holding the wicked looking thing, all black except for a silver shining edge, gingerly turning it over like it was radioactive. "Just put that away somewheres, until it's time."

"Don't you need it? I mean, you seem to be stabbing people a lot."

"Just seem that way to you. Don't worry, I got a lot of knives." Suddenly, three matte black short knives fanned like a poker hand from each of Uriel's sleeves, then disappeared just as quickly.

Parnell recoiled. "Shit, Earle. That's a lot of knives. Why do you have to keep killing people, anyway? What are you, the fucking angel of death?"

"You're funny, Parnell. Fucking angel of death," Uriel said, smiling and chuckling, shaking his head. "Don't always kill people, Parnell. Sometimes just hit 'em with a shoe or something."

"Killed me a lot."

"Yeah, well, it's not like I got a lot of tools to work with here, you know. Not like I can change folks' minds about things, talk sense into them or anything. You know, throw my voice into a burning bush or something. Pretty much the blade's the only play I got, most times."

"When all you got is a hammer, Earle..."

"Yeah, shut up, asshole. You're looking more and more like a nail every time I gotta eat a meal with you."

"Not too many more meals, huh?" Parnell asked as they got back to the hotel.

"No, don't think so. Tomorrow's gonna be a busy day, I think. Listen, Parnell," Uriel said, catching the other man's elbow and stopping him in the lobby on their way to the elevators. Parnell was still carefully holding the knife, turning it over in his hand as they stood. "One thing about this business I haven't really explained," Uriel said, nodding at the knife. "I know you don't wanta kill the girl. Doubt really that you can, even if you wanted to, but I should tell you this anyhow."

"What is it, Earle? You're right, though, don't think it's going to matter. Don't think I can kill anyone. Especially her."

"Yeah, well. You should know this, anyway. I'm sure Pauley neglected to mention this little item, too."

"What little item?"

"If he does succeed in having her excised, it'll have implications."

"So you said, earlier."

"Implications for you personally, Parnell. I don't know everything about you in this life, but I know enough to believe that you're pretty closely bound up with her, in this life at least."

"So?"

"So if she does get excised, I doubt you survive the event. Just thought you should know." The knife slipped from Parnell's hand, striking with a musical tonk into the parquet floor of the lobby. It quivered there, point buried deeply in the wood, having narrowly missed Parnell's own foot. Uriel bent and plucked it from the floor, then flicked it straight up in the air with a slight flick of his wrist. Parnell watched it sail up past the high chandelier.

"Why did—"

"Here," Uriel said to him, getting his attention. Uriel carefully handed another knife handle-first to Parnell, who had turned white. "That one's dull now." Uriel said.

"But, you're saying I might die tomorrow, if—" Parnell said, taking the knife and looking about, then suddenly jumping back as he saw the silver-black blur streak down in front of his face, between the two men.

Uriel caught the falling blade neatly and restowed it in his sleeve with a motion almost too fast for Parnell to follow.

Uriel nodded. "So you might want to hold on to that one, just in case. 'Night."

Julius spent a good portion of the day laughing at his friend as she flew in front of the boat. Eventually, she had had enough fun for one day and he reeled her aboard one last time. Once she had showered again (only the second one today, she remarked as she skipped below deck), she rejoined him on deck in shorts and tee shirt, which had become her standard boating uniform.

The day had gotten hot again, another cloudless afternoon. Julius spent time working at sailing stuff, stowing the spinnaker from the morning's fun. Mostly, though, Julius kept stealing glances at Grace, lying face down on a towel in the middle of the deck, sunning herself with Jack snuggled in the hollow of her waist.

After another hour, Julius poked Grace in the side, awakening her. Grace smiled at him dreamily as he pointed to the light lunch he had laid out on the table. They ate as Jack continued to sleep in the sunshine. It was mostly salad anyway.

"You're not eating again," Julius remarked. "Still out of sorts?"

She nodded. "Sort of, yeah. Sort of out of sorts, I guess. Sorry, I'm not much of a lunch companion. Listen, Julius—"

He put his hand on hers and, shaking his head, cut her off. "I know, Grace."

She looked at him; she was surprised, seeing in his face that she felt much sadder than he looked. "I'd like to, Julius. Really, I would. I try to picture what it would be like, being with you, sailing in the Caribbean and all. It would be great, I'm sure. It's just that, I don't know, I'm feeling more and more—"

"Out of sorts?"

She grinned at him sheepishly. "Yeah, exactly. It feels like I'm swimming around in someone else's skin or something. It's weird, I know."

"Doesn't sound very pleasant."

"Not painful or anything. But I can feel it getting worse, squeezing me. It's feeling more and more wrong, being here. I'm sorry, Julius. I wanted you to have your piece of happiness, you know, before I—"

"I still have it, Grace, for a little bit, at least. And maybe after, too. Who knows?" he said thoughtfully, twisting the ring unconsciously.

"We'll head for New York, then?"

He nodded. "We've been heading north since early this morning, Grace."

"You knew?" she asked, disappointed. He nodded.

"Yeah, Grace. I could tell. Maybe even before you, I don't know. I could tell."

"How long...?"

"Can't say exactly, but if the winds hold, probably tomorrow morning. I don't want to try to navigate New York harbor in the dark. Especially without a transponder—they might try to blow us out of the water or something. See, if you hadn't gone all Sawzall on my boat, we could've just switched it back on as we came into harbor."

"Had to be done. Sorry."

"Yeah, right. Come on, Grace. A little extreme, don't you think? I mean, the thing was turned off, after all."

She looked at him quizzically. "I keep forgetting what you don't know about the world, Julius. You're so innocent, for a priest and all."

"What do you mean?"

"You look at that metal box and just because the little lights are dark, or it's not making any beeping sounds, you think it's powerless, that it's not doing anything. You think you understand everything about electricity and shit, about how the world works. You don't really see the whole world, Julius. You think you do, but you're only looking at one side. That thing was off to you, but there are forces at work that you don't understand, still functioning, forces other than electricity. You don't know what that thing was capable of, even though you think you turned it off. I had to throw it overboard."

He shook his head. "Sounds crazy, Grace. I'm sorry, I don't mean to say you're crazy, but—"

"Don't worry, Julius. I've been a little crazy, so I know. I thought I was really crazy, before. Turns out that a lot of crazy shit I believed, really wasn't so crazy after all. And a lot of the regular stuff, the stuff you just take for granted every day because you know it's true, turns out to be some pretty crazy shit."

"But you said it yourself, before. After you're dead, nobody even cares about this place anymore."

"Almost no one does, or so I thought. Regular people don't, that's for sure. I mean, it's all so different, and you just move on, mostly. But I'm starting to realize, not everybody is regular people. There are forces at work—there, just like here. Major forces, and they're not above influencing what goes on here. I think maybe it's a big part of how they work. Now that I see it, it's pretty fucking scary, I tell you."

"I have no idea what you're talking about."

"Of course you don't, you're not supposed to. You feel like you're in charge of your life, like you have some control. So when you don't, when things don't work out, you blame yourself. Huge forces that might not even care about you, not really—but the forces are so strong that we're all buffeted by them. You know it happens, you've seen it, you've lived it. I lived it." Grace looked out over the water, her expression distant. "It's like that one day, you're driving home from picking up your two little girls from daycare, after you've put in a tough day at work. You're busting your ass, trying to put food on the table for your little girls. Driving home, exhausted, and you need to put some gas in the car or you're not going to make it to work in the morning, so you pull into the petrol station. You turn off the engine and you see that the cost of the gas has gone up, again. Up again, it's way too much, and you look at the money you have in your purse, because it's all the money you have, and you look back at your two little daughters smiling in the backseat—and you put your head down on the steering wheel and start to cry, right there in the petrol station, with the attendant knocking on the window, because it just hit you—hit you like a punch in the stomach, that no matter how hard you keep working, no matter how hard you try—you can't do it. You're not going to make it. If you buy the gas, your little girls are not gonna eat tonight. But if you don't buy the gas, you can't get to work, and you're not going to have a roof over their heads tomorrow. So you just sit there, sobbing, because you see now, you see with sudden perfect clarity, that you will be giving your precious little girls up for adoption. Maybe tomorrow, even—the only reason that you breathe will be gone tomorrow, because not to give them up would be even worse. Not for you, but for them, and you know in that split second that your two beautiful girls will grow up spending their entire lives hating you, hating you for what you're going to do, hating you every moment for the rest of their lives as they struggle to survive without you..." Julius watched Grace as she turned to him, her green eyes now blinking with tears. "Shit, Julius, sorry, I'm so sorry, all I do in this life is cry, cry and take stupid showers. I never used to cry, before. It's not fair to you, I'm sorry..."

"It's okay, Grace," he said, holding her hand in his while reaching over with the other and trying to wipe tears from her cheeks. "It's okay. Don't be sorry. I didn't even know you had any children. I'm so sorry—"

"Me?" She almost laughed, the sound strangled because she was still crying a little. "Kids? No way, Julius. No, I'm talking about my Ma, that's who I'm talking about. And she was right, too. My sister and I spent every day hating her, grew up hating her every waking moment. She was right. But after, once I died, and I could see so much more, see her sitting in that car. My sister showed me. I hated her for so long, for my whole life really, for no reason, when she tried so hard, all by herself, before the forces just swept her aside like a dead leaf. No great plan was aimed against her, no celestial forces targeted her. She was nobody, a victim. Just a victim of everything else that was being manipulated around her, and she was powerless. She never even knew why, but she was destroyed by it, by losing us..."

"When did you finally meet her?"

Grace shook her head. "I never did. She died not long after she put us up for adoption. Pills."

"How did you find out?" Julius asked.

"After. After I died."

"Did you get to see her, then? In the next life?"

"I don't know, Julius. I'm not sure. Fiona, my twin sister, said she was there, close. She stayed away, though. Maybe when I get back, if I get back—"

"You'll get back, Grace." She pulled her hand from his so she could wipe away all the tears, straightening up. "I'll get you back. I promise."

She shook her head, no longer crying. "Don't say that, Julius. I know you'll try. I know you will. But like I was just saying; there are forces involved. I don't really understand what's going on, but something is. Something powerful has taken an interest in me, and not in a good way. Too much is going on, too much that I can't explain. It seems too big, somehow."

"I'll get you back, Grace."

"Don't keep saying that, Julius. Don't. You may not be able to, you have to be prepared for that. I know that you'll try, that'll you do your best. But there are things that are out of our control, Julius, and your best may not be enough. I can't bear to think of you, after, if this doesn't work out. I'll be okay, I promise. You have to be okay, too. No matter what happens, you have to promise me that you'll be okay, Julius."

"I'll get you back, Grace. I promise."

"You're not listening to me, please, Julius, I can't—" but by that point he had her in his arms again, so she couldn't even tell him, to make him understand, that she couldn't even think of him after, even if things did work out—which she was beginning to believe, was probably not going to happen...

Hey, the dog grunted awake as he caught Grace's heel in his ribcage. *Is it lunchtime?* Jack stood up and stretched in the sun, watching his two shipmates. *Geez guys, get a room or something; I'm trying to sleep here, okay?* Jack looked over at the table and saw the two plates still sitting on the table. He walked over and jumped up on the cushions, looking over the lunch Julius had prepared. *Chicken salad, huh? Well, you got that half right.* Jack carefully ate the pieces of chicken, avoiding the rest of the salad. He occasionally stole glances up from the table. *Gad, it's like watching a car crash in slow motion, you know? You want to look away, but...* Jack shifted over to the other plate. *Doesn't look like anybody else is really interested in lunch, anyway. Pretty rude not even to call me.* He looked up again. *That's just not right, not right at all. I mean, I'm sure they told me the dude was neutered and all, when I took him in as a room mate. Neutered, my ass.* Jack finished the chicken from the second plate. *I'm sorry, but this is going on way too long, guys. You need me, I'll be below.* Jack dropped down from the table and lumbered, unnoticed, back down to the cabin. *Gonna need a walk a little later, just warning you. No hurry, guys. You young folk have your fun, I'll be fine, really.*

Pauley sat in the little room, back in the archdiocese. He closed the book and set it down, taking another sip of his drink. He realized that he hadn't eaten anything at all today. He really should head down to the dining room, he thought. He sat, looking at the closed book, no longer wondering about the miraculous nature of the thing. Its nature had been eclipsed by the bigger issues at hand. Pauley considered all that he had read since leaving the restaurant earlier, since the effrontery of that evil man, whoever he was; Earle or Uriel, didn't matter. The evil little man was right, Pauley thought. It didn't change a thing. He knew, both in his heart and—seeing the event play out—in his mind, that he was going to do it. He was a man of God, after all. He had a duty, he told himself. This was important, and he would do what was required of him. It was nothing, he thought to himself, just a touch. He knew that all that was required of him was the briefest contact, and the thing would be done. He would do what he had been asked to do. He was a man of God. He put down the drink and stood shakily, swaying for a moment. He would go to evening mass, he decided.

CHAPTER 29

Grace lay with her head on Julius's chest, feeling the sun bake down on them, the pendulous motion of the deck beneath them mixing with the rise and fall of his chest as he breathed.

"You like it there, it seems," Julius said into the red cloud of her hair.

She nodded, smiling unseen. "When I do this, I can hear the ocean," she said.

"Well, yeah, no surprise. Probably the other ear, actually."

"You're just not a romantic, Julius," Grace said.

"No, I'm just not a conch shell. I'm pretty romantic."

"For a priest."

"Especially for a priest."

Grace poked him in the buttock with her finger. "So who's this, Romeo?"

"Who's what?" he asked, looking down at her back.

"The tattoo. The name—your ex, I presume."

He shook his head but she couldn't see it. She pushed him onto his side and looked closer at the script. "Salome?" she read. "Guess she wasn't Irish, was she?"

He rolled back. "Quit staring at my ass. It's not the name of my ex-wife. I told you her name."

"You did?" He nodded. "So who, then? Some cheap tramp from Afghanistan? Not that I'm judging or anything."

"It sounds like you're judging."

"Maybe, a little. Who was she? You don't strike me as the type that tattoos a chick's name on your butt. Even if you were a sailor."

"Technically, that's my hip. And it wasn't a girl. See the quote marks around it? Not the name of a person."

"What then?"

"That was the name of the operation. My last mission in Afghanistan."

"The one that killed that family?" He nodded. "Oh. Sorry. Kind of a morose thing to carry around on your ass, Julius." She settled back onto his chest.

"I never knew their names, Grace."

Grace waited for the subject to die. "You should get back to your class, Father Zimmerman. Your class needs you. Maybe have a thing with the Asian girl."

"What Asian girl?" Grace raised her head from his chest to give him a look. "Oh, her. Don't think so. Priest, remember? Besides, affairs with students are unseemly. Semester's half over, anyways. Pauley arranged for someone to take over, I'm sure."

"You're a good teacher, Julius. You should go back, when this is over."

He nodded behind her. "Maybe I will. If they'll have me."

"Of course they'll have you, Julius. I'm sure you're the best they've got, especially for that stupid course." Jack sauntered back on deck and thumped down beside them, stretching. "Hey, Jack. Where you been?" Grace asked the dog. Jack didn't honor this with a reply. They were, after all, on a boat.

Julius reached down and scratched Jack's head between his ears. "It's not a stupid course. It's important for them, at that stage of their lives," he said.

No, it's a pretty stupid course. I've been there, believe me.

"You say so, Julius," Grace said, also reaching over to scratch Jack's head. "Stupid name, at least."

"What? 'The Problem of God?' What's wrong with it? I think it's cool."

"Cool? You're such a Jesuit, Julius. It's stupid. You got the wrong word there."

"Cool?"

"No, not cool. 'Of.' You got the wrong participle or something," Grace said.

I'm sorry, 'participle?' Are we speaking your second language here, I hope? You mean 'preposition,' darling.

"Do I?" Julius asked. "Blame the guy who wrote the book. Which does kind of suck, I'll admit."

"Blame anybody you want," Grace said. "It's not 'The Problem of God.' It should be 'The Problem with God.'"

"Don't get the difference."

And they let you teach children. Amazing.

" 'The Problem of God' makes it sound like you're talking about whether God exists," Grace said.

"Well, yeah, Grace. That's kind of the point, you know. 'Is God in our lives?' That sort of thing."

"Well, that's stupid, like I said. It's not whether God exists, that's the wrong question."

"Oh, really?" She nodded on his chest, but said nothing. "So what's the right question, then? What's 'The Problem *with* God?' "

Grace sat up then and hugged her knees to her chest, meeting his gaze. "The problem with God," she said, staring at him, "is that He doesn't give a fuck."

Okay, I'm pretty sure we're gonna be hit by lightning now.

Parnell crossed the floor to the sound of insistent knocking and opened the door of his hotel room, bleary-eyed. Uriel stood in the hall, dressed in another new suit.

"Come on, get dressed. We gotta go," Uriel said.

Parnell rubbed his eyes. "Go? Go where? What time is it?"

"It's 4 am. Get dressed."

"Where are we going at four in the morning?"

"Get dressed and meet me in the lobby. Car's waiting."

Parnell came downstairs dressed in the new suit he'd worn to dinner. He found Uriel pacing near the door.

" 'Bout time," Uriel said, walking out as the door was held open by the bellman with a nod. Parnell followed Uriel into the waiting limo. The limousine moved off.

"Where are we going?" Parnell asked again.

"Reconnaissance," Uriel said. "Lot gonna happen today. Best we be ready."

"To the Guggenheim? At four in the morning?"

"No, not the Guggenheim."

"Where to, then?"

Uriel looked pointedly at Parnell. "The other portal."

"What other portal?" Parnell asked.

"How come you never told me Wright built another portal in Manhattan? Huh, Parnell?"

"I don't know what you're talking about, Earle. What other portal?"

"Hmmph."

"What, you don't believe me?"

"Nope," Uriel said.

"Well, you should. Wright designed the car dealership in '54. You killed me in '14, remember? How am I supposed to know about that?"

"Seems you know about it," Uriel said, watching the lights of the city outside his window.

"Don't know a thing about it."

"Obviously."

"So you think the Mercedes dealership is another portal?" Parnell asked.

"You tell me, Shylock. Wright designed it in '54, died in the operating room during routine surgery in '59. Only thing is, the grave with his name on it in Wisconsin is empty."

"Is it?"

"It is," Uriel affirmed.

"So you think that Frank—"

"I don't much care what Frank was or isn't. Just seems a little weird that the most famous architect of the twentieth century takes the time to design a car dealership as his final, crowning achievement, you know? Then he dies. Then his body disappears." The limo came to a stop at the curb on Park Avenue. The glass partition behind the driver slid down silently.

"We're here, sir," the driver said over his shoulder. "Just across the street there."

Uriel opened his door and climbed out. He poked his head back in the car. "You comin'?"

Parnell shook his head. "Why? Why do you need me?"

"It's the middle of the night. Might be some evil folk lurking about. Best to have a skinny white guy with me, keep 'em distracted."

"Oh. Actually, I think I'll wait here then, if you don't mind. Let me know how it goes, Earle."

"No help at all," Uriel said, straightening. He looked over the roof of the car at the building across the street. Despite the darkness, he could make out the large windows of the dealership, dark and empty. He walked, hands in pockets and head down, up the block to the corner. He crossed the street at the corner with the light, noting a young man standing in the doorway to the building next to the dealership. He kept walking along 55th Street until he came to an alley. As he ducked into the alley, he looked back and saw the young man, Caucasian and dressed in dark slacks with a white shirt, follow him around the corner. Uriel walked briskly down the alley to approach the dealership from the rear. He stopped short as he saw movement in front of him. Shit, he thought, realizing that he was now trapped in the alley. He silently slid a knife into his right hand and froze next to a dumpster, listening. As he stood, he heard noises from the alley in front of him. He quietly approached in the darkness, seeing nothing. Uriel stopped again, listening. Again, a scraping noise and then the muffled crack of a window pane being expertly broken. He moved forward more quickly. It was almost pitch black here, but Uriel could make out the shape of a small individual dropping into the building through a cellar window. Uriel moved to follow, then stopped as another man appeared at the far end of the alley.

Uriel palmed his knife and walked purposefully towards the man, stealing a glance at the broken basement window as he hurried past. The other man, not the same one he had seen before but similarly dressed, stood still before him, waiting.

"Got a light?" Uriel asked him, hand at his side and ready to strike.

The man looked Uriel up and down. "Don't smoke, old man," the young man said, shaking his head.

"Not too old to start" Uriel said and walked past him, the knife disappearing back up his sleeve. He walked back to the limo.

"We can go now, Jimmy," Uriel said to the driver, closing the door.

"So?" Parnell asked as the car started up.

Uriel smiled. "We might just be okay," Uriel said.

"Really? What makes you say so?"

"Think your message got through, Parnell. Your Mormon friends got the place covered tight, front and back."

Parnell nodded. "And that's going to make everything okay, huh?"

"Just might, Chuck. Just might. They know about this place, sure as shit they got the Guggenheim covered real good. Gives us a shot, anyway."

Parnell shook his head. "Could've figured that out in the morning and gotten a good night's sleep, Earle."

"Don't think anybody's getting a good night's sleep tonight, Charles. Leastwise, nobody we care about."

Julius cooked the remaining steaks on the little grill at the stern of the boat for dinner. Again, Grace ate little, giving most of her leftover steak to the dog. She kept looking up from the table, watching puffy white clouds scuttling across the sky, watching the sails billow brightly in the sun, snapping loudly with the occasional gust.

"Don't worry, Grace," Julius said. "Just a little blow overnight. Nothing too bad. I'll probably need to stay on deck tonight for a bit, though."

Grace looked at him, brow furrowed. She nodded. "Can we sleep up here tonight, Julius? On deck?"

"Sure, Grace. If you want. This table turns into a bed, actually. Why?"

She shrugged. "Just want to." He stared at her. "My last chance to see the stars, Julius." He nodded at that.

"Okay. I'll make up the bed after dinner. Might be a little chilly, later."

"You'll keep me warm, won't you, Julius?" she asked, trying to smile.

"I'll do my best, Grace. What's up?"

She stared back at him. Grace shook her head, but said nothing. She stood and gathered the plates, avoiding his eyes.

Julius made up the bed as Grace did the dishes, then took Jack for his walk. Grace joined him on deck at the wheel as he trimmed the sails and adjusted their course. The wind had grown brisk and the sea choppy. Grace clung to his waist and he put one arm around her shoulder. They watched the sails ahead changing color in the reddening light of the evening.

"We're going to be okay," he said, squeezing her shoulders. Night fell and the moon, now waning, disappeared behind thickening clouds.

Grace awoke, naked and alone. She was shivering. She opened her eyes and could see nothing in the darkness. Grace looked up from where she lay, but the moon and the stars were gone. Only darkness. Struggling to stand, she held onto something hard as the floor lurched crazily beneath her, nearly knocking her off her bare feet. A cold wind buffeted her, her hair whipping around her face. Grace could see nothing, could hear only the tearing moan of the wind as her world reeled and heaved. It had happened, she realized. She was lost. She started to scream.

Julius heard her screaming. He wanted to go to her, to tell her it would be okay for the fortieth time tonight, but he couldn't. Not just yet. He was too busy trying to make sure they'd really be okay. The squall had come up quickly. He had checked the weather before they had gone to bed on deck and knew there was a strong possibility of storms in the area. He wasn't surprised when he felt the wind come up and the boat heel over. Now he was back at the wheel, steering the boat through suddenly cross seas, sawtooth waves sending sprays of dark white foam over the rail. Julius had severely reduced sail, now flying a double reefed mainsail and just a small triangle of the jib as a storm sail. They'd be okay, he'd been through much worse before. Probably wouldn't last more than another half hour, he thought, glancing at the radar. Open ocean ahead and the whole of the Atlantic Ocean to leeward, they could ride this out no matter how bad it got. Julius listened to the wind, felt the forces on the wheel, adjusted his course and trimmed the sails. A hard cold rain suddenly swept like a heavy curtain across the deck. Julius tried to block out the sound of Grace, still wailing pitifully, her screams carried back in shreds by the gusting storm. He tried to call out to her, to make her realize that he hadn't left her, that she wasn't really alone, but the gale snatched his words away.

By the time he found her, Grace had stopped screaming. Julius waited until the storm had passed, until he was certain that he could trust the autopilot to maintain a safe course, before he moved forward out of the cockpit in the dark, calling her name. There was no response. He slid his feet carefully along the rain-slicked deck, scared that he couldn't see her, that she may have stepped overboard in the storm, in the dark, looking for him. Nearly panicked, calling out her name, he almost fell onto her as he stumbled, catching himself as he saw her lying on the deck, wet and shivering, curled up on her side in the dark, clinging to something soft. He knelt down, pushed her wet hair back from her face, and saw her eyes squeezed tight shut, saw her holding tightly onto Jack. The dog must have come on deck in the storm, fur wet but nuzzled tight to Grace's chest, licking her face, shivering himself. He looked up at Julius.

"You're one crazy-ass dog, Jack," Julius said, holding the two of them. "You could've been swept right over, never see you again, dog." He shook his head.

She was scared.

By dawn, the storms had passed. The sea had settled into a rolling undulation. Thick metallic clouds gave way to puffy white cumulus once again, scuttling before them as the sky went from red, to white, to blue. The wine colored sails were again full and tautly curving ahead of Julius as he stood at the helm. He had gotten Grace and Jack dried off and swaddled in a blanket on the big bed in the master's cabin a little while before dawn. When he had last looked in on them, they were both snoring peacefully.

Julius scanned the horizon, picking up the small flecks of other sailboats in the distance. He checked his instruments and the radar. The ship had weathered the dirty night without a wrinkle. She was a good ship, Julius thought. He'd miss sailing her. He focused on the sailing, trying not to think of what the rest of the day would bring.

Julius watched as the low dark line of the horizon resolved into the skyline of Manhattan, at first just flashes of reflected sunrise from the tall buildings. He turned up the radio and listened to the chatter of New York harbor ahead. He wondered if their arrival in a couple of hours, lacking a transponder announcing their identity, would pique any official concern. He contemplated a few tactful responses should inquiries arise, none of them claiming Baltimore as their home port. His piratical summers in the Caribbean had taught him a few techniques for obfuscating various port authorities. Of course, this was the US Coast Guard and New crazy paranoid York he was sailing into; he doubted that promising the harbor master a couple of bottles of Jameson upon arrival would be up to the task. He'd have to think of something better, should the need arise.

Grace and Jack appeared on deck a couple of hours later. Grace had showered and dressed in the blue jeans and sweatshirt that she had worn the day they stole this boat. Landlubber clothes. Julius was overtaken with sadness, realizing how much he had loved sharing 'their boat' for the past few days. They were about to step back onto land, into the real world; a world that was not well fitted to his friend. He said good morning and was greeted with a weak smile. Grace sat on the cushion next to him and surveyed the harbor ahead, watching the other boats about. Jack walked to the bow and lifted his leg to pee over the side like he had been born to the sea. He walked back, surveying the deck, eventually coming to sit next to Grace, dropping his head on her lap.

"Want some breakfast?" Julius asked them. "Going to be too busy in a little bit to leave the wheel. Now or never." He immediately regretted the last comment.

Sure. Steak and eggs, over easy. You can forget the hash browns this time, sharkbait.

Grace smiled more broadly at him but just shook her head. Julius pointed ahead.

"Statue of Liberty." Grace leaned to see where he was pointing past the eclipsing sail. She nodded. "Ever been?" he asked, just wanting to hear her say something.

"Once, with Gabe. Did the steps all the way to the crown." She smiled, remembering. Julius was relieved. She wasn't dead yet, sounding more like the Grace he knew.

"Ellis Island? Did you take the tour?"

"Yup. Did the whole tourist thing. It was great. I'm an immigrant, you know."

"Actually, I don't know. Thought you went to Catholic school."

"In a fashion. Not the way you think. Born and raised in Ireland."

"Were you now?" Julius asked, feigning a brogue.

"That's just awful," Grace said, laughing. "It's *'Were you now?'* " she said, lapsing into her native accent. Julius smiled, feeling more relieved as she spoke.

"Where abouts in Ireland?"

"Dublin. You ever been?" He shook his head, adjusting their course to give a wide berth to the commercial boats leaving the harbor. "You should go."

"I'll try," he said, trying not to think what he would do, after. He was listening to the radio, fearful that he'd hear them being hailed at any moment. He kept scanning the sea as they approached the harbor. The giant green statue loomed larger as they approached, the forest of tall glass office buildings glittering in the sunshine off their right bow. He realized that she was staring at him.

"Will you do me one final favor, Father Zimmerman?" Grace asked in her Irish lilt. He looked at her, puzzled. "If it happens that I need burying, Julius. Will you do me a last favor?"

"Of course, Grace, but—"

"I know, Julius. You told me 'bout a hundred times last night and I thank you for it. But if it happens that I can't get back, that I die here today," she held his gaze with hers, "it would be a comfort to me."

"Anything, Grace."

"There's a small cemetery in West Dublin, called Mulhuddart, on Church Road. It's where we buried my sister, Fiona. If it's not too much trouble, Julius, I'd like you to see me buried there, if you could."

"Of course, Grace. If it comes to that, I'll take care of you. You know I will."

"Thank you, Julius. I'm sure you'll say something nice. Thank you— for everything. No matter what happens, thank you."

Julius went back to watching the sea, unable to think of anything else to say to that.

CHAPTER 30

Father Pauley dropped the empty whiskey bottle into the trashcan with a thunk. He shuffled into the bathroom to shower. He felt old. It promised to be a difficult day. As he opened the door to the bathroom, he chanced to look at his hand, there on the doorknob as he pulled it open with his remaining four fingers. He paused, wondering if his hand would be whole by this time tomorrow. He hoped so. He prayed it would be so.

Uriel pounded insistently on Parnell's door again. He kept banging until the door swung open.

"I just got to sleep, Earle," Parnell said, rubbing his stubbled jaw as he turned to let the other man follow him into the room. "What do you want now?"

"She's coming. You want some breakfast before this all starts, we better get downstairs." Parnell sat heavily on the bed, staring sleepily at him. He yawned widely. "I'd suggest it," Uriel said, "Odds are pretty good it might be your last meal."

"You are one depressing son of a bitch, Earle."

"Yeah, I can be. Dress nice, something you'd like to be buried in. Just in case. And your magic underwear. You'll want to wear them, I'm sure."

399

"Don't have the underwear."

"You don't? Thought all good Mormons wore the underwear."

"They do. Those that might be making the journey to the other world, so if they pass through they'll be presentable."

"Magic underwear survive the trip, huh?"

Parnell nodded. "That's why they're magic. Never really applied to me, though. So no underwear. I mean, nothing special, just the usual boxers."

"More than I care to know, Chuck. I'll meet you down in the restaurant."

"We're checking out?"

"You are."

Julius steered them beneath the soaring span of the Verrazano Bridge under full sail. It promised to be another beautiful, sunny day. Tide and wind were favorable, much to his relief. He had never sailed these waters before, but Julius knew their reputation for tricky currents and challenging commercial traffic. He pointed the boat between the Statue of Liberty and the park at the tip of Governors Island.

"Listen, Grace," he said, turning to make sure she was listening. She was, forcing him a smile. "This last bit is gonna be a bit of a goat rodeo, I'm afraid."

"I'm sorry? What about riding goats?"

"Goat rodeo. It's a military term. The last part of our little cruise may be a bit challenging."

"Clusterfuck, you mean."

"Yeah, exactly. But 'goat rodeo' more elegantly captures the need for us to accomplish a series of highly unlikely maneuvers in very short order or we're gonna be—"

"Clusterfucked."

"Exactly."

"Why, what's the problem? I figured you'd just run us aground somewhere and I'd go tearing off down Fifth Avenue."

Julius shook his head. "Uh, no."

"Can't just drop me at the Guggenheim?"

"No."

She shrugged. "Okay, Captain Dubious. What's the plan?"

He didn't want to give Grace the impression that he was just now making up a plan to successfully end their excursion, seeing as the whole cruise had been his idea. Unfortunately, he only had a rather hazy idea of how they might end up safely on shore in Manhattan, and he was pretty much winging this last part. He remembered a particular exercise from his SEAL training days that might apply. Late in the training, the instructors were forced to come up with a couple of additional missions to get more candidates to drop out. Usually, the attrition rate was astronomical, candidates ringing the bell that signaled that they had had enough almost every night. In his group, however, they entered the last week with too many candidates still standing despite going through Hell Week and SEAL Basic. The instructors, an inventive group, had decided to split the remaining candidates into two teams and have them compete in a series of missions, losers going home. On one mission, Julius recalled, they were required to use inflatable Zodiac boats to simulate an assault on an enemy vessel. Julius had led his team in stealing away all the Zodiacs the night before, severely hampering the other team's ability to mount a successful attack. The other team's panicked search in the hours before dawn netted them a couple of life rafts with oars before mission start. It was pathetic. Julius's team won easily. He thought maybe he and Grace could use the technique he had invented on that occasion to appropriate a Zodiac for themselves.

"We can't just pull into a dock in Manhattan," Julius explained. "I mean, we're not exactly inconspicuous and they're probably looking for us up and down the entire eastern seaboard."

"You're just thinking of this now, Captain Clueless?"

"No, of course not. I've got a plan."

"Of course you do. I'm listening."

"Lots of boats tie up farther out, to a buoy. It's cheaper than renting dock space and you don't need a reservation."

"Sounds great. How do we get to the shore then? And you better not say we're swimming for it or I'll kick you in the balls again."

"No, of course not. That would be very suspicious, anyway. No, we just use a small inflatable boat to get in."

"Really? We have a small boat? Where? Must be really small, Julius."

"No, actually we don't. We left before Mark brought it back from service, remember?"

"Oh. Great plan, otherwise."

"So we're going to get one."

"Really? How are we going to do that?" Julius laid out his plan, the same one he had used to steal away the other SEAL team's boats in the night. They would trawl slowly past another boat that had a Zodiac tied up astern and hook the mooring line with a grapple, pulling it in. Then they'd cut the line and take the Zodiac in tow. He smiled at her. "You have got to be shittin' me," Grace said, shaking her head.

"Why? No, it'll work. I've done it."

"You've done it? In broad daylight? With a girl who doesn't know her ass from an admiral and a dog as your team? Are you fucking crazy, Julius?"

"It'll be fine," Julius said with feigned confidence. "You just take us close in to the yacht club up ahead there, and I'll grab the Zodiac."

"You are fuckin' nuts, Julius. You think I can drive us close enough to do that without going right through the other sucker's boat? No fuckin' way. I can't even drive this thing in the open, let alone—"

"You're whining like a virgin, Grace. You can do this."

"Don't get sarcastic with me, Padre. This isn't a stickshift we're talking about. If we're really going to try this stupid shit, it's going to have go down with you driving and me making the grab."

"You think so?"

"Yeah, I think so, Captain Clusterfuck. Not gonna work, anyway, might as well be you crashing us into the docks."

They passed Battery Park, sun glinting off the tall glass buildings crowding the southern tip of Manhattan. Julius struck the sails with a few button pushes on the electric winches and began to motor up the Hudson River. He slowly approached the yacht club in Hoboken on the New Jersey side, stealing looks through a pair of binoculars to find a boat far enough out in the offing with a Zodiac tied astern. Thankfully, traffic this morning was still light on the river. Through the binoculars, he picked out a large sailboat in the yacht club ahead, tied to a buoy at single anchor, with a gray inflatable Zodiac bobbing behind.

"Tally-ho," he said softly. He turned to look over at Grace, who had changed into another bathing suit bottom and tee shirt. She had donned the life vest, just in case things went horribly wrong. Julius tied a safety line to the vest. He had tied another length of line to a five gallon jug half filled with water. She looked game, like the old Grace, bouncing up and down on the balls of her bare feet. "Okay, I see a likely victim," he said. "I'm going to bring us up slowly athwart their stern. You grapple the mooring line and haul it in, cut it, and make it fast to the aft stanchion. Got it?"

"What the hell you sayin', Leopold?"

"Throw the water jug so you catch the line holding the rubber boat. Pull in the line and cut it, but hang on to the end attached to the boat. Is that better?"

"Hold on to which end, again?"

"Stop screwing with me, Grace! We're hot in two minutes here."

"Aye, aye, Number One. Make it so. Still think we should just tie the rope to Jack and toss him into the little rubber boat, be easier." Jack squinted at her.

Been nice sailing with you. Enjoy New Jersey.

Julius brought the sailboat up behind the other boat slowly. He was pleased to note that nobody was aboard. The sea was calm and the tide slack. At first, he thought it was going to be okay, but as they got closer, he realized this wasn't going to work. The mooring line holding the Zodiac to the stern of the yacht was too short, no way Grace would have enough slack to pull the line in close. As they passed within five feet of the other boat, Julius called out, "Shit, Grace, it's not going to work. The line's too—"

Julius was interrupted as Grace screamed something he didn't understand. Julius turned, horrified, as he watched Grace take a running leap, knife clenched in her teeth, from the stern.

"HOLY SHIT, GRACE! What the fuck are you—" He had to look ahead to make sure he wasn't steering them into the next boat, then looked back to see Grace land with a bounce on the rubber Zodiac and roll into the bottom. Her head reappeared immediately as she clambered upright.

"Give line! Give line!" she yelled. It took Julius a second to understand what she meant, then he dove to make sure the life line that he had secured to her jacket had free slack. He watched incredulously as Grace dove to the front of the Zodiac and swung her knife in a broad arc, cutting the mooring line to the other boat just as tension came on her safety line, pulling the inflatable along in his wake. "WOO HOO!" Grace yelled, disappearing as she fell back onto the bottom of the little boat and pumping both fists in the air, one still holding the wicked looking knife. Julius steered them back out into the middle of the river, looking astern. Nobody seemed to have noticed that they had just stolen the guy's boat, despite Grace's whoop. Julius set the autopilot and went astern to pull the other boat close in. He secured a better tow line to the Zodiac. Grace almost fell between the two boats as she tried to jump back aboard, but Julius caught hold of her vest and hauled her back on deck. She clung to him.

"We did it!" she enthused, holding onto him.

"You're nuts, you know that?" he said, taking the knife from her so he could hug her briefly, then shook his head.

"What? Why? That was fun!"

"Yeah, fun. Well, we got ourselves a boat. Nice job, Blackbeard." He helped her off with the life vest. "What was that you yelled, when you went all crazy piratical?"

"That, Captain, was the *Diord Fionn*."

"The what?"

"The war cry of my people, the brave Fianna."

"You have people? And your people have a war cry?"

"Aye, my people," Grace said, slipping deeply into her brogue. *"Glaine ar gcroi, Neart ar ngeag, Beart de reir ar mbriathar."*

"Come again?"

"Purity of our hearts, Strength of our limbs, Deeds to match our boasts! It's our motto, you know."

"Oh. You have a motto, too. Swell motto, Braveheart."

"Not him, silly. Wallace was a Scot. The Fianna! New York or Death!"

New York *and* Death, Julius thought to himself.

Parnell and Uriel finished their breakfast. They took the limousine to the Guggenheim Museum and got out into the morning sunshine, standing on the sidewalk. Pedestrians streamed past in every direction.

"You sure she's coming here?" Parnell asked the other man.

Uriel nodded. "Yup."

Parnell watched the people on the street, the people moving in and out of the doors to the museum. "Shit, Earle."

Uriel was also standing and watching the people flowing about them. "Shit, yeah. Looks like it's going to be a fuckin' party, after all." They both watched as a large number of people, almost all young men who appeared to be in their early twenties, streamed about the building. Many moved in and out of the museum, others just standing about on the sidewalk near the building or positioned in the lobby just inside the glass doors.

Parnell said, "Looks like a freakin' Mormon square dance."

"Yeah, I guess you got their attention, Chuck." Uriel shook his head. "Let's check inside." They walked in, a half dozen young men dressed in unconvincingly casual attire watching them. Uriel stood in the middle of the large central lobby and looked up at the iconic spiraling ramp surrounding them, tracing the crowded rampway with his eyes up to the circular glass roof high above.

"This is crazy, Earle," Parnell said, looking about. "This place is huge. There must be a couple hundred LDS in here, just from what I can see where we're standing. Maybe more."

"I can see, Chuck. I told you, this is going to be complicated. Might not matter too much, though. Just one of her, no matter how many others they bring in. It's only about her, Parnell. Just focus on the girl. You bring the knife I gave you?"

Parnell nodded, patting his jacket pocket. "So what's the plan?" Parnell asked.

Uriel sat down on a bench to the side of the lobby, watching the main doors. "We wait."

"What if we see Pauley?"

"Try to kill him."

Julius skirted the maritime traffic as he slowly maneuvered his sailboat up the Hudson River, crossing to the Manhattan side on the eastern shore. The radio crackled with dense commercial banter, but he was relieved not to hear any Coast Guard hails directed their way. Grace reappeared on deck. She looked about, nodding at the panorama of tall buildings drifting past on their starboard side.

"Are we there yet?" she asked.

"Almost," Julius answered, pointing ahead. "Seventy-ninth Street boat basin, up ahead there. We're putting in there."

Grace strained to see what he was pointing at and saw a smattering of boats docked up ahead on the right. "Really? They going to let us in?"

"Should work. It's a public dock."

"You're just winging this, aren't you, Julius?"

He winked at her. "Pretty much, yeah. Keeps the element of surprise on our side."

Grace nodded. "Yeah, surprise. Great." She flounced down on the cushions next to where Julius stood at the wheel. Jack padded over and jumped up to lie next to her, dropping his muzzle on her lap so she could scratch his head.

Julius turned to glance at the two of them, smiling. "Gonna be okay, Grace. You'll see."

"Like you have any idea, Julius."

"I'm optimistic, by nature."

"The confidence of the ignorant." He gave her another glance, not smiling this time.

"You know something I don't?"

"Not a lot, Julius."

"Well, might be a good time to tell me the little you do know. You know, just so I can try to help, when the time comes." Grace shrugged. "Not helpful."

"What do you want me to say, Julius?"

"Let's review. We put in up ahead there, tie up, and take the Zodiac ashore." She nodded at him when he paused to turn and make eye contact briefly, before turning back again to navigate the boat. "Once ashore, we head to the Guggenheim, right?"

"Right."

"Then what?"

"Then I die."

"Just like that? Walk in, pay for your ticket, fall down dead? Not taking the audio tour or anything? Oh wait, I forgot. We don't have any money. So forget the audio tour. Or the ticket." She shrugged again. "Quit shrugging like that. I can't see you when I'm steering and it's pissing me off anyway."

"Sorry. I just don't know, Julius. I'm not trying to be difficult."

"You don't know how to use the gate, to get back?"

"Not a clue."

"Are you sure the Guggenheim is a gate?"

"Not really. Just winging it here, Captain, just like you. Wright designed it. Hope it is. Looks weird enough."

He sighed and continued to scan the river as he sailed upstream. "How about opposition? You think we need to worry about people trying to stop us, maybe even when we make our landing?"

"Yeah, good point. There'll probably be people trying to stop us. Or kill us. Or try to get us to make a contribution to the Guggenheim foundation. Maybe lock us up in a SOHO loft and ply us with some cloying, overrated Cabernet until we promise to buy a fractional timeshare. Maybe lots of people, maybe people with guns, again."

"Really, Grace."

"Well, what do you think, Julius? I mean, based on your short but spectacularly entertaining relationship with me, what do you expect? New Yorkers streaming from their rent controlled apartments to lead us into the spiral white temple, handing us glasses of a local craft beer and chanting Krishna blessings for my safe passage to the hereafter? That what you think is going to happen when we get off the little dingy thingy?"

"Now that you put it that way, probably not. I just can't see crazy guys with guns again, giving us the jump at the Guggenheim in broad daylight, that's all."

"You can't? I can." He turned to face her so that she could appreciate his incredulously elevated eyebrows. "What, you never heard of the New York City Police Department?" Grace asked.

"You think the cops are in on this? The NYPD is part of the conspiracy to keep you from making the jump back to your husband?"

"Yeah, when you put it that way, it does sound a little crazy, doesn't it?"

"Sure does."

"Well, let's just see how this plays, Julius. Maybe I'm a little paranoid. I don't know. Just out—"

"—of sorts. I know." She nodded.

Pauley closed the book and looked at his watch. He wondered if he had the time to get to the West 79th Street boat basin before they made their landfall. He was all the way on the east side on 56th and First. It would take a miracle to make it across town in time to ambush them. Or a police escort. Not much chance of either, especially the police escort. And if he missed them, he might never catch up—they could take any number of routes to the museum. He shook his head. The damn book helped, it was a great tool all right, but the damn thing wasn't giving him the information he really needed, and not when he needed it. Pauley felt like he was always a step behind, lacking just enough information to succeed. He shook his head, again wondering about the mechanism of the book's ongoing revelations, and its authorship. That Earle guy was probably right, Pauley thought, probably some dead, low level functionary in the Church Triumphant, just pounding away on whatever was the heavenly equivalent of an obsolete computer, probably still running Windows Vista. Pauley guessed he should be thankful the thing worked at all. He stood and stretched, and replaced the now careworn book in his breast pocket. He'd have to make the touch at the museum, that's all. He could make the museum in plenty of time, just uptown from where he was, without a problem. He picked up the phone to arrange for a driver.

Julius brought them expertly up to the anchor buoy farthest from the boat basin and killed the diesel. He ran forward to help Grace secure the boat. They looked up at the city, then stood awkwardly for a moment, surveying the boat.

"I'm going to miss this boat," Julius said. Grace nodded.

"What about Jack?"

Not so much, to tell you the truth.

"What about him?" Julius asked.

"Does he stay here, or come with us?"

Depends. Any steaks left?

Julius said, "Who knows what's going to happen? He might end up stranded here, no one would even know. I can't just leave him here, Grace."

Maybe you can. How many steaks?

"You don't know what'll happen if he comes along, either, Julius."

"No, I can't leave him here."

Sure you can. Just leave the steaks on the table.

"You're probably right, Julius. Steaks are all gone anyway."

Abandon ship! Nothing keeping us on this tub. Let's roll, team.

Julius held the Zodiac close in to allow the dog and Grace to clamber aboard, then followed. He gave the big sailboat a fond goodbye pat on the stern as he pushed off. The small motor started easily and he steered them towards the shore. The docks looked empty, so he brought them in smoothly and tied up, again holding the boat fast so the other two could climb out. He pointed east and the three of them started off at a leisurely walk along 79th Street.

"Is it far?" Grace asked.

"Couple of miles, cutting across Central Park. Not too bad."

We should stop for brunch. Not like we're in a hurry, right? No sense rushing to your own funeral. Am I right? I think Sarabeth's is up around here somewhere.

They began to walk as fast as they could without losing Jack. On several occasions Julius had to pick up the dog and carry him away as Jack tried to dive into restaurants. "Later, Jack," Julius kept saying, but they both knew he was probably lying.

They crossed the grounds of the Natural History Museum on their way into Central Park. As they stepped off the curb to cross Central Park West, it was Grace who noticed the half dozen young men who suddenly started down the massive front steps of the museum in their direction.

"Don't look now, Julius," she said as they crossed the street. Julius looked in the direction she nodded.

"Shit. They look like the guys who were looking for you at the train station."

"Yeah, well, all those skinny white guys look alike, don't you think?" she said as they crossed briskly into the park. Julius led them off the sidewalk and started walking cross-country on a jogging path across the Great Lawn.

"How do you think they picked us up like that? So quickly?" Julius asked.

"I'm afraid it implies that there's a lot of them, Julius."

"No, way, Grace," Julius said, stealing a glance over his shoulder as they walked. Jack was making a valiant effort to keep up. "We could've put in at half a dozen places onto this island. Not to mention that it's been days since we left Baltimore. Nobody has that kind of resources."

"You're still not getting it, Julius. Not seeing the big picture."

"Well, I sure as shit don't like the little part I'm seeing. Try to lose them or straight to the Guggenheim?"

Grace took his hand as they walked faster. "We're not going to lose them, Julius," she said, indicating another group of young men approaching obliquely from their right with a tilt of her head.

"Aww, shit. What is this, a Mormon convention in town? Not sure what they're planning," Julius said, checking over his shoulder again as he stooped to pick up the dog. The group from the museum had broken into a run as they reappeared behind them. "They're not armed."

"Yeah. Well, at least it's not the cops coming after us. You can handle these guys."

"What do you want me to do?" They were walking briskly now that Julius was carrying Jack, angling away from the group approaching from the right as they crossed the lawn.

"Just don't let them get me, Julius. Keep them off me and I'll make a break for the museum. You can catch me up there."

"Maybe we should split up now, see if—"

"No!" Grace said. "Stay with me as long as you can, Julius. They don't want you."

Julius just nodded as they trotted forward, watching the slow ballet play out. He was thinking hard, flashing back to his SERE training so long ago. Survive, Evade, Resist. But the Escape part—not bloody likely, Julius thought. Julius tried hard to remember, but it was a long time ago, it seemed like a different lifetime—and he was pretty sure he wasn't carrying a forty pound bulldog around when he did the training course. He looked ahead, studying the terrain and evaluating for usable advantages the way he had been trained when he took the SEAL sniper course. He had failed that course, he recalled inconveniently.

Up ahead, the path they were on came out at an intersection on Fifth Avenue, the eastern edge of the park. Straight up Fifth was the Guggenheim, he recalled, only about four or five blocks. He wouldn't have to buy much time for Grace, he thought, she was damn fast when she wanted to be. Jack, however, would be on his own. He stole another glance over his shoulder, checked their three o'clock and estimated how much time before all three groups came together. Up ahead, he saw a cop directing traffic at the intersection. He made a mental calculation, shook his head at the result, then decided it was pretty much their only chance. He trotted faster, Grace keeping abreast.

"Grace," he said. He indicated the intersection ahead with a tilt of his head, carrying the ridiculously overweight dog. "I'm just going to have to believe that the cops aren't part of this whole conspiracy. We're going to hit that intersection just as these two groups of yahoos make contact. Straight into the intersection, yell something to get the cop interested. I'll try to keep them off you so you can make a break for the museum."

Grace scanned in front and looked worried. "Where, Julius? Where's the museum?"

"Make a left at the intersection, four or five blocks north, on the right. You can't miss it." He smiled.

"I can't believe you just said that. What about Jack?"

"He'll be okay. I hope." They picked up their pace even more, trying to make the timing work as the group behind was jogging ahead faster. "You're on your own, Jack," he said, stooping momentarily to set the dog down. He pulled Grace into a jog.

No problem, guys. I got this.

"Bye, Jack," Grace called back over her shoulder.

"Where in the museum?" Julius asked her, now in a flat run. The group to the right was close now, the intersection coming up.

"I don't know, Julius," Grace said, biting her lip. "I don't know! Just find me."

"Yeoww!" they heard someone yell from behind, close. "What the heck?" Julius and Grace looked back as they ran, saw Jack latched onto the leg of the leader of the group behind. The guy fell, taking two others down with him. The others stopped to help. They heard Jack snarling and barking as Grace and Julius kept running, one from the group behind starting to run after them again.

Julius and Grace made the intersection as the guy from behind grabbed her shoulder. Grace spun into him and punched him in the throat, staggering him, but now the other group had caught up and converged on them as they all fell into the busy intersection. Julius grabbed the shirt of the closest guy and flung him into an oncoming taxi. The guy bounced up over the roof, getting the attention of the cop, a broad shouldered African-American woman in full uniform with a whistle in her mouth. She threw up both hands and spat out the whistle.

"What the hell is going on here?" the cop yelled. Traffic came to a confused halt around them. Several attackers grabbed at Grace as Julius tripped another into the street. Horns blared.

"Rape! Rape!" Grace screamed at the top of her lungs, still spinning and punching as more of the men tried to grab her.

"Not in my damn intersection, girl," the cop yelled, pulling out her baton and wading into the frenzy. Julius dropped a man with a kick to his knee, then had to dodge a punch from another. He grabbed the guy's arm and struggled with him momentarily before the man was laid out by a blow from the cop's baton.

"Run, Grace! Now!" Grace ran.

CHAPTER 31

"There!" Parnell said, pointing. Uriel looked and saw Pauley, dressed in black suit and white collar, standing at the bottom of the broad ramp. Pauley met their gaze as they watched, quickly turned and headed up the ramp with the crowd of museum patrons. "What should we do?" Parnell asked, turning to Uriel, who was still sitting on the bench.

"You go kill him. I'll wait here."

"Really? You think I should?" Uriel nodded and made a dismissive gesture, still watching the entrance. "Okay, I'm going." Uriel nodded again. Parnell moved off through the crowd, following Pauley up the ramp. Uriel shook his head as the other man moved off.

Grace pounded up Fifth Avenue, her breathing ragged. She looked about her as she ran. On either side of the street, there were dozens of young white men staring at her, moving after her. She kept running, dodging cars as she flew across intersections heedless of the traffic lights against her. Someone behind her grunted loudly as he was caught by the fender of a turning car. She kept running, and now could clearly see the spiraled white edifice of the Guggenheim only two blocks ahead. But then what? she kept thinking. Then what? Look for a shower to dive into? In a museum? Was it even a gateway, and if it was, where the hell was it? How would she find it, even if she wasn't being grabbed at by an army of coffee-scoffing white kids? She shook her head as she ran, trying to fight down panic. "Just winging it, just winging it," kept repeating through her head. And then she couldn't help smiling, she smiled broadly as she ran closer and closer to the broad white structure, almost burst into laughter before yelling out loud between ragged breaths, smiling, "Well, fuck me sideways!"

A huge banner hanging from the side of the museum proclaimed "The Art of the Dead." Grace pounded faster and faster as she read the two story tall sign, "Album and Poster Art of the Grateful Dead, 1967-1995." She ran straight through the crowd gathered on the street in front of the museum, hands grabbing at her, pulling at her as she burst through the glass entrance doors and came sliding to a halt in the crowded lobby, looking about, still smiling because she knew now, she knew she had a chance, she just had to find—there, a sign on a stand at the bottom of the main ramp, "THE DEAD, This Way," with a sixties era poster style hand pointing up the ramp. Two men from the crowd lunged at her as she sprinted between them, catching one in the neck with her elbow, the other missing with his grab as she reached the foot of the ramp and raced up through the crowd.

Uriel stood and watched from the lobby. He looked up and could just make out Pauley on the highest circle of the museum, Parnell following but being buffeted and shunted this way and that by the crowd. As he watched, Parnell was pushed back, almost falling, as a group of young men moved *en masse* down the ramp, heading for the girl as she ran upwards. Uriel shook his head. He never had much hope that Parnell would get anywhere near the priest.

Uriel turned to the sound of a commotion from the entrance in time to see Julius slam the door shut behind him onto the arm of a young man trying to follow. The man fell back and Uriel watched as Julius grabbed an umbrella from the stand next to the door and slid it through the handles, barring the door to a crowd of white shirted young men trying to follow him into the museum. Julius turned and ran in Grace's wake. He was smiling, too, having seen the sign and knowing that Grace was going to make it. Uriel walked behind purposefully, watching as Julius ran ahead up the ramp, grabbing white shirted young men by the collar and pulling them down as he jogged quickly up the ramp, trying to catch up to the commotion that marked Grace's passage two turns of the spiral above him. Uriel watched as the pageant unfolded on the spiraling ramp above and he smiled, too. The girl might make it after all. Might not have to kill anybody today, he thought to himself with relief.

Parnell was forced to flatten himself against a wall as the crowd surged around him. No matter how many times he tried, he couldn't make any headway towards Pauley. He could see the priest, though, see him standing at the very top of the ramp, watching. Parnell had his knife in his hand but felt like an idiot. Uriel was right, there were forces at work here, tidal forces against which it was futile to struggle. He kept his eyes on Pauley, feeling impotent. As he watched, he saw Pauley begin to walk purposefully back down the ramp. The priest was looking towards the lower spiral and as Parnell followed his gaze he saw the commotion moving up the ramp, a knot of struggling activity with Grace at its center, moving up the ramp. Pauley was moving to meet her.

Grace just kept moving, moving and fighting, moving upward and forwards so the hands couldn't get a grip on her, pushing ahead. Julius would have her back, she knew. She just had to move forward, keep moving forward. She was almost there, pushing up the ramp, passing the encouraging signs at each level pointing upwards, signs saying "This Way To The Dead," moving as quickly as she could against the crowd. She thought the crowd grabbing at her might be thinning, her progress growing easier. Fewer hands tried for her as she raced upwards, now seeing the last turn of the ramp ahead. But suddenly Grace was hit by a wall of people, a sudden surge against her that stopped her short. Hands clawed at her, somebody yelled, "We got her," as she punched and kicked. Grace cursed as she was knocked to her knees, struggled to stand but there were too many of them, they held her down, yelling. "No way, no fucking way," she whispered to herself, she was too fucking close, too close but now they were pulling her hands behind her back and she screamed, screamed the *Diord Fionn*, and then Julius was beside her, punching and pulling people off her, yelling for her to quit with the stupid Irish war crying bullshit and just RUN, dammit! She ran.

Grace ran up the ramp, leaving her Julius behind. For the third or fourth or fifth time, she had lost count, the guy had been there, and saved her, and she was going to miss him, she hoped she'd miss him, hoped she ended up somewhere where she'd remember him, but for now she ran.

Parnell stayed flattened against the wall, knife in hand, watching Pauley as the priest slowly descended the ramp, eyes fixed on Grace. Parnell could see Grace emerge miraculously from a scrum of bodies, yelling and running now, knocking the few remaining people aside as she sprinted up the last turn of the ramp. The crowds had passed here, the ramp now empty. Parnell stepped out onto the broad ramp. He stood knife in hand, feet apart, and waited for Pauley to come down to him. Pauley came around the turn of the ramp just above him and stopped short.

"Stop there, Pauley," Parnell said, trying to sound authoritative. It came out as more of a squeak. He held up his knife. "Don't try it. You're not going to do this. No excision. If you try, I'll kill you, Peter. I will." Pauley shook his head in disbelief.

Uriel moved up the ramp purposefully, stepping over fallen patrons, pushing others aside. He could see Grace as she broke free from the crowd and headed up the ramp unimpeded now. And now he also saw Pauley, standing at the spiral just above, facing off with Parnell. What was the guy thinking? Why didn't he just kill the man? Uriel wondered. He knew, though, that Parnell wasn't going to kill anyone—not on purpose, anyway. A knife slid into Uriel's hand and he paused, considering a throw. No, he realized, shaking his head. Not upwards, he couldn't. He was good, but Pauley was too far away, the angle wrong. Fate, it seemed, was against them. Uriel wasn't good enough for that. Maybe the girl, then? She was closer, but she was moving fast, he'd have to throw very soon, before she made the last turn that separated her from Pauley. Uriel raised his arm and held his breath, gathering his strength as he aimed. He could hit her square between the shoulder blades, he was sure. She'd be dead before she knew what happened. Better dead than what that monster was about to do, he started his throw and froze—Pauley had turned.

The priest had turned, had started back up the ramp. Uriel lowered his arm, sheathed his knife. The girl would make it.

"That's it, Pauley! Damn straight," Parnell gloated. "Get out of here. You're not excising anyone, brother!"

"Donovan!" The priest froze in place, his back to Parnell and the ramp below. It was Grace who had yelled. Pauley and Parnell both turned to see Grace running up the last turn of the spiral behind them, her shirt torn and bloodied, her hair a tangled red mass chasing after her. "You motherfucker! You murderer!" Pauley tried to move faster, tried to run as fast as his old frame could carry him, tried to race away from what he was going to do, race upward to the top of the ramp, to get out of there. He was too old, too enfeebled, too laden with guilt to outrace the girl. Grace pounded past Parnell, who stood agape, unable to think of what to do for a split second. Then he remembered what Earle had told him, that he was the last line, better she was dead than excised, and he lashed out with the knife in his hand as she sped past him, catching her in the chest and spinning her, tumbling to the floor of the ramp.

"What?" Grace asked, rising to her knees, clutching her chest with one hand as a red stain blossomed across her blouse. She looked up at Parnell, amazed. "Chuck? Why?"

Parnell dropped his arm awkwardly at his side, the knife clattering onto the floor. "I'm sorry, Grace. I had to. For both of us, I had to."

Grace struggled to stand, holding herself upright with one hand on the low wall of the ramp, the other hand trying to hold closed the rent in her chest, her shirt sticking redly to her side. "You're an idiot, Chuck," she gasped, shaking her head. She turned and watched Pauley struggling up the top of the ramp, about to reach the last sign, the one that said, "The Dead," without pointing any farther. Grace stumbled to follow the priest. "You motherfucker, Donovan, you killed my sister. You killed my sister." She moved faster, pulling herself along the railing of the ramp.

"No, Grace," Parnell yelled. "Don't! Leave him! Let him go!" But he saw Grace shake her head and, miraculously, break into a staggering run, a thick line of dark blood trailing up the ramp as she ran.

"Donovan!" she yelled and the priest stopped. He turned to face her, face pale with horror. He shook his head, held his deformed hand before him to ward off his attacker. "I'm dying, Donovan!" Grace yelled at him, approaching. "You motherfucker, I'm dying but I'm taking you with me! You hear me?" Grace lunged for the old man and grabbed him, wrapping her arms about him tightly and, as she embraced him, Grace launched herself backwards over the wall of the ramp. They fell together, both screaming, Parnell screaming, Julius screaming as they watched, Grace and the old priest falling down the center of the spiral, tumbling, falling and striking with a sickening snapping thump onto the museum floor below. Julius stopped dead, cursing, staring over the side of the ramp wall, looking at the body inert on the floor below. "Grace!" he yelled, staring wildly, but she was gone, she wasn't there. On the floor of the museum, Pauley lay crumpled, broken and lifeless, alone. Grace was gone. Her name echoed around the strange space, around Julius and Uriel who still stood, watching, until the sound of her name too faded away.

Julius looked over the side of the ramp and saw that Grace was gone. He believed for a brief moment that they had done it, Grace had made it through the gateway, back to where she belonged. Julius was happy for a split second before a stabbing, searing pain cut into his chest and his breath caught, unable to scream, and he crumpled to the floor.

Uriel heard Julius cry out, looked to see the man fall to his knees. At that moment, Uriel knew. He flew down the ramp, ignoring everyone else standing and gaping at the body in the center of the lobby. Uriel stood over Pauley's lifeless, broken corpse. He grabbed the old man's hand and saw it was whole, five fingers of his right hand restored. And Uriel knew that Grace was lost. He dropped the dead priest's hand in disgust. Uriel straightened, shaking his head at the unfairness of the world, hearing the wailing from Zimmerman above him. Uriel watched as the dog went running up the ramp to his friend, and followed.

Parnell had a brief instant to watch Grace fall, to wonder at how close he had come to saving them both, before he felt his heart burst with her disappearance, too much of him suddenly cut away. He gasped, and in the instant before he died, hoped he would remember his friend, next time.

Uriel shuffled sadly up the ramp to find Zimmerman slumped against the wall, barely gasping with life. The dog was at his side, licking at his face. As Uriel arrived, Zimmerman slumped to the floor. Jack whimpered once, then looked to Uriel. Uriel went down on his knees next to Julius and gently shook the other man. "Zimmerman," he said. "Zimmerman, God damn you! Open your fuckin' eyes, man!" Julius opened his eyes, full of pain. Uriel hauled Zimmerman upright and leaned him against the wall. Julius stared straight ahead, struggling for each rasping breath. "Listen to me, Zimmerman. Listen, God Damn It! You're not dead."

"She's gone," Zimmerman rasped in a hoarse whisper. I can feel..."

"Damn right, she's gone," Uriel said. "You gotta fix it, Zimmerman. We fucked this up, you and I, but you go and find her. You goddamn fix this." Uriel sat with a grunt next to Zimmerman on the floor, his arm around the other man's shoulders to keep him from slumping over. "I know it hurts, Zimmerman. I know you're in pain. But you're not done, not yet. You got to fix this. Find her and make it right."

Zimmerman shook his head weakly, staring at nothing. "I don't know," Julius wheezed, "Don't know where to find her. She's gone."

"Yeah, she's gone. Julius, listen to me," Uriel implored. A knife slid into his free hand. Zimmerman turned to look in the other man's face, staring with wild, pain-filled eyes. "I'm going to get you started, Julius. Don't let me down, Father. You promised her. You can do this. You gotta do this." Zimmerman's breath caught as Uriel slid the knife between his ribs, his eyes focusing on the other man, questioning. The tip of the knife found the apex of Zimmerman's heart. "Find her, Zimmerman. Get her back." Zimmerman's head fell back as he died.

CHAPTER 32

Julius stepped out of the shower. He looked about, listening. It was quiet. A suit and shirt hung on a hook next to him. Attached was a note: "Hope Antonio got the size right. Good luck, U." Zimmerman dressed in the suit, donned the shoes and socks he found on the floor beneath. He left the house and turned left on the sidewalk, walking quickly. Thoughtlessly, he twisted the heavy ring on his hand as he walked through the predawn darkness.

At first, Julius thought he might be too late. He walked faster, following the side of the busy expressway as the sun started to rise. Then he saw her up ahead, moving quickly. Zimmerman broke into a trot. She was getting away from him.

"Grace," he yelled, but she kept walking, the noise of the morning rush hour traffic drowning out his call. He ran faster. His chest caught as he breathed. "Grace," he called again, more loudly. She stopped. He saw her turn as he kept running. She stood, waiting for him, standing at the side of the bridge. Julius ran up, panting. Grace shielded her eyes with one hand against the dawning sun, blinded. With the other hand she held closed the shower curtain she had wrapped around herself.

"Who are you?" Grace asked, squinting at him. Julius came to a halt in front of her, trying to catch his breath.

"Grace," was all he could get out at first, the stitch in his side catching him up.

"Who are you? How do you know my name?"

"It's not important. Listen, Grace—"

"I think it's important. I'm not listening, asshole, until you tell me who—"

"Oh, fuck me sideways, Grace! Just shut up for a second. It's not going to work. You have to go back."

"What are you talking about? Who are you?" Grace implored, holding up both hands to try to shield her eyes from the intense sun behind him. "I can't even see you."

"Listen! Go back, now! Go back to Gabe. The rest isn't important. It doesn't work—it's not worth it. Do you understand?"

"I don't believe you, I don't know who you are," Grace said, plaintively, trying to see him, squinting against the bright sunrise. "Tell me who you are, so I can believe you." She raised her arms, imploring him. "Who are you?"

Julius sighed in exasperation. "Someone who loved you," he said softly. And then he pushed her; both hands straight to her chest and pushed hard. Grace tumbled backward, cursing, over the side rail of the bridge. Julius watched her fall. He saw the splash, saw her disappear beneath the surface of the water. Julius looked up and watched for a few seconds as the small boat below struggled to turn around. "Good luck," he said, turning to walk back the way he had come. Julius stopped for a moment. He could hear the man in the river below him yelling at his dog to stay in the boat. Julius just shook his head at that. He twisted the ring from his finger. Julius held it in his hand for a moment, then kissed it gently. "God keep you, Grace," he said softly, and then tossed the ring over the railing to the river below.

EPILOGUE

I should quit now, but I can't help indulging myself, just for a bit. Who knew that I'd actually enjoy this writing shit. It served its purpose, anyway. I would feel bad, however, if I just stopped here. The girl was right—the title sucks. So I'm taking her suggestion, not that it's ever going to matter. As a tribute, sort of. Since I didn't dedicate the book to her or anything. Obviously, that wouldn't have worked out so well. Anyways, here goes:

THE PROBLEM ~~OF~~ WITH GOD

That's for you, Grace. I hope it sells a million copies. Not a rat's chance, but you deserve it, girl. You always gave me the biggest portion and I miss you.

And by the way, if you just happen, by some semi-religious miracle, to be a big-time Hollywood producer who's reading this, for fuck's sake don't cast me as a bitch. I know you guys all like to do that, because the bitches have the nice curves and have the rep of taking direction better (which is not really true when it comes to English bulldogs, trust me on this), but WE CAN TELL. Please, some consideration, since from where I'm sitting, it doesn't look like I'm getting anything on the back end of this deal.

Namaste, brother.

Jack

~~~END OF THE SECOND BOOK~~~

ENDNOTES

I hope you enjoyed reading the second book in *The Claddagh Trilogy*. Hopefully, you read the first book, **God Bless the Dead**, before reading this one. If not, I do encourage you to read **GBTD** now—it'll all make so much more sense. Well, maybe not a lot more sense, but a bit more sense, anyway.

As always, this is a work of fiction. Any resemblance of characters in this book to actual persons, living or dead, is purely coincidence and not the intention of the author. And, as always, the rest of this stuff is true. At least, true like I see the truth. As in **GBTD**, this book interprets factual events in a manner which I find intriguing. If reality, or your sense of reality, differs, well I think that's just fine. I hope that I have not offended your sensibilities.

In particular, I apologize to anyone offended by my characterization of Catholicism, the Church of Jesus Christ of Latter-Day Saints, Mormons, or Jesuits. Once again, I have taken liberties with the sum and substance of the doctrines relating to these religious organizations. I mean no offense and again wish to emphasize that certain elements are depicted in a fictional way for the purpose of story. I don't actually believe that the Roman Catholic Church has a practice of excising souls from the universe, nor do I think that the Pope would ever condone the excision of a potential Messiah. Just a story.

Now that that's out of the way, allow me to emphasize what is indeed true in the book. Georgetown University does have a course required of all of its undergraduates entitled "The Problem of God." It is taught, in large part, by Jesuit faculty. The course references a real book of the same name. To my knowledge, however, it is not a "magicky book." Jack, an English bulldog, is the university mascot. He does live with a Jesuit instructor in campus housing. I don't know if he ever pretends to be an advisor to Winston Churchill.

The events described in the history of the Mormon religion are true. The Great Migration occurred as described, though the cause for the

THE PROBLEM WITH GOD

multiple evictions that I put forward is pure speculation on my part. There was an incident known as The Mountain Meadow Massacre which occurred as described. The motivation of the Mormon attackers is not known. Again, my assertion is purely imaginative.

There is actually a large, underground bunker complex constructed and maintained by the LDS Church in Granite Mountain, Utah. Fascinating videos of this complex are available for viewing on YouTube. I have no real evidence that the facility is being utilized to bring back the dead, however. The practice of surrogate baptism is a principle of the LDS church and continues to this day. The Granite Mountain facility, according to church statements, is used to facilitate and maintain the genealogical records relating to this activity. The controversial nature of this practice has been the subject of a great deal of reporting in the press. In response to protests, the LDS Church has stated that the practice of the post-mortem baptizing of Jews, particularly Holocaust victims, has been discontinued.

The historical events related to the life and death of Frank Lloyd Wright, Mamah Borthwick, and the fatal fire at Taliesin are true, as is the manner of injury and death of Grigori Rasputin. The landmarks and locations referenced in the novel are accurate. The shower in the Robert Llewellyn house may not be capable of interdimensional transport, however.

As the close reader with a penchant for fact checking will also realize, many other nuggets within the novel also have a basis in truth. For instance, the phrase "Surrender, Dorothy," really is spray-painted on a bridge over the 495 expressway in Washington, DC. No, not because I put it there—nobody knows how it appears or repeatedly reappears after it has been removed. I'll leave the discovery of other little truthful tidbits from the novel to the over-curious.

I wish to extend my heartfelt appreciation to my great friend and technical consultant, Dr. James Droesch, for his expert assistance regarding all things nautical. Any technical inaccuracies are due, I am sure, to my own inability to take his expert advice. A debt of gratitude is also owed to Kristen Droesch for her excellent editorial assistance.

As always, I could accomplish nothing of substance without the continued support and indulgence of my cherished wife, Sheri. Thank you for everything. Thank you also to the kindly, helpful, and nonjudgmental advice of my alpha, beta, and gamma readers, my children Kaitlin, Sarah, and Ethan.

God bless you, dear reader.

Evan Geller
September 2013

ABOUT THE AUTHOR

Evan Geller is a surgeon and critical care specialist living on Long Island. He is happily married and the father of three extraordinarily pleasant children. He writes on the side.

ALSO BY EVAN GELLER

God Bless the Dead
Book One of The Claddagh Trilogy

Available online and at most independent book sellers.

"The truth will not set you free. The truth will get you killed."
 -Screamin' Jay Hawkins

Gabriel Sheehan is in the truth business. He has invented a technology making it possible to read the thoughts of others. But his wife, Helena, is no friend of the truth. Gabriel knew she was something of an enigma when he married her, but now it seems that she might be slightly more catatonic than enigmatic. And he definitely has the impression that she may have killed someone, though he's not quite sure of the details.

While his company is a success, the change his technology works upon society attracts the attention of powerful forces, both in and outside of government: the kind of forces that his wife has been carefully hiding from for her entire life. But now she can't hide anymore. And those forces are intent on using his new technology in ways that Gabriel had never anticipated. In ways that may lead to his wife's final disappearance.

Made in the USA
Lexington, KY
11 February 2014